Making a place for yourself in a world where you don't belong takes courage.

So does moving in with a warlock.

What readers say about the Books of Waterspell:

"An extremely well written fantasy story ... flows well with a very readable style that holds your interest throughout. The world building is solid and intriguing, the magical aspects well drawn and versatile and characterisation is energetic so that you are immediately invested in their future. All in all a marvellous addition to the fantasy genre and I would recommend it for lovers of magical mystical tales." — Liz Wilkins

"The entire Waterspell trilogy blew my expectations out of the ballpark. What a brilliant and unforgettable story! I devoured it ... literally consumed by the originality and depth Deborah brings to her characters. She provides a strong balance between action, adventure, fantasy, and romance and Carin's combination of pride and vulnerability make her a fabulous character! Quite frankly, I am just astounded by the emotions this book stirred in me. It is simply extraordinary." — Lady Vigilante

"This book made me FEEL — and strongly! I also loved that this story was so completely unpredictable. It's one that I'd find hard to forget ... it is one of those rare stories that will stick with me." — Ali's Books

"If you like epic fantasy that sweeps you to amazing, immersive worlds and while following intriguing characters, be sure to add this series to your to-read list." — Once Upon a YA Book

"It's a great medieval tale, and would be equally as interesting for men as women. (It's no wispy piece of fluff fiction!) ... plenty of mystery and twists and turns." — Beth Hobson

"I adore the world building of the novel. It just felt like a thin mist crawling in ... rearranging the landscape. Everything was so detailed and full of imagery." — Fire Star Books

"Wonderfully written. I was hooked right away and loved that I couldn't predict what was to come next. 5 out of 5 stars! Highly recommend to young adults and older." — Memories Overtaking Me

"As soon as I started to read it, I was hooked. Five stars!" — The Book Lover's Report

"A new mystical world ... the characters and setting most definitely will leave you wanting more." — Let's Get Booked!

"Deborah J. Lightfoot just really has this way of bringing the reader into her world." — My Reading Addiction

"This author has woven such a spell ... I can't seem to get enough of this series." — Once Upon a Book

"Lightfoot does a wonderful job at creating a story. She has created an environment that is easy to understand yet complex enough to keep the reader thinking through her story. Her writing style is engaging and she has great pacing." — Bookworm Lisa

"The story just keeps getting bigger and bigger." — Book Briefs

Waterspell Book 1:
The Warlock

Waterspell ·

For Savvy,

Waterspell Book 1:
The Warlock

May your days be filled with magic!

Deborah J. Lightfoot

My best to you,

Deborah J. Lightfoot

Dec. 2023

Seven Rivers
Publishing

Seven Rivers Publishing
P.O. Box 682
Crowley, Texas 76036
www.waterspell.net

Cover design by Tatiana Vila
Vila Design
www.viladesign.net

First Paperback Edition: October 2011
First Electronic Edition: November 2011
Revised Print Edition (repaginated with minor text edits and updated cover):
January 2022

Waterspell Book 1: The Warlock
A Fantasy by Deborah J. Lightfoot

Summary: Drawn into the schemes of an angry wizard, Carin glimpses
the place she once called home. It lies upon a shore that seems
unreachable. To learn where she belongs and how to get there, the young
misfit must decipher the words of an alien book, follow the clues in a
bewitched poem, conjure a dragon from a pool of magic—and tread
carefully around a tortured, emotionally scarred sorcerer who can't seem
to decide whether to love her or kill her.

ISBN 978-0-9728768-3-4 (E-book)
ISBN 978-0-9728768-4-1 (Paperback)

Boxed sets containing this title:
ISBN 978-1-7377173-2-4 (Ebook: Waterspell, The Complete Series)
ISBN 978-1-7377173-1-7 (Audiobook: Waterspell, The Complete Series)

For F.C.L., who told me, early on, "Don't let them change it."

With thanks to all of my colleagues—writers, editors, and literary agents—who offered valuable advice that helped to improve this book (and its sequels) in ways great and small.

Special thanks to the members of the Dallas/Fort Worth/Arlington Four Star Critique Group who patiently sat through my endless readings and inspired me with your astute and incisive pointers. You helped me curb my excesses, clarify my thinking and my wording, dig deeper into the layers of my story (and my psyche), and more fully realize the potential of this long and complicated history of a Far Country.

To protect the innocent among my fellow writers and critique partners, I will not name you here. But each of you must know how deeply grateful I am to you for your insights, expertise, questions, patience, and enthusiasm. Thank you for supporting me in my grand obsession, all these years.

—D.J.L.S.

CONTENTS

*Not everyone immediately recognizes
a piece of flotsam as a possible bridge
to a shore that seems unreachable ...*

— Theodore Zeldin

Prologue

The Path Ahead

The wisewoman never asked directly, never demanded of Carin: "Where do you come from, you strange, surprising child? Who are you?" But she breathed her questions in an undertone when she thought Carin couldn't hear.

Time passed, and the woman watched with shrewd regard, ever wondering. *What's going on, girl, behind those cool green eyes that view the world with such detachment? You've borne up patiently these five years, with your gaze cast groundward to hide your thoughts from those who think you have none. Oh, you're a self-contained little wight, as guarded in your speech as in your glances. You pretend to be indifferent to your past and resigned to your present. But I have seen you puzzling beside the millpond, gazing into its waters, wondering: 'What brought me here? Where did this journey start, and where do I go now?'*

The seasons turned, and at last the wisewoman drew Carin aside. "I have considered carefully. Indeed, child, I have thought of little else. Still I cannot fathom where your journey began. But I clearly see the path that lies before you now."

The woman did not point. She would not risk drawing anyone's eye to the pair standing apart. She merely tipped her head, keeping her hand hidden in the folds of her shawls, tightly gripping the amulet she had fashioned against this moment.

"Go north, girl," she ordered, her gaze locked with Carin's. "Run from here. You have no home in this village. Granger is much too hidebound and suspicious for the likes of you. Your place is in the North. If you belong anywhere, child, you belong there."

Chapter 1

The Swordsman

Carin felt the hoofbeats before she heard them—a barely noticeable tremor underfoot, hardly enough to suggest the approach of a rider but enough to stop her mid-stride.

She turned and studied the leafless trees. Nothing moved. No breeze rattled the branches, no acorn fell to earth, no dead limb snapped. Nothing relieved the woodland's emptiness.

But she was no longer alone under these oaks. A season on her own had taught her what solitude felt like, and it didn't feel like this.

Every impulse that had brought her to this place screamed at her to get out of sight. *Don't get caught* – not now, after all this time and all that way, those long miles that stretched behind. And not here in this high, pathless woodland that had seemed to hold no life.

The papery dry leaves under her boots barely rustled as Carin darted into a thicket. "Unh!" she gasped at the cold and darkness enveloping her. The pale autumn sun didn't penetrate here. To a passing rider, she would surely be invisible.

She grew still and listened. But the woods stayed silent, with a hush like the calm while the storm-clouds build.

Carin tensed. A shiver ran through her.

There –

She caught them again, tremors in the earth: hoofbeats, now unmistakable. As she hid in the shadows, her breath suspended, she followed their rhythm, the cadence they struck at the threshold of hearing.

Nearer the hoofbeats came—ever nearer and more distinct. They broke to a gallop.

With a sudden sharp burst of noise, a great snapping and splintering of brittle limbs and underbrush, the horse came crashing into the thicket.

"Stop!" Carin shouted. She had no time to run. She couldn't even straighten from her crouch before she was bowled over onto her back. Instinctively she put up a foot, struggling to boot the animal away. "Get *off!*" she yelled. "Get off me." She aimed a kick at the animal's foreleg but the horse sidestepped and she hit nothing.

A blur dropped from the horse's back. Steel flashed. And Carin felt the point of a sword touch the hollow of her throat.

"Oh sweet *Drrr*—" She almost rolled out an oath. But it died on her tongue.

The swordsman was glaring down at her with the angriest, most frightening eyes she had ever glimpsed in a human face. They were as black as volcanic glass, but they burned like fiends'-fire. Their unnatural luster hinted of … insanity? Demonic possession? She couldn't say what she saw in their depths, but they took her breath away.

The man leaned in slightly. His weapon nicked the skin of her throat.

"No!" Carin yelled. *"Don't."*

He pulled up, just a fraction. His eyes scorched her. And when he spoke, he sounded as furious as he looked.

"Can you show cause why I should not remove your head at once?" he snapped. "The boundaries of my land are clearly marked. Those who would dare to enter here know the offense they commit, and the penalty for it. Do you have a defense to offer? Or shall I execute you now and save you the trouble of arguing your case?"

"Wait! Let me explain!" Carin demanded, blustering a little, attempting a show of outraged innocence. It fizzled. Her voice quivered and muffed the effect.

The swordsman pulled back another fraction—not enough to let her up. But he allowed enough space, between his sword and her skin, that Carin could heave a breath without risking major blood loss.

He gave her a curt nod. "Whatever you have to say," he growled, "say it quickly."

Why'd I tell him I'd explain? she thought, aghast at herself. *How do I explain what I don't understand?*

"I'm … not from around here," Carin ventured, feeling her way with him. "I came up from the south—from the plains. And I'm only passing through. I'm not a poacher, I swear." She wiped her sweating palms on her leggings and tried to sound convincing. "I haven't even seen a game trail to follow. Not that I would —follow it, I mean. I didn't come up here to hunt."

She resisted the impulse to touch the sling that she wore concealed under her grubby shirt. With the weapon, she had killed enough prairie hens and rabbits to stay just shy of starvation. That was down on the plains, though. These high woods harbored no sign of game—no tracks, no droppings, no fresh scratches on a tree trunk.

The swordsman didn't budge. "Poachers do not concern me," he snapped. "I accuse you of trespassing. And your presence here, on my land, is all the proof I require. Your guilt is clear."

He leaned in again, poised to stab the blade through her throat.

"*Stop!*" Carin shouted. She raised both hands, palms open. "I haven't done anything. I just climbed up a hill." Her hands shook uncontrollably, which made her mad. She clenched her fists and demanded: "How was I supposed to know this was private property? There's no fence on that hillside where the grass ends and these trees start."

The man's eyes flickered. The sword in his hand wavered, very slightly, but enough to make Carin press on, talking fast.

"I swear I wouldn't be here if I'd seen anything that said 'Keep out.' But the way I came, there's nothing. Maybe the sign's down. Or," she hazarded a guess, "somebody stole it." She gulped a breath and added, "Let me up and I'll leave — right now. Just let me go and I'll clear out of here."

The swordsman was staring intently at her. *Is he a bit thrown by my accent?* Carin wondered. *People often are.*

She tried to look the man in the eye. But she caught a gleam so strange, like a flame deep in the darkness of his eyes, that she recoiled. Carin found herself studying his throat instead, where a burnished badge fastened his cloak of black wool. One half of the badge was a crescent moon worked in silver. The horns of the crescent locked around the red-enameled, golden-rayed sun on the design's other half.

"Cock and bull," the swordsman snapped, whipping Carin's gaze back to his. He gave her a look that, like a cautery knife, burned as it cut. She flinched, but she didn't cry out —

— Not until he flicked the point of his sword up to her eyes. The blade was so close, she couldn't focus on it. She couldn't see much of anything, nor hear much over the pounding of her heart in her ears. But still she caught every word the man said next.

"I had planned to show mercy and kill you quickly," he growled. "But you deserve a slow and painful death for your poor attempts at lying. It is not possible for any mortal to 'steal' the warnings that protect these woods from interlopers. Nor is it conceivable that any living thing could fail to notice those warnings. Your own words condemn you."

"I can *prove* it!" Carin yelled. By now she was breathing so hard and so fast, she could barely talk. "I'll take you — show you. There's nothing. You'll see."

The blade was too close. She couldn't look. Her eyelids clenched shut in a spasm of terror. Her body went rigid and her senses threatened to desert. For a moment, there was nothing: no brambly undergrowth pricking her skin. No spicy scent from the autumn woods' decay. No sound of her own ragged breathing.

Something prodded her leg. Carin screamed—a cry like a cornered animal's. Her eyes flew open, and she was back in the moment.

"Get up," the swordsman barked. Again he jabbed her calf with the toe of his boot. "Walk. Take me to the boundary. I wish to see this impossible thing. If you have the proof, show it to me."

The instant the man stepped away from her, Carin was on her feet. But her legs didn't hold her up. She stumbled and fell to one knee and had to scuttle aside as the man's horse loomed over her again. The animal was a tall, charcoal-gray hunter. It didn't snort fire from its nostrils, but its rider was surely possessed of the devil.

"Walk," he repeated. His eyes glittered hotly. "Show me where you entered this land."

Carin pried herself up, pushed the tangles of dirty hair off her face, and pointed unsteadily. "The hill's this way," she said in a strangled tone. "It's about an hour by foot … my lord." Carin added the honorific as the man's natural due. She had no experience with the nobility of this region, but the title seemed to fit him. His good horse and riding gear, and his highlander sword, showed him to be wealthy if not highborn. And he was clearly accustomed to being obeyed.

She faced back the way she'd come and swung into the ground-eating stride that had already consumed many miles that day. Carin watched for the broken twigs and crushed leaves and boot prints in patches of bare dirt that confirmed she was retracing her steps.

In no time, her feet began to feel heavy. And the farther she backtracked, the heavier they got.

This is all wrong, warned a feeling deep inside.

This forced march was taking her in the wrong direction. To reverse course now was not an option, not with every instinct—

every compulsion—pushing her northward. If this woodland wasn't her ultimate destination, it *had* to be close. Up in this highland of oaks, here in the hard-won north, she might find the place where she belonged.

But not if she kept retreating like this.

Carin fingered the sling that hung around her neck, hidden and waiting. Palm the weapon, fit it with a pebble, whirl, knock the swordsman unconscious with a single precise throw: could she?

It'd be a risk. If her first shot missed, the man following her would be alerted to his danger. Then he would ride her down and either trample her or take her head off.

She threw a glance over her shoulder. The swordsman was not staring a hole in her back. Something else held his attention, at the eastern edge of the clearing they had just entered.

Carin followed the rider's gaze and saw movement—a flickering in the branches, not the sun but something equally bright, sparking through the bare-limbed trees. It kept pace with her like a shadow made of light.

She watched the light and not her feet, until her left boot slipped sideways and sent her leg out from under her. "Mother of—!" Carin bit off the oath as she pitched forward and her right knee came down on a spur of stone that was as sharp as a knife.

It happened too fast to hurt at first. But, oh! the blood—lots of it, streaming from a gouge that crosscut her knee.

She hunched over the wound, her masses of unkempt hair tumbling around her face, strands of it trailing in the gore. Blindly Carin fumbled in her belt-pouch for something to stanch the bleeding. Her fingers met only flint and steel for fire-making, pebbles for arming her sling, and a length of twine that was useful for everything from tying back her shaggy auburn mane to rigging a brush shelter.

Abruptly a hand grasped the shank of her leg, and another shoved at her shoulder. "Straighten up," her captor snarled.

Carin threw back her head and flung the hair out of her eyes. "You!" she gasped. "But—" She hadn't heard the swordsman's approaching footsteps—a seeming impossibility through the crunchy carpet of autumn leaves. Yet here the man was, crouched beside her and brandishing a dagger. Carin's hand flew to shield her throat, but it was her knee he put the blade to.

Stay away from me! she wanted to shout at him. She couldn't get the words out—not in a way that made sense. As sometimes happened when she came unglued, Carin lapsed into a language of her own. The sounds that passed her lips weren't gibberish, but no one ever understood a word she said when she got like this. Carin yelled at the man, in her own private language, and tried to wrench free of his grasp.

"Stop your noise," he barked. He held her leg tighter and waved his dagger in her face. "If you can't be quiet, I'll cut out your tongue."

"Unhh—" Her words choked in her throat. She pulled back and let him cut away the blood-soaked fabric of her legging. Rapidly now, the pain welled up with the blood.

Don't faint, she told herself.

Carin gritted her teeth, and trembled only too visibly, but she didn't faint. She didn't take her eyes off the man's hands. A nobleman he might be, but his hands knew work. They were muscular and lean. The fingers were long, almost elegant, and bore the scars of labor old and new. The blunt nails were well cared-for but stained at their edges. And from his left hand, he was missing his little finger.

When the swordsman had sliced away enough of Carin's legging to lay the wound bare, he reached inside his coat and drew out a pair of small leather packets. One held a bronze-colored powder; the other, a matching amount of a green dust.

"Hold the knee still," he ordered as he dosed the wound with the bronze stuff. "This will burn."

8

Burn, however, was not the word to describe it. A glowing coal dropped into the cut would not have blazed hotter. Tears streamed down Carin's face but she kept still and made no sound, even as she bit her lip hard enough to draw blood.

He glanced at her face as he set aside the bronze powder and picked up the green.

Sweet mercy, what next? Her fingers dug into the cold ground under her.

But when the man sprinkled the green dust into the wound, the fire in Carin's flesh died. Her knee went numb. The gash, though alarmingly deep, no longer bled or throbbed. Carin freed her lip and tasted the blood she'd bit from it.

The man resealed the colored powders and slipped both packets back inside the black leather coat that he wore under his cloak. From another pocket, he produced a square of linen and bandaged her knee.

He stood then and walked to his horse, but he did not immediately mount. "Get on your feet," he snapped.

He's demented. Carin eyed him, more than a little confused. *He's insane.* One minute, he was threatening to kill her. The next, he was doctoring her hurts. And now his anger seemed rekindled.

She pushed up from the rocks and teetered, the toe of her right boot barely touching the ground. The sun hung low in the west. She had to hurry or night would be on them before she could lead this strange man to the edge of the trees and prove her case.

Get on with it, Carin ordered herself. She put one foot ahead of the other and tried to ignore her injury. But she could barely hobble. The numbing effect of the swordsman's medicinal powders wore off fast. With each step, she stifled a groan. She didn't get far before the pain shooting through her knee forced her to brace against a tree and give her sound leg her weight.

"If you continue to try my patience," the swordsman growled, "you will discover how limited it is. Move!"

Carin glared at him. "I can't walk," she snapped in a tone that was as sharp as his. "If you want me to show you that hill I climbed, you'll have to let me ride."

The man scowled. He muttered an oath—something about "guts and gall." But after a moment in which he seemed to weigh his options, he led his horse up beside her.

"Mount," he ordered brusquely. "I am determined to see this place along my borders that you claim is unmarked. Even a blind man must heed those warnings and turn aside. Though you are a clumsy creature, you're not blind. I *will* have you show me what you claim not to have seen."

I didn't see it because it's not there, you lunatic, Carin thought. But she said nothing more, only stretched for the pommel and pulled herself up. She barely managed to get her throbbing right leg over the horse's rump. And she hadn't quite straightened before the man swung up behind her. He pressed her forward on the flat huntsman's saddle and gathered the reins in both of his hands.

"Oh—!" She flinched, swallowing another oath, finding herself trapped between his arms. Only the damned should be this close to a devil who had the fires of the abyss in his eyes.

As they rode south at a canter, the swordsman sought no guidance from his captive. Carin would not have been able to direct him even if he had asked. From horseback in the darkening woods, she could see no traces of her previous passage. But the man seemed sure of the way, as if he knew right where she had set foot on his property.

So why make me show him the spot? If he knew the place, then he must know it was wide-open to any traveler.

Covering the remaining distance far more quickly than Carin could have walked it, the man reined up. He had indeed brought them to the slope where these wooded highlands met the grasslands below. Though the day was far gone, enough light remained to pick out a distinctively scarred tree on the hilltop.

Carin recognized it. The white mark on its trunk looked like a dolphin. When she had passed by here earlier, she'd particularly noticed the dolphin because it looked so out of place, suspended between the golden plains and the leafless oaks.

She started to point out the tree, to tell her captor that this was the precise spot. But the man behind her spoke first.

"Show me!" he demanded, so forcefully that his hot breath ruffled the hair on the back of her head. He pointed down the slope. "If you value your life, show me the break you claim to have discovered along my well-protected borders."

What does this madman want from me? Carin half twisted around to vent her frustration on him, but stopped when she thought how close that would bring her face to his. She jerked her head down instead, and brought up her arm. With a sweeping motion, she indicated all of the landscape that lay before and below them.

"What are you talking about?" she exclaimed. "What are you *looking* at? You can see for yourself that there's no wall, or fence, or signpost." Carin pointed out a glade down on the hillside. "The lower you go, the fewer the trees. That's all *I* see." She shook her head. "Sir, I don't think much of your 'well-protected border.' If you want to keep people out of these woods, you need more than a few scarred oaks and an imaginary fence."

"By the blood of Abraxas!" the man swore in her ear. "You're a brassy chit."

Carin swallowed hard and waited for him to hit her. Whenever her old master, the wheelwright of a small southern town, had barked at her like that, he'd always finished by clouting her.

But the swordsman didn't hit her. He only urged his horse forward, muttering something so far under his breath that Carin didn't catch it.

The horse took two steps, then stopped of its own accord. It snorted nervously and pawed the ground, clearly unwilling to descend the slope.

Its master did not force it. The man dismounted and ordered Carin down.

She dragged her stiffening knee over the horse's back, slid past the stirrup iron, and managed to land with all of her weight on her good leg. As Carin wobbled on one foot, the swordsman caught and steadied her.

"Show me," he ordered again, his voice tight. With the hand that had helped her off the horse, he gave her a push—not enough to unbalance her, but enough to make his meaning clear. He wanted her to go down the hill, back toward the plains below.

Do what he wants. Get out of here. Find another way north.

Carin half hopped and half limped down the slope. Pain lanced through her knee. She had to stop, far above the foot of the hill, and brace against an oak. She closed her eyes and tried to master the pain through willpower alone. She did not succeed.

But in her stillness, Carin again became aware of the silence that pervaded the woodland—a silence in which not so much as a whir of wings nor the distant call of a bird could be detected. The profound hush that had made these woods seem peaceful and promising, when she'd first entered them, now impressed Carin as sinister. No tomb for the dead was more oppressive than this place.

Go, whispered her fear. *Get off this hillside.*

Carin took a step. "Aaahh!" she cried as the pain buckled her leg under her. She collapsed into a pile of leaves.

Sweet mercy, her knee *hurt.* The tears came again, wetting her face. She ducked her head to hide them, but an avalanche of profanities made her look sharply uphill.

The swordsman was striding down toward her, swearing with his every step, shattering the stillness. Though the oaths he spoke were unfamiliar to her, she could recognize the inflections of violent cursing when she heard them.

The man stopped swearing just before he reached Carin. He crouched on the slope so that his eyes were only a little above hers. He stared at her, hard.

Don't scream. Carin beat back a deep need to do so as she endured the searing intensity of his gaze.

Her breath came in short bursts. She grabbed one and panted out, "Got to stop … knee's gone … won't take my weight." She squeezed it tightly. The pressure helped the agony and helped to steady her. As her breathing eased, Carin demanded more coherently: "Leave me here. I'll sleep under a tree. Tomorrow, I'll head down." She pointed to the flats below them. Pain sharpened her voice as she added, "You won't see me again. I promise."

The man didn't answer her. If he altered his expression at all, it was only to deepen his scowl. The sun had set on the hill, but in any light her captor's eyes would be easy to see. They remained fixed on her. He studied Carin as if he doubted what he saw. His face didn't give much away, but she detected a veiled astonishment.

"How have you come through the barrier?" the swordsman asked, finally breaking his silence. "Tell me: do you perceive nothing here? Feel nothing? See nothing that alarms you?"

"The only alarming thing I've seen all day is you—sir." The tacked-on courtesy sounded like she was mocking him: unwise, under the circumstances. But her misery was loosening Carin's tongue. "You want to know what I'm feeling?" she snapped. "My knee's killing me. I'm dead tired from walking a thousand miles, and I'm hungry." Ravenous, in fact. She'd long since walked off her last meal of rabbit and redberries. "I'm cold, too," she added as she shivered so violently that the leaves under her rustled audibly in the stillness.

The man shook his head. "None of that matters. Tell me: what is here?" He pointed to the ground under her. "What do you sense in this place?"

"Sense?" Carin paused to consider her answer, for she'd gradually become aware that she did in fact perceive something—a kind of tingly energy, diffuse and thready, all around her. "It's hard to describe." She looked around, as another shiver traveled over her. "But it feels a little like the air does when a storm is building. You know, when it's thundering and lightning but the air is so dry it crackles, and the rocks are throwing off sparks the way a wool blanket does on a winter night."

She refocused on him. Though the man's expression was unrevealing, his eyes narrowed—not enough to hide the glint in them. Carin shuddered, wishing for a good wool blanket to cover her threadbare clothes.

"That feeling in the air is easy to miss," she added, dropping her gaze to avoid his. "It's weak. I never noticed it when I came this way the first time. I barely feel it now that I'm sitting here freezing to death. When I passed through before—this afternoon, when I climbed up and went on in to where you found me—I didn't sense it at all."

A thought came to her then. Incredulous, Carin snapped her head up and demanded: "Is this little tingly feeling supposed to be guarding your borders? That's ridiculous! You claim your lands are protected, but there's nothing on this hillside that would stop a butterfly."

In response, Carin's captor raised his right hand and made a motion with his thumb and fingers, as if flicking away an insect.

Then the man rose to his feet. He loomed over her.

"Come away from there," he growled. With his three-fingered left hand he grasped Carin's arm and drew her up. His right fist drove at her face. The blow landed.

Or did it? Carin's head snapped back from the force of it, and yet the fist had failed to connect. Half an instant before striking her, the man's fingers straightened and arrowed at her eyes. They seemed to go right through her as a cold white flash engulfed her and nearly popped her head off.

She knew every agony, every torment that human flesh could endure. For a moment, Carin hurt as she had never hurt before.

Then all things subsided. Pain, hunger, and weariness slid away, leaving only a vague, lingering bewilderment. She wasn't entirely gone to insensibility. The white flash had banished vision, but she caught a breath of night-crisp air that carried the scent of the woods.

And gradually, an awareness of movement asserted itself: she or something touching her was in motion. The action had a rhythmic quality, soothing as a baby's rocker. Carin retained enough mindfulness to know she was back on the horse, swaying with the animal's steps. She could almost hear the plop and crunch of hooves on earth and fallen leaves.

Soon these impressions faded, all becoming white and smooth and peaceful. The whiteness filled and took her. And the two voices that came to her then, as if from a great distance, had no power to revive Carin. The words of the two seeped through her brain, like snowflakes melting, leaving no residue —

"The girl makes a pretty picture, mage, resting in your arms."

"Faugh! A drowned cat would look better … and smell better."

"She is another, you know."

"Another what, pray tell?"

"Another like me."

"How so?"

"Unbound by the laws of your world, mage, or by your spells. She is from elsewhere."

"A fanciful notion, sprite, hardly to be credited. She is a serving-maid, more like, running from her master and ill prepared to fend off starvation in the winter that comes."

"How then do you explain her utter disregard for your imprecations?"

"Not so. She sensed the magic. She succumbed at the last."

"Scarcely! And by slow measures, only after swimming in your spells for long enough to drive the sanity from any of your countrymen. You know I speak the truth. Take care how you deny it. I was there. I saw."

"Be off with you, woodsprite. I find your chatter tedious. Though I may be powerless to banish you from this land, I won't abide your insolence. Begone, and do not let me see you again."

"As you wish, magician. I'll leave you to ride home through the dreariest patch of woods that ever grew. But mark my words: you shall find that this traveler who's asleep in your arms belongs here no more than I do."

Chapter 2

The Puzzle-Book

"Myra! Come in here!" a man shouted, loudly enough to wake the dead.

Carin did not wake. Barely sensing a disturbance, she didn't hear the shout so much as feel it. It made a slim dark splinter that stabbed the whiteness enshrouding her.

Presently, a quantity of particles joined the splinter. The particles were recognizably words, but they drifted over Carin's confused senses like a soft blizzard carried on a woman's voice.

"Here you are at last, my lord! How I did worry, when the supper dishes were cleared and the sun had gone down and the stars were out and still there was no sign of my good master. I bade the stableboy ride out to look for you, but he would not. He would only skulk about the stalls and fret that one of his charges was absent. I do believe he cares more for that horse than for you, my lord."

"It pleases me to hear it, Myra," said the voice like a splinter. "Lanse knows I face no danger in these woods. But he also knows the harm that hard use can bring a horse. His fears are rightly placed."

Something moved. As before, Carin registered the motion but was vague about her own part in it.

"I grow weary of this burden." The splintery voice jabbed at her. "Where would you have me drop the creature?"

"A visitor!" the soft blizzard cried. "My lord, how you do surprise me! We've had no visitors for many a year. But always I have hoped—and kept a room ready for any such blessings that might befall us. The blue room, master, at the top of the stairs. Come, if it please you."

17

More movements followed, an impression of climbing. Then the voices drifted past again:

"Lay her here, my lord."

"This creature is filthy," he complained. "She'll begrime bed-linens."

"No matter. Sheets will wash, and so will she. There'll be time on the morrow for scrubbing clothes and bodies. What's needed tonight is rest, for our tagrag visitor and for you, my lord. Lay her gently here, then be off to your bed. I will tend our guest."

"I leave her to you. Gladly."

Another motion, quick and rough, so unsettled the blank void of Carin's existence that she almost roused. But her senses could not marshal themselves before the whiteness again smoothed itself across them.

"Look and you will see a covering on one knee," the splintery voice said. "The cloth protects a wound. Leave it until tomorrow. The treatment needs no interference."

"Do you take me for a simpleton, master? I well know that your cures are not to be meddled with. To bed with you now, sir. The wee hours are upon us."

This time the movement was definitely far distant. Carin felt frozen in place, as quiet and stilled as pond ice in winter. Words settled gently on her, a last flurry from a woman's voice that strew them about like a force of nature.

"Now, dearie, you'll sleep the night through. My master's seen to that. Sleep as late as you like on the morrow, and when you wake I'll have a good breakfast for you. And I'll hear of all your adventures. My! What wondrous adventures you shall have had! Few come this far north. Travelers through this land are uncommonly few. I do wonder ... yes, I wonder how a maid comes to be in this realm, and comes to my kitchen door like a bundle of rags in my master's arms. Mysteries upon mysteries.

You can't have seen sixteen winters yet, but wondrous adventures you shall have had, for all your short years. On the morrow, I'll hear all. Curious as a cat, I am …"

To the subsiding blizzard, Carin was oblivious. The last fragment of awareness left her and she knew no more.

* * *

Sunlight dappled the bed through lace curtains. If it was morning, it had to be late.

Carin stretched between smooth sheets. Then she sat bolt upright and studied the room to which she had been brought in the night.

This can't be a dungeon, she thought, astonished. *It's too pretty.*

The "blue room," as she'd heard a female voice call it, was aptly named. Linen of periwinkle blue covered the walls. The color repeated in the cushion of a three-legged stool at the mirrored dressing-table beside the bed. On the table were a hairbrush and a comb, both of an iridescent blue shell reminiscent of the jewel-toned beetles Carin had seen in the southern grasslands. An azure vase held the bright feathers of bluebirds. The coverlet on the bed, and the cushions of a chair in the corner, were a deep indigo. A cloth of sea blue draped a small table by the latched entry door.

On that table were a pitcher and a plate of bread and cheese.

Carin sprang out of bed, sprinted to the table, and was devouring the food before she even thought of her injury. While ripping into a chunk of bread, she drew up her right knee for inspection. The knee felt stiff but moved with none of yesterday's ache.

She unwrapped the bandage. "Oh!" she exclaimed, so startled that she momentarily neglected to eat. The gash had healed, leaving only a pale scar in place of a bloody wound.

The colorful powders her captor had sprinkled into the cut: did they do this? Could they heal a wound so quickly? "Potent stuff," Carin mumbled with her mouth full again. If she could steal a supply, she ought to pack some along when she quit this place.

This place? Where was she? Carin finished everything edible, then began a closer examination of the room. She was drawn to a set of doors like tall shutters, painted a shiny blue, which closed a floor-to-ceiling opening in the wall to her right. The shutters' narrowness suggested that a smaller room—a pantry? a closet?—lay beyond.

She was at those doors when a glimpse of herself in the dressing-table mirror brought her up short. The swordsman had been generous in calling her *filthy*. Carin frowned at her reflection, knowing he'd said it but unable to remember when.

He wasn't wrong. Her shirt, formerly ivory, was mud-colored. Her hair, an oily mat of tangles, trapped straw and dead leaves. On her leggings, grass stains alternated with black patches of muck, and the ripped and tattered cloth from her right knee down was stiff with her dried blood.

Carin rubbed her forehead, then her eyes, struggling to make herself think back—or better, think ahead. She succeeded only in deepening her sense that she could do nothing for now, except live in the moment. She ought to be planning an escape, but all she could focus on just now was finding more food—she'd forgotten how good bread could taste—and maybe finding something clean to wear until she could wash her rags. She pulled open the blue shutters.

Neither a closet nor a pantry lay beyond. The doors opened to a cavernous room—a vaulted chamber of stone much bigger than the bedroom, and furnished for bathing.

"What the—?" Carin's mouth fell open as she surveyed the fixtures.

A pedestal of blue-veined marble held a crystal washbowl. From the wall above the bowl, a spigot protruded. Carin thumbed it open. "High holy almighty!" she exclaimed in a rapture of delight as warm water swirled into the basin.

The room's most arresting feature was more delightful still. A perfectly circular pool claimed nearly half the open floor space. Stone steps descended into it. Carin crouched and tested the water. It was warm like the flow from the wall spigot.

She tore off her clothes, and with them her sling. She grabbed a cake of soap from the washstand and slipped into the pool. To bathe warmly and with soap—*glorious*. This was simply glorious. From scalp to toes she scrubbed, and thrice lathered her hair.

As she floated in the pool, Carin scanned the room for the source of the steady light that filled every corner. The cavern had no windows, nor lamps or candles. Yet the chamber was well lit, with a diffuse glow like sunlight through clouded crystal. Were the walls not the solid rock they seemed? Were they made of split horn or another material that let the sun in?

The gentle current that stroked her body continually freshened the pool. Where was it coming from? When she had finished scrubbing and the water cleared, Carin dived and located the source of the inflow: an opening in the rocky bottom the size of a serving platter. Surfacing, she found outlet holes between the upper steps. This pool was fed by warm springwater that welled up continuously and drained out the sides.

The design, ingenious, was unmatched in her experience. Could that devil-eyed swordsman of the woodland be the architect of this heavenly pool? Carin wondered, remembering her captor's strong, work-stained hands.

Another memory of his hands, less distinct, struggled to shape itself. They'd grabbed and beaten her—*hadn't they?* She pressed her palms to her eyes, trying to remember. She touched her face where the blow had been aimed. No soreness there, nothing to suggest she'd been struck.

But something had happened last evening, some violence she couldn't fully recall. A persistent mental sluggishness burdened her thoughts and blurred her memories.

Carin left the pool, squeezing rivulets from her hair. Wrapped in a towel, she returned to the bedroom. At the dressing table she took up the comb and attacked the snarls in her long, wet hair.

"Ouch!" and "Ouch!" again. After several minutes of painful and unsuccessful yanking, she dropped the comb and began to search the table's drawers for a knife.

The first yielded only white kerchiefs embroidered with blue flowers. As Carin tugged at the second drawer, a soft knock came at the bedroom door.

Carin jerked her hand away and stepped back from the table. She would have retreated further, had her visitor given her time. But the latch lifted, the door opened, and in bustled a short, sturdy woman.

"Oh my, dearie, aren't you a sight!" the woman exclaimed. "Awake already, and scrubbed. So clean you are, I'd swear 'twas not the same tatterdemalion my master carried up the stairs in the wee hours. Against skin that fresh, you'll be wanting good clean clothes, not those rags we put you to bed in. Let's see how this shift fits."

Carin stood staring, doubly dazed by the woman's sudden, chattering appearance and a sense that the feeling was nothing new, although the woman was a stranger to her. "Who ... ?" she started to ask, then decided it didn't matter. She wouldn't be here long enough — wherever "here" was — to get to know the inhabitants. With a nod, Carin accepted the shift that the woman offered. As she pulled it over her head, her towel fell to the floor.

The woman fished with both hands in the pockets of her housedress and drew out a length of blue fabric. This she twisted several times around Carin's waist, snugging up the folds of crisp linen.

"Now, sit yourself down and we'll comb out those tangles. What a mane you have!" she said admiringly as she pulled Carin's damp hair from under the shift's neckline.

"Ma'am, where can I get a knife?" Carin asked. *A knife? Careful*, she warned herself. *Don't alarm the nice lady.* She flicked a strand out of her eyes and added, by way of explanation, "It's hopeless. I'll have to chop most of this off before I can get a comb through it."

"Oh no, dearie! We needn't cut your lovely hair," the woman replied. "I wouldn't see any guest of this house so disgraced." She dived again with both hands into her roomy pockets. "It only needs a bit of coaxing ... Patience, patience," the woman mumbled—to Carin? to herself?—as she rummaged around. After much searching, she produced a flask and unstoppered it. "This will tame those tangles." She poured out a dollop of a creamy liquid and began massaging it into Carin's hair.

Heavenly. Another blissful sensation suffused Carin, as good as her soak in the pool. Her already draggy thoughts slowed to a crawl. Entranced and dreamy, she watched in the dressing-table mirror as the woman combed out the tangles. It took what seemed forever, but under her deft touch the snarls relaxed and Carin's hair fell down in waves.

"Now then, you're fit to appear at the court of any king," the woman said, rousing Carin to attention. "I've never seen the master's tonic to fail, be it scurf, snarls, or the baldness that troubles ye!"

"The master's 'tonic'?" Carin asked, suddenly wary.

"Aye, dearie. My good master can stir up a potion to cure 'most any ailment. 'Tis a wondrous gift he has."

"The swordsman? *Him?* He's an apothecary?" Carin pressed her.

"Apothecary and alchemist. Herbalist, metalsmith, and worker in stone. There's little in this world that my master cannot turn his hand to for benefit."

Are we talking about the same bare-fisted brute? Carin wondered.

She twisted around on the stool to face the woman. "Yesterday, when I tripped on a rock in your master's woodland and busted open my knee, he sprinkled some powders into it to stop the bleeding. Now, the cut's closed up." Carin showed the woman her faint scar. "It's healed already, like magic. I've never seen any medicine work that fast. Did your master make it?"

"Aye, indeed," the woman said. "I've used the stuff myself, many a time. And Lanse, and the old gardener—the horses, too. So long as the cut does not reach the vitals, the master's healing dusts will stitch it up in no time."

All the better for me, then, that he didn't make good on his threat to remove my head, Carin thought, and shuddered a little. *He couldn't have stitched it back on, dusts or no dusts.*

"Goodness me, child!" the woman said so suddenly that Carin jumped. She walked to the window and pushed back the bedroom's lacy curtains. "If I'm any judge of the sun, I've stood here chatting the morning away. 'Twill soon be time for the master's midday meal. And you, dearie—you've barely made a start on your breakfast with those morsels I left to whet your appetite. Oh my, a good wind could blow you away, so thin you are! You need meat on that spare frame. And aren't I the one to fatten you up? Come along now, down to the kitchen, and I'll fix you a bowl of porridge with bacon, and bread dripping with honey."

Carin wiped her hand across her suddenly watering mouth. She trailed the woman out onto a landing, down a narrow wooden staircase, through an unfurnished foyer, and along a connecting passageway to the kitchen. She sat on a bench at the table and watched the cook throw together the promised breakfast. The meal was served with a mug of hot mint tea and another of fresh milk. Carin delayed only long enough to say a sincere

"Thank you," then attacked with firm intent to leave no crumb or drop.

Only when she had eaten partway through her second full breakfast did she begin to pay less heed to her stomach and more to the swordsman's housekeeper—as she'd decided this woman must be. The latter had been chattering ceaselessly while chopping vegetables and stirring a pot over the fire. Her talk was a running commentary on the weather, the shortcomings of Lanse the stableboy, and the faults of someone called Jerold. He, presumably, was the gardener previously mentioned.

Not once did the woman speak of Carin's late-night arrival. If she had questions, she did not ask them.

Carin volunteered nothing. She only ate and listened and nodded politely, and made her plans to leave. Soon now. She must go soon, while she had only this gabby housekeeper to contend with.

But she wouldn't leave empty-handed. A coarse bag hung on a wall of the kitchen between bunches of dried fruits and herbs. It would comfortably hold whatever bread and jerked meat Carin could pilfer on her way out the door.

And don't forget the medicines. She'd also have to check this room for the swordsman's cure-alls. Given those dusts' impressive healing powers, she shouldn't take off without her own supply. She hadn't been safe for a very long time, but those powders that could close a wound and keep the lifeblood from draining away would make her a little safer, a little less likely to die before she found the place where she belonged.

Thirty-odd pots and jars lined the shelves. As Carin eyed them, wondering which to search first, the kitchen door opened to the courtyard beyond. Through it stepped the swordsman.

He belonged in darkness—not in this cheerful, caraway-scented kitchen. The man wore black, as before, but his garments today were of fine wool, not the leather of his riding gear.

"Myra, is my—?" He bit off the question as his gaze found Carin at his table.

Now she was standing behind it, and she had no memory of getting to her feet. Her head swam and could produce only one thought: *Run.*

But she couldn't run. She couldn't move. She could only stand and stare at him as a coldness surged up from her stomach and jellied all her senses.

He stared back. Fleetingly, he looked surprised. Then his expression grew guarded, aloof.

The housekeeper—Myra by name, obviously—greeted the man warmly and prattled on: Her master's meal would be served in an eyeblink, and hadn't their midnight visitor cleaned up well, just as Myra had foretold?

The swordsman made no reply as he unclasped his cloak and hung it by the door. Carin caught a gleam from the silver badge that fastened the garment. In the sunlight that streamed through the open door, the horns of the crescent moon flashed like sparks from a firestone.

Carin's captor took the bench opposite her. Silently he nodded his thanks to the efficient Myra as the woman set ale on the table for him. He sipped from the tankard and continued his wordless study of a stock-still Carin. Finally, he answered:

"Myra, I am humbled to the ground by your talents in these matters. I scarce gave credit to your claims last night that the revolting creature I carried aloft could shed the muck and emerge a human. Though it doesn't alter her vagrant nature, the outward change assuredly is welcome. At least she does not *stink* now."

Carin clenched her fists at her sides so tightly that her fingernails cut her palms. For a moment, she had no voice. Then she found it.

"Try losing your horse," she snapped, "and walking all summer, with no clothes except the ones you're wearing. Try it, and

see if you don't get as dirty as me and every bit as ripe. Or riper —
to the point of a real stench … sir."

That's enough, muttered her reflexive aversion to bodily harm.
*You know you can't talk to him that way. Like your old master told you
every time he belted you: "Remember your place."*

But of all the nerve … If her unwashed state offended the man,
he should have left her where he found her. *I suppose he's accustomed to abducting a better class of person —*

Carin planted her fist on her hip and grated out her words in
much the same tone she used when swearing. "*Thanks* for letting
me wash up in that hot-spring pool upstairs where the walls
glow. I've never seen anything like it. It's amazing." She gave a
little sniff, trying to appear disdainful.

*But the pool IS amazing. And I sound like I actually AM thanking
him for punching my lights out and manhandling me here.*

Desperate to avoid giving any impression of gratitude, Carin
added, "I can't guess how a marvel like that came to be. Who
gets the credit? Not *you*, I wouldn't think." She cut her eyes at
the man's scarred hand, the one that was short a finger.

No sound greeted Carin's attempts at sarcasm except the bub-
bling of the stewpot on the fire. Even Myra had fallen silent. The
woman kept her eyes lowered and said nothing as she heaped
meat and vegetables on a platter for her master's lunch.

When Myra had set the dish before him, the swordsman buttered a slab of fresh-baked bread and balanced it on the platter's
rim. Then, with the butter knife, he waved Carin back to her seat.

"I hardly hoped to find so much wit in you, to know a marvel
when you see it." He looked across the table at her. His tone,
though sharp, was more dismissive than angry. "The pools—
two of similar design are in this house—are extraordinary, as
you say. They were crafted by my noble ancestor whose estate
this was long ago, and whose descendants, myself among them,
have abided here in an unbroken line since the family's estab-
lishment."

The swordsman paused to take bites of bread and stew. Then he sipped his ale and eyed Carin speculatively.

"As you have nothing but rags to ward off autumn's chill," he said, "and you travel—by your own admission—on foot and without provisions, I take you for a runaway bondmaid. Undoubtedly you carried off whatever you could steal from your master. But it seems your thievery has proved inadequate for your journey. Starvation would have found you, if I had not."

Hold on there, Carin protested, but only inwardly. She wanted to say that she had borrowed—not stolen—from her old master. To survive, however, in the months since leaving him, she'd played the thief time and again. Remembering her plan to ransack Myra's kitchen, she kept still and let the accusation stand.

Now it's coming, she thought. He'd demand to know where— and to whom—she belonged. How much did she dare reveal?

The swordsman's next question, however, was not what Carin expected.

"Do you know your letters?"

She stared at him blankly. "Sir?"

"It is a simple-enough question," he said, raising a bite of stew to his lips. "Can you read?"

She considered, then shrugged. "I'm not sure."

He scoffed. "The question does not lend itself to much uncertainty. Can you, or can you not?"

"The people I—" Carin broke off. *Slaved for*, she'd started to say. But why confirm his suspicions? "The people I used to live with," she amended, "owned one book. I learned to read it. I don't know if I can read any other books. Do you have one for me to look at?"

"I do. None here can comprehend it. Since you are from elsewhere, perhaps you can make it out."

To his housekeeper he said, "Myra, go to the library and open the bottom drawer of my desk. Bring me the book you find there."

"I obey, master, with as much haste as these old legs can make," Myra responded. She bustled off into the passageway that connected the kitchen to the house. Her footsteps trailed away on the ground floor past the foot of the staircase.

The hairs rose along Carin's arms. *Breathe,* she told herself. *You've been doing all right with him. Don't lose it now.* But where was he going with this "Can you read" business?

Sitting alone with the swordsman, Carin felt her nerve-ends prickle as if he were again holding a blade to her throat. She had to lock her hands around her now-empty tea mug to keep from clutching her neck — a defensive gesture that would only tell him how vulnerable he made her feel.

But a man with a sword was an understandable threat ... not like his second, bare-handed attack, when he'd knocked Carin senseless. Why could she remember the cruel hurt, but no fist-to-flesh contact? Sitting at the mirror this morning while Myra combed her hair, Carin had had ample time to examine her face for cuts or bruises. There were none. If her captor had hit her hard enough to put her out cold for the night — and wasn't that what he had done? — she should be wearing his mark now.

The man scraped his platter clean, noisily spooning up the last of the stew. He did not otherwise break the silence that filled the kitchen in Myra's absence.

And mercifully, he did not look at Carin, though she studied him with many sidelong glances. She'd never seen a face like his in the south. For one thing, his skin hadn't been tanned to leather by the elements. The northern sun must be less brutal, or the summers milder here. He lacked the windburned, sun-scorched look of the typical low-latitudes male. Different, too, was his narrow, straight nose. Hawk beaks dominated farther south.

The swordsman's mustache curved down at the corners of his mouth to join the beard that traced his jaw. The dark, neat line of the mustache was thinner than any plainsman would sport, and the beard more closely cropped. He wore his hair swept back from his forehead. It fell to his shoulders, crow-black and straight. His hair was silvering at the temples, but the noontime sun that spread through the kitchen picked out no other gray strands.

His age? Unguessable, she'd say. And not particularly important in defining him. A durableness about him suggested that ordinary concepts of age might not apply in his case.

His housekeeper, returning from her errand, fluttered in like a plump, tame goose. She placed a book near the swordsman's hand. Nattering on about what a lovely day it was for so late in the season, and how many fine books filled the master's library, Myra began clearing the table.

As his housekeeper worked around him, the man picked up the book and flipped through it briefly. Not speaking, he held it out to Carin.

She wiped her greasy fingers, took the book, and studied its red and gold cover. After a moment's puzzled hesitation, she opened the volume and skimmed its first pages.

How? Where ... ? Carin couldn't fully form her questions. She could only stare at the pages. The writing was in a language she couldn't remember seeing before ... but there was so much she could not remember, and other things that she *knew*, in the deepest levels of her mind, without knowing *how* she knew them. Though she hadn't remembered what this language *looked* like, though she couldn't remember ever seeing it written down before, she definitely knew what it *sounded* like. This was her own private language — the one she thought in, and the tongue she lapsed into whenever she came unstuck.

It's here. My language ... it's real. It's not just in my head.

Carin looked up from the volume to find the swordsman studying her fiercely, as if he were trying to divine her thoughts. *Don't let him know,* said every experience that had taught her to keep her brainwork to herself.

Avoiding the man's strangely luminous gaze, she whipped her attention back to the book. Part of her — that voice of caution with its whispered warnings — wanted to close the book, hand it back to him, and feign ignorance. But the stronger part leaped at this chance to show off, to raise herself above the level of a scruffy runaway servant.

From the poem that began the book, Carin chose two stanzas to read aloud. She easily translated them for the swordsman as she went:

> *"Child of the pure unclouded brow*
> *And dreaming eyes of wonder!*
> *Though time be fleet, and I and thou*
> *Are half a life asunder,*
> *Thy loving smile will surely hail*
> *The love-gift of a fairy-tale. ...*
>
> *"Without, the frost, the blinding snow,*
> *The storm-wind's moody madness—*
> *Within, the firelight's ruddy glow,*
> *And childhood's nest of gladness.*
> *The magic words shall hold thee fast:*
> *Thou shalt not heed the raving blast."*

Carin closed the volume and pushed it across the table toward her captor. "Yes, sir," she said with a shrug, as if it didn't matter. "I can read this book. It's called *Through the Looking-Glass.*"

Chapter 3

Secrets

Myra clapped her hands like a delighted child.

"There, my lord! Didn't I tell you? A runagate, you called her, and a vagabond and a beggar. But *I* — I saw right off that she had a good head on her shoulders. 'A smart young thing, she is,' I said. 'Bright as a new copper,' I said. 'Had to have her wits about her,' I said, 'to be traveling all alone, poor dearie, and fending for herself,' this far from nowhere. 'Give her a go at the puzzle-book,' I said. A bright young thing like her — 'tis no surprise to me, my lord. No surprise at all."

The swordsman scowled at Carin, ignoring the flurry of words from his housekeeper. Then he shoved back his bench and stood. He snatched up the book, stepped back a pace, and pointed, indicating the passageway to the foyer.

"Come with me."

Deliberately — she would obey, but not too meekly — Carin gave her mouth and fingers a final wipe and rose from the table. She thanked Myra for her double breakfast, which sent the housekeeper into a pother of thinking-out-loud about preparations for supper. The woman flew about the kitchen, gathering ingredients for the evening meal. She was left talking to herself as Carin followed the swordsman down the passageway, past the foot of the staircase, and into a hallway that opened off the foyer.

Indoors on his own two feet, the swordsman wasn't as imposing as he had seemed astride his tall hunter out in the woods. Carin, trailing along behind him, judged him to be not much over the common height. And though he was muscular, he was too lean to be described as brawny. The grace in his movements spoke of a confident and well-conditioned strength.

They reached the hall's end. The man pushed open a door and held it for her.

Carin took two steps into the library and halted. "Sweet mother of mercy," she softly swore, her eyes widening.

Books lined the walls from the tiled floor to the high, painted ceiling. Every inch of shelf space was filled, and the overflow buried the room's flat surfaces. Books covered a massive oak desk under arching windows. Books spilled from a low table between two cushioned benches. Books sat piled on the floor. Even the windowsills and the fireplace mantel sprouted books. Carin—who had wheedled her former master's fourteen-year-old daughter to teach her to read the one book in that household—stood in awe of the swordsman's vast collection. She had not imagined so many books could exist in all the world.

The library door thudded closed behind her. The swordsman brushed past her shoulder, so close she could smell him. Coming from the man or his clothes was the odor of calendula oil, a musky scent that mingled with the woody, leathery smell of old books.

He wheeled to face her. "Explain yourself," he demanded, holding up the book he carried. "I have studied the ancient languages and I cannot read these words. How is it that you can?"

"No idea," Carin said and tossed her hair back. "I just look at the words and know what they mean. I can't tell you how I do it."

He took a step toward her.

Don't! snapped her inner voice as she almost backed away from him. By a wrenching effort of will, Carin stood her ground. But she could not look the man in the face and risk seeing too deeply into his glimmering, unquiet eyes.

"I warn you, do not provoke me." His voice was steel. "I am in no mood for games. The language of this book is foreign. You claim to know the tongue. Tell me where and when you learned it."

"Sir, I honestly can't say." Carin's tone was calm—firm, almost. And with her hands fisted at her sides, he wouldn't see that they were shaking. "I don't know where or when or how I learned to read the language of that book you're holding. I can't remember ever seeing words written like that before. There's just some part of me that knows what they mean."

The muscles tightened along the man's jaw. Carin braced for a blow. She had taken so many blows in her time as a servant, she was good at seeing them coming.

But the swordsman didn't strike her. He turned on the heel of one boot and crossed to the fireplace. With an exasperated sigh, he dropped onto a bench and gestured for Carin to be seated opposite him, with the book-strewn low table between them.

"Tell me, pray, what you *do* remember," he demanded. "Do you know your name?"

"Of course. I'm called Carin."

"Good. That's a start. Now, tell me where you come from and why you have trespassed on my land."

He makes it sound simple, she thought, *like I ought to be able to give him plain answers. Well it is simple, I guess, if I don't tell him everything.*

She looked down. Her ugly scar was showing, the one on her forearm where she'd sloshed the boiling oil while cooking for her old master. She tugged on her sleeve to hide it, and glanced up to find her captor watching. His eyes made her wince. To avoid them, Carin focused her gaze slightly left of the man's temple. Then she began the account of her life as bond-servant to a wheelwright ...

She had come to the wright's household as a half-grown child, strong enough to do the chores her masters set her of cooking, cleaning, weaving and the like. For five years they'd given her meals and a cubby to sleep in, and she'd done what they'd told her to do.

The wheelwright lived in a farming town down south—Carin omitted naming the place. On a warm night early this past summer, some five months ago, she had left the family sleeping, slipped out to the stable and saddled the strongest horse there—a gaunt, striding dun that had little beauty but more stamina than the rest combined. Riding through the night, heading north, she reached a farmstead before daybreak. A wagon loaded with straw stood ready to be driven to town. She dismounted, tied the reins to the saddle, and sent the dun home with a slap on its rump. The horse would make its own way back to the wright's stable—if no one managed to catch the beast and steal it for themselves.

In the predawn, Carin climbed into the wagon and burrowed. She'd barely grown still when the jingle of harness announced the arrival of the farmer with his team. Hitching up, they drove to town. Safe in the straw, she dozed.

Carin woke to the clamor of the marketplace. She dug out and jumped down. In the confusion of wagons and teams, farmers and peddlers setting up to hawk their wares in the open-air market, no one noticed one slim girl dodging carts and threading the throng of horses and people.

"I begged a little food and started walking," Carin said as she neared the conclusion of her story. Actually, she had stolen more than she'd begged. But stealing was not a crime she would admit to. Thieves were commonly rebuked by having their hands lopped off.

"I just kept walking," she added. "Heading north always … all summer. Every league I covered, the country looked the same—grassy and empty, nothing much but hay fields and cow pastures, and then just the prairie. But yesterday, things changed. I climbed the hill and got in among the trees."

She risked a direct glance at her captor to see what effect her next words might have. "Like I told you before, sir, I never saw a wall or any kind of boundary. The way I came, it's all open—

just some trees. And I thought the trees meant I had reached the wilderness. Another league or so, I thought, and I'd be in the old forests where nobody lives" — a place which, until that moment, Carin had never considered as a possible destination. But it would do. She needed to sound like she knew what she was doing and where she was going, even if she didn't.

In closing, Carin shrugged one shoulder, trying to look unconcerned. "You can believe me or not, but I never meant to trespass on your land. I didn't know it was private."

The swordsman heard her out without comment, regarding her through slitted eyelids. As Carin fell silent, he stood and walked to a small cabinet that was set amid the books crowding the shelves. From it, he took a flagon, and poured himself a goblet full of some ruby liquid. Drink in hand, he resumed his seat on the high-backed bench opposite hers.

"I accept the truth of your story, so far as you've told it," he said at last. He sipped his drink. Then he leaned toward her across the table between them and set the goblet down hard. "What you have *not* told me will make a far stranger tale, I'll warrant. How did you come to be a servant in the wright's household? Where is your home? Who are your people? Who are mother and father to you?"

Carin passed a hand over her eyes and rubbed her forehead. These ... these were the questions she never answered ... *could* never answer. Just thinking about them made her head ache. It was like straining to see the stars on a night when clouds blanketed the sky. No pinpoints of light pierced the darkness.

She shook her head. "Sir, I don't have a father or a mother." Her voice caught; she cleared her throat. "I don't know where I was born. I don't remember how or when I came to the wright's house. They told me they found me one winter. I was lying at the edge of a pond where the wright and his family had come to fish. They said I was soaking wet, like I'd almost drowned, and so cold I was blue. The way they tell it, I was scared to death."

Carin paused. It felt unnatural to say so much. She hadn't said this many words in one sitting in maybe ever. But then, this strange man was the first person who had ever said to her: "Tell me about yourself."

He was looking at her, intent, waiting. She rubbed her throat, and her voice strengthened as she continued.

"I didn't talk to them then, or for a year after that. When I did start talking, I couldn't say things right. I mixed up my words. They thought I was 'sheep-headed,' as they put it. But I kept trying until I could talk as good as any of them could. I listened to everybody who came into my master's shop—all the travelers and the people from the town, and the field hands—and I practiced, in secret.

"The youngest daughter heard me practicing out at the mill-pond," Carin added, "but she didn't tell anybody. She wanted to play the game too. When she figured out that I wasn't as dim-witted as they'd all thought, she taught me to read the holy *Drishanna*—it was the only book her father owned." Carin tilted her head, and a strand of squeaky-clean hair came slipping over her eye. She pushed it back. "Around the rest of the family, I just stayed sheep-headed. It kept me out of trouble. If the wheel-wright had known I could think, he would have watched me closer."

This spotty account of her origins and her education earned Carin the swordsman's hard stare—like an archer studying his target. His next question arrowed straight as a fletched shaft to the part of her story that must sound the least sensible, if he made her say it aloud.

"North, always," he muttered, half to himself. Then, a great deal more forcefully, he demanded:

"Why? You aren't the first serving-girl to run from her master, but why strike out for the forests of the far north with winter coming on? How could you hope to survive on your own when the snows begin, and the winds howl, and the air is so cold it freezes in your lungs? You claim to be sound-witted, yet your actions are those of a rattlebrained fool." He tapped his temple. "Fools have no business in the north country. What brought you here?"

Don't let him get to you, Carin thought. But her cheeks burned. Too offended to invent any lie that would serve her better than the truth, she gibbered out the very thing she hadn't wanted to say.

"The village wisewoman told me to go north. She said I didn't belong in the south, I was no child of the plains country — my place was in the north. She told me to go. So I did."

Shut up. You are babbling like the rattlebrain he says you are, warned the voice in the back of her head.

As Carin heeded it and stopped talking, the swordsman gave her a look she couldn't interpret. "The wisewoman … she threatened you?" He lifted his chin slightly. "She bade you leave the town; else, she'd hex you?"

"Hex me? *Meg* — ?" Carin broke off sharply before she fully named the woman. "No! Why would you think — " She stopped again, dumbfounded by the idea of the wisewoman practicing witchcraft. Then she gave a snort of derision. "The woman isn't young, but she's not *that* old. There hasn't been a witch in the village for a long time."

"How would you know that?" the swordsman demanded. "What would a foundling like you know of the village's history?"

"I heard the stories. All the elders tell stories."

"Of witches?"

Carin nodded. "Witches, warlocks, sorcerers — the dark ones who were destroyed. The village priest said that decent people shouldn't talk about such blackhearts, or listen to stories about those days. But that didn't stop the elders from spinning tales. In one story they swore was true, a witch hexed every home in the village. The people went to her hut at noon, when they could be sure she'd be asleep—she roamed nights, cutting the livers out of dogs and fouling the water-wells with their carcasses. At midday the people burned her hut, with her in it." Carin shrugged. "The elders said that was the last witch ever seen in the village. It all happened a long time ago."

"But tell me of the current wisewoman," the swordsman said, raising one eyebrow. "Had no suspicion fallen on her?"

"Suspicion?" Carin started to shake her head, then hesitated. It couldn't be denied that the villagers were a wary lot—mistrustful of outsiders. Some of them had criticized the wheelwright for keeping a servant girl who came from nowhere and didn't seem quite right in the head …

"She's touched, that one," people would mutter, pointing as Carin passed by.

"You can see it in her eyes," their neighbors agreed. *"Ain't no child of Granger ever been born with green eyes. And she's a sneaky little thing, slipping off to see that witchy old woman every chance she gets."*

Witchy. Carin had thought they were maligning the wisewoman for her eccentricities: her colorful shawls, her fondness for her hens, her general disdain for the company of others. Could they actually think that Meg practiced *witchcraft?* What utter and dangerous nonsense! But the woman—Megella, to name her in full—had once mentioned that she, like Carin, wasn't village-born. In Granger, that alone could cast her under suspicion.

"Daydream in your own time," the swordsman snapped. "Don't waste mine."

"Wh—? Oh." Carin shifted uncomfortably. "I was just trying to imagine the wisewoman's neighbors burning her in her bed." She shook her head. "No, I can't see it. Everyone in the village went to the wisewoman when they had a fever or their animals got sick. She set bones … midwifed babies … never turned anyone away. She was stern, but kind—and one of the few people in town who cared anything about me. When she sent me away, she said it was for my own good. I didn't ask her why."

"You were not hesitant to strike out on your own?"

Carin shrugged. "I was miserable in the village with the wright's family. They weren't the cruelest people around, they didn't beat me every day, but … I didn't fit there. I didn't belong." She looked down, remembering. "When the wisewoman told me to go, I never stopped to think about it. I just saddled the dun and headed north."

Most of what you just told him sounds like complete nonsense, you know, Carin thought with an inward sigh. As a child, she'd come bobbing up in a pond like a fisher's float? Five years later, she would walk across half a continent, with no destination in mind except for the ill-defined territory known as "the North" — all on the say-so of a witchy old woman? The swordsman couldn't possibly believe her. She should have kept her mouth shut.

His face wore a noncommittal quality that was beginning to alarm her with its remoteness. But in his gleaming eyes, Carin saw a hint of turmoil. Had something in her story troubled him?

After a long silence, and with the air of someone who had reached a much-debated decision, the man scooped his goblet from the tabletop. He drained it of the ruby liquor. Using the goblet's stem as a pointer then, he indicated the books that were piled on the low table and the floor under it.

"Let us see how well you learned your letters as the wright's daughter taught you from the *Drishanna*. Read to me the titles of the books that lie before you."

"What? I mean … yes, all right … sir."

Carin scooted to the edge of her seat and picked up the nearest volume. She ran her hand over the carved leather binding, and with her fingertips she traced the letters of the book's title, stamped in gold. It appeared to be an alchemist's handbook: *On the Potential of Transmutation.* Other volumes on the table dealt with fire and water, soil and sky, rituals of healing, rites to mark the summer and winter solstices, and the habits of frogs and toads.

She read off their titles one by one, placing each volume beside her on the bench so as not to repeat a title. She went through some dozen volumes before the swordsman stopped her.

"Enough. I am satisfied that the task is not beyond you. You will order the books in this library, by title, with the first volume to be placed on the uppermost shelf there" — he pointed with the goblet's stem to the wall at Carin's left — "and the final volume to go in the hindmost corner there." He tipped his head back, indicating the depths of the library behind him. The afternoon sunlight that streamed in through the conservatory-style windows did not pierce the shadows behind the benches where they sat. But his gesture implied more shelves looming in the back.

"Complete the task to my satisfaction," the man said, "and I will give you leave to resume your journey, ill-advised though it is. Nothing stirs in winter in the northern forests. The bears drowse in their dens under the snow. The birds flee. Even the wasteland dogs desert the snowy places when the winds begin to blow. They gather in mobs along my northernmost borders. Nothing you seek can await you in that empire of ice — unless you seek death." He shot her a quizzical look. "If that is the purpose of your journey, I won't hinder it. Only do the work I have set for you, and you may go."

Sweet mother of mercy, Carin swore again, but silently. She gaped as she looked around the room. The enormity of the task! This library held thousands upon thousands of volumes. Those crammed into its endless shelves were as disarrayed as those on the table and floor. To arrange them as the swordsman commanded would mean removing all from their places, sorting and re-sorting, climbing a ladder thousands of times to reshelve the volumes properly.

Taming the chaos would take her not only all of the winter ahead, but very possibly the springs, summers, falls, and winters of years to come. How could she do it?

How can you refuse? asked the part of her that warmed at the very thought. To not only have a roof over her head again, but to live with these books, to immerse herself in them, to riffle their gilt-edged pages and smell their wood-dust dryness — to lounge by a fire on the hearth as winter sunlight spilled through the windows, offering enough light to read by —

She would steal every chance to read the volumes, as many as she could, when the swordsman wasn't watching. In seeming to do his bidding, she'd pore over the texts in his library, absorbing everything they could tell her.

She might even get the chance to read the "puzzle-book," as Myra called the volume that mystified the swordsman. Quick as the thought entered Carin's mind, her eyes sought the *Looking-Glass* book where it lay on the bench near her captor's disfigured left hand.

But then Carin gave a start and jerked her head up. She'd caught a distant echo, like the whisper of a voice or perhaps only the impression of one — only a memory, possibly. But it gripped her like a compulsion. It repeated, as it always did: *North, girl.* And the force of it nearly drew her to her feet to resume her journey without a moment's further delay.

Carin reached for a book from among those she had piled beside her. She hefted it, as if to test the volume's weight, as if to gauge its ability to anchor her. And she found that the book almost — *almost* — counterbalanced the compulsion. For the first time in months, Carin felt able to resist the urge to tramp onward, or at least to put it off. Just for now, just for a while, she could deceive this man. She could feign acceptance, do the work demanded of her, and live with these books … until the urge to push ahead succeeded in driving her from them.

"Thank you, sir." Carin flashed the swordsman one of her rare smiles. "I accept your offer. I would much rather sort out your beautiful books than cook and clean for the wright. I'll be glad to get started—right away, if you want me to."

He eyed her narrowly, clearly doubting her sincerity. Had she overplayed the role of grateful servant?

But the swordsman did not challenge her. He set his empty goblet on the table before him, picked up the puzzle-book, stood, and strode to the door. With his free hand on the latch, he paused and half turned back to her, as if undecided whether to leave or to continue the interview. Carin had launched into her task already, stacking books in new piles on the floor, marshaling them by the first letters in each title.

"Myra will call you to supper," he said finally. Opening the door, he turned to go but stopped when Carin addressed him.

"Sir, excuse me." She straightened from her work and smoothed the shift that Myra had provided to replace her travel-stained rags. "You're giving me food and clothes and a place to stay, and the best job I've ever had, and I don't even know your name. Won't you tell me what I should call you?"

He gave her a measuring look. "What you 'should' call me? Have you formed the habit of calling me things you oughtn't?"

Several names shot through Carin's thoughts—*devil*, *fiend*, and *prince of darkness* among them—but she shook her head. "No, sir. I don't call you anything. Well," she amended, "in my mind I call you 'the swordsman.'"

He raised an eyebrow, and Carin felt the color rise again in her cheeks.

"In your mind," he said, "you call me worse than that, I'll wager." He fixed her with another of his unreadable looks, then answered her question. "Mine is the name of the House of Verek, who are lords by blood-right of the lands called Ruain. Address me then, as custom dictates and rank demands, by the name and title which are my due."

43

With that, he stepped into the hallway and was gone.

As soon as the door closed behind the said Lord Verek, Carin abandoned her book-sorting and hurried to the desk under the room's tall windows. She rummaged through unlocked drawers and found only sealing wax, sheets of fine linen paper, ink and writing instruments. The bottom drawer, where Myra had been told to find the puzzle-book, was empty. It held no mate to the volume that Verek had taken with him from the room.

Carin turned to the crammed shelves and skimmed the titles of book after book until one fat volume caught her eye: *The Lands and Realms of Ladrehdin*. Pulled from the shelf, it opened to pages of maps — a treasure like gold to a traveler. Would one show her the realms of the North?

She retired to the desk with her prize. "Ruain," Verek had called his lands, but there was no map so named. Page after page was labeled simply "The Interior." Near the back of the book was a map inscribed "The Wildes," but nothing to say whether that referred to the north's old forests. In any case, it was useless — only an outline with no particulars drawn in.

One large map was a detailed drawing of the southern grasslands. A small "x" among several marked the village where the wheelwright and his family lived. An irregular blue blob represented the body of water where Carin had been found as a child.

Minor landmarks she had passed in her journey northward — settlements, streams, and the welcome stretches of broken country — might provide clues by which to trace her travels. It was hard to be sure, because she'd mostly avoided people and she didn't know the names of many of the settlements beyond the wright's village. Painstakingly matching memory to the details on the map, however, Carin guessed at her route cross-country and was astonished to see how far she'd traveled in twenty weeks. The unrelenting compulsion had pushed her onward, over the dip and swell of the plains, through the long summer and into the dregs of autumn, half killing her with hunger and exhaustion. But she had never paused, not until Lord Verek of Ruain forced her off her path at swordpoint.

Maybe, Carin found herself thinking, *I kept going only because I had no reason to stop.* Now, she had a reason. If she stayed here, she might learn things to her advantage—not least, the story of the puzzle-book and why its language was known to her and not to Verek.

An unfamiliar feeling crept over Carin. For a moment, she experienced freedom, as if a hand had slackened its grip on her. But immediately the old urge—the impulse that had kept her moving day after day—reasserted itself and even interjected a counterargument:

You're dreaming about that book, it said, its tone dismissive. *Didn't you notice how his lordship guards it? It barely left his hand. How do you propose to get it away from him? Poison his supper when Myra's back is turned?* What poison could harm him? Myra claimed her "good master"—apothecary, herbalist, and alchemist—could mix a potion to cure any ailment.

Carin shook her head to clear the jumble of conflicting thoughts. Dutifully she placed *The Lands and Realms of Ladrehdin* in its proper pile on the floor, atop *Lucet's Guide to Distillation* and a slim volume with a one-word title, *Ladra*. Then she selected another book to examine: a collection of training exercises for archers. Maybe she could make a bow and arrows and teach herself to shoot as accurately as she could cast her sling. Where she was going, skill with the bow could be useful.

Settling with the book, Carin was soon lost in the volume's well-illustrated pages. She didn't look up; she forgot even to listen for the swordsman's possible return. She read until the sunlight through the windows dimmed to twilight and she could no longer make out the words. Just as Carin slipped a sheet of Lord Verek's writing paper between the pages to mark her place, Myra bustled into the room to call her to supper.

Carin paused in the library's doorway to look back at the multitude of books. Once gone from this place, she'd never again enter a library the equal of the swordsman's. And she would lose any chance, however slim it might be, to read the *Looking-Glass* book.

She studied the bench where Verek had sat, the book at his mutilated hand, its secrets closed to him but accessible to her. What was in that book? Why was it in her language? What could it tell her?

Until yesterday, Carin's purpose had been plain: do as the wisewoman said and go north. Verek had asked about the woman hexing her, and Carin had denied it. But maybe she *had* been bewitched — or enthralled by the hope of a new life in a far country. Now, for the first time, she questioned her goal. *Where is this journey taking me?*

Chapter 4

Questions

On her second morning under Verek's roof, Carin got up before daylight. She had a quick wash in the room with the glowing walls and threw on her old shirt and patched leggings, which Myra had miraculously scrubbed clean. The housekeeper had neatly repaired the damage done by Carin's stumble in the rocks — almost as neatly as Verek had mended her gashed knee. The woman had also found time yesterday to make up Carin's bed with fresh linens, and to prepare an excellent supper of roast capon and spinach tart.

Now in the predawn, Carin found the indefatigable Myra already at work in the kitchen, clearing the remains of two breakfasts. Early though the hour was, Verek had taken his morning meal and left the manor. He would be gone all day, Myra said, and Lanse the stableboy with him. They were inspecting Verek's holdings to the east, the productive farms and dairylands that supplied the nobleman's wealth and stocked Myra's kitchen.

The housekeeper's description of fertile and populated lands nearby contrasted markedly with the lifeless woods where Carin had fallen afoul of the owner. When the housekeeper paused for breath, Carin broached the subject.

"Myra, you must know everything that's worth knowing," she said, to butter up the woman for the prying that she meant to do. "Can you tell me what's wrong with your master's woodland? I mean, it's so ..." She needed a moment to come up with the word: "*Bleak.* I walked through those woods for about an hour before Lord Verek caught me. And you know I never had a clue, that that land was his private property," Carin added, ever alert for a chance to assert her innocence.

"You're not to blame, dearie," Myra said, shaking her head. She did not look up from the dishes she was washing. "I know you meant no harm."

"And even if I had — meant harm, I mean," Carin said, "I don't know that I could have done anything to damage those woods, short of setting fire to the trees. It's an unnatural place, it's so deathly quiet. I didn't hear a bird sing, or a cricket chirp, or even a mouse in the leaves. I didn't see a squirrel. I never scared up a rabbit. After awhile, it just felt *strange* — like I was the only thing that had been alive in there for ages.

"When I heard Lord Verek riding toward me," she added, "it was like hearing a ghost. Like I'd stumbled into woods that were haunted, and the phantom horseman was coming for me." Carin shivered despite the warmth of the fire on the kitchen's huge hearth. She considered telling Myra all that had happened — Verek nearly trampling her, then pinning her at swordpoint and threatening to strike her head from her shoulders. But Myra obviously thought the world of her "good master." She probably wouldn't hear a word against him.

"So what I'm wondering, Myra," Carin went on, getting back to her question, "is why the woods are so deserted and depressing. You were telling me about all the good land that Lord Verek owns. It sounds like whatever is wrong with the woods hasn't spread to the farms. What is it? Some kind of disease? Is there a sickness in the woods?"

Myra nodded. "Aye. 'Tis a sickness of the soul."

Tears came to the woman's eyes. She dug into the pockets of her housedress for a kerchief and noisily blew her nose.

"'Tis a sorrowful tale, dearie," the housekeeper said, snuffling. "Once, those woods were alive with birdsongs and the chirpings of small creatures. The creeks babbled like children at play. There was a lake of the clearest blue water, with white water-lilies and all manner of fish and frogs. The flowers bloomed from early spring 'til frost, and the woods gloried in their colors and scents. 'Twas the loveliest place in the world.

"Every day of good weather, my mistress—the master's lady wife—would go walking in the woods. 'Twas her greatest pleasure, to stroll about and pluck the freshest blooms and bring them in a basket to brighten the rooms of this house."

"The master's wife?" *There's a surprise*, Carin thought, her breath catching a little. "He's married?"

"He was, dearie. And he loved the lady with all his heart. But now he is alone. 'Tis the saddest tale." Myra dabbed at her eyes. "There came a day—a black day it was—when my mistress went strolling as it pleased her to do, through the woods to the lake. At her side, with his little hand in hers, was the lady's and my master's own sweet child. Oh my! You never saw a child more beautiful than the son of my lord and his lady. Never was a babe more adored. They doted on the boy. Many a time I heard them speak together of what a fine day it would be when the child came of age and claimed his birthright. So proud of him, so full of hopes and plans they were."

"What happened? Where's the boy now?" Carin prodded as Myra paused to snuffle into her kerchief.

"Oh, my. Dead! The child is dead, and his mother with him."

At this, Myra burst into a fit of tears. The crying jag lasted so long that Carin despaired of learning any details of the tragedy. After a time, however, the housekeeper's sobs subsided and she resumed her story.

"'Twas a terrible thing. It sorely affects me even now to think on it, these many years later. As the shadows grew long and the sun went to its bed, and my mistress and the child did not come home, my lord went into the woods to seek them. 'Twas in the blue lake he found them, dearie, found his lady and the sweet child. They were tangled in the water-lilies. Drowned! The master's wife and his only child. It sore affects me, even now."

49

Myra sat blubbering at the kitchen table. Carin patted the housekeeper's shoulder. "I'm sorry," she mumbled. She hadn't meant for her questions to call up such painful memories. In awkward silence, Carin set about getting her own breakfast of porridge and bacon. By the time she'd fixed her meal and joined Myra at the table, the housekeeper's tears were drying. Without further prodding, Myra returned to the tragedy.

"The master's grief was terrible to see," she whispered. "He raged against the very powers of creation. He cursed the lake, and the lilies withered, and the stench of rotting fish rose from the water as he drove away the life. He neither ate nor slept, but sorrowed night and day for the loss of his lady and their dear child.

"I feared the master would go mad," Myra confided. "Aye, indeed … I think he did go mad when he cried out a punishment upon the woods that his wife had loved so well. He could not help what he did, for the place had betrayed his lady's trust and his own. And from that day to this, the woods have been as empty as the master's own heart. Didn't you remark the unnatural silence, dearie? 'Tis the master's grief that drives out the life, even now."

Carin stared at the woman. What to make of this tale? Myra clearly believed that Verek had placed a curse on the woods. Was that even possible? The priests of Drisha taught that all those blackhearts who had had the power to lay curses had been destroyed long ago. The evils of sorcery and witchcraft were things of the past—and good riddance to them, the priests said.

In preoccupied silence, Carin stacked her breakfast dishes and started to work the hand-pump. But Myra shooed her from the kitchen.

"Go on with you now. I was drawing water and washing dishes in this house before you were born, and the day's not yet come that I'll sit idly by and watch another do my work. And there's this about it too, dearie," Myra said, tapping her finger on the table. "The master has set you a task of your own, so he told me. I'm to watch and see that you stay to your chore in the library. Best be getting to it. The sun's showing in the east. Come midday, I'll bring you in a bite to eat. So you just go on now, child, and fill your head with all that's in those musty old books."

"Yes, ma'am. I'll try."

Carin hurried down the hall to the library. Though Verek's absence was an invitation to explore the rest of the house, right now she was intent upon a different kind of quest: finding some logical explanation for the woodland's desolation. She'd felt such hope when she'd first stepped off the grassland and climbed through drifts of autumn leaves. The silence of the woods had seemed full of promise, as if the trees held their collective breath, preparing to welcome Carin to the end of her journey. But deeper in, that silence had turned ominous. What was wrong under those oaks? Why did the place both attract and repel her?

Before the library's door had fully closed behind her, Carin was prowling the shelves, seeking volumes on the natural elements. Leafing through scores of books, she put the most promising on Verek's desk, which occupied the best-lit spot in the room, under the windows; even with the morning sun slanting in through them, the depths of the library remained gloomy. To make a pretense of sorting books as Verek had instructed, she stacked on the floor any volumes that she examined but found unhelpful.

When the floor piles were noticeably higher and more numerous than they had been yesterday evening — offering evidence of work done — Carin settled at the desk with the half-dozen books she had chosen to study. The first, titled *Fyr & Waeter, Erthe & Aer*, dealt with the four substances of which everything was made. In the essences might lie an explanation for the woods' lifelessness — something sensible to pit against Myra's notion of a "curse."

But no satisfactory answers presented themselves, nothing to do with patterns of rainfall or eroded soils or anything so prosaic. Carin had skimmed halfway through her third volume when the clatter of the doorlatch interrupted her reading. She shoved back from the desk and whirled to face the intruder, her hands reaching for the nearest stack of books, pretending to be busy with them.

But her visitor was only the housekeeper, who pushed past the door with a tray bearing bread, cheese, plums, and a mug of small mead. Myra had recovered her good humor, her tears of the morning apparently forgotten.

"Here now ... I've brought you a morsel to eat, just as I promised. Shift that pile, won't you, and clear a space so I may set this down."

As Carin moved books out of the way, Myra rattled on:

"Bless me, if you haven't made as much of a muddle as the master does when he's poking about in here, piling books everywhere. 'Tis a wonder that poor desk, sturdy as it is, holds together with all the books you've heaped on it. Two of a kind you are, you and my good master. You've no sense in your heads when it comes to these musty old books—hardly a one among 'em that wasn't writ long ago by somebody dead these many years. But you pile them up around you, like a child with her dollies. With your nose in a book, you'd forget to eat—just like my master—if 'twasn't for your old faithful Myra bringing you in a bite. You're a pair, dearie, you and my master."

A pair! Carin stared at the woman, partly shocked and fairly insulted. She'd never met anyone she felt less affinity for than that grim man with the balefire eyes.

The housekeeper's errand done, Myra bustled to the door, where she stopped to deliver an afterthought. "If you need me for anything else, I'll be napping in my little room off the kitchen. We've had such a stir of late, what with a young person in the house again—and such a bright kitling, too, who can read the master's puzzle-book and take pleasure in his library. Surely, 'tis a change for the better, but I'm worn out from the commotion of it. With the master abroad today, methinks I'll lay me down for a little nap. But you come tap on my door, dearie, if there's aught else you need."

Myra went on her way. Carin returned to her book and propped it open beside the tray to read as she ate her lunch.

Midway through a dry chapter on the elemental nature of water, she stopped mid-chew as it hit her: already her chance had come. Lord Verek and the stableboy were gone. Myra slept in her room. Who would stop her leaving? The only other human Carin had heard spoken of in that household was an old gardener.

"This is it," she whispered. "Go. Now."

She tugged open the door, flitted down the hall and up the stairs, got her sling from hiding, and strapped on her belt-pouch. Carin was halfway out the bedroom door again when her gaze found the dressing table. Its embroidered kerchiefs would make wrappers for food and bindings for wounds, among other possible applications that she could improvise.

Verek called you a thief, and you wanted to deny it ... The thought didn't stop her from yanking open the top drawer and grabbing a handful of the kerchiefs.

Downstairs in the foyer Carin turned toward the kitchen, then hesitated. She'd abandoned a tray of half-eaten food in the library.

Leave it! Why risk this chance just to save an old woman the trouble of clearing up? But on tiptoe Carin sprinted back to the library, shaking her head in disbelief at her own actions.

With the tray filling her hands as she exited the room this time, she had to put her back against the door's mass to ease it closed. The weight, not of the door but of the collection behind it, bore down on her. This chance for flight had come too soon. It felt hasty, disturbing. She had just about settled to the idea of working in the library for weeks, or even through the winter months. By leaving so soon, she gave up any chance to discover the library's secrets. She gave up her shot at reading the puzzle-book.

This is not your place, Carin's uneasiness argued. *Remember what the wisewoman said. And Verek, too. He called you a trespasser, an intruder. Listen to them and get on your way.*

For another long moment Carin remained where she was, unable to step either forward or back. When finally she broke away from the library and hurried to the kitchen, she wasn't acting upon a decision so much as escaping her indecision. With sharp, quick movements Carin sacked up bread and cheese, handfuls of raisins, and strips of dried meat, and slipped one of Myra's broad-bladed kitchen knives into her belt.

Next she inspected the pots and jars on the shelves. Most held dried herbs and spices. A short shelf over the door, however, yielded what she sought: two flat tins containing perhaps a cupful each of the bronze and green powders that had healed her knee overnight.

Provisioned, she tied up her sack and stepped outside. Nothing moved in the courtyard, nor at the stable beyond it. Carin studied the stable. On a "borrowed" horse, she could put more distance between herself and the swordsman.

Leaving the slight concealment of the kitchen doorway, she slipped along the wall to peer around the front corner of the house. "Blind me!" Carin swore under her breath at the sight that met her eyes. Lord Verek's manor house was *huge*. The kitchen, its connecting passageway, and the foyer that gave access to the library and her second-floor bedroom were in a minor wing of the house. Down the wall from Carin, this wing joined the imposing main building at an angle.

In the wide "V" between the two parts of the house grew something more startling than the house itself: a well-kept garden. Trees and bushes flourished between graveled paths, and flowers bloomed in neat beds despite the lateness of the season. Their perfumes filled the air. Clearly, whatever afflicted Verek's woodland did not stunt the garden at his home.

No groundsman was at work among the flowers, only the bees. Carin slipped back past the kitchen door and edged around to peek at the rear of the building. But behind the house, nothing green appeared, only a great slab of rock. In fact, the back of the house seemed to melt into the face of a cliff.

I've gone swimming inside that rock, Carin realized as she studied the union of house and cliff. Her upstairs bathing cave had been carved from the mass of stone. That accounted for the lack of windows.

It did not explain the glowing walls.

She pressed her forehead to the smoothly chiseled cornerstone and forced the questions from her mind. Now was not the time to ponder mysteries. The longer she delayed, the poorer her chance of escape.

Praying that the grounds were as deserted as they seemed, she sprinted across to the stable. Beyond it, a hedgerow grew against the high outer wall. Carin picked out a gap in the hedge and, half hidden in the greenery, a plank door. It was closed and barred with a thick timber but not locked.

She dropped her sack, put the strength of her back into one good shove, and dislodged the timber. Slowly, wary of squeaky iron hinges, Carin pulled the door open and looked out into the barren woods just beyond. The oaks, as stark as the garden was lush, bumped right up to the wall.

After a brief, listening pause that brought to Carin's ears only the quick and nervous sounds of her breathing, she turned back and slipped inside the stable. It smelled of hay and horses, though the nearest stalls were disappointingly dark and empty. But as her eyes adjusted, her heart rose. A larger enclosure down the center held a black mare marked with white stockings and a blaze that gleamed in the light from one unshuttered window.

Carin approached slowly, speaking in a low voice. "Easy now. That's right."

The mare, alert to the presence of a stranger, pricked her ears and whickered but did not take fright. The animal was small. This black wouldn't have the stamina of the rawboned dun that Carin had taken from the wheelwright. But the mare was as tame as a cart horse, readily accepting a bit and bridle.

Unchallenged, Carin led the animal outside and through the hedgerow gap. "Good girl," she breathed into the mare's ear. "You're a sweetheart." She retrieved her dropped bag of food, pulled the plank door shut, then sprang onto the mare's bare back.

She'd barely found her seat before the animal took off at a trot, which quickened in a few steps to a gallop. Carin clung to the mare's mane and bent low to avoid the slaps of tree limbs that threatened to snatch away her sack of provisions.

There was no guiding the animal. The black tilted full-speed through the woods, and Carin could do nothing but hold on, the wind rushing in her ears. Whatever direction they were going, even if it was wrong, the mare was setting a pace that would leave Verek's manor far behind.

After a very long way for such a small horse, the black slowed and settled to a brisk walk. Carin straightened gingerly—her insides felt shaken to a pulp. She looked around. After such an abrupt departure, she needed a moment to get her bearings. The sun, dimmed by autumn haze, was far enough along its daily arc to signal the way west. The mare was heading generally with the sun. Carin reined her in the desired direction: north.

"Well, little horse," she said, "you're one for taking the bit in your teeth, aren't you? But thank you for the speedy escape." And maybe it hadn't been a bad thing, Carin reflected, for the mare to take her well to the west instead of heading directly for higher latitudes. Lord Verek—if he chose to pursue—might assume that her route had been due north. This far off course, he might never trail her.

Around Carin the woods were deserted and dismal. Nothing moved, not a sigh, not the faintest breath. Over the landscape hung a silence so heavy, Carin felt it like a weight on her skin. She rubbed her arms and found herself listening, in vain, for murmurs of the curse and echoes of the madness that Myra had ascribed to this place.

"I'm only passing through," she whispered to nothing in particular.

Nothing here, nothing to see … nothing to do but check the sun and keep the mare headed properly. Into the emptiness, her questions crowded.

What chased the life from this woodland? What had drawn Carin here? Why had Verek insisted that his borders were clearly marked, when signs or warnings were obviously absent?

Where had the puzzle-book come from? For that matter, where had *she* come from, and why couldn't she remember further back than five years?

Sighing, Carin felt for the flat tins in her pouch, glad of their nearness. Facing the rigors of winter in the north, she might need miracle cures.

A shiver traveled her length. The sun was dropping toward the horizon now, and the night promised to be cold. Already she was paying a price for her spur-of-the-moment flight. She'd neglected to steal a blanket.

"Good work," she muttered. "You really thought this through, didn't you?"

Carin began to scan the ground ahead, searching for a fallen tree, an exposed labyrinth of roots, a pit or a hollow that might shelter her for the night. As she leaned over the mare's shoulder, the animal snorted and sidestepped. It threw up its head as if trying to scent the thing that had alarmed it.

"Whoa!" Carin exclaimed. Unbalanced, she almost lost her seat. "Steady now!"

As she regained control she whipped her gaze around. Still there was nothing to see but the webs of shadow that the sun's low angle cast through the trees.

Maybe the mare saw only shadows. Carin stroked the animal's neck and spoke reassurances. "Easy … easy, girl."

But the black refused to step forward. Carin tapped with her heels — gently at first, then harder — and struck the balky horse on the rump. The mare shifted her feet and tossed her head but would not proceed.

"The horse does well to refuse, maid," said a reedy voice out of nowhere. "You would be wise to turn back."

Chapter 5

The Riddle

Carin dizzied herself trying to look everywhere at once. Her temples throbbed with the sudden rush of blood from her pounding heart. The mare, however, had settled down and took no new alarm at the voice that seemed to come from empty air.

"Where are you?" Carin demanded. *"Who* are you? What do you want with me?"

"I'm here before you, in this tree," the voice replied. "I only want to speak with you and to entreat you to go no farther. As to *who* I am: I might ask the same of you — meaning no discourtesy, I'm sure."

"I can't see you," Carin protested. "Why won't you show yourself?"

"I cannot show myself more plainly," the voice said. "Look before you at the trunk of the big oak. See? I blink my eyes and wiggle my nose. Can you make me out?"

A wedge of the tree trunk moved. It did indeed look like two eyes blinking and a nose wrinkling. Carin stared, astonished. The rapid movements ceased, to be replaced by a slit like a mouth forming words.

"Ah," said the mouth. "You've found me. Now we may have a proper conversation. In these lonesome woods, it isn't easy to have proper conversations."

She gaped. A talking tree? Could such a thing exist, anywhere but in a fable?

"Who are you?" she asked again. *"What* are you?"

"The mage calls me a woodsprite," the tree said. "That's merely his opinion. But I've heard from no one else on the subject, so I can hardly argue the point. Perhaps you'll give me your thoughts on my nature — when you know me better."

Do I want to know you? Carin wondered. She gripped the reins so tightly that the horse backed a step.

Through the trees, she caught sight of the sun hanging barely the height of a fist above the horizon. Twilight would soon fall, and she didn't relish the thought of spending the night near a talking tree. Though it seemed friendly enough, this woodsprite was another unnatural aspect of a highly abnormal woodland. She wanted out of this place. If the mare refused to take her on north, now was the time to free the animal and continue afoot.

"Um, excuse me," Carin said as she slipped from the mare's back. "I can't stay to talk. I have to keep moving."

"Ah yes, traveler. You've reminded me of my reason for hailing you," the tree said pleasantly. "Until you drew so near that I could guess your purpose, I hadn't planned to speak. The woodcutters from the villages take it badly amiss when I address them. Such screaming and carrying on—you would think it was *I* wielding the ax at *them*. But you are not so easily frightened, which gives me hope that I may yet call you my friend. Did you tell me your name?"

"I'm Carin." She edged away from the tree and kept the horse between herself and the oak as she knotted the reins around the mare's neck.

"A lovely name!" the sprite said. "If I knew my own, I'd tell it to you and seal our new acquaintance. But I don't remember my name. So call me only woodsprite, and I'll answer."

Busy with the horse, Carin didn't reply. When she was satisfied that the reins wouldn't drag, she slapped the animal's rump to send it home. The mare trotted only a short distance, however, then stood with eyes and ears trained on its former rider as if awaiting instructions.

Carin ran at the animal, waving her arms and shouting. "Get away! Go home."

The mare trotted a few more steps, then looked back again. Carin threw a clod at her. "Go home, or stay in these miserable woods all night—it doesn't matter to me," she snapped. "I don't have time to bother with you."

Adjusting the sack of food so that it rode more comfortably on her shoulders, Carin stepped out briskly. Until she could find shelter well away from the talking tree, she'd walk herself warm. She could walk for hours after dark fell, guided by the stars circling overhead. If her absence from the manor wasn't noticed until nightfall, Verek would have the added challenge of tracking her in the dark on a course that even Carin could not have anticipated she'd take.

That swordsman would have less of a reason to follow this horse-thief, Carin thought, grimly, *if that mare of his would go home.* A glance over one shoulder found the horse still standing where she'd left it.

She cupped her hands and shouted into the distance: "You stupid beast! Go!"

"Loyal to a fault is that animal," commented the woodsprite from very near.

"Oh—!" Carin half jumped, half stumbled away from the scrub oak that had spoken. Gathering herself, she spun around to face it. "I thought I'd left you behind, sprite, in that other tree. How are you managing to follow me?"

"In the forest, I can go anywhere," the creature said. "Though I'm not sure how I came to be a dweller in trees, I find that I may travel through them freely, so long as they cluster thickly. Onto the plains, however, I may not venture. I tried it once and nearly expired before I found a tiny shrub for shelter. For days I lingered in its twigs, gathering strength for the leap back to the safety of the forest. I haven't had the courage to repeat the attempt.

"But I digress," the tree interrupted itself. "Let me entreat you again to go no farther, but to return to your faithful horse and ride back the way you came."

"Woodsprite," Carin said with more patience than she felt, "I can't go back. I've been heading just one way for so long, I'm not sure I'd know *how* to turn back. And besides, it's no good for me to be anywhere Lord Verek can find me." Carin had a sudden urge to duck behind a tree as she thought of the swordsman's intense gaze, the looks he gave her, terrifying and indefinable ... glances that made her want to scream. "If he catches me out here a second time, he's liable to do what he threatened before: kill me the slow and painful way." She shook her head. "I need to keep going, sprite. Please don't try to stop me."

Striding forth again, Carin settled into the ground-covering walk that had become, over a summer of travel up from the south, her natural gait. The trees against the sunset made a pattern of stripes, dark then bright, which blurred at the edges of her vision as she hurried along.

"I—beg—you—stop—at—once," came the woodsprite's disconnected voice as the creature leapt from tree to tree to keep up with her. "If—you—go—on ... you—will—die."

"So I've been told," Carin said, remembering Verek's warning about perils massed along his northern borders. But why believe him? He'd lie, or exaggerate, to keep her scared and obedient.

The trees were silent. Maybe the doomsaying sprite had given up its efforts to dissuade her. Carin paced onward, putting the mare far behind. Had the animal turned for home, finally understanding that its rider was gone and it had to fend for itself? She didn't like to think of the little mare spending an unsheltered night in the woods, probably skittery at being so far from the warmth and security of its stable.

"You—do—not—know—what—waits—ahead."

The woodsprite hadn't left. It clipped its words as it jumped tree-to-tree beside her. "Death—will—find—you ... ere—you—go—far."

Sighing, Carin stopped. The woodsprite's words of warning were only slightly less annoying than the broken way it said them. Conversations with the creature were best held while standing still.

"Then teach me, sprite, what you think I need to know," she demanded. "What waits ahead? What danger could there be in this empty forest?"

"This forest isn't empty, Carin," the woodsprite said, a bit breathless but fluent again. "You speak, I think, of the mage's ensorcelled woods. When you traveled there, then indeed you were quite safe—kept from harm by the mage's spells. I bide in his woods myself, for that reason. No woodcutters trouble the mage's trees. In them I rest peacefully, secure in knowing that my haven shan't be hewn down as I sleep.

"But the mage's woods are behind us now," the sprite went on. "Where your horse took fright at nothing you could see: that was the edge of the magic lands. Here in this forest, beyond that boundary, is the realm of the wasteland dogs. I tell you as a friend, Carin—the dogs are ferocious beasts, and most especially vicious at this time of year. They sense the coming of winter and know they must gorge and fatten themselves before snow and ice deprive them of their prey."

Carin barely heard the woodsprite's warning about wild dogs. She fastened on its talk of ensorcellment and unseen boundaries.

"Sprite, what are you saying about magic and spells? You don't really believe Verek's woods are hexed, do you?" Involuntarily Carin threw a glance over her shoulder, half expecting to see a figure in black riding at her on a tall hunter. "I know the man can be brutal, but you seem to think he's something even worse."

"The powers of the mage and the bewitchment of his woods are plain for all to see ... all, that is, except you, Carin," the wood-sprite softly replied. "I watched as the mage took you to the woods' edge, where his spells dance between the trees. I watched

the magic flow around you but not touch you. I saw the astonishment in the mage's face when he realized that his spells were
nothing to you." The sprite made a whistling sound, as if chuck-
ling at the memory.

"You watched?" Carin stared at the woodsprite. "I *knew* I saw
something moving in the trees beside that clearing." She stood
with her hands on her hips. "If you hadn't distracted me just
there, I wouldn't have ended up on the ground with my knee
split open, bleeding all over those rocks."

And the swordsman wouldn't have come off his horse to doc-
tor her. Carin could still feel his hands on her leg. Verek's eyes
had been inches from hers. She recoiled at the memory, and
shrank as she recalled riding in front of him — his arms enclosing
her, caging her. Sweet *mother* of Drisha, she never wanted to be
that close to the devil again.

"Ah," the woodsprite said. "Indeed I am to blame for your
unfortunate accident. My apologies. I meant no harm. I wished
only to see where the mage would take his captive and what
might come of it. My curiosity overcame me, for until that day I
had known of no one — excepting myself — who wasn't bound by
the mage's enchantments."

Carin rubbed her forehead. She was having trouble taking in
what the woodsprite was telling her. Each question the creature
answered raised a dozen more.

"If the 'spells' don't work on you, then how do you know
they're real?" she demanded. "Maybe you're just repeating a tale
that you got from some villager. Maybe the people around here
refuse to enter Verek's woods because they're superstitious, or
they're afraid of the owner. As I learned myself, the Lord of
Ruain takes a dim view of trespassers. That's really why no one
sets foot on his land, isn't it?"

A patch of bark flickered on the trunk of the tree Carin was
addressing. The sprite's reply looked and sounded agitated.

"Upon my oath, the ensorcellments are real—do not doubt them! Though I am not fettered by them, *I see* the spells that curtain the trees. They are as clear to me as to the villagers. Indeed, all manner of beasts that creep, crawl, run, or fly sense the enchantment, and they stay away. Didn't your mare balk? And the mage's favorite mount, which took you up after your fall? Do you not remember how that horse hesitated at the crest of the hill, putting you back afoot for the final steps to the barrier?"

"There was nothing—" Carin started to argue, then broke off, thinking suddenly of Verek's question. *"How have you come through the barrier?"* he'd asked her.

"It's nothing to you," the sprite said. "But you appear to be quite alone in your inability to perceive the boundary that is raised by magic. All along the edge of the enchanted woods, whether to north or south, the spells weave and twine. Even I won't approach them too closely. I am careful to leap for the safety of a tree that bears no touch of the sorcery. You, however, stand drenched in the mage's spells as the enchantments wash over you with power enough to consume your very being—and yet you pass through safely, knowing nothing of the nightmare visions that swirl around you."

Carin shivered. Evening had closed in as the woodsprite spoke, and the air was cold. She needed to keep moving. But the creature's extraordinary claims held her riveted.

"If I can believe you, sprite, then apparently only you and I can enter and leave Lord Verek's woods anytime we want. For you, they're a haven away from the woodcutters' axes. But how can you stay there? Aren't you afraid of him?"

"Don't think me braver than you are, Carin," the woodsprite said. "The mage is formidable, and I wouldn't wish him for a foe. I find, however—to my relief and his vexation—that he can't touch me. I merely leap, like so"—Carin saw the tiniest flash in the dusk—"and I'm beyond his reach." The woodsprite's voice was no longer near, but came from some distance away. "Then I leap again" — another spark flashed — "and I elude him once more." The voice had returned to a nearby oak.

"It maddened him when we first met," the sprite continued, "and he discovered that his spells were useless against me. Even now, he speaks resentfully whenever our paths cross. But I'm grateful that he chooses to speak at all. In my wandering days, before I settled in the mage's woods, I found no one who would converse with me. All whom I approached ran away in fear, though I spoke courteously to them. All ran ... that is, until today ... this happy day when I offered a friendly warning to you, Carin, and you did me the great honor of accepting me as I am."

What a pitiful little creature, she thought. *It sounds starved for company.* Since it could leap so agilely and match the pace she set, maybe it would agree to accompany her on her journey. After so long alone, she wouldn't mind some companionship either.

Carin started to ask. But the creature cut her off.

"Shh — quiet!" it ordered. "Listen!"

"What?" She strained to hear over the sighing of a light wind in the treetops. At first there was nothing, only a faint whiff of skunk in the air. But then a high-pitched whine floated in on the breeze, followed by frenzied, distant barking.

"A dog!" the woodsprite shrieked. "And where there is one wasteland dog, the pack follows. Run! Run to the safety of the mage's woods. *Hurry!* I beg you, Carin."

Her hand flew to the hilt of the stolen kitchen knife at her belt. If it was only one dog, she could kill it. Was one dog enough of a threat to send her cowering back to Verek's woods?

The sprite screamed at her, its voice thin and shrill. "Carin! Run! You cannot stand against the pack. Wasteland dogs delight in killing. Run — or feel your throat torn out!"

Standing stock-still in the gloom, Carin listened for the single dog that had barked. But a wicked howl rent the dusk, followed by another and another, until the air throbbed with the cries of the pack.

Dark shapes glided through the trees, barely visible in the owl-light just before full night descended. The pack had closed on her with uncanny swiftness. Carin smelled their stench, and gagged. Then she was running, her feet pounding the ground but much, much too slowly. All of reality seemed to go slow, but not the dogs. They flew over the ground, gaining on her with every stride.

Her lungs hurt. Her heart was bursting. She threw back her head but she couldn't cry out, having no breath to spare.

A light flashed ahead. In it, she glimpsed a way, maybe, to live.

"Quickly!" the woodsprite shrieked at her. "Here—to me! Climb for your life."

With the pack's leaders howling at her heels, Carin sprinted for the tree. She couldn't mistake which one the sprite meant for her to go up. A large oak stood in a clearing directly in her path, its limbs glowing with some weird inner light like a beacon to guide her. Barely breaking stride, she launched into the chest-high lower limbs and worked frantically to pull her body higher, out of reach of snapping jaws and tearing teeth.

Something grabbed her. She kicked furiously. But it was not a dog that held her. The sack of provisions on her back had snagged in the tree's branches. She grabbed its cord and yanked violently. She couldn't free it.

"Woodsprite!" she cried. "Help me!"

Tree limbs snapped. "Climb!" screamed the sprite in an anguished voice. "You ... are ... freed ..." The voice trailed off, and the tree's inner glow winked out.

Carin lunged upward as the branches that had held her gave way. The limbs crashed to the ground. Sharp cries from below said the branches had landed squarely on the pack.

She climbed until her feet found a thick limb that grew almost straight out. A wave of dizziness threatened to drop her off it; she hugged the tree trunk until she'd steadied. Then she wedged herself into a sturdy fork and sat gulping air, willing her pounding heart to slow. Below her the dogs yipped and whined, impatient to claim the prey they'd treed.

"Woodsprite?" Carin called softly when she had breath enough for words. "Are you there?" Her voice was little more than a whisper to avoid exciting the hunters below. "Sprite?"

She got no answer.

"Woodsprite!" she shrieked as a rush of ungovernable panic threatened to take her. "Where are you?"

Only the dogs responded. For minutes the forest rang with the clamor of the pack in full throat, baying its bloodlust.

On her branch above the dogs' heads, Carin sat very still, her fingers digging into the tree's bark with such force that they burned. She closed her eyes and took slow, deep breaths.

"Woodsprite!" she called again in a hoarse whisper when the dogs' howling had abated somewhat. "Are you there?"

"I am," came the soft reply.

Her muscles relaxed. She wasn't alone.

"Are you all right?" she asked. "Where did you go?"

"I … had to leave this ancient oak … for a time," the sprite murmured. "The branches …" The voice trailed off anew, filling Carin with fresh alarm.

"Stay with me, sprite," she hissed into the dark. "Are you hurt?"

"I am … undamaged," the sprite replied in a voice thinner and reedier than before. "When I broke the branches to free you, there was … distress. I took myself to another tree, until the … discomfort … had passed."

Carin stroked the tree trunk. But which creature did she attempt to soothe? The wounded oak, or the woodsprite inside it?

"You felt pain when you broke the branches?"

"In the tree, there was pain ... or something like," the wood-sprite said. "I cannot clearly explain it. A feeling of loss and a great hurt overwhelmed me in the moment when I caused the limbs to break. I couldn't abide in this tree—not even long enough to see that you reached safety. But the feeling is gone now. This great oak is distressed no more."

Carin pressed against the trunk. "Sprite, if it wasn't for you, those dogs down there would be gnawing my bones right now. I should have listened. But how soon before they lose interest? I can't stay in this tree all winter."

"Friend," said the voice, stronger now, "the wasteland dogs are as noted for their endurance as for their savagery. When they've treed their prey, they don't leave until the doomed creature falls to them. It's useless to imagine that you can outlast them."

"You're saying I'm doomed?" Carin murmured, her stomach twisting.

"I am telling you only that you cannot trust in time and patience, for the pack has both on its side. Rather, you must hold tight, high in these branches, through the dark hours. By midday tomorrow—sooner, if luck goes with me—I will have brought the one who can save you. For now, I must leave you in the care of this ancient oak. But be of good heart. I'm going now to find the mage."

"What?" Carin cried. "You don't mean Verek? You don't seriously intend to hand me over to him, do you? Did you hear anything I said, woodsprite? If you betray me to him, he'll kill me."

Carin groped in the dark, trying in vain to lay hands on the sprite and shake sense into the creature. "Listen to me! Verek barely stopped short of removing my head when he caught me on his land. Now I've trespassed again. And I told him I'd work for him, and instead I ran. And I stole from him—bread from his table, and a good knife." Carin made a quick mental inventory and realized she had more to account for. "I also helped myself to those amazing healing powders that Verek makes. And to top it all, I stole the mare. Horse-thieving is a capital crime, sprite.

"Tell me this, my faithless friend," Carin demanded. "Why should Verek bother to come to my rescue? When you've found him and told him what's happened, why shouldn't he laugh at you and say, 'Let the dogs have her—she deserves her death—they're saving me the trouble of hanging her'?"

"The mage will come for you," the woodsprite replied with a certainty that discouraged argument. "There are, after all, only the two of us who can give him the answers he seeks. As you yourself remarked, Carin, among all the creatures of this land, both good and base, only the two of us—a thieving runaway and a nameless woodsprite—have the power to pass at will through the mage's enchanted woods. We confound him, you and I. He desires to know our secrets. He can't rely on me to reveal the mystery. He must, therefore, rely on you.

"He seeks you even now—of that, I'm sure. He'll ride through the night to save you. The mage must have your help to solve the riddle that we pose him: the riddle of two lost travelers, maid and woodsprite, who are from elsewhere."

With that, the sprite sparked away into the darkness and was gone. Alone and helpless in her tree, Carin was left to await her fate like an abandoned owlet too young to fly.

Chapter 6

The Mistake

She woke in the early dawn, stiff and trembling with the cold. She'd lashed herself to the oak with the tie-cord from her sack of food, then slept in snatches through the night, rousing often to chafe her chilled flesh and shift her position on the unyielding tree limb.

Now in the gray light of morning, Carin looked down through the branches of her refuge and studied the danger she'd barely glimpsed and narrowly escaped last night: a pack of thirty or more, ragged brutes, most of them larger than wolfhounds. They were filthy. Dried blood, mud, and dung encrusted the mongrels' coats.

Some of the dogs sat with their backs to the tree, eyes and ears to the fore like sentries on watch for rivals that might try to take their prize. The rest of the pack lay curled beneath the oak, frequently growling and baring their fangs even in their sleep. Carin suspected that, should a dog be injured, its mates would tear it apart.

Try it and see? She fingered the knife at her belt. She could throw it into the pack and kill or maim one dog. But after the rest had devoured her victim, they would only settle again under her tree—perhaps hopeful that Carin might dispatch a few more of their number before she herself fell to them. To throw away her knife for a single dead dog would be foolish.

She touched the sling that was hidden under her shirt, but rejected it as even more useless than the knife. She couldn't whirl the sling in the branches of the tree.

So numerous were the dogs, most of the mob could go to water and hunt for prey whenever thirst and hunger drove them to it, leaving a few of their mates to guard her tree. Her enemies need want for nothing while they waited for her to weaken and fall.

Carin undid the cord that anchored her. Stretching cold, protesting muscles, she kneaded them back to life. She turned her face to the rising sun and soaked up its feeble warmth, and was serenaded by a few hardy northern birds while she breakfasted on bread and dried fruit from her sack.

Such a meal needed water to wash it down, but she had none. She hadn't taken a water skin from Verek's manor. During her months of walking—until she stumbled into his woods—she'd never failed to locate a seep, spring, or stockpond when she needed water. In fact, she'd discovered that she had a knack for finding water in the most arid-seeming places. In any event, she'd expected to find abundant water in the north, once she'd gotten away from Verek's cursed lands. To be chased up a tree by a pack of killer dogs—there to die slowly of thirst—was a possibility she hadn't considered.

Her breakfast done, Carin tied up her leftovers. Slowly, taking care with her balance, she stood. At her movements, the pack came awake and yowled for blood. She didn't look at the dogs, but clung to the oak's trunk and examined the branches of her sanctuary. No nearby limbs provided what she needed.

She climbed higher. The dogs responded with furious baying and eager whines, as if hoping to distract her and cause the misstep that would send her to her death.

Well above the sturdy limb on which she'd slept, Carin found what she sought. Where the oak had lost a branch, perhaps broken off in a storm long ago, a circular wound had formed. Within the scar was a rotted-out hollow the size of a human head. She clambered higher until she could look directly down into the cavity. Her reflection stared back darkly.

Water. The cavity still held a measure of the last rain that had bathed the oak. Carin cupped a hand and tested it. "Ugh," she muttered. It smelled and tasted musty, but it wasn't undrinkable. She dipped until her thirst was satisfied.

From this high vantage point, much of the surrounding forest lay open to view. Carin probed the scene for any possible route of escape but found none. She could see no way to move squirrel-like through the treetops. Her sanctuary stood alone, spreading above a good-sized clearing that ringed the tree like an earthen moat. She couldn't jump across the space to any neighboring oak or beech. And if she fell, of course, the dogs would gut her.

Whether by plan or accident, the woodsprite had guided her to a tree from which escape seemed impossible.

The dogs below had yapped and howled without pause since Carin began her early morning explorations. Now, abruptly, the pack voiced a different cry. A challenge sounded in their excited baying.

From her perch, Carin scanned the forest. Eastward, some-thing glimmered — the briefest twinkle. Again, she saw it: a gleam, as of reflected sunlight. She stiffened, and stared intently. Something or someone was coming through the trees toward her.

On the ground below, the pack went into a frenzy. Every dog faced the risen sun, howling, growling, snapping at air. As the dogs' jaws closed on nothing, the cracking sounds reached Carin high in her refuge. No doubt, a bite from those powerful jaws could sever a leg, even crush a skull.

But the pack seemed to have forgotten its treed quarry. Some-thing else now held the dogs' attention: a diversion that could work to her advantage?

Be ready, Carin ordered herself, though the danger she was in seemed to darken and deepen as the glints of movement through the trees drew nearer her sanctuary oak. The dogs, too, sensed what was coming, to judge by their agitated frothing at the mouth. The pack was keying up for battle.

If the curs go that way, hit the ground and head the other direction — fast.

As quickly as she dared, Carin climbed down to the forked bough where she'd left her provisions. She lashed the sack to her shoulders like a beggar's bundle, reaching back to tuck and smooth its folds so that nothing would snag in the tree limbs. Then she dropped to a sturdy branch among the lower limbs and crouched there.

"Phew," she breathed, wrinkling her nose at the stench that rose from the dogs. Her hands were shaking, and sweating, but she kept one hand on the knife at her belt in case a brute jumped at the limb where she waited.

But the dogs ignored her. Every eye was fixed on that which approached from the east. And with a suddenness so unnerving that Carin came near to losing her balance and her grip, the dogs sprang from beneath the tree, racing to the attack as one animal.

Carin squinted through the branches to see what had drawn the pack away. Framed by gnarled trees at the clearing's edge, two bowmen on horseback met the dogs' attack with a hail of arrows — but what extraordinary arrows! The shafts blazed with a light greater than the sun's, streaking incandescent fire into the pack as the dogs sprinted, tightly bunched, across the clearing. Each time that an arrow found its mark — and Carin counted no misses — flashes like lightning shot out from the mongrel the arrow had pierced and consumed the dogs to either side. Four and five deep around each arrow's victim, dogs burst instantly into flame.

It was over before she could fully comprehend the scene. In seconds, flesh became ash. The dogs scarcely had time to yelp their pain.

The blindingly bright arrow shafts had seared afterimages into Carin's vision. Looking past the dancing streaks, past the naked branches that made a poor hiding place, she glimpsed the face of the lead archer. It was like seeing him for the first time.

Really seeing him. Recognizing instead of resisting the truth about him. In the south it was said that no sorcerers still lived. The priests claimed that every master of magic had been destroyed.

The priests were wrong.

A sorcerer was glaring at Carin from across the clearing, with enough distance between them that she shouldn't have been able to make out his eyes. But she did see them, for they burned with the same hellfire that had incinerated the dogs.

For a moment she couldn't drag her gaze away. Time stopped. Thought stopped. Nothing remained but sensation: her scalp crawled.

Then, out of her throat came a cry she'd never heard herself make before. It was high and wild, a frantic command to herself to *"Move!"* repeated at the top of her voice until her muscles finally obeyed. She dropped to the ground and raced across the clearing, heading toward its farther side, putting the oak between herself and her pursuer. This was a thin chance she was clutching at, the thinnest, that she could elude him in the trees beyond, since he'd done her the service of dispatching the dogs.

But she'd barely hit her stride when five wasteland dogs burst from those woods, making straight for her. Her mistake: they weren't all destroyed.

A sorcerer spurring up behind her; ahead, five snarling dogs tearing toward her —

Carin dug in her heel and tried to cut left, glimpsing as she did the second bowman, who was waiting in the distance, at the clearing's edge. But as Carin glanced his way, she slipped on the leaves that littered the clearing. Breaking her fall with a hand to the ground, she pivoted on her fingers and worked her legs, desperately trying to regain her footing.

"Stay down!" Verek shouted. A bow twanged. An arrow blazed over her head and impaled its target. A dog yelped — a short, clipped sound. There was a sharp crackle, then the hiss and pop of meat roasting. Waves of heat rolled over Carin. A sickening odor filled the air, of burned flesh and dog hair.

Scrambling to her feet, her eyes stinging from the smoke, Carin looked for other attackers. But where Verek's single arrow had found the mob of five, nothing remained but ashes.

She spun around, wiping her eyes and gasping, and discovered the slayer of the dogs sitting on his horse, little more than a bow's length from her. Silently he regarded her.

This encounter mirrored her first meeting with the Lord of Ruain: Carin on the ground, so knotted up inside that she couldn't even swear at him; an armed and angry Verek deciding whether she would live or die. The moment felt dreamlike, as though she were fated to reenact the scene until Verek finally got enough. He let the silence stretch on, withering her with his gaze.

"Tell me," he grated at last. "What is it that drives you toward death? Why have you scorned the living I offered you?"

Carin sucked in a breath and let it out slowly. Horse thieves were customarily hanged. Would this warlock respect tradition and kill her that way instead of burning her in his fires?

Or did he truly need her alive to help him solve some riddle, as the woodsprite had suggested last night? That, too, was a terrifying possibility.

She threw back her shoulders, and the best she could, met his gaze. What was there to say to him? *"I'm a thief and I can't be trusted"*? *"Go on and finish me; I know you want to"*?

But instead, she answered him in a voice that didn't shake, though every other part of her did: "Sir, you should let me go. You have no claim on me. My life is my own."

"Your life is your own?" Verek echoed in a flat voice. His jaw was set and the fiends'-fire light burned in his eyes. The fingers of his damaged left hand opened and closed on his bow. Did he imagine them closing around her neck? Or was he thinking of bowstringing her? — a form of execution more quickly carried out than a hanging.

Carin ached with a gut-shredding fear and with the strain of hiding it. She couldn't swallow; her mouth was too dry.

The warlock spat his next words as if they tasted bad.

"Your life became mine, you little wretch, the moment you crossed the barrier and entered my world. My every instinct told me to destroy you." He leaned toward her. "But instead, I took you into my home.

"And how have you fared in my service?" he snapped. "You're made to sleep on featherbeds in the finest bedchamber in the house, to bathe in waters warmed by the world's own fire, to eat bread fresh from the oven and fowl from my best flocks, and to do no work but arrange the books in my library—a task that would seem well suited to a thief. From those volumes you might take all my secrets, and the knowledge of other *wysards* besides. But the work doesn't suit you: that, you've made clear. Nor do you approve of your lodgings.

"Mark me well, you young fool!" he exclaimed. "I'll amend my treatment of you. From today, I'll give you work and quarters better suited to your ungrateful nature."

Carin's knees nearly buckled. He was letting her live. He was taking her back.

Her relief lasted only seconds. Rising up in its place was a terrible new dread. What kinds of punishments could a sorcerer devise for a mortal who had spurned his charity?

Her captor shouldered his bow. Then he reached out a hand and demanded the return of Myra's kitchen knife. Carin fumbled with it, holding the blade so as to present him the handle.

Verek demonstrated that sorcerers required no such courtesies. He snapped his fingers and the knife flew from her hand to his, nicking her forefinger as it winged away.

Carin stuck the cut in her mouth. She involuntarily took a step back.

Verek sheathed the knife and called for the bundle from Carin's back. Then he dismounted and motioned her up. Before she was well seated he swung up behind her. His arms closed round her, hemming her in so closely against him that he must feel her shuddering.

Neither of them spoke as Verek reined the hunter around and urged it to a trot. Quickly they recrossed the clearing and left Carin's sanctuary oak behind. The horse swerved to avoid the ashes of the dog pack that the warlock and his companion had destroyed.

The second archer still sat his horse at the edge of the clearing. As they neared him, Carin got her first good look at the warlock's follower. He was a youth of about nineteen, slender of build and with long brown curls that were darker than her own mane but many shades lighter than Verek's crow-black hair.

Was this Lanse, the stableboy? He stared back at Carin as the distance between them closed. The boy's hazel eyes expressed a cold sort of curiosity but no sympathy.

Verek rode past him without a word. The hoofbeats of the second horse mingled with the hunter's as the boy fell in behind. Verek allowed his mount to set the pace. The hunter trotted for some distance, then slowed to a walk. They rode on, so silent that Carin almost jumped at the occasional trill of a bird or the raspy bark of a startled squirrel.

The sun's position in the eastern sky announced the time as late morning. Carin had eaten enough at dawn to take the edge from her hunger still, but she craved a drink of good water. The rainwater in the oak's rotted cavity might have kept her alive if she'd been treed for days, but her one deep drink of it had left a bad taste in her mouth.

Though Verek's water skin was easily within his reach, she did not ask him for it. Maybe at midday they'd stop to eat and she could swill away the lingering sourness.

But by the time the sun rose to its zenith, an unpleasant taste in her mouth was the least of Carin's discomforts. Her belly ached, her head pounded, and only by constantly blinking could she keep her vision cleared. Did she dare tell Verek how sick she felt? He might leave her to suffer, or he might put her right with two pinches of his healing powders.

The powders. No need to beg for them. She still carried her stolen supply. Verek hadn't taken her belt-pouch.

Moving stealthily to avoid drawing the attention of the warlock at her back, Carin felt for the tins. If only Verek would call a halt—to rest the horses if not the riders—she might dose herself and let the dusts cure her present ailment as speedily as they'd healed her knee.

An eager whinnying invaded Carin's thoughts. The greeting came from in front; the horse that nickered was not the gelding the stableboy rode behind.

Blinking her eyes clear, Carin spotted a small mare just ahead. The animal—black with a blaze and four stockings—whickered and pawed the ground as if barely able to contain its excitement. It was the same horse that had willingly taken her through Verek's silent woods, only to refuse to cross a boundary that— so the woodsprite said—the mare could see but Carin could not. Even now, though the mare was neither tied nor hobbled, she would step no closer, but only bob her head and paw the leaves, waiting impatiently for the riders to come.

The woodsprite had talked of spells weaving through the trees. Were they here, between her and the mare, invisible to Carin but apparent to all other creatures? Rubbing her eyes, she watched for any movement of Verek's hands, which lightly held the reins in front of her.

There —

He made the gesture she'd seen him use before: a small, quick motion with the thumb and fingers of his right hand, as though flicking something through the air. Then he urged the hunter to a trot ... as if to carry them through some spectral gate before it slammed shut. Carin heard nothing—an absence that only confirmed her suspicion that they had reentered Verek's cursed woodland.

Still whickering her pleasure, the mare now trotted to meet them. It wasn't the other horses, her stablemates, that held the animal's attention. She came straight to Carin, stretching her neck over the hunter's withers and nudging Verek's arm aside to thrust her face as near to Carin's as she could.

Carin rubbed the mare's forehead. "What are you doing here, horse?" she mumbled. "Waiting for me? You should have gone home, like I told you to. Except now I'm glad you didn't."

Verek dismounted and dropped his hunter's reins, leaving the horses standing together with Carin still astride. He unshouldered his bow and his quiver of enchanted arrows. To the youth who followed he said, "We'll rest here, Lanse. Only ground-tie the horses, so they may graze. Eat, if you're hungry."

"Yes, my lord."

The boy swung down. Verek moved off a few paces to lean his bow and the quiver against a tree.

As Carin slid from the hunter's back, her legs nearly gave way. She'd been so pleased to see the little mare again, she had, for a moment, forgotten her illness. But the pains in her head and stomach were becoming unbearable.

Steadied between the hunter and the mare that crowded close, Carin lifted the water skin from Verek's saddle, unstoppered it, and drank deeply. Then she worked one tin out of her belt-pouch and opened it. Her hands shook so badly she spilled at least half the bronze powder, but she managed to pinch a bit between thumb and forefinger and place it on her tongue.

"*Aaahhh!*" Carin screamed, so piercingly that both horses skittered away, leaving her unpropped. She collapsed to the ground.

Her tongue was on *fire*. If she'd taken a mouthful of lamp oil followed by a flaming torch, the pain would not have been more consuming. Her shirt got soaked as she tipped up the water skin.

But swallowing great gulps did nothing to quench the fire in her mouth.

Verek and Lanse reached her at almost the same moment. The warlock kneeled beside her, his eyes taking in the flat tin that lay open on the ground at Carin's feet. The tin was empty now of all but a few specks of bronze dust, the rest scattered in the leaves. Verek slipped his hand inside his coat and brought out a small packet wrapped in tallow-soaked linen. He peeled away the wrapper and used his thumbnail to flake off a wafer of the packet's contents.

"Lanse," he ordered the youth who stood over them, "take the water from her."

Carin had no voice with which to protest. The raging fire had burned her tongue to a cinder. As Lanse wrested the vessel away, Verek popped the wafer into her mouth.

It melted on her tongue like finely powdered sugar in a hot drink. Just as quickly, the fire died.

Carin scraped her tongue over her teeth, checking for charred flesh. There wasn't any. She stuck her finger in her mouth and felt only soft, healthy tissue. Her tongue had not been burned from her head. The fire was gone, leaving no trace except a memory of pain so intense it made her puke.

She rolled over on hands and knees and vomited all the water she'd drunk. For a minute or more she remained that way, breathing heavily.

As the nausea passed, Carin took stock of her condition. Pain gripped her belly. A film clouded her sight. The pounding in her head was like a score of tiny imps hammering spikes into her skull. The powder that had set her tongue afire had failed to cure her ills.

She crawled away from the vomit and sat in a pile of dry leaves. Wordlessly, Lanse gave her back the water skin. Nodding her thanks, Carin rinsed her mouth and took a few cautious sips, careful not to start heaving again.

"Come here." Verek's clipped voice sounded near. "I wish to speak with you."

Struggling to make her legs obey, Carin stood and looked around. A dark blur sat on the ground a few paces away, his back to a tree. Wobbly-kneed, she approached him. The blur gestured, but she couldn't make it out.

"Sit," Verek ordered, "before you fall over. You're as unsteady on your feet as a new colt. Tell me: what ails you?"

Carin lowered herself to the ground about two arms' lengths from him. In a strained voice, hoarsened by her retching, she described her various pains. She added, "I drank stumpwater up in that oak. It tasted terrible, but it was the only water I had. I guess maybe I poisoned myself."

Verek stroked his close-cropped beard and regarded her. "And you thought to counter the poison," he said, holding up the tin that had held the bronze powder, "with stolen medicine?"

Carin nodded weakly, waiting for his anger.

But the warlock threw back his head and laughed—a long, loud laugh that he seemed thoroughly to enjoy. It was the first time he'd even smiled in Carin's presence.

She clamped her lips together, holding back indignation. Why should it surprise her that her suffering would amuse him?

"If I did not have the proof before me, I wouldn't believe the tale," Verek said, his stern manner returning. "To ease a sickness in head and belly, you took the powdered *cyhnaith* on your tongue. By Drisha! I who made the mixture would not be so bold. The pain must be exquisite."

Through misted eyes, Carin saw the warlock shake his head. Then he began to pat his clothing as if he searched for something he wasn't sure he carried. Finally, digging deep in an inside pocket, he produced a misshapen pellet about the size of a baneberry. Leaning forward from his tree, he handed her the corpsy-gray lump.

"Hold it in your mouth and let it melt."

Uhh, Carin thought, *it looks deadly.* She sniffed it, then touched it to the tip of her tongue. But she could detect only a wax coating. When another paroxysm in her gut almost doubled her over, she closed her eyes, put the pellet in her mouth, and rolled it around. The coating melted, releasing a surprisingly pleasant minty flavor, and her stomach and head ceased to ache. In a few moments, when she reopened her eyes, she found her vision clearing.

She blinked. "Your medicines work fast."

"My medicines are not to be trifled with by ignorant children," Verek snapped. "Do not meddle further in things of which you know nothing. You've had more good fortune today than you deserve. Some poisons lack remedies. And in the hands of the unlearned, even a cure may kill."

Carin made no reply. He was right. She'd been a fool.

Verek toyed with the tin that had held the powder. "I didn't know you had taken this. What other thefts have you yet to confess? What are you concealing in that bag you're wearing?" He pointed with a corner of the tin.

"Only the mate to the bronze medicine, sir—the green dust you used with the bronze on my knee," Carin answered, too hastily. "Nothing else of value—just some stones for my sling."

"Sling?"

She winced at her mistake. Until that moment, Verek had known nothing of the weapon she carried.

Sighing, Carin pulled the sling from under her shirt. She wrapped the cords loosely around the leather strap, then held the weapon up to Verek's view. "I've only used it to take small game—rabbits and such."

Verek put out his hand. Reluctantly, Carin laid the weapon on his palm.

"Did you steal this?" he asked, examining the workmanship.

"No! —sir. I made it. It's mine."

"*You* made it? Who taught you?"

"No one. I taught myself. My old master's son killed birds with a sling, and I watched him practice. It's such a simple weapon, I knew I could make one for myself. I used scrap leather and bits of cord that other people threw away. It's mine. I didn't steal it."

Verek examined the sling for a few moments more. Dashing Carin's hopes that he might return it to her, he slipped the weapon under the wide belt that circled his waist.

"You've taken many things from me," he said. "I take this property of yours in partial payment of the debt. Now—empty your bag. I would see what hides there. Nothing of value, you say."

Carin gave a half-nod, half-shrug, then lifted the pouch's flap and dug for the stones that lay within. Her fingers touched soft cloth and she started. The kerchiefs: she'd forgotten them. Swallowing uncomfortably, she closed her fist on the squares and drew them out.

"Oh ... these," she muttered, opening her fingers. "I didn't remember. I know they're much too nice to use for bandages, but that's what I took them for—just in case I needed bandages."

Carin spread the wrinkled kerchiefs on her knee. With one blunt nail, she tried to scrape slivers of dry grass out of the delicate embroidery. The dirt off the stones in her pouch had smudged the linens. No longer were they a snowy white.

Verek was strangely silent as Carin finished her poor attempts to clean and smooth the kerchiefs. Shaking them out one by one, she gathered and folded them into a neat bundle. When he made no move to take them from her, Carin rose on her knees and hesitantly held them out to him.

He stared at the kerchiefs as if at a mystical vision. Reverently, reaching with both hands, Verek accepted the bundle from her in the manner of a village priest accepting the holy *Drishanna*.

Carin, still kneeling before him, watched in wonder as the warlock traced the stitches with his fingertips. He pressed the linen to his face. Then he shook himself, as if coming out of a trance, and slipped the kerchiefs inside his coat. Still he said nothing.

It seemed an ominous silence. Nervously, Carin cast about for something—anything—to fill the void. "The needlework is excellent, isn't it," she remarked. "Is it Myra's?"

With the speed of a striking adder, Verek hurled himself away from the tree at his back, knocked her flat, and pinned her shoulder blades to the ground with a force that drove the air from her lungs.

Carin went rigid. In the face that loomed inches above hers, the warlock's eyes blazed with a murderous rage. If he'd had a knife in his hand at that moment, her throat would be laid open.

"The needlework is my wife's," Verek breathed into Carin's face. "It is the last work from her hands, done on the morning of the day that she died and I placed her body in the tomb, with the body of our only child lying in her arms. It is all I have left of her. And for befouling the work of her hands, you dirty little thief, you will pay."

Chapter 7

Darkness

He had her inescapably pinned, his fingers clamped on her arms like iron traps. Under his weight and in his grip, Carin was crumpling. Her lungs felt like they'd folded up. Her heart, too, seemed on the verge of collapse, thudding wildly in the too-small space that was left to it.

Reality began to shrink away as Carin came close to blacking out. But two things wrested her back to full consciousness: the pain she was in, and a piercing awareness of Verek's invisible borderland. She could feel it now, could feel how very near they were to it. The ground under her thrummed. The air felt charged, explosive.

Verek's grip tightened. He was crushing her arms.

Mother of Drisha, they're breaking! Carin tried to pray, or to swear, but she couldn't get the words out. She was fighting for breath that came only in shallow, jerky spasms.

Sweet mercy, *the pain* — her bones *must* snap —

Just when she was certain of it, Verek released her arms. He straightened slightly, still with her pinned under him.

Through streaming eyes, Carin watched the warlock cup his right hand and repeatedly slap the back of it into his left palm, as though the hand were a self-willed thing that he must force into submission. His skin was flushed and his eyes smoldered.

His hands kept up the tattoo until he cut loose with a vicious oath that didn't translate in any language Carin knew. Then he rolled off her, got to his feet and stalked away, grinding dead leaves under his boots, leaving her flat on her back and struggling still to draw air into her burning lungs.

Carin managed to twist her head to follow his departure as Verek walked out to join the horses. He stood among them with his back to her, adjusting some strap or buckle on his hunter's tack.

After a long interval, when she could breathe properly again and force some useful movement from her quivering muscles, Carin pried herself up, dashed the tears from her eyes, and rubbed her arms. Her bones seemed intact, but the flesh of her upper arms was badly bruised. She stumbled to a tree, propped against it and tried to control her shaking hands, at least enough to brush off her clothes. The force of Verek's attack had slammed her deep into the mold on the floor of the woodland.

Footsteps crunched boldly through the leaves. Carin gasped and jerked her head up. But it was no new threat approaching, only the mare renewing its greeting.

Carin stroked the sleek neck as the animal nuzzled her with velvety lips.

"I wish you could grow wings," she murmured, "and carry me far from this evil place. But you wouldn't want to, would you?" Carin buried her face in the mare's mane. "What good are you to me, little horse, when you refuse to take me somewhere that warlock can't hurt me?"

More steps crackled through the leaves. This time it was Lanse striding past. He did not glance at or speak to Carin, but headed for the tree where Verek had left his bow and quiver. The boy carried the weapons to his master, who still stood with the hunter. Verek gave Lanse a curt nod, then shouldered his weaponry, gathered his horse's reins, and swung into the saddle.

Lanse caught up his gelding and rode to where Carin stood with the mare.

"We ride on," he snapped. "Mount. Can you?"

"Of course I can." Despite sounding a little short-winded, Carin edged her words with a brusqueness to match the boy's. Though she still had the shakes, she managed to boost herself smoothly onto the mare's bare back.

Lanse started to ride away, but he stopped when she spoke to him.

"My name is Carin."

He stared at her and made no reply.

"You're Lanse, aren't you?" she persisted.

"Yes," he growled, scowling.

Maybe, Carin thought, *stableboys only talk about horses.* So she tried again: "This little mare is a good horse. What's her name?"

Lanse brightened like a child at Mydrismas. "She's Emrys. And don't be fooled by her size," he added, pride in his voice. "Though she is small, for heart and courage Emrys is the equal of my master's Brogar."

"I don't doubt it," Carin said. "I'm glad to meet you, Lanse."

His frown returned. "Come on." He rode away without waiting to see that she obeyed.

The mare needed no urging. Emrys fell in behind Lanse's gelding as though it were her accustomed place. Verek on Brogar followed at the rear, a dark, silent shadow.

With the warlock's rage firebranded on her memory, Carin squirmed as she imagined his eyes watching her back. Her thoughts strayed to his bow, and to the quiver which still held several of the enchanted arrows that had charred the wasteland dogs to ashes. As they rode through the late afternoon, Carin listened for the twang of the bow. But no sound came from the rider behind her, not even a squeak of saddle leather.

And no sound came from the woodland around her. The birds and the squirrels that had chattered in the forest beyond were conspicuously absent on this side of the boundary, inside the barrier of thrumming, tingling energy that she had distinctly felt but not seen.

They reached the manor just before sundown. Approaching the stone wall that enclosed the grounds, Lanse did not ride to the narrow plank door through which Carin had escaped. He led them around to the main entrance where a pair of massive iron doors closed a wide opening.

Verek rode up and dismounted in front of the doors. Carin expected them to swing open magically at a word or a sign from him. The warlock, however, merely dug into one saddlebag, produced a large iron key, and turned it in a monstrous lock. Under pressure from his hands, the perfectly balanced doors wheeled inward, making no noise on their hinges.

He spoke to Brogar and the horse trotted through, into the courtyard. Lanse followed on his gelding. Emrys hurried to join them, without waiting for instructions from her rider.

It was good that she had a mind of her own, since Carin had been content to sit on the mare's back like a sack of oats all afternoon and let Emrys do the thinking for them both. *Weary* wasn't the word. Carin was tired to the point of numbness. Running from killer dogs, poisoning herself with stumpwater and stolen medicine, and getting the life half crushed out of her by a maddened sorcerer: each adventure had drained her of strength and resolve until she was nearly bereft of either. All she wanted was to fall into bed and sleep.

Please, warlock, she addressed Verek silently, *hold off on punishing me until tomorrow. Whatever you have planned for me, can't it wait?*

They were at the stable, Emrys on the heels of Lanse's horse. The boy dismounted and reached for the mare's bridle as Carin slipped down. Her feet dragging, she stumbled to the doorway that opened into Myra's kitchen.

She found the housekeeper at the fireplace stirring a stewpot that steamed enticingly. Carin drank in the aroma. The bites of breakfast she had eaten at sunrise were now a distant memory.

"Oh my, dearie!" Myra exclaimed at the sight of her. "Here you are, and not dead upon some blood-soaked ground!"

The woman bustled over to take Carin's hand. "How I did worry when I went to call you to supper last night and could find no trace of you, not in my master's library nor in your bed-chamber nor anywhere upon the grounds. What a fright you gave me, child! And when my lord came home and found you gone, and found the mare missing from the stable—what a state he was in! He flew into a rage, the like of which I seldom have seen. Furious, he was, and beside himself with worry.

"'The fool's gone north,' he roared, 'north to her death. The wasteland dogs will have her before morning.'

"Wasteland dogs!" Myra wailed. "Oh my, how I quail to think of them. A pair of those beasts can down a boar bear. A lamb like you couldn't stand against them. But my master wouldn't give you up for dead. He braced his bow and called for the boy to bring his horse. 'Lanse,' he said, 'if she had sense enough to climb, we may find her alive. Else, we'll find only blood and hair.' Oh my, dearie. Whatever did possess you to leave this safe, snug house and take yourself into such mortal danger?"

Carin got no chance to reply. The door burst open behind her: She whirled to see Verek framed in the doorway. Myra made to greet him, but got no further than "Good master, I—"

"*Silence*, woman!" he thundered. Striding furiously into the room, the warlock slapped the flat of his hand on the trestle table with enough force to rattle the dishes that were set for supper. "Do not plague me with your empty talk, for I am much dis-pleased with you. Didn't I order you to keep a close watch on this chit and lock her in? So neglectful are you of your duties that you lie napping while this thief ransacks my house and steals from my stable the finest mare in Ladrehdin. And to your crimes of neglect—grave as they are—I now discover that you have added an affront far worse."

"Master, I—"

"Hold your tongue," Verek snarled. His voice dropped to a menacing whisper. "Years ago, when the pain of losing all I loved was a pike through my heart, I bade you put these out of my sight, for I could not bear to look at them." He reached into his coat, pulled out the kerchiefs, and laid them on the table. Lightly he rested his fingertips on them. "You know the bitter memories these stirred in me, and how they preyed on my mind. I gave these mute reminders into your care, trusting you to keep them safe.

"Treacherous, cold-hearted woman!" Verek's voice rose to a shout. "You took from me these precious things—which I hold dear and yet cannot bear to gaze upon—and you gave them like rags to a worthless vagabond who sees in them no value save for wiping filthy hands and binding festered wounds!"

Myra buried her face in her apron and wept—great, racking sobs that shook her body.

Carin stood by the woman's side and glared at the warlock. How could he be so cruel? His anger at herself, she understood. But to blame a faithful servant for crimes committed by another was a great injustice, and a poor way to repay the housekeeper's devotion.

Seething with indignation, she couldn't hold her tongue. "Stop this!" Carin hissed at him. "I took the kerchiefs without asking, like I took the knife and the horse. Myra didn't know what I was doing. You leave her alone. If you want to punish somebody, then punish me."

Verek bent stiffly from his waist and grasped the edge of the table with both white-knuckled hands, as if he was preparing to overturn it and send the supper dishes crashing to the floor. Carin reached to grab the still-sobbing Myra and pull the woman clear. But Verek released the table without venting his anger on it. He straightened, and turned to his captive.

"In the course of this dismal day," he said, his voice brittle, "I made you two promises, you little fool. Do you remember them? I vowed to house you as you deserve. And I swore that I would exact a price from you for your offenses—a high price for your mockery of my grief. I will now keep those promises. Come with me."

Carin winced as Verek seized her left arm in exactly the spot he'd earlier bruised. He hustled her down the passageway to the foyer. Past the foot of the stairway he turned abruptly, jerking her around.

The sudden turn brought them hard against the wall under the stairs. Verek lifted a latch and flung open a door-sized panel that was angled along its upper edge to follow the rise of the stairs. The panel, grating on hinges squally from disuse, opened to an unlit void. He thrust Carin into the blackness, then released her arm and snapped his fingers. A torch flared in an iron holder.

The firelight revealed steps of stone dropping into nothingness. Verek lifted down the torch, put a firm hand to her back, and ordered her to descend.

"I don't—"

Carin broke off when the hand at her back gave her a shove that nearly tumbled her down the steps. "Oh sweet Drisha!" she cried, twisting, catching her balance by a fingernail. "All right! I'll go." With the warlock close behind her, Carin worked her way down, planting her feet with care to avoid slipping on the smooth, seamless stonework.

At the bottom, a cavernous dungeon stretched away beyond the reach of the torchlight. Iron bars rose on either side, parceling the vault into row upon row of windowless cells. Rust caked the bars. The rock underfoot, unlike the chiseled blocks of the steps, was cracked and pitted. Water trickled darkly down the cavern's walls, flowed in thin threads across the floor, and disappeared like spilled blood into a labyrinth of cracks. The moisture-laden air was icy cold and reeked of decay. A crypt lined with moldering human bones could not have been more ghastly than this sorcerer's dungeon.

A crypt? *Her* crypt? Her final resting place? Carin shuddered. The evil-smelling pit made her breath come short and the hairs lift on her neck and arms.

"In here," Verek ordered. He shoved her into the first cell. Her prison's width was an arm-span; its length, a foot or two greater than her own height. It was, therefore, just large enough to lie down in, but the cell offered no cot or bench, only the cold, wet floor.

Waves of dread broke over Carin. She grabbed the bars and stood trembling.

"Good night," Verek said, his voice sardonic, as he fastened the cell door. "I trust you'll sleep well. You will sleep *long*, for the night is uncommonly long in this place. Indeed, sunrise is as absent here as in the grave. And if day does not come, what is there to awaken to? Only an endless night that is close kin to death itself."

Clinging to the bars, Carin watched the warlock mount the steps, the torch in his hand. The circle illuminated by the flickering light shrank until darkness reclaimed every part of the dungeon except for a bright dot at the summit of the steps. Her gaze fixed on that remnant of light as a starving beggar's would on a crust of bread. Then Verek extinguished the torch and shut the door behind him.

Intense blackness flooded in: heavy, a crushing weight, thick and clammy as mud. The blind nothingness pressed on every side, such a dense, cold, black pall of nothing that it suffocated her.

Easy! she ordered herself. *No one ever died of darkness. Settle down.*

Squeezing her eyes tight shut, Carin put her hand over her mouth with her fingers spread so they wouldn't stop her breath, but on her skin she could feel the warm puffs, and in every quick, frightened gasp she could feel the vital force that was *her – Carin*. She might have been buried alive, but she was still that: alive.

With one shoulder pressed to the bars to keep her bearings in the blackness, she slid down to crouch on the floor. She ran her hand over the pitted stone, hunting blindly for a dry spot to sit on. Finding none, she sat on her heels with her back jammed against the bars, needing to feel the ironwork's solid presence in what was otherwise a formless abyss.

Only a corpse should rest easily in a sealed tomb. It was a measure of Carin's exhaustion that she dozed almost at once … huddled, head drooping, unmoving except for her shivering …

Shivering that grew more pronounced, convulsing her with spasms violent enough to jerk her head up, though her eyes remained closed. In this drifting state, for a moment neither awake nor asleep, Carin felt the presence of death—cold as the stone beneath her and dark as the grave.

No! screamed a voice inside her skull. *I'm not dead!*

But awareness came too late to anchor her. Springing up, Carin lurched on numbed legs into concentrated nothingness. Screams of terror—she only vaguely recognized them as hers— reverberated through the crypt like a chorus of night-fiends.

Their echoes ringing in her ears, the floor slipping out from under her … she was falling. Her head struck stone, and a bright flash penetrated the darkness behind her eyes.

With the fading of the flash, she sank away into silence and stillness, and down into a blackness that swallowed all existence.

Chapter 8

Two Horrors

Carin lay at the bottom of an ocean, achingly cold. She was drowning. Feebly she moved her arms through a frigid slush and tried to swim to the surface. But the mire pulled her back. It clung like mud.

It *was* mud. She was suffocating in a pool of black ooze. Try as she might to reach the surface, she couldn't free herself. There was no escaping: the mire held her fast. One more breath and the ooze would fill her lungs, and she'd die in the depths ...

"Now then, dearie, 'tis time you were awake," said a voice from beyond. "The master says 'twould be better for your poor bruised head if you'd wake up. Can you open your lovely green eyes, for Myra? 'Twould do this old woman's heart good to have you stirring this morning."

Carin moved a hand. It touched smooth linen and soft wool. Her shallow breaths drew in only air. There was no suffocating ooze, nothing dragging her under.

"Wha-a-a—" she croaked, struggling to understand.

"Oh, my!" The excited voice sounded in her ear. "At last! Let's lift your poor bruised noggin just a bit now, and you drink down as much of this potion as you're able."

A warm, pudgy hand slid under Carin's neck and gently lifted her head. With difficulty, she forced her eyes open. Two Myras beamed down. She blinked, and the two became one.

"Here ... take this, child, and ere the week's out you'll be right as rain."

A cup pressed against Carin's lips. Aware suddenly of how desperately thirsty she was, she accepted the drink. It tasted of herbs, and of something unidentifiable. Though its flavor was less pleasant than its aroma, she tried to drain the cup but could swallow only the liquid, not the bitter mash coating the bottom.

"That's right, dearie." Myra eased Carin's head back to the pillows. "A good long draught like that will put the color in your cheeks. The master will be pleased. Last evening when he came home, and early this morning before he left on his rounds, he looked in on you. 'Myra,' he said, 'you're to give the girl this elixir the minute she's awake. Do not delay a moment!' And I nodded and told him — for the twelfth time as surely as the first — that I'd do it. Now I must find the master and tell him the news: our foolish young runaway has rallied."

"No." Carin croaked a protest, but the housekeeper was already out the door and gone.

Whatever else the draught might do for her, it seemed already to be clearing the cobwebs. Her mind focused on one pressing urgency: she wanted Myra's master — that warlock Verek — coming nowhere near her. Would Myra bring him?

Tensing for the effort, Carin made to throw back the bed-clothes and rise. It was useless. Her attempt accomplished nothing, except to trigger a merciless pounding in her skull. She barely had strength enough to lift her hands to her face.

Sweet mercy, she swore in silence. *What … ?* Exploring cautiously, her fingers found that her head had been bandaged. Strips of linen bound a sticky pad of cotton wool to the side of her skull.

And then she remembered: her tomb. The sensation of being stone-cold dead in her grave. Screams echoing through the darkness. And then a brilliant flash.

Carefully she worked a finger under the padding. She touched a swelling on the side of her head and flinched from the sudden, shooting pain.

Carin lay quietly, making no further effort to rise, and the pounding in her skull lessened. From far off she caught a snatch of voices, unintelligible. She kept her face turned away from the window. The brightness of day, barely veiled by the lace curtains, hurt her eyes. Those curtains said she was back in her bedchamber. The vivid light suggested morning.

Scurrying footsteps sounded on the landing beyond the bedroom door. Myra entered, carrying a tray.

"Now then, dearie. The master's potion went down handily, so let's see if a drop of broth won't follow just as quick." The housekeeper set the tray on the dressing table. "The master's medicines work their good with speed to make a body dizzy. 'Twouldn't surprise me to find you strong enough already to sit up and take a little broth. I'll help you. Gently! Gently. Mustn't move too fast."

With Myra's help, Carin raised to a half-sitting position, propped on fat pillows. The effort so tired her that she had no strength to hold the oak-burl soup bowl; she let Myra spoon-feed her. Nothing in recent memory had tasted as good as the warm broth of chicken and herbs.

Between swallows, she tried to question the housekeeper. It was all Carin could do to whisper a few words, but Myra needed little prodding. The woman was adept at one-sided conversations.

"Is Verek ... ?" Carin murmured.

"No, my good master is not in the house. But as soon as he returns, I'll tell him of your recovery. He'll be pleased."

"No!"

"Aye, indeed he will. My master has been anxious about you. When he found you lying senseless in that awful cellar, he carried you up and helped me put you to bed. He fixed a poultice to take down the lump on your head. 'Twas big as a goose egg! The knot pains you yet, I shouldn't doubt, but not half so much as 'twould without the master's medicines. He fixed the potion you drank when first you roused; 'twill ease the ache in your brain and build your strength.

"'Twas a hard blow you took," Myra added. "There's some as don't wake up from such a blow to the head as that. Or if they do wake, they sweat and vomit and go white as a sheet, and can't remember their own names. But you'll be troubled by none of that. You'll be right as rain. The master's medicines will have you out of bed in no time."

"The dungeon ... "

"'Tisn't a dungeon now, only a cellar. Years ago, when there were scores of mouths to feed in this household, the housekeepers who had the post before me filled that great empty cave with crates of roots and kegs of beer, vats of wine and long links of sausages, and all manner of food and drink. Things keep fresh for months in that dreadful cold. But I've no need of such a cellar. I've only to feed the master and Lanse — and Jerold, too, if the old goat would let me — and now you, dearie. I never go down there. 'Tis too dark, and too cold for these old bones."

"Why ... ?" Carin whispered, and Myra understood. She shook her head and sighed.

"I didn't wish the master to lock you in that awful place. 'She's hardly more than a child,' I said to him. 'She'll be frightened out of her wits. It's pitchy black in there, and cold and damp as a dead fish.'

"'Send her to bed without supper,' I said to him. 'Make her stay in her room for a month. Lock her in the library — or out of it, for that might be a heavier burden to one who takes such pleasure in the books. Punish her, my lord,' I said. 'Do punish her, for Drisha knows she's a thief and a scamp and as stubborn as a jennet. But don't put her in that awful cellar. She'll catch cold. And if she slips on that wet floor and cracks open her skull, you'll not forgive yourself, master.' Those were my very words, and didn't it happen just as I had feared?"

The hand that held the soup spoon hung suspended, midway to Carin's mouth, as Myra relived her argument with Lord Verek. It wasn't every day, Carin guessed, that the housekeeper dared to challenge her master. Then Myra's eyes refocused on her patient, and the spoon completed its journey.

"My lord knew I spoke truth," the housekeeper went on as Carin swallowed the broth. "But, oh my! Dearie, he was so terribly angry with you. 'Silence, woman!' he bade me. 'Take care I don't lock you in that black hole with her.' Then he sent me to my room.

"I tried to sleep, but I was too anxious for you, poor lamb. I made up my mind to take a lamp and a blanket and a loaf and some cheese, and go down in that cellar and feed you your supper. I resolved to do it and suffer the consequences. 'If my master wishes to punish me,' I said, 'so be it. I can't leave that child to pass the night, cold and hungry, in that black pit.'

"But what did I find as I reached the door under the stairs? I spied my master climbing up with you in his arms. 'She fell and hit her head,' he said to me. 'We must poultice the knot.' The rest I've told you, of how my master fixed your medicines and looked in on you as you slept. He'll be glad to see you awake and mending."

"No."

Again Myra grasped what Carin packed into the one word.

"Now, dearie, don't judge him too harshly. My master has always had a temper, since he was a boy. And you do provoke him — you know you do. He was wrong to lock you in that dreadful place. It was badly done, and he is sorry for it. When I asked him how it was that he found you lying senseless, he said he was coming to let you out. He said two hours in such a place were enough to teach anyone a lesson. He was just reaching out his hand to open the door 'neath the stairs when he heard you screaming. 'It sounded like the gates of *farsinchia* were breached and all lost souls were wailing in the cellar,' he told me. My master ran to you, but he wasn't in time to catch you."

Carin swallowed the last of the broth. Her head sank back on her pillows. She tried to fight off sleep long enough to beg Myra to keep the warlock away from her. But her lips and tongue refused to form the words. She was descending through darkness, still hearing Myra—

"You'll be stronger ... We'll get some solid food down you ... a bit of veal with ginger ... "

—And then the darkness had her. Deep within it, in a cold horror of a nightmare, Carin fled a mounted swordsman. He pursued her through a forest of silence where gaping pits waited to swallow her. No matter how fast she ran or how well she hid, there was no escaping him, no way to get free. Carin wanted to scream and could not.

But just as it seemed the swordsman must chase her and oblivion snatch at her through all of eternity, a veil lifted to reveal a table, festively dressed. The table groaned under the weight of all manner of meats and vegetables, artfully prepared as if for a Mydrismas feast.

Gradually, Carin's dreams faded, to be replaced by hunger pains so sharp that they woke her. To judge by the softening of sunlight outside the window, she had slept for several hours.

She pushed back the bedcovers and lowered one leg over the side. The move was a modest success. Her head ached dully but she was spared the vicious pounding that her earlier exertions had spawned. She levered herself fully upright. A moment of dizziness threatened to undo her then, but it passed as she braced against the dressing table.

Carin hardly recognized the face that looked out at her from the mirror. Below the linen that wrapped her head, the whole side of her face was an orangey yellow.

She slowly unwound the bandages. The pad of cotton wool was gummy with poultice and peeled off painfully, to reveal a black and purple bruise. In its center was a lump big enough to make her skull look lopsided. Verek's orangey poultice had been slathered on liberally, leaving her hair a sticky mess and staining her skin.

Carin fumbled with the table's drawers and found the length of twine she used as a hair ribbon. She'd been wearing it in the dungeon. The housekeeper must have undone it after the warlock bore Carin upstairs.

Her every nerve prickled, a kind of half-flinching, half-shuddering sensation, as Carin thought of Verek carrying her unconscious body in his arms. If she could prevent it, that sorcerer would not touch her again.

Awkwardly, taking care not to graze the bruise, Carin pulled her hair up, tied it with the twine, and coiled it atop her head. Then she wobbled through the folding doors into the bathing room. With difficulty she stripped off her vomit-soured shirt and leggings. She'd been put to bed wearing every stain of sickness, mold, and rust that she had collected out in the woods and down in the dungeon.

As she sank into the waters of the hot-spring pool and her muscles limbered, Carin scrubbed off the touch of Verek's hands. The warmth was bliss, but she did not linger. Hunger urged haste.

She wrapped up in a towel and stepped into the bedchamber. As her bare foot crossed the threshold, the room's outer latch lifted. Someone was coming in from the landing off the stairs.

Not the warlock! Carin silently shrieked. *Sweet mercy, keep that blackheart away from me!* She stood rooted to the spot, unable to retreat.

The door opened, and in bustled Myra. Seeing Carin afoot and dripping, the housekeeper threw up her hands in surprise and left the door standing open behind her.

"Bless me—you're up and about so soon! Didn't I say the master's medicines would work their good with speed to make you dizzy? I've only come up to see if you're awake and hungry for a bit of veal, and here I find you've quit your bed and had your bath and washed the ocher from your face."

Then Myra was rushing to her side, exclaiming, "Why, you're gray as ash! Sit down, child, before you fall and hurt your head again." With warm hands, Myra guided her to the stool at the dressing table.

The woman studied Carin's face. "You've gotten yourself out of bed too soon — that's what the matter is. Let's get you back between the sheets. The master will have *my* head if I let you crack your noggin again."

Carin kept her seat, resisting the housekeeper's gentle efforts to tug her off the stool. The quick surge of her terror had given her strength; her blood was racing, and its heat seemed to kindle her voice. She spoke in a rush:

"Myra, I don't want to go back to bed. I'm much better, not a bit dizzy, just really hungry. But you scared the daylights out of me when you came in just now. I thought you were Verek — and I'd rather see a death's-head at my door than see him again."

Ignoring the look on Myra's face, Carin let the words spill on out. Her voice grew fierce as she released her pent-up anger.

"How I hate that man! No! He's not a man. He's something that shouldn't *exist*. I've seen him shoot arrows blazing with hellfire. I know he's cast an evil spell over the woods. At a sign from that warlock" — she made the flicking motion of thumb and fingers that she had seen Verek use — "the evil gets out of his way. I can't see it but I've felt it all around me, and I've watched him use it. I've seen him snap his fingers" — again she imitated the sorcerer — "to set fire to a torch or make a kitchen knife fly through the air."

Her heart was pounding. "I don't want to be here!" she cried. "I never meant to come *here*. I'm so sorry I climbed that hill and walked into those woods. This is a horrible place."

As Carin gulped a breath, Myra started to speak. But Carin cut her off.

"You see these?" She pointed to the bruises on her bare arms. They clearly showed where Verek had grabbed her and slammed her to the ground. "Your 'good master' gave me those. He never misses a chance to hurt me. I thought he was going to run his sword through me the first time he ever laid eyes on me, but then I realized it wouldn't hurt me enough. It would be over too quick to satisfy him.

"When your 'good master' does kill me, he'll want me to suffer. Maybe he'll snap his fingers and burn me alive. Or he'll crush the life out of me an inch at a time. Or he'll throw me back in the dungeon and leave me to starve in the cold and the dark."

Carin shivered. All the warmth seemed to leave her. She remembered an abyss so mortally cold it would make the teeth of the dead chatter in their skulls.

Myra was looking at her with an aggrieved expression. It only made her angrier.

"You don't know!" Carin snapped. "You're under the spell of that fiend. All that rot you were telling me about Verek being 'sorry,' about him regretting his cruelty to me—I don't believe a word of it. Myra, he's evil! Don't you know what the priests all say about blackhearts like him? Can't you see it in his eyes, like a ... a dark light?"

That last was not, perhaps, an altogether sensible way of putting it, but Carin could think of no better description for the shadowed glimmer that haunted Verek's gaze.

She paused, finally, to let the housekeeper speak. But for once, she'd left Myra wordless. The woman only stared at her in consternation.

At a noise from the landing, they both turned to seek the source.

Standing on the threshold of the open bedroom door was Verek. From the look on his face—a hard rain at midnight could not have been darker—it was clear what he'd overheard.

Myra gasped. The blood rushed to Carin's face. Fresh from her bath, she wore her hair atop her head like a frayed coil of rope, but under her towel not a stitch nor a thread.

Carin clutched the towel tightly as she spun off the stool and tumbled into the bathing room. "Beggar it *all!*" she swore through gritted teeth as she slammed the shutter-doors behind her. Whatever that warlock might have to say for himself, he would have to wait while Carin threw on her clothes. She yanked the twine from her hair and combed her fingers through the snarls, wincing as her fingertip jabbed the bruise on the side of her head.

But when she had pulled herself together enough to return to the bedroom, Carin found only Myra. Verek had gone.

The housekeeper sat on the bed, dabbing her face with her handkerchief. When Myra looked up, the hurt in the woman's eyes was evident.

"Oh, how it pains me to hear you speak so harshly!" she cried. "I wouldn't have you think this an evil household. I've read the holy *Drishanna* from beginning to end, and I try my best to follow its teachings. Lanse, and old Jerold too, were brought up with Drisha's words in their ears.

"And the *master*—" Myra said, with emphasis. "Why, he knows the book better than all the rest of us together. He's studied it since childhood and knows its whole history.

"Great, too, is the master's knowledge of healing herbs. Comfrey, woundwort, feverfew, *hyweldda, cyhnaith*—he knows which to pick when the moon is new, and which reach their potency on Midsummer's Eve. He can make of herb and flower, salt and sulfur all manner of potions that restore a body to health."

Myra flicked her kerchief at Carin and rushed on. "Think, child! How many times has he healed your hurts? Didn't he mend your knee? And when your belly griped as he brought you home safe from the wasteland dogs, didn't he soothe you with a *glenondew* mint? Aye, the master told me of your foolishness: first to drink of tainted water, and then to take the powdered *cyhnaith* on your tongue as if you wished to burn the flesh from your mouth."

The woman tsked, then added, "And now, this very day, didn't he fix the potion that eases the hurt in your poor bruised noddle? Why, 'tis hard for these old eyes to see the knot—it shrinks betimes, so potent are the master's remedies. Oh my, child! With so much proof before you of the master's goodness, how *can* you call him wicked?"

"Like I said—" Carin growled.

But Myra put up her hand, staving off interruption.

"'Tis true," the woman rolled on, though in a whisper now, as if sharing a secret, "that *some* who have knowledge such as my lord possesses use it for purposes base and ill. They cast spells to do injury to others. They use magic to put gold in their coffers. Their enchantments bring evil and pestilence into the world. But hear me, child, when I say to you that my lord is no evil magician. He uses his powers for good. He's a wise and learned man, and a healer, and to me a kind and generous master."

But what about the cursed land that's just outside the manor's walls? Carin thought. *If Verek uses his powers for good only, and never for "purposes base and ill," then how did he lay waste to a sizable swath of the woodland? How could he have done such damage unless he commands the powers of evil?*

And was it his unrestrained malevolence that Carin felt each time she neared the edge of his stricken woodland, where his spellwork writhed in curtains she could not see?

But now that Myra was finally giving Carin a chance to respond, she decided to repeat no more of her thoughts. A falling-out with the housekeeper would gain her nothing. Carin's quarrel was with another.

"I'm sorry, Myra," she said. "You've been kind to me, and I shouldn't have blown up at you. I didn't mean to hurt you."

She shut the bathing-room doors behind her, then walked over to sit on the bed beside the housekeeper. "I don't like closed-in places, is all. When I was traveling on the plains south of here, I almost never had a roof over my head, day or night. I got used to the wide-open spaces. When Verek put me in the dungeon … uh, the cellar … I thought I was going to die. That *place* … unh. I get the jitters just thinking about it."

"There, there, dearie." Myra patted Carin's arm. "You've had a bad time of it, that you have. Poor lamb! To be so young and traveling the countryside all alone, fending for yourself with no one to look out for you. But that's all past, child. You'll soon be settled and back at the books in the master's great library. Won't that be a fine way to spend the long, cold winter?

" — But bless me!" Myra exclaimed then. She hoisted herself to her feet. "While I chatter away, your supper grows cold in the kitchen. You stay right here in your lovely little room — of all the bedchambers in the master's house, I've always thought this the prettiest — and you rest your bruised noggin. I'll bring a tray up straightaway …"

Myra's words faded as she rushed from the room and down the stairs.

With the housekeeper's departure, Carin reseated herself at the mirror. The face that looked back no longer had an ugly stain down one side. The yellowing from the poultice had washed off in her bath.

Carin inspected her reflection more closely, and her eyes widened as they studied the bruise at her hairline. What had been a deep purple-black an hour before was much faded. The knot in the bruise's center had shrunk to no more than a slight swelling.

"Drisha," she swore under her breath. "Is that even possible?"

She shook her head at her reflection. "Bruises don't fade that fast." As a point of reference, Carin had the marks on her arms. They were still livid. Verek had not poulticed them.

The warlock's remedies worked with speed "to make a body dizzy," so Myra said. Carin had the proof: her knee, healing overnight; and now the warlock's medicines flattening the lump on her head and lightening the bruise almost as she watched.

Did he use only a knowledge of herbal remedies to work his cures? Carin wondered. Or did he weave magic into his mixtures to achieve such uncanny results?

If Verek relied on sorcery to give his medicines their powers, should she refuse the remedies that came from his hands? Could the magic that healed her also taint her with evil? *"They are undone, who meddle with witchery,"* warned the priests of Drisha.

Footsteps sounded on the landing. Myra entered, bearing a tray loaded with food enough for a family. There was a platter of veal, as the housekeeper had promised, and also a baked wood pigeon, boiled salad, herbed soup, mashed peas, and for dessert a honey and hazelnut crumble.

"Oh!" was all Carin could say before digging in. Myra stood silent for a moment, watching her shovel in the feast two-handed, then shut the door and left her to enjoy it all in solitude.

Eating her way through every course took Carin awhile. By the time she'd picked the last bits of flesh from the pigeon's bones and licked the dessert bowl clean, twilight was invading the room.

She grabbed the candlestick off the dressing table and cradled it close. If Myra forgot to come back up to light the candle for her, she'd be left sitting in the dark. And after enduring that black pit of a dungeon, Carin never wanted to be in darkness again.

Of course, she could go in search of a flame. But roaming through the house, she might bump into the warlock.

A shudder ran through her. Which would it be? Sit in her benighted bedroom, fighting off a rising panic, or go to the kitchen for a light and risk a meeting with a sorcerer?

Wait—she had another option.

Flinging herself off the stool with such force that she knocked it over, Carin dove for the bathing room. She yanked open the shutter-doors.

Light streamed into the bedchamber. The glow from the bathing room's stone walls filled every dark corner. The effect was much like moonlight on a clear winter's night when snow blanketed the ground.

The moon—had it risen? Carin crossed to the bedroom's one window and pushed back the curtains. The luminous quality of the world outside said the moon was up, though it hadn't yet come into view over the cliff behind the house. But when it did, its light would shine in to mingle with the glow from the bathing room. She wouldn't have to choose between two horrors—Verek or darkness—after all.

Someone tapped at her bedroom door.

Carin whirled, startled. Myra seldom knocked. When she did, she never waited for an answer but simply walked in, blithely unconcerned about any need Carin might have for privacy. Whoever was at the door, it almost certainly was not the housekeeper.

"Yes?" she croaked, the word passing her lips before she knew she'd said it.

Both hands flew to her mouth as if to catch the sound before it could reach the other side of the door. *Keep quiet!* a frantic voice screamed inside Carin's head. *Wish the fiend away!*

But it was too late. The door opened, and a demon stepped into the room.

Chapter 9

The Note

The figure in the doorway seemed half trapped by the darkness of the corridor behind it, its features sunken, hollow, as indistinct as if charcoaled with heavy, slashing strokes. The eyes were lost in pits of deepest black, but still Carin felt the force of the gaze. It drove her back against the window. It made her draw in her breath: one short, quick gasp followed by another so sharp that her throat constricted. And then it gripped her so tightly that she could not breathe again—

—Not until the figure broke its stillness. Stiffly, it leaned to place a lamp upon the table by the door. And as the light fell upon it from this new angle, the face emerged from the gloom to become recognizably Verek's.

Shadows! Carin told herself fiercely, gulping for her next lungful of air as if the warlock's movements had triggered a reflex. *You're jumping at shadows.* The lamp Verek had held had illuminated his face from directly under his chin, rendering his features grotesque. It was a trick of the light such as children played on Mydrismas Eve to frighten each other with spooky faces.

Carin leaned against the window and kept quiet. With her breath still convulsing her throat, she couldn't trust herself to speak without a quaver—and any tremble in her voice would betray a fear she didn't want him to see.

Verek addressed her in cool, clipped tones. "Be easy. I have not devised new torments for you. I know you loathe the sight of me, so I shall keep this visit short."

He laid a thick volume down, next to the lamp. "This is a book of woods' lore." He rested his finger on it. "I charge you to study it well, for your life may depend on a mastery of its contents. From it you will learn the names of plants that grow wild in the north. You will learn which may be eaten and which are deadly. You'll learn the habits of the beasts that dwell in the far north, how to hunt them and how to escape them. You will learn of glaciers and ice caves, and of snowdrifts deep enough to cover this house. You will study the book until you know it better than you know your own mind.

"When spring comes," he went on, "I will question you to discover the depth and breadth of your knowledge. If I am satisfied that you've mastered every particular of each page, I will allow you to continue your journey northward—if that remains your wish. I think it likely, however, that when you have acquired a true understanding of the rigors of that place, you will see that you have come as far north as you can. Venture beyond my borders, and you will not survive."

Verek paused. He toyed with the one object he still held. It was another book.

In the combined light of the lamp, the glow from the bathing room, and the moonlight that now streamed through the window at her back, Carin easily recognized the red-and-gold volume. It was the *Looking-Glass* book that Myra called a puzzle. She gasped.

The warlock looked at her sharply. "So you have not forgotten the book that defeats me." He hesitated, as if reconsidering the wisdom of what he was about to do. Then, with obvious reluctance, Verek laid the puzzle-book on the table atop the volume of woods' lore.

"I cannot read it." The tone of resignation in his voice made Carin think of a man who had lost his sight and no longer entertained the barest hope of regaining it. "I had thought to make you read it to me. But in your obstinacy you would give a false account of it to deceive me and frustrate my desire to know its meaning. Thus I am thwarted. I can see no course but to entrust the book to you, in hopes of hearing a true report of it when your wounds are enough healed that you can speak civilly to me."

Carin passed a hand over her eyes. They were open; this wasn't another dream. At best, she'd hoped Verek would mislay the puzzle-book—maybe leave it in the library in a moment of forgetfulness to let her spend a few stolen minutes with it. Failing that, she had planned to search the house when the lord of the manor was away on his rounds. But here he stood, handing her the most exotic book in his collection so she could read it at her leisure.

As if he knew Carin's thoughts—did she only imagine he had that ability? Or did he use sorcery to pry inside her mind?—Verek quickly corrected her on the matter of how she was to use her time.

"Do not suppose that you will be free to amuse yourself through the winter," he warned, "reading what you wish—whether these volumes that I have chosen for you, or any others from my library. Your work is what it was on your first day under my roof. You will order the books in the library, from first volume to last. This task you will do each morning, from sunrise until Myra calls you to the midday meal. Then you will do any chore that woman sets for you, be it scrubbing the floors or eviscerating a hen. In whatever time is left to you, you may read, whether these"—Verek touched the two volumes on the table—"or any books you find in my library.

"What say you?" he demanded. "Do you find my terms reasonable, or do you think me a 'fiend' for requiring you to earn your keep in this household?"

Carin flushed at this reminder that he had overheard what she'd said. She cleared her throat, and managed to speak without betraying herself. "That's fair enough, sir."

She paused, then added, "Thank you for the books."

Verek made no reply, but neither did he turn to leave. His eyes on her now were glittering fires in the night.

What more did he expect her to say? Carin couldn't think of anything very sensible, but any blather was better than one of his savage silences.

"Sir," she offered, "I don't want to be late to work tomorrow, but I might oversleep because of this." She pointed to the much diminished lump over her ear. "I had a hard time waking up today. To be sure I rise early in the morning, I should go now and ask Myra to call me."

If Verek heard the intended note of dismissal in Carin's phrasing — "go now" — he didn't show it. Wordlessly he picked up the lamp and strode to face her at the window.

Carin recoiled from him, feeling the glass at her back like a sheet of ice against her shirt. The cold crawled up her spine. Her huge supper of half an hour ago lay in her stomach like a lumpfish swallowed whole. To avoid the warlock's eyes, Carin focused her gaze over his left shoulder. As she stared into the comforting glow of the open bathing-room door, she thought only of holding down her dinner.

Verek shifted the lamp from his right hand to his left and raised the light to Carin's face. Blinded, she could see nothing of his next movements, and started violently when his fingers touched her chin.

"Turn the bruise to the light," he ordered, pressing against her jaw.

Carin squeezed her eyes shut and submitted to his examination, though her every fiber screamed a protest. When his fingers moved from her chin to touch her hair and lift it aside, she couldn't help flinching away from him, her breath a piercing whistle through clenched teeth.

"The bruise remains tender, so it would seem," Verek muttered, evidently misreading her horror of him for physical pain. "There's some purpling yet, and slight swelling." He stepped back a pace and lowered the lamp. "This would now be healed, had the poultice been left in place as I ordered. Who removed the dressing? Myra? Or yourself?"

"I did," Carin whispered, her head still twisted away from him, her eyes closed. "I wanted to wash the stain off my face."

"Hmm. If you had permitted the ocher to mar your beauty for a few hours longer, the bruise would now be gone, and the lump with it.

"No matter." Verek turned on his heel and walked to the door, to replace the lamp on the table. Not looking back, he spoke over his shoulder. "A day's time will remove the last traces of your injury. Therefore, you may spend tomorrow in bed, or with your books, or as you please. But at first light the morning after, be at your task in the library — or answer to me."

Then he was gone, the bedroom door closing solidly behind him.

Carin unlocked her knees. She slumped to the floor, where she had no company for a time except the hammering of her heart and the rush of short, quick breaths.

When her pulse and her breathing began to slow, lucid thought returned, and with it the realization that her feet felt like two chunks of cold meat. Her fingers were icicles, and she was trembling in the cold that seeped through the window above her.

She scrambled up, crossed the bedroom, and stepped from its wooden floor onto the stone foundation of the bathing room. The gleaming rock was warm under her bare feet. Carin stood thawing, glad for the warmth and the light but unable to quiet a faint uneasiness about their source.

Did the fires of Nature warm the stone? Did this rock shine with captured sunbeams?

Or did *magic* give this room an unnatural warmth and light? Was this an ensorcelled place, full of spells that writhed along the walls — spells she couldn't see?

Carin flattened both hands against one wall, seeking the tingling sensation she'd felt on the hillside below the dolphin-scarred tree, then experienced again at the edge of Verek's woodland when he'd nearly broken her arms. Her fingers found only warm stone. She pressed her forehead against the rock. But she could perceive nothing like the forces that trilled along her skin whenever she neared the invisible barrier. If spells like those in the borderland did dance in this room, they kept themselves hidden.

When the chill had left her, Carin returned to the bedroom to retrieve the puzzle-book and the lamp that Verek had brought. She pulled the coverlet and all the pillows from her bed. These she piled on the floor of the bathing room between the washstand and the hot-spring pool. Thus cushioned, awash in lamplight and the glow from the walls, she settled with the book and began to read:

> *Through the Looking-Glass*
> *And What Alice Found There*
> *By*
> *Lewis Carroll*

Rapidly Carin reread the poem that prefaced the book, two verses of which she had read aloud to Verek on the day he first showed her the volume. Turning to chapter one, she was lost in the story before she reached the end of the first page. The warlock did not invade her thoughts again for many hours.

* * *

The bathing room's narrow doorway framed the sunlight that streamed into the bedroom beyond. To judge by the light, the time was late morning. At Carin's hand the puzzle-book lay open to chapter seven: "The Lion and the Unicorn."

Yawning, she picked herself up off the floor to stretch a stiff neck and a sore back. On the stone at her feet, the lamp was out — it had flickered itself empty of oil while she slept.

With the cold lamp and the puzzle-book in hand, Carin crossed the bedroom to replace both where Verek had left them last night, by the door. Heading back for her bath, she stopped and stared —

Draped on the bed was a fine woolen kirtle in a dark, rich shade of red. To one side lay the linen shift Myra had given her on her first morning under Verek's roof. On the other side were blue wool stockings of a length to reach above the knee, with leather garters to hold them up. The clothes were a gentlewoman's finery, not servant's garb.

As Carin stepped close to finger the soft wool, she saw that the tray that had held last night's supper was gone from the dressing table. In its place, a mug now waited. Propped against the mug was a small slip of paper folded in two.

She half sat on the stool and unfolded the slip. The writing, in blue ink in an elegant hand, read: "C — Drink the liquid. Leave the dregs. — V." The four capital letters were large and flowing, gracefully tendriled and dotted like grape-laden vines.

A small thrill shot through Carin. The writing, though it came from a hand capable of evil, was beautiful.

And it was meant for her — the first penning ever addressed to her. No one in the wheelwright's household had ever commanded her in writing. Only the daughter had known she could read.

Carin took the artfully decorated note to slip inside the puzzle-book. Back at the mirrored table, she examined her recent injuries. The bruise above her ear was barely visible — discernible only because she knew where to look. The swelling was gone, leaving behind only a slight tenderness.

She held the mug under her nose. The aroma confirmed her suspicion: it was the same potion Myra had administered after

Carin smacked her head on the cellar floor. The mug held a mixture prepared by a sorcerer.

Did she dare drink it? The potion had healed her — no arguing with that. But what else might it do?

Or did she dare to *not* drink it? If the damage to her head went deeper than Carin could see, she might do herself harm by refusing the warlock's medicines.

In any case, Verek's message hadn't left the choice to her. It did not read: "If the bruise is black and the lump large, drink this elixir." The note ordered: *"Drink."*

So she did — quickly, tasting the medicine as little as possible. Its flavor was as she remembered: less pleasant than its aroma.

Then, vowing not to sleep in her clothes anymore until she'd scrubbed out the sour stains, Carin stripped and went for her bath. This time she washed her hair too, since the bruise over her ear wasn't too sore to prevent it.

Dressed in shift, stockings, and rich red kirtle, she picked up the empty mug and headed downstairs. In the antechamber she paused, listening for Verek's voice. He might be in the house for his midday meal — reason enough to retreat and seek the kitchen later.

Hearing nothing of him, however, Carin slipped along the passageway to the kitchen. She found Myra at the fire, stirring a sauce. A clean platter, knife, and spoon waited at Verek's place at the table — signs that he was expected.

Carin couldn't retreat. The housekeeper had already bustled over to admire her new clothes and the rapid improvement in her health.

"Oh my, aren't you a picture! What a change there's been in you, child. Yesterday you were weak as a kitten. Now here you stand, straight and strong, the color in your cheeks and no lump to be seen. Didn't I say the master's medicines would put you right? He'll be pleased to see you up and about.

"And don't you look the fine one in your new clothes? I stitched up the kirtle while you slept. The color's fit for a queen, dearie, and suits you just as well."

Carin seized her chance when the housekeeper paused to breathe. She thanked Myra for the clothes and made to withdraw.

But the housekeeper seemed determined to prevent her. Myra took her hand and drew her along.

"Oh my, 'tis my fondest wish come true, to have a young person in the house again. And such a bright youngling, who can make sense of the master's books. What a fine thing it is to fill your head with learning. Why, child, the things you'll know after a season in the master's library ... it quite turns my head to think on it ...

"Come to the fire with me," Myra insisted, tugging her along, "and tell me of the books you've read."

But Carin got no chance to name a single volume. The woman did not pause again but chattered endlessly, touching on ten different topics when she'd run through her first.

Carin filled the time by helping with the apple dumplings Myra had been making. She was pressing a generous chunk of fruit into the last of the pastry dough when the door to the courtyard opened behind her. She whirled at the sound, and thoroughly squashed the dumpling in her fingers.

Verek stepped into the kitchen. "Myra, is—"

He hesitated as his gaze found Carin, then finished: "—the meal on the table?"

"It lacks only the doing of it, my lord," the housekeeper replied merrily. "Come, sir, and sit yourself down. There's lamb with sauce, and greens in vinegar. And for a sweet: a hot apple crusted from the hands of my fair helper. Long it's been since I've had such pleasant female company in this kitchen."

The sight of the warlock in daylight affected Carin almost as strongly as seeing him like a demon at her door last night. A sheen of sweat formed on her forehead.

I've been standing at the fire too long – that's all, she told herself sternly. But her legs refused to carry her away from the flames, for that would mean coming a step nearer the warlock. Her body rigid, as firmly in place as an iron pot-hanger, Carin found herself unable to move as the sweat trickled down.

Verek removed his black coat to reveal a blue vest over a white shirt that was open at the throat. This was the first time she'd seen him wear anything but black. As he laid his coat on the bench nearest him, he looked across the table at Carin and gave her a slight nod.

"You are well?" He spoke sharply, turning the question into a challenge.

"I am."

Carin's bit-off words hung in the air, sounding angry. Thinking it might be prudent to temper them, she added, "Thank you for the medicine."

"You drank the potion?"

"Yes."

"All of it?"

By way of answer Carin reached for her empty mug, on the chopping block where she'd left it, and tilted it to show that nothing remained but unpalatable dregs.

"Good," Verek snapped. "Though you are enough of an infant to fear a dark cellar, you aren't so childish as to hold your nose and refuse the draft that the physician orders for you. Not every remedy is as sweet as *glenondew.*"

Myra saved Carin the necessity of replying. She set a platter of broiled lamb on the table. Then she took Carin's hands and pulled her away from the heat of the fire. With her apron, she wiped at the sticky remains of dumpling that oozed between Carin's fingers.

"Oh my, 'tis truth, good master," the housekeeper burbled. "A draught of *hyweldda* can gall the patient's tongue. But our girl drank the potion down, even to the second dose which you bade me leave with your message while the child slept, curled up with her book. Two of a kind you are, my master—you and this bright young thing. Reading till all hours, awake in the night with your noses in books when you ought to be seeking your beds.

"And haven't your medicines worked their good with speed to spin one's head? The lass is quite herself today. She'll have us in an uproar the first chance she gets. It might be wise, my lord, to lock up the horses and bar the gates: mischief is abroad again."

Verek took his place at the table, poured himself a mug of ale, and—to Carin's intense relief—changed the subject.

"Late in the season though it is, Cian Ronnat's bay mare has a fine new foal," he told the housekeeper. "A colt. He'll be wanting a handsome sum for it, if it lives to see the spring."

"Well now, sir, if anyone can nurse a late-born colt through a hard winter, 'tis Cian Ronnat," Myra said as she served her master from a bowl of greens. "He's the finest horseman in these parts, excepting only yourself, my lord."

The housekeeper motioned for Carin to join Verek at the table. "Sit down, dearie. 'Tis time to eat. I'll watch that the sweets don't burn on the fire."

Woodenly, her every movement awkward, Carin took the seat across from Verek. Myra handed her a platter piled as high as his and poured her ale, then bustled to the hearth to turn the dumplings. The scene reached Carin as if she had no part in it. The warlock and his housekeeper might have been players on a stage while she sat in the back of the audience, barely hearing them speak their lines.

"Nay, Myra," Verek was saying. "You've not seen Lanse ride of late or you'd know he is Ronnat's match. The horse hasn't been foaled which that youth cannot gentle with a touch. He

119

himself, I sometimes think, is more horse than human, so clearly does he know their minds."

The warlock looked up from his meal then, and laid his glittering stare on Carin.

In the midst of bringing a bite of lamb to her mouth, her hand froze. Hairs rose along her arms. No longer did she watch the scene, safely detached from it. Verek's attention had swung back to her.

"Lanse tells me the mare Emrys is troubled. She eats but little and mopes in her stall, her spirits as droopy as her head. He thinks she pines for you. Go visit her this afternoon and restore her good heart before her melancholy spreads and dispirits every horse in the stable."

Carin swallowed dryly. "I'll be glad to," she said in a voice that was gratifyingly firm. "It will please me to see Emrys."

"It will please *me* to see you keep to the grounds within the walls," Verek almost snarled, pointing at her with the hunk of bread he held. "Do you mark me well? You are not to stray from the garden paths. Attempt to venture into the woods beyond and you'll find the gates tight shut, well barred and locked. I don't propose to ride again through a cold night to slay beasts that would make dogs' meat of you."

Carin lowered her stalled morsel of lamb and tried to look guileless. "You won't need to. I … I made a mistake before. I won't do it again."

"No more mistakes? Hunh!" the warlock scoffed. "Aim lower. From what I have seen, such an ambitious goal is beyond you."

Turning back to his meal, he muttered something else, a low-voiced aside heard only by his housekeeper. Myra chuckled, glanced over at Carin, then refilled her master's cup.

Carin narrowed her eyes at the two of them but couldn't think what to say.

Presently, Myra loosed a cheerful cloudburst of words, filling the noontime with patter about the health and doings of local farmers and village folk. Her conversation was like rain on the roof—soothing in its monotony. Verek interjected few comments, as if unwilling to make the effort to be heard above the torrent.

Carin ate quickly. Finishing first, she wedged a way into Myra's chatter. "If I may be excused, I'll go see the mare now."

Verek nodded and reached for the apple crusteds. Carin was off her bench and at the door before Myra could serve him the sweets, but she halted her flight at the housekeeper's warning:

"Mind now, dearie, that you don't spoil your new clothes. Menfolk will muck about in the stables wearing their best, but a gentlewoman ought not drag her skirts through the mews.

"Why," Myra continued, "that puts me in mind of Mydrismas Eve—how many winters ago was it, my lord? It stormed for a fortnight and the mud was up to the saddle-girths. A body couldn't stir forth without—"

But only Verek heard the rest of it. Carin swerved from the door and fled down the passageway, then up to her bedroom. She changed the woolens for her still-unwashed shirt and leggings, and put her boots on. Then she was down the stairs, through the kitchen, and out the door while Verek still sat at the table. Rapid strides took her across the yard. Not until she ducked into the stable's shadowy interior did she slow to catch her breath.

A soft whickering greeted her. It came not from the nearest stalls, where the warlock's Brogar and Lanse's gelding dozed, but from farther down the gallery. Those two horses eyed her sleepily as Carin passed, showing no more interest in her than she had in them.

But the soft whickering changed to excited neighs as she approached Emrys' stall. The mare danced on four feet and bobbed her head with such vigor that she threatened to dash out her brains on the crossbeams above.

"Easy, girl!" Carin soothed her. "Quiet down, before you hurt yourself."

At the sound of her voice, the neighs hushed and the dance stilled, but the mare's head continued its eager down-and-up as Carin stroked the graceful black neck.

"I can't take you for another run today," she murmured, "but we can go out in the sun. Your dark master gives us leave to walk the grounds."

Which wasn't precisely true. Verek merely bade her visit the horse, while forbidding her any wanderings beyond the walls. But taken together and viewed in the right light, his instructions could be stretched to accommodate her wishes.

She looped a soft rope around the mare's neck and led Emrys outside. Across the yard, in the garden that grew where the two wings of the house met at an angle, brightly colored flowers waved their heads. The mare made straight for the garden, her ears pricked and her eyes on the flowers. Carin's stride length-ened to match the mare's, and they were across the yard in no more time than a bee could have flown the distance.

At the edge of the flower patch, a graveled path wound between beds of yellow daffodils and blue gentians. As they set foot on it, the gravel crunched under Carin's boots and the mare's hooves with the noise of a small rockslide — an unmistak-able announcement of their presence in the manicured grounds.

At once, a bony face appeared above a cluster of pink roses. Startlingly blue eyes scowled from under wispy white hair and bushy eyebrows.

If this wasn't an elf—Carin's first impression, which she quickly dismissed—then it had to be Jerold, the old gardener Myra had mentioned. Carin addressed the scowling face with a pleasant "Good afternoon." It made no reply.

Not wishing to linger unwelcomed, Carin was at the point of walking on, twitching Emrys' rope, when a thought came to her. This aged being, whether it was Jerold or it was an elf that lived in the garden — *and why not an elf,* she reconsidered, *in a warlock's world?* — this being might know of a way to call the woodsprite. Carin had unfinished business with that traitor. It ought to hear of the trouble its betrayal had brought down on her.

So instead of walking on, she again addressed the frowning face.

"My name's Carin."

One bushy white eyebrow lifted slightly, which did nothing to soften the face's look of displeasure.

"Are you Mister Jerold?"

A curt nod of his head satisfied her on that point: this was in fact the gardener and not some uncanny being.

But did the old man not have a voice? Carin pressed on: "I wonder, sir, if you know the woodsprite."

Though the look of displeasure deepened on the gardener's cadaverous face, this proved to be the right question to loosen his tongue.

"If you mean the fay that lives in the woods — yes," Jerold replied in a voice raspy with age.

Gratified, Carin questioned further. "Have you talked to the sprite recently?"

Jerold shook his head. He started to walk away.

Exasperation rose in her, but Carin managed to keep it from her voice. "Sir, may I ask if you expect to see the woodsprite again?"

This stopped the gardener in his tracks.

"No, I do not, missy," he snapped. "I sent the creature packing, after it wore me out with its chatter — and its silly questions." Jerold eyed her sharply. "I can't abide a talker. And that hobthrust headless fetch-life is a talker."

Carin toyed with the coiled rope in her hands, not sure how to continue. Another word from her, and Jerold might banish her from his garden too. But she needed to know.

"Excuse me, sir. Just one more question. I can't go look for the sprite. Lord Verek has ordered me to stay inside the walls. Do you know of any way I can get a message to the woodsprite to tell it where I am and ask it to come?"

With grave severity, the old man scowled his displeasure.

"The wight's not welcome here—not in my garden," he rasped. "I can't abide it. If I see it here, I'll ax the tree it's in. The last tree that hid the creature bears the mark yet. One good chopping blow from me and the fay lit out like the cowardly thing it is. Don't try to call it back, missy. I won't have it."

He shuffled off and began pruning a myrtle tree that grew near the rose bushes. Their unsatisfactory conversation was clearly at an end.

"What a grouch!" Carin whispered to Emrys.

The horse blew softly through the nostrils, as if in agreement.

Continuing her walk, Carin led Emrys down the graveled path, winding through the fragrant garden for some distance. The path ended in a curve that turned away from the large main wing of the house. There, the trail became rougher and less distinct, as though this section hadn't been used in years. The shrubs and flowers strayed from their beds and overgrew the path, and vines draped the tree limbs, forming a curtain dense enough to block the way.

If Carin meant to explore the garden past this point, Emrys must stay behind. Small and agile though the mare was, the undergrowth here was too tangled to permit a horse's passage.

"Emrys," she addressed the mare in a conspiratorial whisper, "I'm going to see what's up this way. You wait for me here. I won't leave you alone long. I don't want either of us coming to grief. Your dark master might not like me roaming around back here. This place looks like a jungle, and he told me to stay in the garden.

"As for you, horse: you'll be in trouble with Jerold if he catches you eating his flowers. Stop that!" Carin tugged at the rope to bring the mare's head out of the hyacinths that Emrys had begun to nibble. "Just graze the grass while I'm gone, and stay put. If anybody sees you're on the loose again, I could end up back in that fragging dungeon." Carin's heart convulsed at the thought.

She looped the rope over a low-growing bush, gave the mare a final pat, and pushed past a screen of vines into an untamed profusion of greenery. A few steps beyond a long-abandoned bed of asters, Jerold's garden became a wilderness. There was no sign here of a human hand at work. Flowering vines festooned the trees. Ferns and creepers vied to cover the ground. Saplings fought for space and light.

Making headway through the tangle would have been impossible if not for the vestiges of a grass-grown track that meandered away from the house, leading deeper into the garden gone wild. In places the remnant path was detectable only as a patch of ground too firm for the rampant plant life to invade.

Carin picked her way along the barely visible trace, following it for some minutes before the jungle began to open up. The undergrowth thinned enough that she could see more than an arm's length ahead. Through the greenery, a stone wall appeared.

The path led up to the wall, and thence along it. Carin paused, resting a hand on the stonework's mossy surface. Should she return to the mare and save further exploration for another day?

Two minutes, she bargained with herself. *Just two minutes along the wall to see where it leads. To a door? A stile? Then back to Emrys.*

At the end of her allotted time, what came into view was nothing formed by human hands, but the bole of an oak so massive it dwarfed the tree that had saved Carin from the dogs. The oak grew so close to the wall that its roots had undermined the stone foundation and its thick limbs breached the wall halfway up. The damage, however, left no weakness in the fortifications surrounding Verek's manor house. The massive oak plugged the holes it had made as effectively as stone and mortar.

Drawn to the tree as to a temple, Carin approached almost reverently. She put her hand on the bark. Her widespread arms couldn't reach a sixth of the way around the bole, but on impulse she hugged her body to the great oak and stretched to embrace as much of its roughness as she could.

"My friend, words fail me," came a reedy voice in her ear. "I'm more pleased to see you than I can say."

Chapter 10

The Mirror Pool

As Carin jumped away from the oak, a feeling of relief mixed with annoyance replaced her momentary shock.

"So you're here, you traitor," she snapped at the tree. "A little while ago I was begging the gardener to help me get a message to you. After the way you betrayed me to Verek, I thought it might amuse you to find out he didn't kill me. But now you're here, you can see for yourself that Verek kept his prisoner alive, and I'm still more or less in one piece.

"Tell me something, you faithless creature!" she demanded, not giving the oak a chance to speak, although a shape that looked like a mouth worked helplessly in the bark. "When the dogs attacked, was it only by chance that you led me to a tree that stood all by itself, like an island? Or did you trap me there on purpose, knowing I couldn't escape, so you could be sure Verek would find me exactly where you left me? Was that all part of your plan to betray me?"

"My friend." The mouth in the bark drooped at its corners. "It is as I feared: I'm to feel your anger for leading the mage to you. Can you not see that I had no choice? Without his help, you would have perished. The dogs would not have given up the siege until you fell to them—or you died aloft and your body wedged in the tree, there to shed the flesh that tempted them. Whatever you may think of me now, I served you well in bringing the mage to you. He had gone miles astray before I found him, bound north when your sanctuary oak was to the west—

"To answer you on the question of that tree," the woodsprite interrupted itself, "as to whether it was luck or foresight that made me lead you to it: good fortune alone must get our thanks.

That ancient oak waited in its clearing as if the passage of centuries had prepared it for one purpose only — to take you up and protect you from the beasts. You could have reached no other tree in time. Among the ancient's neighbors, no other oak let down its lower limbs near enough to the ground to accept your leap, but not so low that the dogs could follow. No — Thank luck, fate, or whatever gods you pray to, but don't thank me for putting such a sanctuary in your path. I had no part in that good fortune, save to guide you to it.

"But I digress. The mage, as I say, was riding well to the north when I located him. So anxious was he for your safety that he greeted me with none of his usual malice, but as a soldier meeting an ally in the field.

"'The maid lives!' I told him. 'The dogs came for her, but she escaped up a tree and waits there now, helpless but defiant.'

"'She's unharmed?' the mage demanded to know. 'She suffered no bite from those jaws? Such a wound festers quickly.'

"'She's unharmed,' I assured him. 'Our traveler flung herself up an oak so fast that dogs' jaws closed on air alone.'

"'Your traveler is my runaway, and I mean to have her back!' the mage bellowed at me, his old manner returning with the knowledge that you were safe. 'Lead me to her.'

"'I will,' I told him. 'But first, I require a promise from you.'

"'*You* require a promise of *me?*' he shouted. He was furious by this time, Carin, as you may imagine. 'By the powers,' he swore, 'if I catch you in a twig I'll use it for tinder and laugh as you burn. What is this *promise* you want before you'll lead me to the girl?'

"'Only that you won't stop her speaking with me, once you have returned her to safety,' I told him. 'She's the only friend I've found in all my travels. She doesn't scream and run, or threaten me. She talks to me. I'll wish to visit her when she's back with you. Give me your word, magician, that you'll do nothing to prevent it.

"'And promise me also,' I added as the thought occurred to me, 'that you'll speak to the gardener who tends the grounds, to dissuade him from attacking with his ax the trees in which I rest!'"

The sprite's more scared of Jerold than of Verek. Surprised, and sensing a chance to learn something useful, Carin tipped her head and listened well as the creature rushed on:

"The mage did not waste time arguing, but assented readily to my first demand. 'If I don't scrag that thieving chit' —small chance of it, Carin, when he so desperately craves your help— 'then I won't stop her speaking to you,' the mage assured me.

"But in reply to my second request, he said only this: 'As for Jerold —he answers to no master but himself. Deal with him as best you can. His methods may prevail against you better than mine.'

"With that, we were away —I leaping through the trees with all the flashing and sparking I could manage; the mage and his boy following. I led them to your refuge and watched the rescue from a distance. Though the mage's spells cannot touch me, if his fire-arrows had set the forest ablaze, I could have been in mortal danger. When I saw the mage carry you clear of the smoke and ash, I knew my task was done. As the sun warmed the forest, I found a quiet tree and took my rest."

A few moments of silence followed the woodsprite's narrative as Carin mulled over the creature's words. Its story would merit careful reflection, when she could think it through. But for now, there were details of her recapture for which the sprite had yet to account.

"You didn't follow us afterward, then, back through Verek's woods to this house?" Her question was half accusation.

"No, Carin, I did not follow. After the night's exertions, I was content to drowse away the day and rely on the mage to convey you safely home. You and he had no mishaps, I trust?"

"Mishaps?" she echoed. "No, I was battered, buried alive, and nearly brained, but otherwise that warlock didn't lay a hand on me—as you can see." She pushed up her sleeves to reveal the bruises from Verek's iron grip.

A mouth as round as a full moon in the oak's bark told Carin she'd struck home. While the creature gaped, she related the events of her forced return to the manor, dwelling particularly on Verek's violence over the stolen kerchiefs, his entombing her in the cellar, and the head wound she'd suffered there. By the time her tale was done, the woodsprite was sputtering with indignation.

"That—that—*snake*," the sprite managed to hiss after several moments of shaping words which found no voice. "My friend! I never thought he'd deal with you so harshly. You are right to be angry with me. In the forest, when you warned of what would happen if I let the mage have you back, I thought you were over-wrought—your fears exaggerated by the circumstances. But now I see that your brief acquaintance with the mage has given you a better understanding of his nature than I have gained in all my time dwelling within his woods.

"Forgive me, Carin!" The sprite's voice rose until it resembled the highest notes of a reed flute. "I *have* betrayed you. I've handed you to a serpent. I do not deserve your friendship."

The mouth in the bark emitted cries so misery-filled, they would have broken a heart of stone. Carin stroked the tree trunk—her hand on the bole was a barnacle on a leviathan—and tried to take it all back.

"Hush, sprite," she whispered. "I don't blame you for what happened … not really. I know you meant to do the right thing. And you did. If you hadn't fetched Verek, I would have died just the way you said—torn apart or starved to a skeleton. Wood-sprite, we're still friends. You ignored what I said I wanted, and gave me instead what I needed. I know it takes the best kind of friend to do that."

At this, the creature gave a hopeful-sounding little hiccup, and Carin went on.

"Honestly" — while she was at it, she might as well confess what else she knew — "it's me I'm mad at, not you. I messed up my best chance of getting away. Verek won't be that careless again." Carin looked over her shoulder, perpetually on alert for the warlock. "When I'm around him, I feel like a tongue-tied dormouse." She rubbed her sore arms. "There's lots I'd like to say to him, but I'm too paralyzed to get it all out. Instead, I jump down your throat. I'll try not to do it again, all right?"

The woodsprite's reply was lost in a sudden commotion that came from the direction of Jerold's garden. First there was a shout, then the sound of a large, four-footed body crashing through shrubbery.

"Jerold's found Emrys!" Carin exclaimed, wondering briefly if the sprite had the least idea of what she meant. "I have to go. Meet me back here tomorrow. If I can, I'll be here at the same time."

Carin sprinted down the trail as fast as she could without losing the nearly invisible trace. In minutes, she was back on the graveled walk beside the main wing of the house. Emrys wasn't there.

A startled horse would head for its stall.

But almost as quickly as the thought sent Carin running down the path toward the stableyard, she stopped short, sending gravel flying. There stood Emrys, on an expanse of lawn between beds of primroses and violets. The mare wasn't browsing. She stood frozen in place, her muscles corded, her head flung up, eyes white-rimmed. Facing Emrys was Jerold, his right hand tracing patterns in the air.

The scene was distinctly unnatural. A horse so obviously frightened should race away, not stand rooted to the spot. A hand drawing pictures in thin air should not leave behind a tracery that—for the briefest instant—*glowed* before fading to invisibility.

Carin's brain resisted the evidence of her eyes. Gardener, he was. Elf, he might be. But *sorcerer?* Jerold—a warlock? *Another one?*

She shook herself from awed stillness and sprinted down the path. "Mister Jerold!" she called. "I'm really sorry. It's my fault. I shouldn't have let the mare wander off. I hope she didn't eat too many flowers. Or trample them. If you'll excuse us, I'll take her to the stable now."

Carin's flurry of words bought her time to reach the mare's side. She seized the trailing rope and came to the end of her overlong apology at almost the same instant. Just as she slipped an arm under the mare's neck and twined her fingers through the mane, Jerold ceased his midair tracings and dropped his hand.

Released from the spell, Emrys started back. She snorted her alarm but didn't break away. Neither the rope nor the arm hugging her would have held her, had she been determined to run. But Carin's nearness calmed the mare enough to stop her bolting.

"Good girl," Carin whispered, stroking Emrys' neck with the hand that held the rope, the fingers of her other still knotted in the mane. "Easy. Let's get you back to your stall." She glanced at the lawn where the gardener had set the air aglow, but the old man was no longer in sight.

The stable was as welcoming as a temple's inner sanctum. Brogar and Lanse's gelding dozed in their stalls; Lanse himself was absent. Emrys skittered down to her own enclosure, a horse clearly glad to be back on familiar ground.

Carin latched the stall door, then lingered in the comfortably dim stable to consider the significance of the afternoon's events. Her troubles multiplied with every day she spent under Verek's roof. Living in close winter quarters with one hot-tempered warlock would be tricky enough. But now she'd turned up a second sorcerer on the premises, and she had managed to antagonize him in a space of minutes.

Jerold, at least, might be easier to avoid than Verek. The silent, unsociable old man seemed never to leave his garden.

That it was an enchanted garden, Carin couldn't doubt. How else to explain the riot of flowers, the green grass and leafy trees this late in the year, with the days growing short and a chill in the air signaling the coming of winter?

And how else to explain the luxuriant growth of Jerold's garden in the midst of Verek's blighted woodland? It was as if the magic of the garden called up vigorous new life to battle the spells that desolated the woods.

The thought gave Carin pause. Could the magic garden be a sign that Jerold and Verek were adversaries? She considered the evidence. Jerold "answers to no master but himself," Verek had told the woodsprite. "Deal with him as best you can."

Myra, too, had suggested a rift when she said that Jerold — "the old goat," she'd called him — wouldn't let her cook for him. Myra was Verek's loyal servant. If Jerold would not eat food that Myra prepared, maybe he didn't trust the woman. Maybe he feared the housekeeper would scheme with her master to harm him.

If ill will existed between Jerold and Verek — the one championing life, and the other calling on the forces of destruction — could Carin turn it to her advantage?

If you want the old man to be your ally, you've made a bad start with him, she chided herself. *He probably won't let you back in his garden — with or without Emrys — after you chattered away and asked too many questions and upset him over the woodsprite.*

But to set things right with Jerold seemed worth the attempt. At worst, it might gain her the freedom of his enchanted garden this winter. At best, it might aid her against Verek.

Carin left the stable, strode purposefully across the courtyard, and stepped through the side door into the kitchen. She found Myra busy with early preparations for the evening meal.

"Here you are, dearie!" the housekeeper greeted her, cheerfully waving her to a seat at the table with the knife she wielded. "Sit awhile. 'Tis a long visit you've had with the black mare. How fares the coddled beast? Did you raise her spirits, as my master wished? The affection of a trusting animal is a fine thing. The master's Brogar would leap from the roof of the world, he would, if the master asked it of him. Aye, I've always thought it the surest test of anyone's character—how kindly he treats the dumb brutes and the loyalty they give in return. People can be fooled … *och*, people can be, and often are, but not the dumb brutes. They'll soon know a man for what he is."

"Um, Myra?" Carin spoke up when the housekeeper paused to dab at her eyes, which were tearing over the onion she chopped. "While I was out with Emrys, I accidentally upset Jerold. I took the mare for a walk in his garden. Mister Jerold didn't like her being there. He drew bright lines in the air, like this"—Carin imitated his tracings as nearly as she could—"and Emrys turned to stone. She was scared but she couldn't run. She just stood like a statue, rolling her eyes. It was the weirdest thing."

Myra quite forgot the onion in her hand. She stared at Carin and said nothing for the space of several heartbeats—a rare silence that she seemed to reserve for extraordinary news or events. Then she laughed and dropped her bulk onto the bench opposite.

"Oh my, dearie! I didn't think the old goat had any tricks left in him." She chuckled again, a sound like the simmering of cabbages in the pot. "Bless me, child! What a change there's been in this household since you arrived, poor lamb, all rags and tatters on our doorstep. Jerold hasn't practiced the craft for lo these many years, but has been content to putter in his garden.

"Did the old goat banish you?" Myra continued in the same breath. "If I had a copper for every time Jerold threw me out, I'd have riches enough for my own garden, indeed I would. But mine wouldn't be such a pretty place to walk in winter. 'Twould be only a common garden, where flowers wilt and grass dies. Nay, I'll not be wanting my own as long as there's such a garden in all of Ruain as Jerold keeps, where the green things grow through the cold months and flowers bloom in the snow." Myra sighed. "There's magic in that garden still."

Carin hung on the housekeeper's every word but made no reply. Until she knew what might unite or divide the members of this small, strange household, she'd keep her own counsel.

Myra heaved herself back to her chopping block, and talked on. "Don't trouble yourself about Jerold, dearie. He's an easy one to tame. Only go to the master's books and find one with pictures of flowers in it. Not pictures drawn dully, but sketches done up in glorious colors, and the biggest you can find. Take the book to the greensward and sit out there to read it. Mind, now, that you open it to a picture of the brightest, grandest flower. Keep your eyes on it as though you wished with all your heart for a real flower to burst from the page.

"You won't sit there long, child, ere you'll have Jerold peering over your shoulder and telling you all about the care and keeping of that flower—whether it likes mulching or wants the soil bare round its roots, how to tease from it the biggest flowers and the best, what seeds it makes and how deep to plant them for a sturdy crop of seedlings. Talk to him of flowers, and you'll soon have the old goat eating out of your hand."

It sounded like a plan worth trying, but not today, Carin thought. Better to let the gardener's annoyance fade first.

While Myra chattered, Carin spread pastries with curd cheese and raisins to make a dessert for the evening's meal. When the pot-herbs were chopped and a well-seasoned pork loin was roasting, filling the kitchen with the aromas of garlic and pepper, Myra settled her wide frame at the table and closed her eyes.

"Run along now, dearie, and give me peace. Methinks I'll rest these old bones a bit, while the dinner's cooking. You know I feel it in my bones ... Winter's coming ... and ... and other things ..."

The housekeeper's gentle snoring followed Carin down the passageway. At the foot of the bedroom stairs she paused, considering. A good hour of daylight remained. How best to spend it? By probing deeper into the great house in Verek's absence?

But was the warlock absent? She had seen nothing of him since midday, when he bade her visit Emrys — never suspecting, Carin felt sure, that she would also manage a private talk with the woodsprite, or provoke old Jerold into displaying his powers.

No, she wouldn't nose around now. Verek might be secretly about the house, mixing magical elixirs or conjuring up nightmares. The thought of interrupting the warlock in some arcane ritual sent a shiver through her flesh.

Her best course would be to return to the puzzle-book that was lying half unread in her bedchamber. Carin climbed to the blue room and stood there clasping the book in her arms, looking for a good spot to take up her reading. The bathing room was adequately bright, especially when she added lamplight to its own mysterious glow. But for curling up with a book, its stone surfaces were not the most comfortable. The bed and the corner chair were both too far from the window to catch the late-afternoon sun, and too heavy to move. Undeniably the best place she'd found for reading, in her limited explorations of the house so far, was the big desk under the windows in Verek's library.

She took a moment to change out of her smelly old clothes before padding downstairs. As she approached the library, Carin whispered to the unseen warlock, "Please don't be in there."

He wasn't. The library, warmed by a fire on the hearth and hospitable in its untidy stacks of books, harbored no sorcerer behind its door. Carin settled at the desk and opened the puzzle-book to the page she'd reached before sleep claimed her last night.

The light through the windows was noticeably dimmed when she looked up again, two chapters later. Myra would soon be putting supper on the table. Carin closed the book, using Verek's elegantly lettered note as a marker. She rose to return to the kitchen.

But as she pushed back her chair, a creaking came from the lightless depths of the library opposite the windows. It was the sound of a door opening on dry hinges.

Verek emerged from the darkness, his white shirt aglow in the failing daylight, his shoulder-length black hair swinging with the rhythm of his stride. Discovering Carin at his desk, he stopped short. Both stared.

For a moment, silence reigned, broken only by the crackling fire. The warlock crossed his arms, seeming to distance himself. But then he stepped forward and greeted Carin as casually as if finding her in his library at sundown was normal household routine.

"I see you are well along in your reading." His unquiet eyes took in the puzzle-book that was lying closed on the desk. The elaborately worked initial "V" was clearly visible where his note to her protruded from the volume. "Is it to your liking?"

He made the question sound offhand. But Carin doubted that the warlock's interest in the alien book had cooled as much as his manner suggested.

"Yes, sir," she answered him as serenely as possible, given that her mouth had gone dry. She slid the book off the desk. "I do like it. It's a little hard to follow, though. I don't understand all of it. Maybe by the time I get to the end, the confusing parts will make more sense to me than they do now." Carin glanced at the closed library door, wishing fervently that Myra would appear and save her from this conversation. "Myra hit the mark, I'd say, when she named it the puzzle-book."

Stop talking, Carin warned herself. *For pity's sake. When I'm not tongue-tied, I'm babbling.*

But it was too late. Verek's curiosity, though he might have held it at bay to that point, was now fully aroused. He crossed to the benches that were paired before the fireplace, took one, and waved her to the other.

"I will await a full account of the book until you've read it through," he said, "but give me now a puzzle from its pages, or read me some part that frustrates you. I might have knowledge that will aid your understanding." He wouldn't be denied; his balefire eyes flashed with interest.

Carin riffled the book's pages to give herself time to think. Of all the puzzles in the story, which one to pose him? It would be simplest to begin at the beginning, she decided, with the title and the impossible act it described: *Through the Looking-Glass.* She opened the book to the first chapter and to a drawing of a child who was pushing her way through a mirror.

"If you'll look at this, sir," she said, and handed him the open book across the table between their benches. "The little girl in the picture is named Alice. When the story begins, Alice is playing with a kitten and prattling about this and that, the way children do. She tells the kitten that she'd like to go through the looking-glass that's hanging above the mantel. She wants to get into the strange house that she's convinced must lie on the other side. And that's what she does. As soon as Alice names her wish, the glass gives way, and she goes through. On the other side she finds a house that isn't like hers.

"I don't know how that would work." Carin glanced at Verek and was glad to see him studying the book, not her. "To get through a looking-glass, anybody would have to break it first. Alice doesn't break it. But all the same: even if a person *could* do it, what would be the point? If a mirror hangs on a wall, there's nothing behind it but the wall. If it hangs above a mantel, there's only a chimney at its back. But in the story, Alice finds a new world beyond the mirror. It's a bizarre world, full of odd creatures." Carin shrugged. "Like I said, I haven't read the whole book yet. Maybe everything will be explained in the end."

She heard skepticism in her voice, and was proud of it. Not long ago, Verek had called her a rattlebrained fool. Whatever he might think of her mental powers, though, she was smart enough to recognize nonsense when she read it.

Verek studied the drawing a moment longer, then handed the book back.

"You are thinking of only one kind of mirror—the kind that's hard and impenetrable." He leaned back against the cushions of his bench, his fingers laced together and slipped behind his head. His eyes fixed on her. "Haven't you ever gazed into still water and seen your reflection, the same as if you'd looked into a glass? Isn't the surface of a reflecting pool a barrier between two different worlds? If you were to pass through that definite but yielding surface and enter the pool below, you'd find a strange realm—where finned creatures fly through water as winged ones through air, where objects float upward instead of falling downward, where beasts may have eight legs or no legs, but seldom walk on two or four as is common in the domain of men. Perhaps Alice's looking-glass is like a reflecting pool. Another world waits beneath its smooth surface."

Carin opened her mouth to reply, but shut it again without speaking. Verek had thrown a new light on the matter. He seemed to find substance in the tale. As she considered his analogy, other aspects of the story began to lose their absurdity.

"I hadn't thought about it like that," she said finally, "but I see what you're saying. The surface of a pool of water is strong enough for insects to skate on. A leaf that falls on a still pond will float on the water. But anyone Alice's size would easily pass through that surface. And once she's through, she might find creatures that are not common to her own world … not just fish and crabs, but others that are stranger … living chessmen and talking flowers, and a big egg with a human face, and a queen who becomes a sheep, and …" Carin's voice trailed off as she recalled the curious beings that Alice had met in the looking-glass realm.

"Good." Verek's clipped voice interrupted her thoughts. "You begin to see that the surfaces of things may hide their deeper meanings."

He dropped his hands and leaned toward her. "I will be pleased to hear the rest of the tale of Alice through the looking-glass when you have read it all and wish to tell it to me. There is, however, another tale I also desire to know the ending of — or rather, its beginning. And that is the story of your unexplained appearance on the shores of the lake where the wheelwright found you, years ago."

Carin's heart quickened at this sudden return to a subject she had thought closed. "I swear, sir, I've told you everything I know — "

The warlock raised one hand, cutting off further protest. "That you *remember* nothing more than you've told me, I believe. But there may be means of going deeper, beneath the surface of your memory — to find the other world that waits there, as Alice finds a realm of marvels waiting beyond her looking-glass."

Carin's alarm must have shown in her face, for Verek added: "This delving that I propose, to discover what may lie hidden in your memory, poses no danger to you. You will not be harmed. You won't feel pain. If I am correct in believing that your buried memories can be brought to the surface, they will reveal themselves as other memories do: as images only, with no substance, no solid form to shape a threat."

"But — "

A knock sounded at the library door. Myra bustled in, cutting off Carin's objection.

"Here you are, my lord!" the housekeeper said. "And my fair helper too, whose hands made the pastries that fain would flutter from the dish, so light they are. If it please you, master: the meal is ready now and needs eating while 'tis hot. There's pork peppered and roasted, and broad beans fried with onion. Will you wish to eat at table tonight, my lord, or in your rooms as ofttimes is your habit?"

"In my quarters, Myra, if you please," Verek replied. "I have preparations to make."

He fixed Carin with an unsympathetic gaze, clearly not interested in hearing how she felt about him poking around in her mind. "When you have eaten, meet me here," he ordered. "We will proceed as I have said."

With furrowed brow, Carin trailed Myra to the kitchen. After helping to prepare a tray for Verek and seeing the housekeeper out with it, she sat down to her own meal but ate sparingly on account of the butterflies in her stomach. Myra hurried back, all a-chatter about nothing much, and relieved Carin from any obligation to keep up her end of the conversation.

Supper finished and table cleared, Carin drifted from the kitchen down the dim hallway, obeying Verek's summons as slowly as she dared. She found him standing at the fireplace, waiting for her. The fire cast the only light in the night-darkened library. It illuminated features sharp with impatience.

"At last!" Verek beckoned Carin into the room as she hesitated one step inside the threshold. "Come." Turning from the fire, he disappeared into the library's shadowed recesses. A door creaked — the same door, by the sound of it, through which he had entered the room earlier and caught her at his desk. A rectangle of soft reddish light appeared; the door led to some chamber that was better lit than the library.

"Come," Verek repeated from out of the darkness.

Carin forced her unwilling legs to obey. She crossed the room to stand in the shadows and look through the doorway. It opened onto a narrow landing and a flight of stone steps. The stairway curved as it descended, hiding what lay at its foot. The steps were very like those she had climbed down into the black horror of the dungeon—smooth, seamless, well-worn. The only clear difference was that these steps led from a dark room above to a brighter chamber below. Where they were lost to view around the curve, their edges cast firm shadows in the stairwell, suggesting a light-source steadier than candles at their foot.

The unseen illuminator was not enough to tempt her to descend. "No," Carin said in a tone that revealed none of her dread, only her determination. She would not follow these winding stone steps to another nightmare like the dungeon.

From that one word Verek seemed to grasp her reasons for refusing the stairs, and even to understand them.

"No dark cellar awaits you," he said. He stood off a ways, this side of the doorway, and was cloaked in the library's dimness. "Do you recall your words to me, on your first day under my roof, when you said that you had never seen the like of the springwater pool in the room with the glowing walls? And do you remember my reply? I told you there were two pools of similar design in this house."

He pointed, only his hand emerging from the gloom to indicate the stairwell. "At the foot of these steps, you will find the second pool. It's larger than the spring in which you bathe; its waters are deep and still, but it is recognizably a sister to the pool that comforts you with its warmth. The light coming up from below is cast by the walls that enclose the pool. They glow as do the walls in your bathing room, with a light older than the sun's. I know you don't fear that light, for I have seen you use it to ward off the darkness that distresses you. Therefore, put aside your fears and come with me. In the chamber at the foot of these steps, you do not risk the terrors of the cellar."

When Carin didn't reply, Verek left the shadows, brushed past her, and descended the steps to the point where they curved from view. Pausing there, he looked up and waited, his stance relaxed — as if prepared to wait for her all night, if need be.

Carin drew a deep breath, stepped haltingly through the doorway, and took the stairs stiff-legged, puffing out her held breath with each downward step until she reached Verek. Neither of them spoke as he continued around the curve and down, with Carin following close behind.

After a winding descent that seemed to plunge to the world's core, the stairwell opened to a huge stone vault. It was many times the size of Carin's bathing room and less brightly lit. The dimness was not merely because the walls had a larger space to illuminate. These walls glowed with a duller light, faintly red, while the light in her bathing room was a strong yellow-white like sunlight through panes of polished horn. One would be hard put to read a book by the glow of these walls, but the illumination was adequate for Carin to make out details of the chamber —

— Not that there were many to see. The floor was stone, as level as a tabletop and polished like a marble slab. Centered in the smooth expanse was the pool Verek had described. A perfect circle, it could have held seven or eight pools the size of the one in Carin's quarters. Verek had called its waters deep and still, but he hadn't mentioned its mirror sheen. A lustrous reflection of the chamber's ceiling of rough stone — the roof of an enormous cave — glinted from the pool's glassy surface.

Without waiting for permission, Carin left the stairwell and stepped deeper into the cavern. She paused behind the nearest of four stone benches that were arrayed around the pool. The backless benches were spaced equally, like the four cardinal points of a compass. The nearest one appeared to have been hewn from a single block of stone, and was undecorated except for a crescent moon carved into its surface.

The crescent drew Carin's fingertips as a lodestone pulls a needle. As she traced the smooth curve, she knew where she'd seen the design before. The same crescent moon, worked in silver, formed half the badge that Verek had worn at his throat on the day he caught her trespassing. The other half of the badge had been a sun, resplendent in gold and red.

Avoiding the edge of the pool, Carin circled slowly to the next bench. It was identical to the first except the shape chiseled into it was that of a key. The third stone seat—which faced the bench of the moon across the pool—bore the symbol she expected to find on it: the sun, radiating flames. Cut into the final bench—the one paired with the key—was the outline of a fish.

What meaning did the symbols hold for the sorcerer who stood quietly near the foot of the steps, watching her circle the pool? Carin could only guess at their significance: the sun symbolizing day, fire, light and wisdom; the moon representing night, water, darkness and mystery; the key, with its power to open—to unlock secrets?—and the fish, perhaps symbolizing the depths of knowledge or the unearthliness of other realms. Seeing this pool and the fish carved into stone, Carin easily understood why the sorcerer, when posed the puzzle of Alice's looking-glass, had thought at once of a reflecting pool and the strange creatures one might discover below its surface.

Completing her circuit of the pool and its four benches, Carin approached the water's edge and looked down at her reflection. The pool cast up a perfect image, unmarred by the slightest ripple. In the eerie reddish light of the cave, she could see individual hairs in the auburn mane that fell around her face. If Verek hadn't said the surface was water, Carin would have sworn on the holy *Drishanna* that it was glass, a flawless sheet of it, impossible to penetrate without destroying.

A sudden urge had her crouching on the pool's rim, her fingers stretching to dabble in the water and disturb its mirror-stillness. But a half-formed apprehension of danger closed over her as fast as the impulse, and stopped her. To meddle with the forces that emanated from the walls and writhed just below the pool's perfect surface—she couldn't see them, but every fiber of Carin's being said they were there—such meddling would be to invite disaster …

For this was a place of power. Magic was palpable here. Tendrils of it brushed Carin's arms, urging restraint, warning against recklessness. Any mortal who would ask audience of the forces that ruled this place must leave willfulness at the door—and it wasn't fear of Verek that inspired Carin's caution. Even that warlock had grown quiet in the presence of the pool. He now moved toward her with the hushed demeanor of an acolyte in a temple.

Carin hastily retreated from the pool's rim. As Verek joined her, she asked him in a whisper, "Has that water always been so still and so smooth? Or did this used to be a flowing spring? Did it have a current stirring it like the pool upstairs does?"

Verek looked almost pleased, the way a teacher might beam if a dull student suddenly posed an insightful question. "Far back in the night of time … yes, these waters flowed," he murmured.

"Did these walls cast more light back then?" Carin persisted. "Did they glow as brightly as the walls in my bathing room do?"

Verek seated himself on the bench of the crescent moon, with his back to the mirror pool. Though there was room beside him, he did not wave her to the seat. No matter—Carin was disinclined to sit so close to either the sorcerer or the pool.

"Your speculations come near the mark," he said. "So shall I put an end to your conjecturing, and tell you why this wellspring daunts while the smaller one delights? Isn't that what you wish to understand?"

Verek looked searchingly at her. Carin nodded.

"Very well," he said. "This place was once as bright and animate as the chamber you call a bathing room. In an age so distant from ours that the mists of time have long hidden it, the first of countless generations of *wysards* began to work magic in this cavern. They drew power from the depths, using the forces that flow in stone and water — shaping them, directing and refining them, and over time, subtly changing them. The power is here, undiminished from the dawn of time, flowing through this rock and water as unfailingly as when the world was new. But the magic that springs from it has also tempered it, subduing the glow of the walls and stilling the waters of the well.

"These forces also flow in the walls and water of your bathing room. There, the power is untapped and unaltered. No magic has touched it. In its primordial state, the chamber soothes and comforts you. The walls glow and the water moves with forces akin to sunlight and the ocean's tides. A flower turns its face to the sun; fish swim in on the tide. You feel as naturally as they the forces in that chamber. You find them pleasing and benign.

"Because magic has been worked, however, with the power that dwells in this cavern, you feel the forces here as altered. You feel a sense of awe. Though you haven't the mastery to see the forces clearly, still you sense what flows through rock and water here. You sense the power that is both the raw power of the world and the creative potency of magic, and it unnerves you."

Getting no comment from Carin, Verek went on: "Much of this you have, I think, guessed already, though perhaps you haven't formed your thoughts clearly. What you have not suspected, I'll wager, is that the chamber you call a bathing room was given to you as a test."

"A test, sir?" Carin blinked at him. She stirred out of the stillness that had fallen over her. "What do you mean?"

Verek shifted on the bench, and looked past her as if the words he wanted were to be found on the red stone behind her.

"You should not be here," he said at last, in a tone that expressed perplexity more than resentment. "The spells that wall off my woodland should have turned you away, as they turn away all others who would venture there. But you not only defied the magic, you proved insensible to it. No mortal creature that is natural to this world could have lingered on the hillside at the edge of my woodland, in full view and sway of the wizardry, and yet claim to neither see nor feel the spells. A man trapped in a burning building could as easily feign unawareness of the flames. Pretense would turn to horror as the fire seared him, and in blind terror he would claw his way toward safety. Yet I saw you resting quietly on the hillside as the spells twined about you, and I knew it was no pretense. I knew you must be oblivious to the magic's very existence. Else, you would have run screaming, or fainted dead away.

"Only two explanations are possible," Verek went on. "The first is that you are a sorceress powerful enough to break a spell I believed unbreakable."

"Me? A *sorceress?*" Carin exclaimed, appalled. "You can't believe that!"

"Now ... no. I am convinced that you have no mastery of the art. But when I saw you defy the magic of the woodland, I believed you answered spell with spell.

"Therefore, I made no strong objection when Myra proposed lodging you in the blue bedchamber. The barn, I thought at the time, would have served more suitably" — Verek ignored Carin's sniff of indignation — "but the blue room upstairs offered what no other quarters could: access to the springwater pool. So I allowed Myra to install you in the finest bedchamber in this wing of the house ... and I waited.

"Were you a sorceress, you would know the pool for a place of power, and you couldn't help but work magic there, drawing on its potent life-force. Such a great, untapped pool of *gê* energy" — Carin didn't know the word, but she could guess at its meaning — "would be a treasure beyond price to a worker of wizardry. And when you tapped the force, when you turned it to your own ends, I would know."

Verek sighed, then went on mildly: "But as a sorceress, you proved a disappointment. You used the pool for no purpose but to bathe and splash about like a child at play."

"That was the test?" Carin interjected. "To let the pool show you whether I was magian or mortal?"

Verek nodded. His eyes, which for a time had focused on the wall behind her, shifted suddenly and locked onto Carin's. Only a quick tensing of muscles stopped her backing away a step, so forceful was his gaze.

"By such means, I was well satisfied that you are a mortal creature," Verek said, his glittering eyes holding hers. Neither of them moved as he awaited Carin's reply.

What could she say to him? They were agreed that she certainly was no magician. What was the point of repeating the obvious?

But as Verek continued to look at her with dismaying intensity, a phrase from his lips popped into Carin's mind:

No mortal creature that is natural to this world ...

"There are only two possible explanations—that's what you said, isn't it?" she addressed him finally. "The first one can't be right, because I *am* a mortal. I don't have powers like you have. That leaves only the other thing: You believe I'm *not natural* to this world."

"Yes."

In the silence that followed, the forces alive in the cavern seemed to whisper to Carin as the music of the stars plays in a person's fancy on a still, moonless night. Wrenching her eyes from his, Carin looked past Verek to the pool.

"In the library before Myra came in," she whispered, "you talked about another world ... one you think I've forgotten." She stared at the water, trying without success to see below its surface. "Is it really possible to look into my memory and search for it? Is the pool the way?"

Verek nodded. "With the power of this place, we may learn your origins, how you arrived on the shore where the wright found you, and—of utmost importance—what brought you here." Rising, he offered her his bench. "Take a seat, and we'll begin."

Carin pointed one bench over, to the image of a fish. "May I sit there instead?"

The sorcerer looked puzzled but nodded assent. "Yes, all are equal. Why do you choose that one?"

Why, indeed? As they walked over, Carin groped for words of explanation but found them as slippery as minnows. "I don't know. The fish ... it just fits somehow. It's free to go anywhere in the water, so maybe it can go where I can't—in my mind."

His head tilted thoughtfully, Verek nodded. "Yes. The fish swims in the depths. Perhaps it will be a guide to fathoming this mystery." He gestured at the chosen bench. As Carin settled onto it, facing the pool, the sorcerer stepped behind her. He brushed aside a hank of her hair and put his hand on her shoulder. This time, she did not flinch away from him.

"Look into the pool," Verek instructed. "Breathe deeply and slowly; clear your mind of all thoughts except for the village of the wheelwright. Picture it: its cottages, shops, streets. Think of it not as you last saw it, when your mind was full of plans for escape, but as you remember it from your years in the wright's household."

Staring at the pool's glassy surface, Carin called the village to mind in as much detail as she could remember. Well down from the wheelwright's work-yard was the mill; up the street in the other direction were a shoemaker's shop and a tailor's, a weaver, a candlemaker, a baker and a barber. The lane was narrow and gloomy. The living quarters above the shops, jutting out above the ground floors, turned the street almost into a tunnel.

As the village took shape behind her eyes, the pool in front of her lost its mirror sheen and became transparent. Carin saw steps leading down from the rim, wider and with a greater rise than the steps of the springwater pool in her bathing room. They descended endlessly, through crystal-clear water.

But as her gaze followed the steps downward, the water fogged in the depths, and the pool's surface grew misty. Out of the mist, as Carin watched open-mouthed, rose a perfect image of the village called Granger, matching the picture in her mind in every detail.

"Good," breathed the warlock behind her. "Now we search for the other world that waits beyond this one."

Chapter 11

Oblivion

The hand on Carin's shoulder tightened as Verek leaned to place his mouth near her ear.

"Think now of the pond where your master fished," he whispered, "the pond where you were found, a frightened child lying cold and wet upon its shores. Make a picture of it in your mind and take us there."

Many times Carin had walked from the wheelwright's shop down to the millpond. The way came easily to mind as she pictured the mill with its great waterwheel and the dam that created a head of water for driving it. In summer the pond above the dam was a pleasant place, its banks thick with willows, lilies, and red poppies.

As she thought of it, the village scene dissolved in the mists that played over the enchanted pool, to be replaced by an image of the millpond. But this was not the pond in summer. The whip-like branches of the willows were stripped of leaves; the banks were bare of flowers. The air around Carin, which had been comfortably warm to that point, suddenly chilled. Though Verek had said this delving into buried memories would call up only images — nothing with substance or solidity — Carin could *feel* the wintry scene as well as see it. She smelled it, too, a dampish odor rising from frost-killed foliage.

Something moved at the edge of her vision. Carin turned her head to view it more clearly. Verek followed her gaze, his head nearly on a level with hers as he leaned over her shoulder. A spot of color on the pond's far bank held steady for a moment; it might have been a scrap of cloth washed up from the water. But then it moved again, revealing arms and a bare, golden-brown head. It was a child, dressed in bright blue and green. Its hands clutched at bare willow limbs. Its legs, partially submerged, struggled to push itself higher onto the bank, out of the cold water and the mud.

"Fix your eyes on the child," Verek breathed into Carin's ear — as if any power existed that could have torn her gaze from the image of the half-drowned foundling trying to pull itself to safety. "Go back with that child, back to the moment which brought it to this juncture."

Go back? How? The scene was completely unfamiliar, the child unknown. How could Carin picture events she hadn't witnessed?

But even as she started to protest, the mists that drifted above the magic pool began swirling — slowly at first, but then spiraling precipitously downward to turn the image of the millpond into a frothing, howling whirlpool. Before her eyes, the child in blue and green plunged within the whirl, disappearing into the vortex like a nosegay of violets sucked into the eye of a storm.

"No!" Carin shrieked. She sprang up from the bench and reached for the image, as if to pull the child back. But the whirlpool had emptied of everything except hissing, swirling water and the mists that curled into the maw at its center.

"Stop!" Verek shouted over the roar of the vortex. "You can do nothing for the child. The images are from the past. All that you have seen *has already happened.*"

Carin probed the mists that spun down into the whirlpool's mouth, searching for a glimpse of color. But she saw only gray vapor and foaming water. The vortex grew steadily larger, tilting toward her until the bottomless opening at its center loomed only inches from her face.

She twisted away from it and tried to run, but something held her. Struggling to free herself, Carin clawed at the restraints and felt cloth ripping.

"Keep still!" Verek shouted in her ear. "It is illusion. It cannot harm you if you stay clear of the pool. Look! The image of the vortex fades, and another scene takes its place. This is a bed-chamber — a child's, by the look of it."

It was true. The whirlpool had dissolved, leaving behind only wisps of vapor that curled through the small room which now rose in the mists. Furnished with a four-posted bed, a chest of drawers, and tall shelves above a scaled-down desk, the room was clearly meant for a child. Brightly colored fish hung in mobiles from the ceiling and papered the walls. Playthings and books filled the shelves and covered the desk.

Most of the toys were plush likenesses of animals, several of them terrestrial — horses, a lion, a unicorn, an eagle, a clowder of cats. Dominating the collection, however, were salt-water creatures: whales, dolphins, parrotfish, starfish, a green sea turtle and a blue crab.

Looking down on the menagerie from the topmost shelf was a big egg with piglike eyes, a wide mouth, and booted feet. It was the very image of the "Humpty Dumpty" character from the puzzle-book. Hooked over the egg-man's left foot was a neatly lettered sign that read, in the language of the puzzle-book, *Karen's Zoo.*

The words held Carin for a moment. Then her gaze shifted to the cornerpost at the head of the bed, and to a crystal that hung from it on a golden chain. The crystal caught and reflected light from some unseen source. Its winking was, for long moments, the only motion in the room …

Until something stirred under the coverlet on the bed. An arm — sleeved in blue and green — flew up, to come to rest atop the bedcovers. The fitful sleeper rolled over, revealing a head of golden-brown hair before settling again into stillness.

"The child is alive," Carin whispered. "She wasn't killed in the whirlpool."

"She is most certainly alive," Verek said. "Do you not understand? That child is *you*, as you were years ago, before the vortex plucked you from your bed and spun you into the void between worlds, finally bearing you up through the waters of the mill-pond to cast you upon the bank where you were found. What you witnessed moments ago was the journey as it happened — the events depicted backward through time."

On legs that felt suddenly unsteady, Carin sought the bench behind her. Helping her to the seat was an arm wrapped tightly around her, its white linen sleeve ripped open from elbow to wrist. As she dropped onto the bench, still facing the pool, the arm released her. Its owner sat down beside her, his face turned opposite, toward the wall. Neither of them broke the silence as Carin watched the image of the child's bedchamber fade and the pool resume its perfect mirror surface.

"Do you remember these events?" Verek asked finally.

Carin shook her head. "Not at all — not the bedroom, or the whirlpool, or the child. You're telling me that a whirlpool carried me off, and that's how I ended up nearly drowned in the mill-pond?" She waved one hand dismissively. "I don't believe it. That's completely round the bend. If something like that *had* happened to me, how could I not remember it?"

"Fear and shock may have entombed the memories so far below the surface of your mind," Verek said, "that only the methods we have used tonight could have power to uncover them. The void between worlds is a place so alien that the mortal mind must recoil in terror if ever it be exposed, by chance or wizardry, to that dark oblivion. It's no marvel that a child caught in the vortex would lose all conscious memory of it. The greater wonder is that you did not lose your reason as well, and become a whimpering lunatic."

Verek stood, signaling an end to the night's "delving." With his disfigured left hand, he helped Carin to her feet.

She tested her legs, and finding them strong again, started to walk to the steps that led up to the library. The hand on Carin's arm, however, guided her around the pool, toward the wall that curved behind the bench of the carved key.

"The hour is late," Verek said. "This way leads more straightly to your quarters."

Though no opening was visible in the wall, he ushered her up to it, then pressed the palm of his right hand upon it. When he moved his hand away, a section of the wall swung inward on unseen hinges. The door opened to another stairwell. The reddish light that spilled onto them from the cave showed these stairs to be grander than the steep, winding stairway to the library. These steps were of wood, not stone, and they climbed upward in wide, straight, gradual flights separated by landings.

As Carin and Verek stepped through to begin the ascent, the opening in the wall closed silently behind them. With the light from the cavern cut off, the stairs fell into blackness.

Swallowing a shriek, Carin gasped at the sudden darkness. It weighed on her. It squeezed the breath from her.

An orb of clear white light appeared in the right hand of the warlock at her side. He held it with his fingertips far away from her, where it lit their way up the stairs—and threatened her as little as possible? Carin glanced at him. Could he actually be trying not to unsettle her with sorcery any more than he already had tonight?

Verek noticed her glance. He brought the magical orb a little closer. As they climbed, he twirled it in his fingers. "It's a light without flame," he murmured. "Cool as distant starlight ... incapable of causing harm."

Carin did not reply. The orb seemed like an unremarkable bit of magic compared to the other wonders she had witnessed tonight. Her mind raced back over the events and images.

Had the enchanted pool, now two flights of stairs below them, really caught a reflection of the past, of the bedroom she had occupied as a child? Had a frothing whirlpool plucked her from that life and dropped her, stripped of memory and identity, into this one?

If the vision revealed the truth, it suggested that she had once had a home. Carin rolled the word around in her thoughts, trying to make it mean something. But it remained an empty concept. "Home" was not a place she knew. Neither her memories nor her experiences told her what or where it might be.

The stairway's third and topmost landing opened onto a long corridor. The hall was moonlit through high, round windows at infrequent intervals. As they neared the corridor's far end, Carin suddenly knew where she was. This was the hallway that opened off the landing which her bedroom door faced.

The evening's adventures had taken her in a great, multi-storied loop: from her bedroom, puzzle-book in hand, downstairs to the ground-floor hallway and library; from the library down a plunging stairwell to the chamber of the magic pool; and from that cave up three long flights of stairs to this upper corridor that led back to her room.

They were at her door. Verek released the arm that he had lightly held since guiding Carin from the bench at the pool's edge. He lifted the latch and pushed the door open. Carin's bedroom was lit only by the moon shining through the open-curtained window. The doors of the bathing room were shut, preventing the glow of those walls from mingling with the moonlight.

"If Myra has left lamp or candle for you, this will light it," the sorcerer said. He lobbed the magical orb in his hand toward the ceiling of her bedchamber. The orb shattered, showering the room with sparks. In an instant, the chamber exploded with light to rival the sun's, blinding in its sudden intensity.

"Drisha!" both swore together, jumping back from the threshold in unison as if joined at the hip like Cethren twins.

The room was awash with light from every possible type of lamp. There were candle lanterns tall and short; shallow saucer lamps with flaming wicks floating in fat; covered oil lamps of every description, some clean-burning, others smoky; and candlesticks single, triple, and branching. One treelike specimen held more than twenty tapers. The flames alight in the bedroom, all ignited at once by Verek's glowing orb, would have adequately illuminated the great hall of many a manor house. Ablaze in such a confined space, they threw off enough heat to toast the faces of the two astonished onlookers in the doorway.

Recovering his composure, Verek snapped his fingers; more than half the flames died as if buckets of water had been thrown into the room. With one eyebrow arched quizzically, he surveyed the numerous fires still burning.

"Pray tell," he said, turning to Carin. "Are all these here by your design?"

"No," she said, emphatically. "The last time I saw this room, there was just one candlestick on the dressing table, and the oil lamp that you left here at the door."

Verek nodded. "This bears Myra's mark. To ease a child's fear of the dark, she would burn down the house." Abruptly he turned back to the hallway. In a voice more annoyed than concerned, he threw a warning over his shoulder: "See that you do not set afire the bedclothes, the curtains, or yourself." Then he was gone, retracing his steps down the moonlit corridor.

Alone in her room, Carin extinguished all but a pair of lamps — the original left by Verek last night, and one from among Myra's multitude that cast a similarly steady, clear light. Then, stripped off to bare skin, she crawled into bed. Sleep must come quickly tonight. After her day of courting trouble in Jerold's enchanted garden and time-traveling through Verek's pool of magic, she felt thoroughly ground down.

Despite the lateness of the hour, however, Carin's mind was too agitated to let her sleep. Answers had come tonight like tithes to the temple on Mydrismas Eve: answers to the riddles of an unremembered childhood, of glowing stone walls, of spells that were invisible to her while horrifyingly apparent to others ...

even a possible explanation for Verek's hostility toward the runaway he had found hiding in his woods. For a time, he had believed her to be a sorceress—a blackheart powerful enough, maybe, to break his spells and challenge his rule. If only briefly, during those moments when he'd held a sword to her throat, he had supposed himself to be in danger.

The thought provoked one of Carin's rare smiles. For a little while anyway, the warlock had feared her.

In the vision they had seen tonight, there was also a hint about the puzzle-book's origins and why Carin knew its language. Many books crowded the shelves of the child's bedroom that had risen in mists above the mirror pool. Had the puzzle-book once been among them? Had it, in fact, once belonged to *her*, a companion to the egg-man toy that seemed cut on the pattern of the Humpty Dumpty from the book?

If so, how had the volume come into Verek's possession? If an unnatural whirlpool had dumped Carin in a millpond on the southern grasslands, then why hadn't the vortex also borne her book to that pond?

She sighed. It had been the same since her first hour in Verek's realm: every question answered summoned two more to take its place.

Lying awake, Carin stared into the flame of the short, round oil lamp on the table by the bed. Its steady light filled her mind. She waited for sleep to come.

But what crept over her instead was a growing anxiety. The feeling drew her to her feet to stand at the window, looking for ... she didn't know what ... in the moonlight outside. The rocky cliff behind the house dominated the view from this window, which overlooked the corner of her jutting bedroom where it joined the long roofline of the upper-story hallway. A small section of the stone wall surrounding the manor grounds was just visible. Beyond the wall, Verek's cursed woodland appeared not desolate, but peaceful in the moonlight.

The woodland wasn't the source of the apprehension that now fell around her like a heavy veil. Carin crossed to her bedroom door, pulled it open a crack, and looked out at the landing, listening for any sound. All was silent. And yet feelings of despair and foreboding drew her gaze to the long, empty corridor that led to the cavern of the enchanted pool.

She closed the door and dressed quickly in only her shift. Then she lit a candle lantern from Myra's multitude, stepped out onto the landing, and turned to the corridor down which Verek had vanished. He'd left her at her door not an hour ago, to judge by the moonlight through the corridor's windows. The light seemed little altered since her previous passage.

Gliding silently down the hallway on bare feet, Carin reached the wide staircase that descended to the cave. Beyond the head of the stairs, set into a wall that closed off the corridor at an angle, were large double doors. Carin hadn't noticed them before. Her thoughts as she passed this way with Verek had been too full of questions and revelations. But beyond those doors must lie the larger, main wing of the house.

Pausing, Carin closed her eyes and opened her other senses to the feeling that had drawn her to this spot. It beckoned, not from behind the closed, latched doors, but from the great stone vault at the foot of the stairs.

Am I a moth drawn to candlelight? she wondered uneasily. *Am I going to my doom like an insect that flies into the flame and gets burnt up?*

Slowly, with many pauses that brought nothing to her ears but silence, Carin descended the three flights, passing from the moonlit world of the upper stories into the dark depths below ground. It was impossible to know the exact moment of transition, as the walls of the stairwell were paneled from top to bottom in some dark wood that absorbed light from her lantern as wheat boiled in milk soaks up the liquid. At the bottom of the stairs nothing met her eyes but dark paneling. The door to the cave was well concealed.

Lightly brushing her fingertips over the paneling, Carin felt for any break. On the third pass, her fingers found a gap in the wall a handbreadth wide. She raised the lantern to the opening and stared, dumbfounded. Her eyes could detect no break in the smooth surface. Yet her fingers were up to their second joints *in* the paneling, as though stuck into soft rye bread. She felt nothing; her fingers met no resistance. She wiggled them. Their movement was apparent up to the knuckles but invisible beyond.

More fascinated than afraid — was this how Alice had passed through the unresisting looking-glass? — Carin thrust her hand into the gap until her wrist and lower arm disappeared. Her fingers felt a metal bar: a latch. She lifted it and pushed. A section of the paneling yielded the merest bit, moving silently away from her. She had found the door to the cave of magic.

Setting the lantern down, Carin closed and fastened its curved visor to darken without extinguishing it. Then she put both hands to the paneled door and pressed gently, moving it by fractions until a sliver of reddish light shone through a crack. Also slicing through was a voice, the words distinct and brittle like shards of glass.

"Show me the past, *Amangêda!* I beseech you: take me through time. Return me to days of happiness, before this ghastly scene. You have shown only this brutal image in answer to my every plea. It is burned into my brain. I see it waking and sleeping. Blot out this image, wretch, and grant me respite! Show me my lady and the child as they were in life — not as they linger in my nightmares, in this scene that repeats endlessly in a tortured mind."

For a moment, silence leaked from the cave. Then the voice — barely recognizable as Verek's — cried out in anguish: "*Amangêda!* Have pity! Would you show the mortal *fileen* the dark magic that bore her between worlds, yet deny your servant the slightest glimpse of light or beauty, love or laughter? *You are a monster!"*

These final words were screamed in a rage that upended the hairs at the nape of Carin's neck. The voice conveyed a fury beyond any human capacity to feel or to express.

She pushed the door open far enough to get her head through the crack, just in time to see the image against which Verek railed. Rising from the surface of the enchanted pool was the scene that Myra had described to Carin on her second morning under Verek's roof: a tangle of water-lilies, a woman and a child caught in the twining stems, their drowned bodies hideously bloated. The skirts of the woman's gown and the tendrils of her long hair floated up like smoke.

So vivid was the image that, for an instant, its strange perspective escaped Carin's notice. She—and the sorcerer who was standing on the lip of the pool—did not look down on the scene, as they would view it from a lake's shore. They looked *up* through the image as though they stood on the lake bottom. The stalks of the water-lilies reached from the pool's misty surface to sway above Verek's head like a forest of slender, interlaced tree trunks. The bodies of the woman and child hung high in the stems, both face-down, suspended more than an arm's length above him. He looked directly up into their dead eyes.

Screaming with pain and rage, the sorcerer swept his arm like a scythe through the lilies' stems. The slim, translucent rods shattered glasslike, sending drops bright as diamonds raining down into the pool. The illusion, destroyed, returned instantly to the water from which it had been formed. The images of water-lilies and two drowned bodies roiled together as water crashed down into the pool with the force of the sea through a burst dike. The deluge caught Verek. It knocked him into the pool and swept him under as the flood poured over him.

It was finished in seconds. The macabre images sculpted from water were gone. Like quicksilver, the waters of the enchanted pool flowed into the basin and stilled, not sloshing or splashing but coming to rest as if suddenly made glass. The pool's un-rippled surface was flawless, a perfect mirror.

Verek had vanished.

Chapter 12

Suspicions

Carin tried to call his name and found she couldn't speak. She made to run to the pool, and found she couldn't move. Her body was one with the stone of the cave's walls and the glass of the pool's surface: fixed, immobile.

This wasn't terror that held her. She'd been frozen with fear often enough in a week's acquaintance with a warlock to know the sensation of it. This was something else. Her muscles didn't merely refuse to obey. She might as well command the stone of the cavern to melt as to order her rock-rigid limbs to move. They were cold and lifeless fossils.

Only her eyes remained under her control. Carin fixed them on the magic pool, searching for some sign of life. Behind her wild stare, wilder thoughts raced.

Was Verek dead? In destroying the reflections of his drowned wife and child, had he caused his own death by drowning? Or had he angered some demon or spirit that dwelled in the magic pool? He'd called out a name—"Amangêda"—as though he addressed a sentient being. Had his words, or his destruction of the water-sculpted images, so enraged the demon-spirit that it had killed its servant?

Without Verek to release Carin from whatever spell now held her, she might remain in the cave's doorway through eternity, as unmoving as the walls of rock. Was this how the pool dealt with intruders—by turning them to stone? Neither of the entrances that Verek had shown her had been locked or barred. Both the door from the library and the door in which Carin now stood were hidden, but once their locations were known, it required only the lifting of a latch to pass through either. Did the force that ruled this place choose not to exclude intruders, but rather to admit them just this far … then punish them in ways worse than death?

Carin's imagination fed on itself until thought collapsed into panic. But she couldn't scream. She could only stand and stare at the pool—

—Where bubbles had appeared under its glassy surface like air pockets beneath the ice of a pond in winter. Joining the bubbles were two hands, palms pressed upward. The surface lost its brittle sheen and became liquid. Through it burst Verek, gasping for breath. His black hair shed glittering droplets that shivered away like crystals of ice and chimed with a faint ring when they hit the pool's surface.

He swam strongly, throwing up fans of the uncanny liquid. Though the well might once have held drinkable water, the properties of the fluid were now so altered that he seemed to swim not through water, but through liquid glass. It rolled off him—quite literally like water off a duck's back—leaving him dry as he reached the pool's top steps, crawled up them on his hands and knees, and heaved himself onto the rim. Collapsing on his side, he sucked air deep into tortured lungs.

The moment Verek escaped the pool, the spell released Carin. She again had command of her limbs. They tensed instinctively to flee, and it took all of her self-control to remain where she was, only shifting her weight slightly and craning her neck for a better view of the pool's rim and of the warlock who had barely avoided drowning.

Except for the rush of his breath, Verek lay unmoving. His face was turned to the bench of the sun, away from the doorway and away from Carin. She watched him for a few moments more. Then the door closed silently upon her retreat.

* * *

Carin slept late. Dawn was long past when she rolled out of bed, splashed her face, and pulled on clothes.

As she raced downstairs to the kitchen, she breathed a plea to both Verek and his housekeeper: "Please be somewhere else." Myra's patter would only further delay her. And the warlock's temper — after what he'd gone through last night — was bound to be raw this morning. If he caught Carin coming down at this hour, she would pay a price. Verek had warned her to be at her task in the library at cockcrow today — or suffer his wrath.

Luck seemed to favor her: no one waited in the kitchen. Carin poured a mug of thin ale, grabbed two cheese and raisin pastries that were left over from last night's meal, and carried her makeshift breakfast to the library. It too was empty.

She set to work sorting and stacking books, determined to make up for the morning's lost hours. As she worked, Carin kept a wary eye on that section of the library, opposite the windows, which lay perpetually in shadow. She listened for the creak of a door that would warn her of Verek crossing the shrouded threshold.

But no noise reached her from anywhere in the house — no thudding door, no voice, no rattled pot in the kitchen. No one came to check on her. When her stacks of books towered high enough to prove that she'd been working, Carin propped open the library door — meaning it for an invitation to any passerby to stop in and review her progress. But none did.

Past midday, she quit the library and went in search of Myra and a meal. The kitchen was exactly as Carin had left it, the jug of weak ale on the table, the platter of stale pastries beside it. Looking further, under a cloth on the cutting block she discovered a loaf of good wheat bread, a round of goat's cheese, and several ripe apples. Had the housekeeper meant this for her? Or for someone else? Shrugging, Carin cut thick slices of bread and cheese and took them with two apples out to the stable. She'd share her lunch with Emrys.

The mare whinnied a welcome — eager, but not frantic as it had been at Carin's approach yesterday. Neither Lanse's gelding nor Verek's hunter was in the stable.

"That accounts for the absence of the sorcerer and his apprentice, doesn't it, Emrys?" Carin said as she fed the mare an apple. "It looks like your dark master wanted some time away after what happened last night. I wonder where he's ridden off to."

Emrys munched noisily but didn't so much as bob her head in reply.

"I've been around Myra too much," Carin muttered. "I want to talk to somebody, and no one's here."

Company might be found, however. The woodsprite was a great talker, as Jerold had complained, and Carin had promised to meet the creature this afternoon at the great oak behind the main wing of the house. She could walk Emrys around the grounds and still meet the sprite at the appointed time.

"If you are *quite* finished, horse" — the mare had polished off her apple and claimed the better part of Carin's as well — "we'll go walk in the yard. But you mustn't eat Jerold's flowers."

This time, Carin avoided the flowerbeds in favor of an unexplored section of the property. Behind the stable the tall hedgerow curved into the yard instead of hugging the wall that enclosed the grounds. The hedge rejoined the outer wall behind the kitchen, near where the back of the house blended into the cliff face. The greenery cut the corner in such a way that a triangular space must lie hidden behind it.

"Let's poke into that corner," Carin said as the mare walked alertly at her side. "Maybe it hides a treasure house. Or a maze. Or a temple ... if not to Drisha, then to the spirit of the magic pool that your master calls *Amangêda*." She watched for any reaction, even a flick of the mare's ears, but Emrys seemed not to know the name.

As they rounded the end of the stable and approached the curve where the hedge took leave of the wall, an opening appeared, easily visible in the greenery. The place was unguarded and proved to be a disappointment. It concealed nothing more interesting than a grape arbor and an orchard that was thick with apple, hazelnut, and plum trees. Sound asleep under one heavily laden apple tree lay the old gardener, his wispy white hair teased by a gentle breeze.

So peaceful was the expression on Jerold's formerly scowling face that Carin found it far easier to think of him as an elf than as a sorcerer. But she had seen the old man paralyze Emrys—as she herself had been made a statue on the doorstep of Verek's cave of magic.

"We won't risk waking Jerold," she whispered in Emrys' ear. "I've had enough of turning into stone. And I bet you don't want to go through that again, either. We'll raid the apple orchard another time."

Departing quietly, Carin led the mare toward the cliff that backed this section of the house. More of the rock face showed from this angle, and a closer examination supported the ideas she had formed on the day of her escape attempt. The back of the house joined the cliff so seamlessly that it was impossible to tell where the stonework of the building became the solid rock of the cliff. The stone face reared behind the house in an imposing mass, its upper reaches broad and steep, towering above the wall that encircled the grounds.

"How much magic is buried in that mountain of rock, Emrys? My bathing room is there"—Carin pointed at the union of house and cliff, as if the mare could have any interest in such matters. "Your master says the cavern with my springwater pool holds power, ages old, for those who know how to use it."

But much deeper, inestimably farther under the ground than Carin's lofty pool rose above it, lay the cave of magic where she had glimpsed another world. Picturing the layout of Verek's mansion, with its subterranean dungeon and its caves penetrating deeply like roots, gave Carin a slight chill, despite the warmth of the late-autumn sun on this beautiful afternoon. On their next pass by the cliff, she studied the house through narrowed eyes. Maybe it stood upon this spot for no other reason than to give generations of sorcerers ready access to the forces that flowed in rock and water here.

Sometimes sharing her thoughts with the mare, sometimes keeping them to herself, Carin walked Emrys in a circle seven times from stable to hedge to kitchen door to the green turf of the garden, and around again to the stable. At each pass by the garden, the mare eyed Jerold's flowers but made no effort to escape Carin's grasp.

Stabling Emrys after their exercise, Carin groomed the mare with a wisp of straw, then took her leave with a promise to walk again tomorrow. She slipped back through the orchard entrance and verified that Jerold still slept. Good. She could cross the old elf's garden unobserved.

Retracing her steps of yesterday afternoon, in short order Carin was down the graveled path and along the remnant track to stand at the great oak that breached the wall.

"Woodsprite!" she called. "Are you here?"

"Indeed I am," replied a reedy voice. "And no happier sight than you have I ever seen. Are those new clothes you're wearing, my fair friend?"

Carin glanced down at the red kirtle, then looked at the oak and frowned.

"Yes, I'm afraid they are. I completely forgot to put on my old rags before I came outside. Myra—she's Verek's housekeeper, have you met her? She made these for me. They're the best clothes I've ever had. I hope I haven't torn them on the brambles out here."

"Come a little closer and turn around slowly," the sprite said, "and I'll look for rips."

Carin raised her arms and did as she was bid.

"Be easy," the creature chirped. "I see no damage. And by re-turning to the house through a doorway that is quite near here, you may avoid the dangers of thorns and brambles."

"A door here?" Carin asked. "Will you show me?"

"Gladly. I need not merely point it out, but can lead you over its threshold. When I leap to the rowan that grows just before the portal, I may spread with the tree's roots over the doorstep and into the house. It's the only place I have found where I may enter the mage's home. Come! Fol−low−the−flash−of−my−pas−sage," it said, leaping away.

The sprite sparked like a purposeful firefly as it jumped from tree to tree. It led Carin to the end of the house farthest from the kitchen doorway. The garden here, though not groomed as in the V-shaped tract between the house's two wings, was more open and freer of brambles than the tangle that grew near the big oak at the wall.

"This is the door I spoke of," said the sprite, its muffled but unbroken voice signaling that it had come to rest. "When I follow the tree's roots over the threshold, I look up and see on the door's inner side a thing that might be a hasp. But there is much rust. Maybe the lock is weak. Can you try the door, and force it with a little effort?"

Carin studied the portal to which the creature had brought her. That the door hadn't been used in a score of years or more was evident from the mature rowan that grew directly in front of it. The silvery-gray trunk made a thick post centered in the doorway. Some of autumn's red berries still clustered at the branch ends. The tree's roots, as the woodsprite had said, had grown under the door into the room beyond, splintering the threshold boards and the door's bottom rail. What was left was weather-beaten and as fragile-looking as a sheet of birch bark.

Slipping between the tree trunk and the jamb, Carin leaned her shoulder against the door. Its rotted hasp and the top hinge broke instantly. It tottered inward, kept from toppling by only a scrap of a lower hinge. She caught the door and held it, and stood staring into the space beyond.

The room was huge: three stories high, open to the rafters, well lit by arched windows at each gable end and eight pairs facing across the immense central space. A balcony, reached by a stone stairway, looked down from the long wall opposite the doorway Carin had opened. Five long tables, each fronted by a bench of equal measure, were aligned lengthwise with the room.

At the far end, under the gable windows, was a raised platform on which stood a table—the high table, obviously. There was no mistaking this room for any other than the manor's great hall, a place for banqueting and entertaining visiting nobility. In the wall to Carin's right, across the open space from the high table, were elaborate gates through which guests would once have entered.

But no guests had dined in this hall for many years. A thick layer of dust coated the tables and benches. Beetles and mice rustled the dry leaves and catkins that had blown in through broken windowpanes. Much of the balcony's railing was missing or dangled precariously. Spiders spun fantastic creations in the highest corners. The room smelled of dry rot. Carin wrinkled her nose and coughed.

"The place reeks, doesn't it?" The woodsprite spoke from just in front of Carin's feet, where the tree's roots had cracked the floor tiles. "The wood in here is decaying. With a great leap I can reach that first table, but its lumber is so old and dry I cannot bear to linger within it. I've explored no farther. Even from here, though, the weakness of that railing yonder is clear to see. If you go that way, you must take care. I know the treachery of rotted wood. It cannot be trusted.

"Come," the voice piped. "Let's retreat to fresh air and to sound and healthy timber." The creature leapt from the rowan to the trunk of a good-sized oak a few feet away.

Carin propped the door closed as best she could. Then she joined the woodsprite and sat on an exposed root.

"That door is a good find," she said. "Thank you for telling me about it." She leaned to touch the sprite's tree. "I've got something for you, too. I'm sure you'll want to know where I went last night, and what I saw, deep in a cave with Verek."

"In the depths with the mage?" the sprite said, its voice lifting. "Tell me everything!"

Not everything, Carin thought. She wouldn't talk about Verek's anguish or her glimpses of his dead wife and child. That was neither the sprite's business nor her own.

But every other detail from last night, Carin related fully: The cavern with the redly glowing walls. The mists rising from the enchanted pool, forming images. The child appearing at the mill-pond. The vapors whirling them away to another world—the child's world—where toys took the shapes of exotic animals, and books might be written in a language incomprehensible to the sorcerer Verek but familiar to Carin.

"You saw your homeworld!" the sprite broke in, sparking brightly. "This is tremendous news. It gives me hope that a return journey to my own world is possible. I have been stranded here for a long time. I want to go home. I don't belong here. And neither do you. That other place with the books and the toys is where you should be."

"Do you think so?" Carin tilted her head, struggling with the idea. "But I don't remember that place. For all I know, it doesn't exist. Everything I saw may have been a fraud—a magic trick. And even if it was real, it might not be there anymore. Verek said we were looking back in time, seeing things as they used to be." She sighed. "I don't know where that place is or how to get there. I'm not drawn there." Not in the way she'd been drawn north to Ruain. She had had to come *here*; she felt no similar compulsion, however, to go *there*.

"The fact is," Carin muttered, mostly to herself, "I don't have a home. If I don't belong in Ruain, I don't belong anywhere."

And that's just the trouble. I am well and truly lost. Carin had been sent packing by a southern wisewoman, and now she had a northern warlock telling her just as bluntly: "You shouldn't be here." So where to next? Stumbling around in search of a place she could truly call home, could she end up in the void between the worlds? That was a place of oblivion, Verek said. Carin stared into the distance, imagining herself emptied of being, without thought, dissolved away into nothingness.

"I'm counting on you, my friend," the woodsprite was chirping, reclaiming her attention. "I don't know how I can ever go home without your help. The mage speaks to me hardly at all, and never as openly as he spoke with you last night. You can learn from him. Has he given you a sign that he knows what force or power brought us here, or why? Though I think we come from very different worlds, Carin, I suspect the same agent may have spirited us to this one. We must discover what or who that agent is, and — most importantly — whether it can send us back the way we came. Does the mage know, do you think?"

Carin shook her head. "When he took me down to the pool of magic, Verek said it might show not only how I got to the mill-pond, but also what brought me there. He said *that* was the main thing." She lifted both shoulders in a don't-ask-me shrug. "All I know is what I saw. And even then, I'm not sure how much of it to believe. As real as those images seemed, Verek admitted they were illusions."

Had he, however, been using the word in a way she didn't fully understand? Carin wondered. His was the language of sorcery, after all.

And one language Verek doesn't know, Carin reminded herself, *is written in the puzzle-book.* How could he have put even two words of that language into a false illusion, if that sign in the child's bedroom was a fiction he'd invented?

"But you'll keep digging, won't you, Carin?" the sprite pleaded. "You'll attempt to learn what the mage knows?"

She nodded. "Maybe when Verek gets back—his horse and Lanse's are not in the stable, so they must be out riding—maybe this evening, if I see Verek, I'll get a chance to find out more."

"The mage does not ride today," the sprite said. "From a tree outside the wall, I watched as the boy and a plump, graying woman drove a wagon and team through the main gate and headed off to the east, early this morning. The wagon was empty except for bundles of sacks and canvas. And tied to the back were both the mage's great horse and the boy's saddle steed. The mage himself was not to be seen …

"I confess, my friend," the sprite added, "that I have often lingered in the trees outside these walls, hoping to see the wizard emerge in such a mood that would permit at least a brief conversation. For until we met, Carin, I had no one else with whom to speak. I never addressed the boy or the woman—

"Is the plump woman your friend Myra?" the sprite interrupted itself. "The mage's housekeeper who made your new clothes?"

Carin nodded. "That's her."

"Then I must do something kind for the lady … perhaps shoo a flock of songbirds through her window," the creature mused, half talking to itself and forgetting its tale of the wagon.

Impatiently, Carin drummed her fingers on the oak's trunk.

The sprite sparked under her hand, roused from its meditations. "But I digress. What was I saying?"

"That you never talk to Lanse or Myra when they go outside the walls."

"Oh, yes. Thank you. I never speak to them, you know, for fear of sending them into fits of screaming and carrying on, like the paroxysms of the village woodcutters. But several times I have watched the boy and the woman—this Myra—take the wagon out empty early of a morning and bring it home loaded just before sundown. I suspect they travel to some town or market to buy goods. Why the boy sometimes ties saddle horses to the wagon's tailboard, I can't say. I've never followed them, preferring always to wait at the gate on the chance the mage would come forth and speak a civil word before bidding me begone. Do I sound quite pitiful, to be spending my days hoping for only a kind word or two?"

"No, you don't," Carin said. "I often wished I could hear a few kind words when I was walking up from the south. But I never talked to people either. It was too dangerous. Someone might suspect I was a runaway." She paused, remembering how it had felt to be a fugitive, keeping to herself and trusting no one. "I know what you mean about wanting company. When I woke up this morning and couldn't find anybody, I decided I wouldn't mind ever again about Myra talking my ear off—

"Sprite," Carin added, suddenly inspired, "if you want conversation, then get to know Myra. I don't believe that a 'talking tree' would upset her in the least. After all, she keeps house for a sorcerer. I'll bet Myra has seen things weirder than you. Be polite and flatter her, and you'll make a friend for life."

At this, the creature excitedly piped its thanks. But Carin's thoughts were moving back over the sprite's story about the wagon. She returned to a passing mention that troubled her. *Tied to the tailboard were the mage's horse and the boy's saddle steed. The mage himself was not to be seen.*

If Lanse and Myra had taken the horses this morning, and Verek was not with them … where was he? If not out riding Brogar, then where? Verek often disappeared for hours at a stretch, but his and Carin's paths usually crossed at least once a day—if not in the kitchen for meals, then over a book in the library.

Carin's throat tightened as she pictured the warlock where she'd last seen him: lying half-drowned beside a pool of magic. Maybe she had misjudged the reason for his daylong absence.

She stood. "Sprite, there's a book in the library I want to finish while I've still got the sun to read it by. But first I'm going to explore this end of the house. I'd like to find some way to come and go that doesn't take me through the kitchen. Everyone's eye is on me there. If I can slip out sometimes through the rowan door, I'll be able to get away easier to meet you."

Carin touched the sprite's tree in parting, received its farewell, then returned to the servants' entrance of the great hall and eased open the weatherworn door. She walked the length of the room, crunching bird droppings under her boots, and stepped up on the platform of the high table. The room had been thoroughly stripped. No shred of a woven tapestry hung on its walls. Not a single trencher or spoon had been left behind, nothing to hint of extravagant feasts in years gone by.

Down from the platform, she scuffed through debris to the foot of the stone steps. They led her up to a balcony that ran the length of a wall which was pocked with nooks and crannies.

Carin searched along the wall for a means of admittance to the main wing of the house. She found wide double doors filling the third alcove. The doors' shared latch was rusty, but it yielded to her determined, two-handed shove. One door's hinges seemed fused into solid metal chunks, so firmly did they resist movement. But the other door, squalling like an injured cat, gave just enough to let her squeeze through.

She stood at the end of a long, dusty corridor. Sunlight filtered through high windows of the same design as those in the upper-story hallway that Carin had traveled last night. Doors lined the corridor, spaced well apart, leading to guest quarters perhaps. She tried each as she passed, but all were either locked or firmly stuck.

Another set of double doors closed the facing end of the corridor. Their latch was in better repair than the one Carin had just forced. It lifted easily.

Through those doors was the landing she knew from last night. The darkly paneled stairwell descended from it to the cave of magic. The hallway continued past it, heading for her bedroom at an angle. The two upper corridors met in the point of the wide "V" that was formed by the master and minor wings of the house.

Stepping through to the occupied part, Carin turned to shut the doors behind her—and froze, her gaze on the dust motes that danced in the corridor. Her passage had stirred up a cloud of particles that twinkled preternaturally, catching the sun like tiny crystals. For a moment she saw, not the dust of disuse, but the glittering droplets that had fallen from Verek's hair when he broke the surface of the enchanted pool, gasping for his life's breath.

Hastily she shut and latched the doors. Then she stepped to the head of the stairs and peered down the stairwell.

"Are you there, warlock?" Carin whispered. "Are you dead? Maybe if I'd stood and watched you a little longer, I would have seen you stop breathing. Or maybe you're still alive down there, but barely—and wishing that somebody would come help you. But who's brave enough to open that door? I'm not. I won't—not after last night.

"But maybe," she added more audibly, "there is one person around here who will risk it. If Myra can't vouch for your whereabouts, warlock, then I'll tell her what I saw last night. I'll tell her my suspicions and ask her to send Jerold down to help you. He has power. Maybe he can hold off the magic of the mirror pool with a spell of his own and not turn into a statue the way I did."

"Do you strew riddles upon the stairs?" snapped a familiar voice at her back. "Pray face me and speak plainly."

Chapter 13

A Susceptibility

Carin whirled, and had to grab the handrail to keep from tumbling backwards down the stairs. Verek stood with his arms folded and his feet apart, eyeing her crossly. His long black hair, normally smoothed back from his forehead, hung around his face in disarray like a Drishannic monk's. His bloodshot eyes were sunk in shadows. The beard that edged his jawline was untrimmed. The tear in one rolled-up sleeve identified the rumpled garment as the same shirt he had worn last night during the "delving." He looked altogether like a man in need of, first his bed, then his barber.

"Good afternoon, Lord Verek." Carin addressed him formally, struggling to appear calm. "Are you well?"

"Well enough," he growled. He gestured at the stairs behind her. "What business have you here? What has Myra to do with my whereabouts, or Jerold with anything but his garden? What are these 'suspicions' you're muttering about? And in what fashion have you become a statue? You seem lively enough, if eyes may judge."

Carin gripped the handrail tightly, her thoughts racing. How could she answer him without revealing where she had been and what she'd seen last night? Would his fury have limits if he learned what she had witnessed — the ghostly drownings and his torments?

Trying desperately to concoct a plausible story in a span of seconds, Carin stammered out: "It's only that … that the house has seemed so empty all day, s-sir. Myra isn't here. I started to … to worry when I didn't see her … or you … from the time I got to work in the library this morning until I went to the kitchen to eat. I—"

"Let us adjourn to the kitchen now," he interrupted. "I've eaten nothing today—your mention of a meal interests me almost as much as this tale you're weaving. Come." He turned to the hallway and waved her to his side with a quick, peremptory jerk of his hand.

"Speak truthfully," Verek demanded as they strode toward her bedroom, "and dispense with the effort of crafting a story that will topple like a wall raised on sand. Already you've laid a weak foundation with this talk of an empty house. If you have noted Myra's absence as well as my own, then why do you not try *me* with questions as to *that* one's whereabouts?"

He answered for her. "No. Your worries are not for Myra. You speak as though she were expected momentarily, and I not at all.

"Tell me," he continued, dismantling Carin's powers of invention as he attacked her story from another angle: "In these roles you give us, as though to make of us mere players on a stage, why do you cast Myra as the warden, yourself as herald, and Jerold in the hero's part? Pray cease your attempts to compose a motley drama, and tell me plainly what you mean with your talk of suspicions and spells and statues."

They'd reached the landing fronting her bedroom. Verek paused at the head of the stairs. He gestured for Carin to precede him down them, sweeping his arm theatrically as might a speaker who steps forward from the chorus to introduce the play's next act.

She bristled at him mocking her.

"You're right, sir," she snapped. "I'm not a good liar. I can't make up a story on the fly. So I'll tell you the truth, since that's what you say you want. You won't like it, though, when you hear it."

Her mind on the events she was about to relate, Carin hardly noticed when they reached the kitchen and she flipped back the cloth that covered bread, cheese, and fruit. She cut wedges of cheese and slapped them onto a trencher with a hunk of bread and the ripest of the remaining apples; she and Emrys had polished off the best pieces earlier. She plunked the trencher down in front of Verek, poured him a tankard of ale, then seated herself opposite, nearer to the cold fireplace than to him.

Verek said nothing, only pared and ate his apple slice by slice and watched her expectantly from across the table.

"All right then," Carin began, her tone declaring her reluctance to recite the tale. "Last night, after you walked me to my room, I went straight to bed. But I couldn't sleep. I got this feeling that something was wrong. I didn't know where the feeling was coming from. But it was strong, and sad, and heavy, like something weighed me down. And it called to me. I couldn't ignore it." Carin frowned, remembering the power of that summons.

"So I got up," she said, "and went where the feeling told me to go. It led me downstairs to the cave of the mirror pool. I felt around for the door in the paneling and found the latch and pushed it open a crack, and I heard you talking to ... well, it seemed like you were talking to the water in the pool. You were asking it to show you ... some good memories. But it wouldn't. I heard you getting furious at it. I wanted to see what was happening, so I opened the door wider, just far enough to stick my head in."

Carin paused, feeling like a swimmer who was rapidly getting out of her depth.

Verek stared at her with eyes that were unnaturally luminous. His lunch lay untouched in front of him. Presently, he took a sip of ale. Then: "Go on," he breathed, his voice barely above a whisper. "A story so boldly begun must be told to its finish."

Carin took a deep, shaky breath.

"I don't know how to tell you what I saw," she murmured. "The pictures are hard to put into words. It took me a second to figure out that I was seeing the stalks of plants growing up out of the pool. I almost felt like I was in the water, like I was a fish in a pond that was choked with water-lily stems. The stalks

179

reached up toward the cave's ceiling … and two bodies were caught in them, tangled up, over where you were standing.

"I watched you knock the whole thing apart," she said. "When you hit the stalks, the pictures collapsed. I could see then that they'd been made of water. The water poured back into the pool and took you with it. That's when I got turned into a statue. I couldn't move or do anything except stare at the pool and wonder if you'd been drowned. I thought you must be dead, and I figured I wouldn't get out of there alive either.

"But then you surfaced. I could hear you breathing so hard, I knew you must be hurting. The thing is, though, I could move again. The second you came up, I wasn't paralyzed anymore. So I didn't stick around to be sure you would live. You were out, you were breathing, and I wanted to leave.

"Even if I could have done something to help you," Carin added softly, "I figured you wouldn't have been happy to know I was standing in the doorway. I don't understand why I was brought there to see what I saw. I doubt that you would willingly have shown me those things."

Avoiding Verek's gleaming eyes, Carin hurriedly concluded. "When you heard me talking to myself, I was making up my mind to tell Myra what had happened. She could have sent Jerold to help you, maybe. Jerold can do magic—I've seen him petrify a horse. He was the only one I knew of who might have been able to go down and get you. Maybe it wasn't much of a plan. But I didn't know what else to do."

The silence that followed was profound. Carin didn't dare look at Verek, for fear of the rage she might see in his face. She heard him rise from across the table and saw, out of the corner of one eye, that he walked toward the fireplace where she was sitting.

She half stood, but found nowhere to run. Verek could easily cut her off if she tried to flee through either the side door to the courtyard or the passageway to the foyer. There was only the door to Myra's bedroom at her back, and no certainty that she could reach it before the warlock caught her, or that such a retreat would gain her more than a few seconds of safety.

Carin forced her gaze to the sorcerer and found him staring at the banked coals that, in Myra's absence, hadn't been fanned to a fire on the hearth. The face that could express consuming rage, but more often wore an unreadable cast, lay fully open to her examination. Emotions moved over it as plainly as clouds scudding across a stormy sky. Each temper threw its own distinct shadow over Verek's countenance—each, for an instant, identifiable before giving way to the next.

Anger was there, certainly, but it yielded by turns to shock, distress, doubt and wonder, and a moment that Carin took for pure revelation. Once, Verek's lips writhed back from his teeth in a grimace that might have been a prelude to the violent rage Carin expected. One glance, however, at his now-subdued eyes told her it was pain that contorted the warlock's face, not fury.

What finally settled over him was an attitude of resolve tinged with resignation. When Verek turned his face to Carin's, he had the look of a man who had reached a decision he found distasteful but necessary.

"Tell me more," he said firmly, in a voice that betrayed no inner turmoil, "of this 'feeling' that drew you from your bed to descry my private concerns. Did it take the form, perchance, of voices in your head?"

"No, sir," Carin protested as she retook her seat. "It wasn't anything crazy like that. It was just a feeling, and as hard to explain as any other feeling that suddenly comes over a person." She struggled to give him a good example. "Have you ever come to a fork in the road and decided, on impulse, to go left instead of right? Have you ever felt the urge to look over your shoulder? Do you look? Maybe you don't listen to your feelings, but I listen to mine.

"When I was walking up from the south," Carin added, "I learned to trust my instincts. I always paid attention when something whispered to me that I should take one path and not another, or I should keep walking and not settle for the night in some haystack that seemed as safe as a temple. Trusting my gut is how I stayed alive and free." She rubbed her forehead. "I don't know what came over me last night, but I can tell you that it was the strongest feeling I've ever had about anything. I had to listen to it. I had to go where it told me to."

Verek was looking at her with a sort of preoccupied skepticism. Abruptly he left his spot by the fireplace. He sat down directly opposite her, reached across, and rested his right hand, palm up, on the table between them.

"Give me the hand that found and opened the hidden door to the cave of the *wysards*," he demanded.

Reluctantly, Carin eased her right hand onto the table to rest near his; she couldn't bring herself to lay it in his open palm. For a moment then, he examined her hand with only his eyes.

She, too, looked at it, seeing it as if it weren't hers. Months ago, when she fled the wheelwright's house, her hands had been reddened and calloused from years of chores. Now they might almost be called pretty, Carin realized with surprise. Her feet had borne the brunt of her journey across the grasslands. Her hands, with little more to do than steal food or skin a rabbit, had healed. Spared of any task in Verek's quiet household except to handle his leather-bound books, her hands had regained the pale, unveined smoothness of youth.

Slowly the warlock reached for the hand that Carin had laid on the table. He lifted it into his. It fit in his palm like an oyster on the half shell. He turned it to study the back, knuckles, palm, and each ringless finger individually. And he picked off a wispy cobweb that clung to Carin's wrist, the residue of her snooping in the great hall.

Verek rolled the dust-flocked spider-silk into a tiny ball. Then he released Carin's hand.

She snatched it back to the safety of her side of the table.

"Unmarked, untouched," the warlock growled, "when—by Drisha—you should now have nothing at the end of that arm but a charred stump. I would give much to know whether you were saved by your own otherworldliness, or by the same unguessed susceptibility that drew you to the portal."

They were interrupted by the sound of a wagon and team arriving in the stableyard. Myra and Lanse had returned.

"Speak no word of these events to my housekeeper," Verek ordered as he rose opposite Carin. "That simple woman is not so privy to my affairs as you may suppose. Myra can do nothing to help with any of the tasks that face you and me. To confide in her may gain you a sympathetic ear, but will alarm her needlessly. If you care for her, hold your tongue."

From the table, Verek picked up the trencher that held his un-eaten bread and cheese. Turning, he stepped with it to the passageway. "Only tell Myra that I am occupied and will require dinner in my rooms. These bites will not long take the edge from a day's hunger."

He paused, his dark gaze on Carin. "As for you, little spy: You'll do well to resist, by any means, those unfathomable 'feelings' that call you to the chamber of magic. The spells which safeguard that vault are meant to burn to cinders any hands laid uninvited upon either of the door-latches. I think you will not risk again such an agonizing punishment, unless you are *quite* certain that whatever protection you enjoyed last night will not fail you."

As the warlock disappeared down the passageway, Carin sat staring after him. Waves of hot and cold traveled over her, and for a moment she forgot to breathe.

Slowly she stood, stirred the coals on the hearth, and added wood. The fire blazed up, throwing some life back into a space that Verek had made grim. Carin picked up the apple core he'd left on the table and threw it into the fire. Then she hung a kettle over the flames and went out to meet the returning wagoners.

She found Lanse and Jerold unloading crates and sacks under Myra's watchful eye.

"Oh my, have a care!" the housekeeper called to them as Carin joined her. "Spill the meal, my boys, and it means another long trip to Fintan. And haven't we had enough of busy roads and thronging crowds to keep us for a month?"

Myra didn't take her eyes off the men unloading the wagon, but she reached to slip a plump, strong arm around Carin's waist and give her a hug. "Oh my, dearie! Had you given us up for lost? We left so early this morning that I hadn't the heart to wake you to tell you. But didn't I spend the day fretting that our absence might trouble you? And most especially that you might go hungry? Did you find aught to eat in that barren kitchen? And what of the master? Have you seen m'lord today? He gave me no answer when I tapped at his door this morning to remind him of our errand. Do you know, child, whether my good master has eaten the least morsel this long day?"

"Yes, Myra." Carin patted the pudgy hand that gripped her waist. "Lord Verek and I ate the cheese and apples you left. That was plenty for me. But I think he's hungry for a hot meal. Nearly the last thing he said to me today was, 'Tell Myra,'" she repeated in her best imitation of the warlock's clipped voice, "'that I require dinner in my rooms.'"

Carin's mimicry threw Myra into a frenzy.

"Oh my, dearie! What am I to do!" the housekeeper cried. "I've all these new-bought goods to stow and store, and a fire to build, and water to heat, and two brace of hare to season and stew. They're skinned and gutted already, thank Drisha, as I bought them fresh from the butcher's this very day, but I've got pot-herbs to chop and—"

"Easy, Myra!" Carin interjected. "There's time. I'm sure Lord Verek only meant that he wanted to eat alone tonight. He's not expecting to be served a meal in the next five minutes.

"Now," she continued as Myra's fluster began to fade, "tell me what to do to start supper while you finish out here. I've already built a fire, and water's on to heat. I'm not the cook you are, Myra, but I can help."

"Bless me, what a joy it is to have you in this house," Myra almost purred. "Start with these, dearie."

Springing into action with as much agility as her bulk would allow, the woman gave Carin a bunch of leeks, with instructions to slice them thickly. From another sack that was tied to the wagon's side, she produced leaves of fresh savory for Carin to chop.

"Then take a garlic from the string above the kitchen door," Myra added, "and finely chop six cloves. By the time you're done with the herbs, I'll have my hands on the meat that's in this jumble somewhere. And together, child, we'll cook up such a kettle of stew as to make mouths water all around."

As Carin hurried off, Myra's voice filled the yard. "Oh my, Lanse, you foolish boy! Would you crush a gross of fresh eggs with that great cask of vinegar you're rolling about like a—" The kitchen door closed on what was not, Carin suspected, a comparison in the stableboy's favor.

Quickly she prepared the seasonings. She was mincing garlic when Myra came in carrying four fat hares on sticks. The skinned, headless carcasses hung by their back legs, two to a staff. Carin helped cut up the meat and brown it in butter with the garlic and leeks. Then all went into the kettle to boil. While Myra cheerfully bubbled with news of market day in Fintan village, the pot simmered an accompaniment. And when the meat was perfectly tender, into the kettle went the fresh savory for the crowning touch.

Myra took Verek his meal, then carried two steaming bowls out to the yard for Lanse and Jerold. When the housekeeper — with a long, tired sigh — finally settled her frame at the kitchen table, Carin served up the cook's supper and her own. Then she sought the answer to a minor mystery that had puzzled her for days.

"Why is it, Myra," she asked between bites of stew, "that we — you and me — always eat in the kitchen, and even Lord Verek eats in here by the fire when he's not in a bad mood, but Jerold and Lanse don't come in? Don't they like a little company at dinner?"

Myra shook her head. "The fault is Jerold's," she said, sounding vexed. "That old goat seeks no company but his own. In all my years as housekeeper to m'lord, Jerold's never set foot in this kitchen but to carry in firewood, or to bring me a sack of apples from the store-shed. He cooks for himself in that crib he calls a bedchamber, in the loft over the horses' heads — and mayhap he'll set the place ablaze someday with a spark that catches in the hay, and kill himself, the boy, and all the luckless animals below!

"But dearie, 'tis a sterner story with headstrong Lanse," Myra went on. "That foolish boy ate every meal at this selfsame table, right up to the day when you wandered in like a lost lamb." Myra reached across and patted Carin's hand — the very hand, Carin realized with a start, that she would now be missing if the warlock's spells had worked as he intended.

"Um ..." she began.

But Myra kept talking: "The boy has not been persuaded, since, to keep a civil tongue in his head and join us at table. He eats instead of the messes Jerold slops together, and refuses any dish from my hands unless I take it to him in the stable — as I did just now, out of pity for the weariness he must feel almost as sharply as I do after this long day.

"I've believed for a week — and expected every day — that when Lanse tires of Jerold's dreadful cookery, he'll show some sense and return to this table, where he can get the nourishment a strapping boy needs. But he's as hardheaded as Jerold. He vows never to sit at table with you, child."

"Huh?"

What Carin felt at this snub must have shown in her face, for Myra rushed to add: "Don't ask me why. I don't know, and the boy won't say. I suspected, at first, that the foolish cub was tongue-tied in the company of a pretty girl, and hid himself away to avoid the strain of speaking to you, like a love-struck Galen who fears to approach fair Dara. But, alas, I've come to doubt that Lanse's reasons are anything so pure as love. I do believe, dearie, that the foolish boy envies you bitterly."

And what have I got going that Lanse could envy? Carin wondered, astonished. She mentally inventoried her situation: imprisoned in a mausoleum of magic, at the mercy of a quick-tempered sorcerer who wasn't above throwing her into his dungeon; and vulnerable to strange nighttime beckonings that threatened her with paralysis and possible dismemberment.

But, Carin conceded silently, *I do have my own bedroom, a hot bath whenever I want one, and the library.*

"Does Lanse resent me staying in the house," she asked Myra, "while he's sleeping in the stable? Or does he envy me my job in Lord Verek's library? He may think I have it easy, but maybe he doesn't realize how heavy some of those books are. The hugest ones, I can barely move. Or does Lanse resent me having Lord Verek's permission to read in my spare time? Would he like to take books from the library too?"

The housekeeper shook her head. "Nay, dearie. The boy has no head for books. He doesn't love them as you and my master love them. He cares only for his horses. He sleeps, by preference, in the hayloft to be that near to them, though he has his choice of any bedchamber in the great empty wing of this house."

Myra sighed and took another bite of stew. With her exceptional talent for eating and talking at the same time, she continued:

"What the boy begrudges you, child, are the hours you spend with our master. He fears to lose—to you—his place at the master's side. Before you came—and don't doubt that your coming to this house has brought *me* great joy—but before you, no day passed that the master and Lanse did not ride together. They shot targets together and hunted deer. They tested one another's hand with horse and sword. The boy is an apt pupil, dearie. He's spent many an hour learning from his master fine horsemanship and skill with bow and blade."

The housekeeper leaned across the table, and her voice dropped to a whisper. "Once, dearie," she confided, "Lanse did aspire to learn the arts of alchemy and magic. But that was not to be. The boy hasn't the gift."

Sitting back, Myra went on briskly: "No one knows better than I, how mistaken this old woman can be when she lets her thoughts gallop unchecked. But I've told you what I think. I do believe Lanse fancies himself angry with you—you blameless child—for drawing to yourself the notice that he craves from our good master.

"'Tis a foolish notion the boy has, isn't it, dearie? For well I do know, since the fright my master gave you in that awful cellar, that you've done your best to stay out of his way. But with the three of us tucked up in only this wing of the house, the grander part closed off long years ago, there's little chance of any one avoiding the other two. So be easy in your heart, dearie. I've talked too long and said too much—'tis my greatest weakness. I ought not to have told you of Lanse's spite. 'Tis only boyish nonsense, and 'twill pass.

"But before I say good-night and take these weary bones to bed," Myra said, rising from the table, "I'll tell you one thing more, and also ask a thing. The question first: Did you find, among the lights I took up to your bedchamber, brightness enough to chase the fears that followed you up from that black cellar?"

"Oh! Yes. Lights," Carin stammered, surprised into recalling the blazing multitude in her room. "Er, thank you. You're right—I don't like the dark. It's silly, I know. But after thinking I'd been buried alive in that horrible cellar ..." She finished her excuse with a shrug.

"*Och*," Myra commiserated, reaching to pat Carin's hand again. "You'll not be needing so many lights in the night when you've forgotten that awful place. But till you're over your fright, you're to have as many as you wish. Just take care, child, that you don't set yourself afire—or the curtains or the bed!" The woman's warning, offered in words almost identical to Verek's last night, was spoken with what seemed a far more genuine concern for her safety, Carin noted.

Myra stacked her empty bowl with Carin's. "Be off with you," she said. "These few dishes will wait for the morrow to be washed and put away. I'll call you early, child. If you're not in this kitchen by daybreak, you'll hear me rapping at your door. For you've work to do in the master's great library, and no time to be a slugabed."

The housekeeper was nearly through the door to her bedroom when Carin remembered the other half of the woman's closing promise.

"Wait, Myra," she called. "You said you had something else to tell me, didn't you?"

"Oh my, dearie—yes," Myra exclaimed. "So weary I am, I quite forgot. When I took supper to my master, he bade me tell you ... " Her voice trailed off, her eyes stared blankly, and for a moment Carin feared the woman had forgotten the message. But Myra was only preparing to deliver it in faithful imitation of the warlock's voice—her mimicry being in earnest, unlike Carin's in the stableyard. "He bade me tell you three things, dearie, and these were his very words: 'The waters are still. Do not heed the phantasmic summons. It needs but a thought to break the spell of stone.'

"His message was skimble-skamble to me, child," Myra added, her hand on her door. "But I did not ask its meaning. 'Twas likely, I thought, that you'd spent the day, the two of you, trading secrets among the dusty tomes or picking out some riddle from that puzzle-book — and so you would know of what the master speaks. He bade me say, also, that you'd left the puzzle-book in the library. As you'd only a brief bit yet to read, he wondered if you wouldn't finish soon — then to tell it to him.

"Now I've done my duty, child," Myra said, pushing her door open. "You've the master's message, and I've the weariest bones in all of Ruain to put to bed. Good night."

"Sleep well."

With the house to herself again, Carin lit a candle at the kitchen fire and headed for the library. Verek's reminder about the puzzle-book had been unnecessary. With only four short chapters left to read, she would have finished the book that afternoon, if the warlock hadn't caught her brooding about him, above his pool of magic.

The library was pitch black. In Myra's absence, no fire had been lit that day. Carin hadn't needed one in the bright morning, but had warmed herself with the motions of sorting and stacking books. Now, however, she hesitated on the threshold, straining to see in the candlelight. The fears that had beset her since the suffocating blackness of the cellar-dungeon prodded her like invisible cudgels. How could she enter a room so dark — especially one that hid, as she now knew, a spell-shrouded portal to a vault of sorcery?

What are you doing here then? Carin demanded, sharp with herself. *Do you want the looking-glass book? Then go get it.*

Gulping a breath for courage, she threaded her way between stacks of books that were piled like guideposts on the floor and dashed to the bench she'd occupied yesterday evening while Verek questioned her. She snatched up the volume, retreated nimbly through the stacks, and was in the hallway heading for the foyer before she took her next breath. The candle in her hand flickered wildly throughout this foray, but remained lit.

Upstairs and safe in her bedroom, Carin lit a score of Myra's multitude. Then, stripped to her skin, she dove under the bed-covers and opened the puzzle-book to chapter nine—"Queen Alice." Thanks to the housekeeper's overindulgence in lamps, Carin had ample light for reading, even without adding the un-canny glow of the bathing room to the ordinary light of many flames.

Three chapters later, her long anticipation turned to disap-pointment.

"A dream!" Carin grumbled. She slapped the book closed with such force that it made a loud *pop* and sent fluttering Verek's note, which had served her as a marker. "It was just a dream!" The chess pieces that came to life, the talking flowers, Tweedledum and Tweedledee, Humpty Dumpty and the clumsy White Knight: all of them were only a sleeping child's fantasies. Or was Carin to believe that the Red King dreamed it, and Alice merely had a part in *his* fantasy?

"Beggar it all," Carin swore, as her old master the wheel-wright used to. "I could tell a better story than this, and it would all be true. I've met a *real* talking tree, and I've watched a gar-dener freeze a horse. I've even helped a sorcerer conjure up images made of water."

Still grumbling, she crawled out of bed, picked up Verek's note, and slipped it back inside the volume. Then she dropped the offending book onto the table by the door, snuffed all but two flames, and resumed her pillow. Tonight, she would *not* let rac-ing thoughts keep her awake until all hours.

But Verek's three-part message, delivered by a drowsy Myra, crept unbidden into Carin's mind. *The waters are still*, the sorcerer had said — an obvious reference to the waters of the magic pool.

Did he mean that those forces were again at rest after last night's raising of water-sculpted images? Or was Verek thinking of Carin's brush with the spells that guarded the vault? Did he mean to imply that the demon-spirit of the pool had not been lastingly angered by her intrusion? Carin quivered at the thought that some wrathful specter might yet revenge itself upon her … in its unimaginable ways.

Verek's second admonition — *Do not heed the phantasmic summons* — seemed a restatement of his earlier warning. Did he doubt the power of his words, when he ordered her to resist any unexplained "feelings" that might call her back to the cave? If so, he could rest easy. Carin had no faith that whatever had kept her from harm would protect her if she reached for the invisible latch a second time. How could she trust in such continued protection when she had no idea from what source it sprang?

The final part of the message seemed the most cryptic. *It needs but a thought to break the spell of stone*, Verek had said. The words wove through Carin's brain like a mournful lullaby. The spell of stone … flesh becoming rock … Emrys petrified … her own body made stone, as lifeless as a sculpture …

It needs but a thought? What thought? What must she think? Where was the meaning in Verek's words? Carin couldn't make it out. Presently she slid into sleep, to dream of monstrous chessmen that moved about as freely as the living beings they mirrored, turning their glittering black eyes upon her from faces of cold, dead stone … faces forever grimacing with pain.

Chapter 14

A Dragon

Gray dawn found Carin at work and the puzzle-book lying where she'd tossed it—with a contemptuous flick of her wrist—upon entering the warmly firelit library. The book awaited the sorcerer atop a stack of volumes on his desk. He could have it. Carin no longer wanted the volume. She didn't care whether it had once been among "her" books on the shelves of the child's misty bedroom.

The twilight through the library's windows did not brighten appreciably as the morning wore on. Outside, storm clouds shrouded the sun. By midmorning, a hard rain pelted the windows. The tempest cast such a pall over her work that Carin needed not only the light from the fireplace, but also a half-dozen of Myra's multitude that she brought down from her bedroom, their resettlement requiring three circuits of the stairs.

"Oh my, dearie!" the housekeeper exclaimed as she bustled in to call Carin to the midday meal. "We'll need boats to get about in, if this keeps on. 'Tis more rain than we've seen in these parts in a year or more. Leave off with those musty old books now, child, and come to the table. There's a plump hen in a fair broth of mushrooms and raisins, with fresh-baked bread. You needn't go hungry today, dearie. You'll not be wanting for a meal on the table while I've strength enough to drag these old bones from their bed of a morning."

Carin followed the woman into the hallway, glad to put a hard morning's work behind her. Some of Verek's oversized books weighed as much as small casks of wine. To remove them from the highest shelves, Carin needed all the strength in her upper body to slide each volume onto her head as she propped unsteadily on a ladder. Then, lowering herself to the floor with one hand grasping the rungs, she had all she could do to keep each book precariously balanced. A long morning of such labor left her ready for easier pursuits.

Verek was in the kitchen when Carin reached it, already at the table, sipping a mug of hot cider.

His appearance was much improved over the disheveled, sunken-eyed creature who had confronted her yesterday. His hair was combed neatly back, his beard and mustache trimmed. He wore a clean white shirt under a vest that, except for its color, was the twin of the dark-blue garment he'd worn on the day of the delving. This one was a deep shade of plum. His eyes were clear, and they fixed on Carin dispassionately. He greeted her, his manner reserved but civil.

Carin fashioned, with difficulty, an attitude of detachment to match his as she took her place opposite him at the table.

"On such a wet and stormy day as this," Verek commented, "I think of no better place to spend the morning than in my library. How goes your work there?"

"I'm making progress," Carin replied in a clear voice that gave no hint of her chronic uneasiness around him. "Things are going faster than I expected, actually. I've cleared the shelves in the corner next to the desk. Now I'm starting to pick out the books that belong there. I think I've found the one that will have to come first, when I start reshelving them in order. It's called *Aabalwynd*."

"Oh my, good master!" Myra chimed in. "The girl is ever so steady in the work, and she hides in that thin frame a strength like a Trosdan deer's. Why, she's shifted books that I could never budge, so thick and heavy are they. She's too proud to call for help, but maybe she ought to seek a stronger back when there are such books to move about."

The warlock nodded. "As ofttimes is your wont, Myra, you see what I do not. Summon me to the task, or petition Jerold to make himself useful and answer to your call, or this adept's" —

he raised his cider-mug to Carin—"when a man's strength is needed. Though in truth," Verek muttered, "I had expected no such devoted effort from her to do the work that I set her."

Carin ignored his grumbling. Her mind was otherwise occupied. She was fairly bursting with questions for Verek—questions inspired by the events in the vault of wizardry, and by her encounter yesterday with the warlock at this same table. Her curiosity had gone unsatisfied when the wagon's arrival cut their meeting short. So quickly had Verek retreated to his rooms, with the air of an unsettled man who was seeking his privacy, Carin had had no time to discover what he'd meant by a "susceptibility" that drew her to the cave of magic. She hadn't learned what "tasks" they faced, with which Myra could not help. Her wonder at all of this had only intensified last night, when the housekeeper delivered Verek's message.

For once, she was less interested in avoiding the sorcerer's company than in getting him alone. As long as Myra remained within earshot, she couldn't talk about their night in the magic cave, or about yesterday's drama in this kitchen. "Speak no word of these events to my housekeeper," Verek had warned.

There was one magian subject, however, that must be safe around Myra. The woman seemed comfortably familiar with the looking-glass book. In fact, there had been a mention of it in Verek's message through Myra last night—urging Carin to finish her reading and give him an account.

And so she would. The book would be the means to draw him to the library, out of Myra's hearing, where she could question him.

"Lord Verek." Carin spoke up during a break in the housekeeper's indictment of the weather. "I got done last night with the puzzle-book. The ending surprised me. It wasn't what I expected. If you'd like, sir, I could go with you to the library, when you're finished eating, and read you the book. Maybe not all of it this afternoon, but the first chapter, if you wish."

Whether Verek felt pleasure or astonishment—or any other sentiment—at the offer Carin made him, it couldn't be read in his face. But he accepted at once.

"Good. A better enterprise for a gray and rain-soaked day could hardly be wished for. Come with me now and we'll begin."

They headed down the passageway, leaving Myra exclaiming to their backs over the twin marvels of the strange book and "the smart young thing, bright as a new copper," who had mastered it.

Outpacing Carin, Verek's long stride carried him down the hallway like a man who was hastening to claim a lost treasure. When the warlock reached the library door, he shoved it open and stood on the threshold, propping the heavy oak with one hand.

Verek's white shirt under the plum vest glowed spectrally in the firelight that escaped through the open door. But his dark eyes caught no glint, making his face, from that distance, a blank and lifeless mask.

Carin's steps faltered.

Are you insane? cried reason. *The blackheart who's waiting for you has threatened you with steel, laid you out cold, locked you in a crypt of black horror, dragged you underground to a cave crawling with sorcery, and shown you things no mortal should see. And now you seek his company, hoping to ply him with questions? You're a fool! He'll tell you only what he wants you to know. He's the master. You're his pawn – nothing more. The Looking-Glass book has put ideas into your head. Maybe Alice can advance from pawn to queen, but only in her dreams. Verek is no toy chessman from a dream. How can you hope to beat him at his own game? That sorcerer can choke out your life as easily as he snuffs a candle.*

This tumble of thoughts so unnerved her that, as she approached the end of the hallway, Carin could not force her eyes higher than the point of Verek's chin. They refused to meet his eyes, but gazed fixedly at the half-lit, half-shadowed hollow of his throat.

She brushed past him into the library. Wending her way through the stacks of books, Carin made for the desk where the puzzle-book lay, to scoop it up and hold it close:

Exactly like a frightened child would clutch a familiar toy, she thought, disgusted with herself. But her disgust didn't loosen her hold.

Verek worked his way through the uneven stacks on the floor to his usual bench in front of the fireplace. He motioned for Carin to take the seat opposite.

As she did so, a white light flew at her and stuck in her hair.

With a startled cry of "*Drisha!*" Carin swatted at the thing, a move that only shifted it from her hair to her hand. It clung, giving her a glimpse of a shining orb, something like a sweetgum ball radiating light. Carin's fierce, unthinking reflex permitted her only the one quick look. An eyeblink later, with a violent shake of her hand she'd loosened the orb and flung it at the fire. It never reached the flames, though. As soon as it left her fingers, the light ceased to be.

And Carin found herself sitting and staring at Verek, her hand still raised, her heart racing and her breath coming short.

The warlock was leaning toward her, his chin in his hands, both elbows propped on his knees. For a long moment he only gazed at her, a slight frown furrowing his brow. Then he leaned back against the cushions of his bench and brought up one booted foot, resting it ankle on knee. His right hand kneaded the propped ankle deeply, as if to ease a sprain. He was a man, by all appearances, who bade himself sit and be easy despite a desperate desire to make things happen.

The hand kneading the ankle grew still. Then it stiffened, with the fingers pointing to the ceiling, the wrist resting on the ankle, and the palm toward Carin, as if willing her to motionlessness.

Willing it, or compelling it by sorcery? Carin wondered. If the warlock was trying to quiet her under a spell, it was having little effect. Her scalp still crawled and her hand tingled from her brief battle with the uncanny light.

Finally, Verek broke the silence. "You will agree that on such a sunless, rain-darkened afternoon as this, firelight or the flickering of these few lamps makes a poor light for reading."

It was more a statement than a question, but he paused as if expecting a reply. In truth, the library was gloomier now than when Carin had abandoned it at lunchtime. Half the lamps she'd brought downstairs from Myra's multitude were dark, their oil consumed. To Verek's statement, therefore, no response seemed possible but her assent.

When Carin had given it, quietly, Verek went on:

"You will also agree that sunlight, when no clouds dim it, serves best for reading, for it is a bright, steady light that does not tire or strain the eyes."

"Yes, sir."

"You will further agree that I am a demon, a warlock, a fiend who summons fire to do his evil bidding —"

Verek broke off, and wagged his upraised hand once to the left and then to the right, as if to rub out his words.

Carin's blood rushed to her face at this reminder of what she had said, while wearing nothing but a towel, after she revived from her fall in the cellar. But even as she blushed, she wondered: Had her words stung the sorcerer so deeply, that he would return to them in this sudden and unexpected way?

Verek began again, his hand relaxing and his voice less edgy.

"As I have the power — which you have seen — to call forth a light that is clear and steady as daylight, but which burns flameless and cool, you'll agree that I should give you such a light to read by? If you had objections, surely you would have voiced them on the night you first saw the orb, when it lit the stairs by which I led you from the chamber of *wysards*."

Carin couldn't fault Verek's reasoning. The light he'd summoned to his fingertips had been of small concern on that strange night. Then, Carin had made no protest. But this was another day, and her concerns had multiplied.

"Please explain it to me, sir," she answered him cautiously. "What is that light? What's it made of? Does it have a name?"

"I cannot tell you its true name," Verek said, "nor explain to you its substance. I won't repeat the false name given to it by the ignorant and the superstitious, for their words would merely deepen your suspicions. I will tell you only this: The light, like the glow of the walls in your bathing chamber, is as old as the world and as natural. It belongs here as surely as do antelope on the plains and trees in the forest."

And that's how he'll answer all your questions, Carin warned herself. *He'll talk and say little, he'll draw pictures that show nothing, and when everything's said and done he'll leave you just as confused as you are now.* But she pressed on, wondering if rainy afternoons always put him in a mood of such rare patience.

"Sir, you mentioned the chamber of wizards. I believe the message you sent me last night must have something to do with that cave." Carin pointed down, toward the cavern far under the library. "I didn't understand all of it. You said the 'waters are still.' Does that mean the, uh, powers down there have, um, forgiven me for opening the door?"

Verek flexed his knee, returning the propped foot to the floor.

"You give my words more weight than they'll support," he said, his frown deepening. "I spoke not for the forces that flow in that place, but for myself alone. And that I spoke at all, to send Myra to you with that ill-considered message, I regret. The words sprang from a troubled mind."

The warlock looked at her sharply, the force of his gaze pinning Carin to her bench. "If I had any hope that you'd obey me, I would command you to dismiss the remark from your thoughts. But that, you will not do, as I well know. Without some explanation from me, you will build from those few words such intrigues and mysteries as might confound the greatest mind to be met in any book on these shelves." Verek gestured at the vast collection that surrounded them.

Then he sighed, a sound that was both nettled and tolerant. "So that we may proceed with the business at hand—which is, as I recall it, the reading of the looking-glass book—I'll give you an explanation. I will tell you what was in my heart when I spoke to Myra of still waters and phantasms. You were meant to understand that my private affairs would not again be put on display. Despite what you may feel, hear, see, think, or sense in the small hours of the night, you must imagine the waters of the well as always still, always at rest. What I do in that chamber—alone— or what I see in that chamber—alone—does not concern you. If ever I require your presence in the vault, I will summon you by means more tangible than any vague feelings of disquiet. That is the gist and pith of my message: In the waters of the *wysards* there is nothing to interest you, until such time as I may tell you otherwise, and until such time as I may summon you, by means you will find unmistakable."

Carin swallowed. The undertone in Verek's cool voice made her reluctant to continue this line of questioning.

The warlock, however, needed no prodding to take up the third part of his message. "As for the final words I bade Myra speak to you—'It needs but a thought to break the spell of stone'—the meaning is easier shown than said."

Lazily lifting fingers that had rested on his leg, Verek pointed across the table between them to Carin's empty left hand. It lay idly on the bench at her side, while her right hand cradled the puzzle-book in her lap.

At once, her idle hand became a stony lump, cold and dead. She could neither move nor lift it.

"No! Stop!" Carin's protest climbed the scale to at least an octave above her natural voice.

Verek's customary impatience returned in a rush.

"Quiet!" he barked. "No harm will come to you. The spell of stone is the first learned by any novice magician. It is a spell as easily broken as cast. It needs but thought, I say."

He leaned forward, lacing his fingers around his knee. "Think of your hand as an egg — softness inside a hard, brittle shell. Or imagine it dipped in thin, wet clay, which has now dried and hardened to a brittle overcoat. However you achieve it, you must form in your mind the clear image of your hand — warm and sound, throbbing with life — encased in a shell. The moment you have that picture firmly in your thoughts, imagine a hammer tap-tap-tapping the shell, shattering it to bits. Once the crust is broken, your hand will be free, the spell also broken."

Closing her eyes against the warlock's unsettling gaze, Carin composed her mind and built the image Verek described. She could easily picture her hand in a shell of clay: it harked back to a favorite memory. On those rare times in her earliest days when the wheelwright's household hadn't needed her, she would slip away to the millpond to make mud pies on its banks. Vividly Carin recalled the sensation of mud drying and cracking on her hands. She had even spread them with varying thicknesses of wet mud to see which flaked off most readily when dry. Too thin a coat, and the mud would only turn to powder when she flexed her hands. Too thick and it wouldn't crack at all, leaving a hard cast to wash off in the pond. But somewhere between those extremes lay perfection. When the mud dried, a gentle flexing of her hands would craze the coating with many cracks, flaking off chips as thin and brittle as eggshell.

Carin pictured her bespelled hand encased in that perfect coating of brittle mud. Though she couldn't flex the inert lump at the end of her arm, she could imagine, as Verek had said, a small hammer gently tapping it all over, breaking the dried mud into chips. In her imagination, the chips fell away. Her hand was free. Carin crooked her fingers and opened her eyes.

"Nimbly done," the warlock said. He leaned back and drew up one leg to return that ankle to its resting spot on the opposite knee. "Remember that trick the next time you are rendered a statue. Although," he added, "you may find stillness a better course than action, in some predicaments."

Verek's level gaze discouraged further questions. So did a renewed curtness in his voice. "Enough of this. You promised me a reading from the book. I hold you to it. The skies grow ever darker and this room with them. Will you accept the light I offer, and take up that infernal book and read?"

The library had indeed grown dimmer. Rain slashed at the windows. The storm's black clouds turned the day beyond the sweating glass to night. Carin glanced at the cover of the book in her lap. Even the large letters of its title were indistinct. She couldn't argue the point: to read in this gloom, she needed the warlock's eerily glowing orb.

Not quite returning Verek's gaze, Carin said, "Please show me the light again ... only this time put it in *your* hair — not in mine."

Something that looked almost like a smile flitted across Verek's face for the briefest instant and was gone before Carin could be sure it had ever been. He didn't oblige her by calling the light to the top of his head or to the ends of his shoulder-sweeping hair. Instead, the hand that rested on his propped ankle rolled palm up, and instantly a ball of clear white light shone in it. Glancing at Carin — perhaps for assurance that she wouldn't lunge across the table and try to kill the light — the warlock held the orb for a moment. Then he rolled it along his resting leg from ankle to knee. Catching it in his left hand, Verek turned the orb a few times between thumb and three fingers, then lifted it to his shoulder and there let it rest.

"Cool to the touch, without flame — harmless," he said. He plucked the light from his shoulder and held it out to her. "Will you take it?"

Hesitating only briefly, Carin reached for it. The orb rolled from Verek's fingers to hers. It filled her hand with a tingle no more distinct than the tickle of a feather. Yet its glow had a surface of sorts—Carin could roll it in her hand as the warlock had done and feel its shell, a bit clingy and crinkly and more fragile than a casque-bug's. Slight pressure between thumb and forefinger would crush it to … what? Sparks? Razor-sharp, gleaming slivers?

She did not try the experiment. Pushing her hair back, Carin rested the orb on her shoulder. Then she opened the puzzle-book. Verek was right about the quality of the orb's light. Clear and white, yet soft and easy on the eyes, it lit the words as steadily as sunlight but without the sun's harsh glare.

From the title page, she read aloud: "*Through the Looking-Glass and What Alice Found There.*"

"Good!" Verek exclaimed. "At last—we proceed." He stretched himself full-length on the cushions of his bench.

Should she, Carin wondered, tell him her low opinion of the story? That it was nothing, just a silly dream?

No. Verek wouldn't tolerate any more delays. Now she must read, and let the warlock discover for himself that the most intriguing book in his collection was nonsense.

In a strong voice, Carin began. "'One thing was certain, that the *white* kitten had had nothing to do with it—it was the black kitten's fault entirely.'" She read with good animation that conveyed none of her disappointment in the tale, giving Verek as faithful a translation as she could. The rain battering the library's windows and the fire crackling on the hearth were fitting backdrops for the wintry tale of Alice and the kitten.

Verek asked no questions as the story unfolded, following Alice from her comfortable drawing-room through the mirror into Looking-glass House, where living chess pieces walked among the cinders on the hearth. Carin read effortlessly, translating without much trouble until she reached the incomprehensible poem, *"Jabberwocky."* Here, she paused.

"Sir," she said, lowering the book, "I don't know the right words, in the language of Ladrehdin, to substitute for the foreign words in the poem that Alice reads. If I knew what the poem meant, I'd just tell you and skip to the next page. But even Alice, after she's gotten through it, admits that she can't make sense of it. So I'll just read it to you in its native language. The words sound good together, anyway."

The warlock said nothing. A lazy wave of his hand was the only proof that he heard her and was not dozing on his bench.

Taking Verek's hand-wave for assent, Carin read aloud, in the puzzle-book's alien tongue, the opening stanza of the poem:

> *'Twas brillig, and the slithy toves*
> *Did gyre and gimble in the wabe:*
> *All mimsy were the borogoves,*
> *And the mome raths outgrabe.*

The reclining warlock sprang to his feet with a speed and vigor that quite took Carin's breath. For the briefest moment, Verek stared at her wild-eyed. Then he sprinted for the dark depths of the library and yanked open the door that was hidden there.

"Come!" he shouted. "Quickly! Bring the book." His voice echoed up from the winding stone stairs; he was already well down them to the cave of magic.

Carin reacted to his command as would a wild deer to a snort of alarm from the herd's stag. Reflex subduing reason, she rushed after Verek and was a good way down the stairs before it occurred to her to doubt the wisdom of following him. Not an hour ago, he'd warned her to keep away from the waters of the wizards — "until such time as I may summon you," he'd said, "by means you will find unmistakable." Clearly he had just summoned her, and urgently. But why? Toward what was she rushing? What had there been in her reading from the puzzle-book to send the warlock careering down to a cavern that held great danger even for him?

As she slowed her descent, Carin realized she was clutching the puzzle-book tightly in both hands. She'd lost the shining orb, however. The only light in the stairwell was the fixed reddish glow that came up from the cave below.

Also rising from that vault of writhing forces, Verek's voice welled up. "Quickly!" it boomed.

His authority acted on her. Carin could resist it as little as a feather the gale. Down the winding stairs she plunged.

At their foot, as she emerged into the cave, she barely avoided colliding with the warlock. Verek stood motionless, gazing at the enchanted pool.

Rising from the pool's shape-shifting mists were the watery images of the strangest creatures Carin had ever seen. In the foreground was a colony of animals about the size and shape of badgers, but they had white hair, hind feet tipped in claws like lizards', and snouts that twisted as tightly as corkscrews. The "badgers" were busily scratching, and with their coiled snouts, boring holes in a hillside that was sculpted from the magical waters.

Above the creatures, topping the hill, were rows of sundials on pedestals. Huddled nearby, crouched over their nestlings, were thin, wingless, miserable-looking birds with untidy feathers. The birds, which looked like flightless parrots, squawked unhappily at the burrowing badgers.

Bursting quick as hares out of the watery hill were smooth-skinned beasts that resembled piglets with long ears. The pig creatures also scolded the badgers, squeaking at them solemnly.

As Carin studied the scene, she became convinced that the piglets and parrots were fighting to defend their nests. With only squeaks and squawks as weapons, they were trying to chase off the badgers before those burrowing corkscrew snouts could destroy the smaller creatures' homes in the hillside.

Beside her, Verek roused as if from a trance. He leaned to place his mouth near Carin's ear, and said in a whisper: "Quietly … slowly … read the rhyme again, pausing as you end each line. Let us see which words conjure up which creatures."

Carin obeyed, in a soft voice but one which seemed to echo round the vault. "*'Twas brillig, and the slithy toves …*" she read. Out of the mists rising from the pool, the "badgers" doubled their numbers.

Seeking something only half-remembered, Carin thumbed forward to chapter six: "Humpty Dumpty." There it was — the egg-man telling Alice that *"toves"* were a bit like badgers, and they nested under sundials. Carin, reading late at night by the glow of the bathing-room walls, had been half asleep her first time through Alice's talk with the egg. She had thought little of it — then. But now Carin looked at the book in her hands with new respect. Maybe the story wasn't nonsense. If it recounted only a child's dream, why would the waters of the wizards' pool respond so vividly — and literally, it appeared — to the alien language of the *"Jabberwocky"*?

She flipped back to the poem and continued aloud with the next line: "*Did gyre and gimble in the wabe.*" The "toves" vigorously scratched and bored holes in the hillside. "*All mimsy were the borogoves,*" she recited, and the shabby-looking parrot-birds squawked miserably at the "toves." The final line, "*And the mome raths outgrabe,*" provoked from the piglets more solemn squeaks, and also noises that seemed to mix bellowing, whistling, and sneezing, just as Humpty Dumpty had described to Alice the sound of *"outgribing."*

But there the egg-man's explanation of the verse ended. He did not tell Alice what a *"Jabberwock"* was.

Carin raised the book to the eyes of the sorcerer at her side. She pointed at the next stanza. "Should I keep going?" she whispered. "There's more to the poem."

Verek nodded. "But say only a single line, then pause," he whispered back. "I would see more, but this thing must be done carefully."

In a voice no louder than before, but which again seemed to reverberate in the cave of magic, Carin read the next line. *"Beware the Jabberwock, my son!"*

The illusion of the badger-infested hillside collapsed in a torrent of falling water. But barely had the rush of liquid struck the pool's surface when it reformed itself into a long-necked, dragon-winged monster that rose howling from the mists.

The creature's tail churned the pool's crystalline waters to foam. In a head made hideous by a bony crest that protruded between eyes of flame, jaws bristled with fangs. From its gaping mouth exhaled a hot, putrid breath. The dragon reared on scaly, muscular hind legs to tower above Carin's head and Verek's. It slashed at them with hooked claws as long and sharp as scimitars.

Sorceress or not, Carin had just conjured up the instrument of what promised to be a bloody and brutal death—for both of them.

Chapter 15

A Test

She screamed, and the sound mingled in her ears with the dragon's roar. The puzzle-book slipped from Carin's fingers.

Verek grabbed it, thrust it back into her hands, and with the same motion shoved her into the stairwell behind them.

"Run!" he yelled above the Jabberwock's heart-stopping howl. "Take the book from this house!"

She ran. Up the steps Carin spiraled, to burst into the library like a wayward gust from the storm that raged outside. The only light in the room came from a few glowing embers on the hearth. All of her lamps had burned themselves out, and the neglected fire had dwindled to coals. Carin fought her way through the gloom, stumbling over stacks of books, tripping, falling against the hall door.

She yanked it open and raced down the hallway to the kitchen. There she met no curious Myra to delay her. But as she flung open the door to the courtyard, rain slanted into the kitchen with such stinging force that Carin stumbled back, momentarily repelled.

More intent on protecting the puzzle-book than keeping herself dry, she wrapped the book in a snatched-up piece of sacking and hugged the bundle to her chest. Bent almost double to shield it from the rain, she dove into the storm.

In moments, she was drenched to the skin and slogging through mud up to her ankles. Carin leaned into the wind-driven rain and struggled across the yard to the stable door. Lurching inside, she nearly fell on her face as the abrupt cessation of wind left her overbalanced. She panted for air, half strangled. Water streamed from her hair. Her saturated clothes hung heavy, and under them she shivered.

The stable was full of shadows and the musty smell of damp hay and horse dung. Carin headed instinctively for the familiar comfort of Emrys' stall. But the moment she reached it, welcomed by the mare's soft whickering, she knew she must turn around and go back.

Though Verek might already be dead. Carin felt covered in frost, crystals of it piercing her skin and chilling her heart, as she imagined the Jabberwock's teeth and claws buried in the warlock's flesh. If he'd been slaughtered, and if the dragon escaped from the cave of magic, forcing its way to the surface, this entire household might end in just the same carnage.

Carin whirled so quickly that she startled Emrys. She lunged into the empty stall across from the mare's and shoved the puzzle-book under a pile of hay.

With the refrain, *What have I done? What evil have I done?* running through her mind, she turned for the stable door. She must get Myra out of the house. And when she had Myra, Jerold, and Lanse all together in the relative safety of the stable—the two men were probably nearby already, chased indoors by the storm—Carin could tell them of the dragon she had raised from the pages of an alien book. Would they believe so improbable a tale? The new housemaid conjuring a dragon from words and water? She had no explanation for what she had done, only a sickening sense of responsibility for the consequences thereof—

Carin's darting thoughts ended as if they'd hit a wall. She had barely taken a step toward the stable door when a hand grabbed her shoulder and wrenched her around.

Lanse stood glaring into her face, his eyes bright with anger. "Thief!" he shouted. He drew back the hand that had seized her, fisted it, and smashed it into her face.

The blow knocked her to the hay-strewn floor. Carin fell heavily and lay still. She only hazily became aware of her lips throbbing. She tried to bring her fingers to them and found her arm slow to answer the command. In her mouth was the taste of blood.

Her dimmed vision picked out Lanse leaning over her. He caught her arm and jerked it, yanking her shoulder off the floor.

By a supreme effort, Carin raised her head and focused her eyes, in time to see Lanse fisting his other hand and drawing it back, preparing to deliver a blow more vicious than the first.

"Hold, boy!" Verek's clipped voice reached Carin through her fog of pain. "Drisha's teeth! What are you about here?"

"She's a thief, my lord." Lanse released Carin's arm, dropping her jarringly to the floor. "I watched her sneak into the stable and hide a parcel. A moment pray, my lord, and I will return your property to you."

Carin struggled to pull her dazed senses out of the fog and her body upright. She had only partly succeeded with either effort when strong hands caught her arms from behind and lifted her to a sitting position. Verek crouched at her back, supporting her with his arm around her shoulders.

"Ice, if you please, Jerold," he muttered. He pointed at a water trough. "Already the swelling is pronounced."

From the direction of Emrys' stall, the old gardener approached. Wordlessly Jerold plunged his hands into the water, closed his eyes as though in deep concentration, and pulled out a chunk of ice, cradled in his palms. He balanced the chunk on the trough's rim, then dug into a pocket of his shabby coat and withdrew a handkerchief that was as startlingly white in the stable's gloom as his wispy hair. Jerold wrapped the ice in the linen and handed it to Verek. Then he backed away half a step and hunkered down, bringing his wizened face to their level.

Verek pressed the ice to Carin's throbbing lips. "Take this," he said. "Can you?"

The hand that Carin raised to his was shaking. Her muscles felt like putty, but she managed to grip the ice and hold it to her mouth. The cold began to numb the pain.

Verek stood, leaving her on the floor with Jerold crouched nearby like a grumpy elf who'd rather not be bothered. The warlock stalked toward Emrys' stall, his stride so quick that his black oilskin rain-cloak billowed out behind.

He met Lanse emerging from the empty enclosure opposite, the sack-wrapped puzzle-book in the boy's hands. The look of triumph on the stableboy's face turned to confusion as Verek grabbed him by his jacket collar and slammed him into the boards of the stall, sending a frightened Emrys skittering to the far side of her enclosure.

Lanse, though his master's equal in height, was a willow to Verek's oak. Yet the boy showed no fear. Watching them from her sprawl on the floor, Carin read only anger and defiance in the boy's bright eyes and set jaw.

"The girl is a thief, my lord!" Lanse cried, waving the sacking bundle. "This is the parcel I saw her hide. I found it just now, buried in the hay. She thought to be clever and do her thieving in a storm that would hide her acts from watchful eyes. But I wasn't fooled. I saw her enter with this bundle, then I watched her turn to leave without it. Her acts were patently those of a thief who hides the goods to return for them later."

Verek, his fingers knotted in the boy's collar, yanked Lanse away from the stall, then shoved him back against the boards so violently that Carin heard the wood splinter.

"Her acts were in answer to my commands," the warlock said, his growl directed to the boy alone and barely reaching Carin above the noise of the storm. "I bade her take the bundle from the house, and I am well pleased with her swift obedience. Even in the face of this storm, she did not hesitate."

Keeping his grip on Lanse's jacket, Verek continued in a voice loud enough now to carry throughout the stable. "But with you, boy, I am gravely displeased. Do you presume to take upon yourself those privileges which are mine alone? Do you think to raise yourself by usurping my rights? Oh, no! It will not do. I tell you distinctly, boy: this matter wears a serious cast."

He stepped very close to Lanse. The boy looked pale, but he didn't flinch.

"So grave is your transgression," Verek went on, "that I declare before these witnesses"—he tipped his head back to indicate Carin and Jerold behind him—"that I will tolerate no further affronts of this kind. Dare you to raise a hand again to any member of this household except by my express orders, and I'll do worse than strip you of privilege and dismiss you from my service. I'll invoke my right as High Judge of Ruain to order you flayed for your crime.

"Do you mark me well, Lanse? The girl enjoys the same protections under my roof as do you and Myra. If you suspect her of stealing, then bring your suspicions to me. But on no account presume again to 'punish' her. I will not stand for it."

The warlock released the boy's collar, snatched the bundled book from Lanse's hand, and turned so sharply from him that the hem of Verek's rain-cloak snapped at the boy's knees. Verek neither awaited nor, obviously, expected an answer to his reprimand. Slipping the bundle inside the coat he wore under his oilskin, he walked to Carin and Jerold on the floor.

She tried to rise to meet him, but lost her balance, nearly dropped the chunk of ice, and in her struggles to right herself discovered that her lips were bleeding freely. The ice's linen wrapper was soaked.

Verek took Carin by the arms and lifted her onto her feet. He rewrapped the ice in an unstained corner of the cloth and gave it back to her. Her lips felt swollen to hideous proportions but, despite the bleeding, there was little pain now. Jerold's conjuration had numbed them to any sensation but pressure.

"Can you walk?" Verek asked, his dark eyes examining her face.

Carin nodded. She didn't lower the ice and she didn't try to speak, being fairly certain that she couldn't, just yet.

"The wound needs tending," Verek said, "and for that I want you inside." He reached for the clasp of his oilskin. "You should have a cloak for your return—though another drenching could hardly leave you wetter than you are."

"No point *you* taking a soaking, Theil," Jerold said, and rose from his haunches. "She'll have mine. 'Tis a better fit anyhow."

The old man led the way to the stable door, beside which hung the promised rain-cloak. The gardener's was made of an oiled cloth less lustrous and supple than Verek's, but its length, as Jerold said, suited Carin better. The hem reached only to her calves, whereas she would have dragged Verek's cloak through the mud.

She pulled up the hood and slogged into the storm on legs she barely trusted. The yard was a quagmire, and the wind threatened to knock her down. But she splashed across to push open the side door and step into the kitchen, admitting buckets of rain.

Verek entered on her heels. For a moment the warlock struggled with the door, his muddy boots slipping as he forced it shut against the gale and shot the bolt home.

"Oh my! *Oh* my!" Myra exclaimed from across the kitchen. "Whatever has possessed you both, to be out in such a storm!" She hurried to them, staring at Carin's face as she helped her shrug out of the dripping cloak. "Dearie? What has happened? You've been kicked by one of those brainless horses! That's the trouble, isn't it."

Carin put down the stained cloth with its partly melted lump of magical ice and tried to shape a denial. She wouldn't have Emrys or any of the animals blamed for the injury that Lanse had done her. But she could force no intelligible sounds past her numbed and swollen lips. Her mumblings might have been in an alien language, so incomprehensible were they.

With a speed that startled her, Verek grabbed the ice and pressed it back to Carin's lips, silencing the noises she was making. His reaction was so emphatic and firm, she couldn't help but read a warning in it.

He's taking no chances, Carin realized. *He doesn't understand what I'm mumbling about, any more than he knew the words in the puzzle-book rhyme that called up the Jabberwock. He just knows he doesn't want me gibbering away in what sounds like a foreign tongue. For all he can tell right now, I could be muttering another magic spell. I've scared him, haven't I? Maybe as much as I've scared myself.*

Carin accepted the ice from him, and with a little nod to say that she'd gotten his message, she held it tightly to her mouth.

Verek stepped away, and still watching her, doffed his cloak. "No horse is at fault," he said, directing the comment to Myra but keeping his gaze relentlessly on Carin. "The girl has only herself to blame. Nothing would serve her but that she see the black mare, even on such a day when wiser heads keep covered. She hazarded the storm, slipped on wet hay in the stable, and fell on her face. A bloodied lip is small penalty for such foolishness. She's lucky she didn't break her nose."

Throughout the telling of this lie, the warlock's eyes bored into Carin's. She could make no protest beyond a sharp intake of breath, but at the sound of it Verek raised one eyebrow and shook his head almost imperceptibly. Again, his meaning was clear. She was not to contradict him, either now or when she regained the power of intelligible speech. Myra wasn't to know the true cause of Carin's injury.

Myra dabbed a wet cloth at the blood on Carin's mouth. "What's to be done first, my lord?" she asked. "A poultice for this wound, or a hot bath and dry clothes for the rest of her?"

Verek had bent to remove one muddy boot. Before he pulled off the other, he straightened and looked Carin up and down.

"Attend first to the matter of drying her out," he said, "for truly she looks half drowned. Make her warm, for a cold in the head won't improve on a split lip. Lastly, send her to me for the poultice. I'll be in the library, warming at the fire."

The warlock kicked off his other boot, then headed that way, striding past Carin in his stocking feet.

But just before he disappeared into the passageway, Carin hooked her fingers like talons and clawed the air, mimicking the Jabberwock. Then she opened her hand, palm up, and shot him a questioning look.

Verek paused, his head atilt. Slowly, he nodded.

"You're asking about that story you were reading to me," he said with a casualness that sounded forced. "Be assured—you've gone far enough with it for now. Before proceeding, I will wish to consider all that I have learned."

He put his finger to his lips, then added, pointedly: "In any event, you're in no condition to continue the reading. Keep silent … so that you do not aggravate the damage."

With that final admonition, he left her with Myra.

The housekeeper—launching into a complaint about the caprices of weather and of young people—managed with difficulty to loosen the sodden leather laces of Carin's kirtle and strip her of the hay-flecked wool. Carin let herself be led to a bench at the table so Myra could remove her mud-covered boots and soggy stockings. She retained her last garment, however—the shift that clung damply—to cover her retreat upstairs to the privacy of her bathing room.

There in the hot-spring pool, Carin scrubbed the blood from her face. The water stung her lips, but its warmth eased a pain that had settled in her left cheekbone. By the time she'd washed the hay out of her hair, the soreness was leaving muscles that felt as if Lanse had nearly wrenched them off her bones.

Lanse can go to the devil, she thought with a huff of contempt as she climbed out and twisted her hair up in a towel. He was a minor problem compared to the conjuring of a dragon. What had become of the Jabberwock? What had gone on between it and Verek? Had both survived, or only the warlock?

In her bedroom, Carin found that the always-diligent Myra had been there before her. Dry clothes—gray breeches and a white shirt—lay on the bed. The breeches had a drawstring waist, deep pockets, and legs tapered to tuck into boots. The housekeeper had tailored them to her perfectly.

Carin pulled the towel from her hair, then drew on the shirt. It did not fit, because it was one of Verek's. The garment hung loosely from her shoulders, its hem fell below her hips, and the sleeves were so long that she had to roll them up in wide cuffs to uncover her hands. But the quality of the cloth was unmistakable. In the glow from the bathing room, the pure-white linen had a sheen like a pearl's. It was the finest that gold could buy in Ladrehdin.

When she had dressed, Carin stood at the mirror and studied her lips. They were split top and bottom, but the cuts no longer bled. Her lips didn't look as swollen as they felt. A worse sight was the bruise that spread from the corner of her mouth to circle her left eye. Lanse's fist had blackened half her face.

A tap sounded at the door. Myra bustled in, as was her habit, not waiting for an answer.

"I put the last threads in those breeches only this morning, dearie—never knowing that you'd be needing them before the day was out. Whatever did possess you to go out in such a storm? Never mind, child." The woman waved a hand and rattled on before Carin could attempt a reply. "What's done is done. There's naught for it now but to keep you warm and ease your hurts."

Myra gestured at the stool. "Sit yourself down. Let me work a comb through that mane of yours, and then you must stay by a fire until every hair is dry to its roots. The master's medicines can chase 'most any chill, but 'tis better not to catch a chill at all.

"Oh my, dearie!" the woman exclaimed in the same breath as she studied Carin's face in the mirror. "Such a big bruise. I've seen a horse's hoof do less damage, and a fisted hand as much." She shook her head and pursed her lips, and kept silent for one full, leisurely stroke of the comb through Carin's thick hair.

Carin, watching the housekeeper in the mirror, read the woman's doubts as easily as if they were written on the glass. Myra didn't believe her master's story about Carin falling on her face. But whether the housekeeper believed she'd been kicked, or — knowing of Lanse's bitterness — Myra had guessed the truth, Carin couldn't tell.

Whatever her thoughts, the woman withheld them. Clucking like a hen with chicks, Myra put the comb down and began digging through the pockets of her housedress.

"The master's shirt swathes you like a sack," she said. "I've no time now to take it up. But stand, dearie, and let's see what can be done without a needle." She produced a bright red scarf and made a sash of it around Carin's waist. This shaped the folds of the oversized shirt into the respectable likeness of a woman's overblouse. "That's better, child," Myra said.

"But bless me!" she exclaimed then. "What am I about? Dawdling with trifles while the master waits with a remedy for your poor bruised face. Didn't he say to send you for the poultice when we had you toasty? Be off with you now. You know the power of the master's medicines. Go to him. Go!" She shooed Carin toward the door.

Carin went, her bare feet softly slapping the stairs.

I only read a poem, she thought, feeling as if she were practicing an excuse, or preparing her defense, as she walked through the quiet house. *I didn't set out to summon a dragon.* Still, as Carin approached the library, she couldn't shake the feeling that something inside her had changed. She'd unsealed doors — first to the cave of magic, and now to a place deep in herself that she hadn't known was there.

The library door was closed. Carin let herself in without knocking.

She found the room far brighter than when she'd stumbled through it in terror of the dragon. The storm raged on, darkening the world outside. But during Carin's absence, her six work lamps had been refilled and relit. The embers on the hearth had been stirred to new life, and the fire fueled with an armload of wood; it now burned brightly. Verek stood before it in his shirt-sleeves, having shed both his black coat and the plum-colored vest he'd worn earlier in the day.

"Come to the fire," he ordered brusquely. "I would see by a good light what damage that fool boy has done."

Filled with her thoughts, but still making no effort to speak, Carin threaded her way through the stacks of books and joined him at the fireplace. Verek cupped his three-fingered left hand around the back of her head and tilted her face up to his.

Carin—swallowing hard in a tight throat—locked her gaze onto the mantelpiece behind him, willing herself to submit to the examination but not letting her eyes meet his. Standing this close to the warlock, she couldn't fail to see that indescribable quality in the depths of his eyes: less than a flame, it was a flicker ... elusive ... something more—or less—than human.

As he cradled Carin's head, his palm warm against her damp hair, Verek raised his other hand to the mantel behind him and flipped open a small jar. He dabbed his fingertip into the glisten-ing, brownish contents, brought it to her lips, and rubbed the ointment into her cuts.

The mixture tasted of fennel. Its aroma blended with the war-lock's own. Carin breathed in the scents of the healing herbs that he carried on his clothes and skin.

Verek reached for a second jar on the mantel, this time using all four fingers to scoop out a dollop of a salve that was lighter in color than the first. This he spread over the bruised half of Carin's face, massaging it with a circular motion that, despite her

knotted nerves, she found entrancing. Her lids drooped over un-
focused eyes — until the warlock's fingertips prodded a little too
firmly against Carin's left cheekbone.

"Ouch!"

She started back, wide-eyed, and jerked away from him.

"What troubles you?" Verek demanded.

"It hurts," Carin mumbled. Slurring her words slightly, she
added, "It's 'sworst right here," and pointed to the pain that
pierced the bone.

"No marvel, that." Verek cupped his hand around the base of
Carin's skull and drew her back to him.

Still partly under the spell of his healer's touch, Carin didn't
resist but resumed her place, close enough to smell him but
staring past him.

The warlock stroked her cheekbone lightly. "Speak out if the
pain returns," he said, then pressed more firmly.

"Ow!" Carin flinched, but Verek was ready for her and didn't
let her leave his grasp.

"The bone is cracked," he said. "Left to itself, it will knit, in
time. But you may forever carry a lump upon the spot — a disfig-
uring reminder of the strange course that events have taken
today. A week ago, I would have given you no other choice.
Then, I believed no true wizardry of mine could touch you. But
that was before you answered a vague summons in the night, or
showed yourself vulnerable to the spell of stone, or conjured a
dragon from the waters of the *wysards*.

"I begin to think," Verek said, "that with each day under my
roof you grow more aware ... more alive to the forces that are
assembled here. I propose, therefore, a test. With your consent,
I'll attempt to heal the bone. You, in turn, will tell me all that you
feel, every sensation of which you are conscious as the healing
progresses. Perhaps this will bring to light some new detail that
will help us to understand what can and cannot touch you in this
world that is not your natural home."

The sorcerer's proposal gave Carin her opening.

"If you can help the pain, please do," she said, her voice sounding thin and cracking a little, then steadying as she got used to speaking again. "But first, I've got to know: *What happened to the Jabberwock?*"

"Silence!" Verek thundered.

His command threw such a hush over the room that no sound remained but the crackling of the fire and the sluicing of rain against the windows. Carin hardly dared to breathe for fear of breaking the sorcerer's immediate and profound state of concentration. He stared into the library's gloomy recesses where the upper door to the cave of magic lay hidden.

Presently, he shook himself and returned his gaze to Carin.

"From afar, the name alone is insufficient, so it would seem, to summon the dragon," Verek said. "Perhaps your presence in the chamber is required. Perhaps a conjuring needs the rhyme spoken in its entirety. Or maybe the final line of the incantation is the key. For now, I am pleased to discover that you do not call the creature with a single word."

So am I, Carin thought, her mouth dry. She'd spoken the name without thinking.

"As to the monster's fate," Verek went on, "I cannot tell you what became of it, for I do not know. Soon after you took yourself and the book from the chamber, the creature began to lose its solidity of form. I don't mean to say that it weakened, for it remained as ferocious as when it first appeared. But gradually its shape became less distinct, as patterns sculpted in ice lose their sharpness when they begin to melt. The creature flung itself from the pool to its full length, but it could not entirely break its bonds to the waters that gave it substance. The very tips of its hindmost claws remained hooked round the pool's rim. So great was its reach, however, that it could, from that position, hack at the cave's walls with its foreclaws. I retreated to the foot of the steps, within the stairwell, and there it could not reach me.

"As I watched it fade from view," he continued, "the thought came to me to test its corporeal nature. Was it illusion, or did it have substance? Was it spectral, or tangible? Moments before it vanished—still howling its rage and clawing the air—I removed my vest and threw it to the dragon. The creature's attack lasted hardly longer than the flicker of an eyelid. But when the image was gone and the waters of the well had regained their customary stillness, I ventured into the chamber and found nothing of my garment but this."

Verek reached into his trousers pocket and pulled out a scrap of plum-dyed wool. Carin took it from his hand, held it in her palm, and stared. The scrap had not been torn from the vest, but cut—as cleanly as by the sharpest blade any metalsmith could fashion. What would those claws do to living things?

The warlock, in his unnerving way, seemed to read Carin's mind. "Such a monster, if ever it were loosed from the bonds that tie it to the pool, might wreak such bloody havoc on mortal flesh as to make our wasteland dogs seem tame. But I am satisfied that it cannot so defy its nature as to leave the waters that give it form."

Verek retrieved the scrap from Carin and stuffed it back in his pocket.

"Now: an end to this tale," he said. "Other matters await. When the dragon was gone—not vanquished, but returned to whatever realm it sprang from—I sought you. A lake of rainwater on the kitchen floor told me you'd heeded my words and taken the book from the house. I followed, expecting to find you in the stable but unprepared for the sorry scene that greeted me there. A moment earlier, and I might have prevented the blow that did this damage." He touched Carin's cheek.

"Let me remind you of our bargain," he said, again cupping his hand around the back of her head. "I will attempt to knit the bone. You'll attend closely to every sensation and tell me all that you feel."

"Yes, sir."

Carin fixed her gaze on Verek's right hand. He pinched together his thumb and forefinger, then eased them apart. A bead of brilliant light the size of a pebble filled the gap. It was far brighter than the witchlight orbs that Verek had previously summoned to his hand. Carin couldn't look directly at it. Squinting, she shifted her gaze to the sorcerer's left shoulder. From the corner of her eye she watched him squeeze the brilliant pebble until it was no bigger than a wheat grain but shone with the intensity of the summer sun. Against that glare, she clamped her eyes shut.

Even through closed lids, however, Carin could detect the grain of brilliance nearing her face. It threw off heat as well as light. A candle flame laid to her cheek would not have been hotter. But she felt no pain. This was heat that did not burn. She felt it touch her cheek, then pass through her skin and settle in the cracked bone. There, the heat flashed like a stroke of lightning — an extreme but incalculably brief sensation of pure fire. At no time did Carin feel the slightest discomfort.

The heat and the light were gone. She opened her eyes.

Verek was looking at her. He stood with his right hand resting on the mantelpiece; his left hung at his side.

Carin blinked a few times, feeling as if she were emerging from a vivid daydream. She raised her hand to her face and felt for charred flesh over the cheekbone that the warlock had bespelled. The skin was smooth and supple. There was no burn. She pressed her fingers firmly against the bone and experienced no pain.

"Thank you," she said. "It doesn't hurt now."

As best she could then, Carin fulfilled her half of the bargain. Choosing her words with care to give Verek the truest account that words alone could convey, Carin described the sensations of heat and light and fire that flashed but did not scorch.

Verek nodded.

"You tell me nothing remarkable, but that is noteworthy in itself. Perhaps we may yet discover a pattern in this puzzle of what is present to your senses ... and what is less to you than nothing."

He turned to the mantelshelf, picked up the ointment jars, one in each hand, and pressed them into Carin's hands. "Tomorrow, apply these as I did—the darker salve to your cuts, the lighter to your bruises. For hurts of that sort, the healer's art serves better than the *wysard's*. The apothecary may mix a multitude of remedies for each solitary cure that is worked through magic—and yet retain the strength, at day's end, to do other than seek his bed."

The sorcerer turned toward the room's shadows. Even the light of six glowing lamps could not dispel the gloom that lay like smoke over that section of the library. The stubborn darkness hiding the upper door to the cave of magic was also a product of the wizard's art, Carin suspected.

"Tell Myra that I wish the evening meal in my quarters," Verek said. "You're at liberty this evening. Tomorrow, we will resume the reading. I have decided I must hear more of the odd adventure of this girl 'Alice'."

Verek walked into the darkness. The door creaked, and for a moment he was silhouetted against the reddish glow that rose from the depths. Then the door closed behind him, with a solid click that suggested nothing more would be seen of the warlock tonight.

Left standing in the well-lit library, Carin listened to the rain, the crackling fire, and the din of her thoughts. A dozen questions darted through her mind, but she would have to wait to ask them.

She put out the lamps and went to eat supper with Myra. After clearing the dishes, she laid her kirtle full on the kitchen table, shaping the still-damp wool to dry flat before the fire. Then she ascended to her room, and took Verek's book of woods' lore to bed with her. But she managed only two pages of it before snuffing her reading lights and surrendering to a deep, dreamless sleep.

* * *

The new day broke in a cloudless sky. The storm was over.

Carin was up with the sun to sit at the dressing table and rub Verek's salves into cuts and bruises that had faded appreciably overnight. In the sorcerer's treatments of her latest injuries, she had found a clue to one troubling mystery: whether his medicines were natural compounds of herbs and oils, or unnatural mixtures with magian qualities. Before working magic on her fractured cheekbone, Verek had — astoundingly — asked Carin's consent. He had never sought her permission before plying her with powders, liquids, and salves. The implication was clear. The warlock didn't scruple to use such remedies, but he felt some duty to obtain the patient's consent before working a magical cure. A sort of wizard's code of conduct? she wondered.

In the library, Carin started her morning's work by shifting the stacks of books that she'd scattered on the floor. Arranging them in neat rows, she made pathways that would give quick access to the hall door from any spot in the room. If she must again beat a retreat — fleeing the warlock himself, or any monsters that might clamber up from his cave — she wouldn't again stumble over badly placed cairns of books.

Next, she sorted through the volumes she had piled at random on the desk. These were books she wanted to read, or at least page through more carefully before assigning them their places in the order that was slowly emerging from the room's disarray.

One volume that Carin had set aside was the book on archery that she'd found during her first exploration of the shelves, on the day Verek put her to work. She settled with it at the sunlit desk and was reading instructions for shaping a bowstave from yew or wild elm, when the hall door burst open and the warlock strode into the room.

He was coatless and wore his shirtsleeves rolled up, as though he'd been at manual labor that morning. In one hand he carried a hemp bag, knotted at the neck. In the other was the puzzle-book, which Carin had last seen concealed in a piece of sacking and slipped under the warlock's rain-cloak.

"Good," he greeted her without preliminaries. "You're here. Come with me."

Verek tucked the book under his arm and walked into the shadows opposite the desk. By sound alone—he was quite invisible in the library's depths—Carin knew that he opened the door to the cave of magic. She heard the hinges creak.

She laid her book facedown on the desk. Slowly she rose and stood beside her chair, with her insides kinking.

Not again, Carin thought. *What can he want with me down there?* Drowned bodies, dark forces, a dragon ... With her every descent of those stairs, Carin felt herself being dragged under, deeper into the dangers of the warlock's world. She half gagged on the intensity of the dread that was welling up in her at the prospect of reentering that realm.

"Come here," Verek snapped from out of the darkness. "If I have to carry you below, you won't like it."

The threat didn't move her. Carin's reluctance to descend to the cave was so strong that she couldn't pry herself from the sunlight that flooded through the windows.

"Please," she managed to say to the shadows that had swallowed the warlock. But that was all. No other words made it past her constricting throat.

Verek reemerged from the darkness, still carrying his bag and the book. He paused in the edge of the sunlight and looked at her with his usual unreadable expression. Then he dropped the bag, and laid the book on the stack of sorted volumes closest to him. Striding between the now-orderly towers of books, he advanced to the desk and stood over her, his arms folded.

Carin prepared to take what was coming.

But in the warlock's stance there was nothing—no muscles knotting in his neck, no clenching of the long fingers that rested on his crossed arms—to suggest anger.

"You're afraid," he murmured. "Good. Only a fool could enter the chamber below this room and feel no fear. In the work that awaits us, a fool would be worse than useless."

He cleared his throat, then went on: "I will not lie to you, and tell you that the events in which you find yourself entangled will pose you no threat. The time may come when I will ask you to embark with me on an enterprise that will endanger both our lives. But that time is not now. At this point, I require your presence in the vault for a purpose that poses little risk to you, and only slightly more to myself.

"The unfortunates that I have brought for this test"—he tipped his head back to indicate the bag on the floor behind him—"may fare less well than you and I. But they're fated to be meat for others, whatever the outcome today, so I think we may bear their loss with good heart."

Verek turned and retraced his steps to retrieve the bag and the puzzle-book.

"Come with me now," he ordered, speaking over his shoulder. "Save your fear for a day when you may need it."

Though Verek's words served only to deepen her uneasiness, Carin pushed away from her bright refuge under the windows. She joined the warlock at the edge of the sunlight, then followed him into the shadows. The open door to the cave of magic showed clearly, a rectangle of red in the darkness. Verek ushered her through it ahead of him. Then he paused inside on the landing to close and latch the door.

So that no monsters could escape? Carin's breathing quickened.

The stairs were too narrow to let Verek squeeze around her, burdened as he was with the bag. Carin was forced to lead the way down. But the moment she emerged from the stairwell, she stepped aside. And when Verek strode past her with the bag, she retreated to the foot of the steps. From there, she watched the warlock take the sack to a spot less than halfway between the stairwell and the pool. When he dropped it on the floor, the bag moved. It held something living.

Verek joined Carin at the foot of the stairs and handed her the *Looking-Glass* book.

"Summon the dragon," he said. "Call only its name. Let us determine if that is sufficient when you stand so close to the waters of the *wysards*." Verek stationed himself between Carin and the pool, then added over his shoulder: "Be ready to take to your heels. I believe the thing has intelligence, and memory. If it remembers its first summons to this chamber, then it may lunge for us at once — to catch its prey, if it can, before we withdraw up the stairs."

Prey?

Carin planted a foot on the bottom step, prepared to fly up-ward with the speed of smoke up a flue. Speaking around Verek's back, she threw the alien name into the cavern like a gauntlet:

"Jabberwock!"

Nothing happened. The pool's perfect surface did not flicker.

"Speak the line that contains the creature's name," Verek instructed.

Carin called it out: *"Beware the Jabberwock, my son!"*

This time, the pool reacted. A ripple moved over it as if a strong breeze gusted through the cave. A heartbeat later, how-ever, the waters had resumed their unbroken, mirror smooth-ness.

"It is as I thought," Verek said. "The incantation must be spoken in its entirety. Open the book and read the words for which the language of Ladrehdin has no equals."

She didn't need to consult the puzzle-book, Carin realized. She knew the words by heart. Taking a breath to steady nerves that were as taut as bowstrings, she recited the opening stanza of *"Jabberwocky."*

On cue, the magic pool misted over. From it rose the badger-like "toves" to bore holes in a water-sculpted hillside. After the "toves" came the unhappy "borogoves" like wingless parrots, and the piggish "raths" squeaking in protest at the destruction of their homes.

"Good!" Verek flung approval over his shoulder. "Now — summon the monster."

Carin's muscles tensed. She recited the line: *"Beware the Jabberwock!"*

Instantly the images of the hillside creatures collapsed in a flood, to be replaced by a bat-winged, scimitar-clawed dragon that reared from the pool, howling like the supernatural thing it was.

Carin sprang up the steps as quickly as Verek flung himself backward to take her place at the foot of them. Just above his head she stopped and crouched, to gaze down at the unreal scene below.

The warlock, in his study of the creature yesterday afternoon, had taken the measure of the beast with life-saving exactness. The monster's talons reached to the opening of the stairwell, but no farther. They slashed at the stonework with such viciousness that chunks of rock clattered to the floor. The claws' razor tips flailed only inches from Verek's face. But the dragon could not reach him. The pool held it back.

With a frustrated roar, the monster gathered itself and pounced on the bag that Verek had left for it. One swipe of a talon laid the bag open, slicing cleanly through the heavy hemp.

Three terrified chickens fluttered up, right into the dragon's jaws. Fangs closed on one bird, then another, snapping with a sharp *crack* like a tree breaking. No drop of blood escaped that maw.

Carin watched, morbidly fascinated, as a single brown feather drifted down to settle on the cave's floor.

"Excellent!" Verek exclaimed, tilting his head back to peer up at her. "If proof were needed, this has provided it. The dragon transcends illusion. It is—as I hoped and did suspect—a killer."

As he *hoped?* Surprised into meeting the eyes that were turned up to hers, Carin recoiled in horror. About them was a preternatural brilliance that expressed excitement barely contained—or madness barely controlled.

Chapter 16

Promises

The warlock gave no sign that he saw the revulsion in Carin's face. He held his hand up to her, demanding the puzzle-book. Then he bade her return to the library.

"Wait for me there. When I join you, I will wish to hear more from the pages of this bewitching book. But first I must see to our otherworldly guest." Verek jerked his head to indicate the screaming monster that, inches behind his back, was slicing the hemp bag to ribbons.

Carin raced upward, her skin damp with sweat, the air in the stairwell chilling her. Whether she fled the Jabberwock or the sorcerer, however, she could hardly say. *What was in Verek's mind?* What evil did he think to do with the dragon she had conjured?

She flung open the door at the head of the stairs. From the unnatural shadows which cloaked that section of the library in endless night, Carin plunged into the sunlight streaming through the windows. She threw herself against the desk, fighting for breath and for mastery of her fear.

To stand against the sorcerer and whatever he planned for "her" monster seemed worse than foolhardy. Verek might feed her to the thing. But she couldn't sit idly while he used the dragon for some terrible purpose she could only imagine.

The warlock lingered long underground. By the time the creaking of the hidden door told her he had returned to the library, Carin was ready — though nervous to the degree of misery — to say what she had to.

"Lord Verek," she snapped the moment he emerged from the shadows. "I don't know what you think you're up to with that dragon I accidentally brought here from the puzzle-book. Feeding it those birds was a *creepy* thing to do. But the look on your face when you saw the Jabberwock kill them—that was even worse." Carin wiped her palms on her breeches and shook her head. "I'm done. That's it. I won't call the monster back, *ever*. If you intended to set the thing free, or use it as some kind of weapon, you can just forget it. I don't care if you torture me, or you lock me in the dungeon, or you throw me into the wizards' well to drown. It doesn't matter what you do. I *won't* summon the dragon to serve you."

Verek heard her out without moving another step into the room. When Carin's words had died away, he stood another moment in silence, eyeing her. Then he walked to the cabinet from which he'd poured himself a drink on the day they first talked in this library. As he passed the bench Carin had occupied then—the same bench she'd taken at every meeting in this room since—he tossed the puzzle-book onto its seat, not breaking stride.

At the cabinet Verek tipped out a ruby liquid from a glass flagon, filling two goblets to the brim. He carried both to the desk where Carin stood.

"Drink this," he said, handing her a goblet. "It will aid the recovery of wits you seem to have lost."

Carin accepted the drink but did not taste it. Her full attention was on the warlock. She studied his face, especially his darkly flickering eyes. Their elusive manic quality remained, but the terrifying brilliance no longer shone in them. Any outward expression of Verek's madness—if madness it was—had been replaced by a circumspect look of surprise.

The warlock returned her gaze, watching her over the rim of his glass as he sipped his drink. He lowered it and asked: "Of what do you suspect me? Upon whom shall I unleash the monster, do you think? Might I loose it on the countryside to murder my tenants?"

231

Carin shook her head. "I don't know what to think, sir. I can't guess your secrets. But when you act happy about the dragon being a killer, I have to assume that you're not planning to use the Jabberwock for anything good."

"Drink," Verek said again, gesturing at the glass Carin hardly knew she held. "You will find the elixir calms the nerves and quiets the mind."

As he raised his own glass to his lips, Carin took a hesitant sip from hers. The liquor was warm on her tongue and in her throat. It tasted of currants, slightly sweet with a tartness.

For a long moment, the warlock said no more. He drained his goblet, then set it on the desk and raised his face to the sunlight that poured over them through the tall windows above. With his eyes closed, he soaked it up like a lizard sunning on a rock.

As Carin studied Verek's profile with its straight nose and firm jaw, she had the startling idea that this warlock might long for sunshine and open spaces, the same way she did. She thought of him as a creature of night and darkness, closeted deep with his spells, working wizardry until all hours. But what had Myra said? She'd mentioned that Verek and Lanse used to pass their days outdoors. Before Carin arrived on the scene, the two of them had ridden together almost daily to sharpen their skills with horse, sword, and bow.

Is it my presence here that drives the warlock underground to face the forces in that cave? Carin wondered. *If I hadn't stumbled onto his property, would he still be the swordsman who used to ride through the woods, and not the sorcerer who's planning something horrible?*

Verek opened his eyes and turned to her.

"You speak of 'doing good,'" he said. "Tell me: do you believe that the sun does good in its daily arcing through the sky?"

"Yes, of course," Carin answered without thinking. "If the sun didn't cross the sky every day, the world would freeze in the dark. The sun is warmth and light. It's life."

"Does it not also bring death?" Verek shot back. "Is it not the searing heat of the sun that shrivels the crops in the fields and dries the ponds in midsummer so that beasts lay dying of thirst? Where then, in the sun's merciless scorching of the land, is the benevolence of which you speak?"

Carin chewed her bottom lip, then took another small sip of her drink so she could hide behind her glass. He was right, of course. The sun was neither good nor bad; it just *was*. On the world below, living things might feel its glow as benign or destructive, but the sun, in itself, was neither.

Verek seemed to know that Carin had realized her mistake. He continued: "Again it's necessary to look beyond the immediate and the obvious to see what may lie deeper — as in the matter of Alice and her looking-glass. You think the sun in the sky is unfailingly good, but upon reflection you see that it may cause harm. You believe the dragon you call to the *wysards'* well is a thing of evil. But are you so sure of its wickedness that you will say it's impossible for the creature ever to serve as an instrument for good, in some peculiar instance that you cannot now imagine?"

The warlock was looking steadily at Carin, but he seemed unaware that he had asked her a question.

"Undoubtedly," he went on, "you think that killing a person is an evil thing. But could you call it a noble act if the killer were reluctant to his very soul, and despite his qualms he did take a life, for no less a purpose than to save the lives of millions? To save life itself, perhaps, on this world and others?"

This time Verek paused, awaiting her answer. But Carin only stared at him, deeply confused. How could the death of one person save lives on such a scale as he described? And where was the Jabberwock's place in all of this, as "an instrument for good"?

Then she made the connection, and she felt the color leave her face. Two alien invaders — a dragon from the abyss and the girl who conjured it ... a girl who "shouldn't be here." Use one to kill the other, and be rid of both.

Involuntarily Carin backed away from Verek, moving a step closer to the hall door. *Don't admit to anything! Don't agree to anything!* screamed her instinct for self-preservation.

"'On this world and others'?" Carin said in a voice far firmer than her jellied insides felt. "There aren't any 'other worlds.' I was born in the south of Ladrehdin to parents I never knew. That place I saw in the pool of magic—the room where the little girl was asleep—that was just a trick." With every sentence, Carin got louder and angrier. "You tricked me! That wasn't a vision of my bedroom from childhood. There was never any whirlpool swooshing me from there to here. You're a sorcerer. You can make me see things that don't exist. You can twist my mind however you want it to go.

"No!" she fairly screamed at him. "I won't call the dragon again, for *any* reason. Whatever your schemes are, you're not getting any help from me. I'm not daft enough to help you set a trap, and then walk right into it. I haven't stayed alive this long by being that thick-witted."

Verek stood looking at Carin, listening, his face an impassive mask. His eyes wore a distant and guarded expression now, as though he strove with conscious effort to avoid any fleeting glance that might betray his thoughts.

He snatched his empty goblet from the desk and spun around. His long strides carried him back to the cabinet in the bookshelves. Verek flung it open and poured himself another bumper of the ruby liquor. He drank a good third of it on the spot. Then he carried his glass—along with the half-full decanter—to his usual seat in front of the fireplace. The hearth was cold; Carin hadn't needed a fire to work in the library on such a sunny morning.

"You mistake me," the warlock said, snapping off his words as if they were sticks of dry kindling. "When I speak of taking a life, I have in mind … someone who is a more urgent threat to this world than you are. Cool down. I won't murder you today. Nor will I ask you again to summon the monster to the vault below. Though the beast does not and will not answer to me, I know its nature now. On that front, my inquiries are ended."

Verek paused to sip his drink. With a preoccupied wag of his empty hand, he waved Carin to her usual place on the bench opposite.

She delayed long enough to gulp a mouthful from the goblet she clutched. Somewhat steadied by the liquor's warmth, Carin made her way through the stacked books to settle across from the sorcerer, with the low table reassuringly between them. The *Looking-Glass* book lay on the bench beside her, where Verek had tossed it on his earlier visit to the liquor cabinet.

"I am much dissatisfied with you," the warlock growled, riveting Carin to the cushions with his dark gaze. "I had thought you must accept the truth of what you saw in the well of the *wysards*. If the world you glimpsed is not your true home, then how do you explain the puzzle-book and your ability to read it? How do you explain your lack of childhood memories? How do you account for the wheelwright finding you in a state of shock and unable to speak a word for a year afterward? Doesn't it occur to you that you could not speak because *you did not know the language of Ladrehdin?* For a year after you washed up on the shores of this world, you were a child learning to talk. Small wonder that the wright thought you feeble in the head. I begin to think he took your measure truly."

The warlock paused again, frowning, and sipped his drink.

Carin swallowed more of hers as well, as much to gain time as to draw courage. Verek's points were difficult to refute. Why she couldn't remember her childhood and how she'd arrived on the banks of the millpond were baffling questions, but other explanations were possible. The only real evidence that she'd come to this world from another was the *Looking-Glass* book and her otherwise inexplicable ability to read it. The book was a key to this mystery.

So what was Verek doing with it? If it had been Carin's on that "other world," how had he gotten his hands on it?

"Sir," she said, looking at him askant, "*if* it's true that the child's room that materialized out of the magic pool used to be my room, and *if* it's true that this book" — Carin picked up the volume beside her — "is written in the language of that other world and used to belong to me there, then the same whirlpool that brought me to Ladrehdin should have brought the book too. So how come I popped into a pond down south, but my book ended up with you?"

Carin paused, but not long enough to let the warlock answer. Her point was not yet made.

"It's more likely, isn't it," she went on firmly, "that the book is written in some obscure language of Ladrehdin that I learned from my parents before I got separated from them. Your library has lots of examples of old languages that nobody speaks any-more. Maybe this" — Carin hefted the book — "is just a story in a dead language. Maybe it doesn't prove anything about 'other worlds,' or about me coming from one."

Verek sighed heavily at her. Scowling, he reached for the flagon to refill his goblet.

If he keeps on at this rate, Carin thought, watching him, *I'll soon be sitting here with a sorcerer who's not only half crazy, but half drunk too.*

The warlock did not immediately drink from his refilled glass, however. He leaned back against the cushions of his bench and cradled the goblet in one hand while he ran the fingers of his other through his hair.

"The book came to me on a cold winter's morning, some five years ago, as I sat reading in this room," Verek said in a voice that was strained but quiet. "I felt a great disturbance in the waters of the *wysards* … as I felt the uproar yesterday when you spoke the incantation that conjured the dragon's heralds. On that winter's morning, I hurried to the pool and found the waters wildly agitated. They seethed and foamed like the sea in a mighty storm.

"I called upon the power of that place to show me the cause of the turmoil. It could form no clear likeness upon the pool, such was the fury of the storm of magic that whipped the waters to foam. But the power in the chamber did impress upon my mind images of a vortex spinning through a dark void … bearing near its center a speck: green and blue like a bunch of violets."

"You saw me!" Carin exclaimed, then clamped her bottom lip in her teeth, threatening to reopen the nearly healed cut. Caught up in Verek's storytelling, she'd forgotten her professed disbelief of the tale.

"Yes, I saw you," the warlock replied, seeming not to notice Carin's slipup. "Then, of course, I didn't know the identity of the bright speck, nor fully comprehend the significance of the vortex in the void. I knew only that I witnessed wizardry of an incredibly powerful nature … magic not of my own working.

"I reached to touch it," Verek went on. "I strove to call forth from the magic itself the name of the master *wysard* who made it. With all of my powers I probed the secrets of that vortex and its creator."

He fell silent. Verek's eyes looked through Carin as if they saw the whirlpool still spinning in the void.

She took a tiny sip of her drink and said nothing. Holding the goblet in front of her, Carin watched the warlock over its rim.

In a moment, Verek shook himself and resumed his story. "Gradually, the magic faded. The images ceased and the waters of the pool stilled. Yet I worked on in the chamber, struggling to lift the curtain of silence. Calling on the forces that are both servant and master to me, I sought their help in discovering the maker of the vortex and learning the nature of such powerful wizardry. But a day spent in hard pursuit of knowledge yielded nothing but speculation ... and the book you hold in your hand."

Verek drank deeply from his goblet, then tilted its rim toward Carin to indicate the puzzle-book she clutched.

"I don't understand, sir," she ventured after a moment, when the warlock seemed to need prodding to finish his story. "Did the book just show up in the wizards' well like a ... a ship on the sea?"

"More like driftwood washed up on shore," Verek replied. "When the waters grew still, I discovered the book on the pool's rim, as one might find the lost cargo of a wrecked ship heaped onshore after a storm. I don't doubt that the book was with you in the vortex at the beginning of your journey through the void. What I do not know is how it came to be parted from you. Perhaps my interference, as I strove to touch the magic, so disturbed the vortex that a small part of its 'cargo' broke free and floated to me, like flotsam after a storm. Or perhaps my efforts had no effect, and the book was simply a bit of debris washing up where the tides of magic took it."

Carin examined the volume in her hand. It was undamaged. There were no water stains or wrinkled pages such as a book should have after even a minor wetting, much less the total submersion that Verek described. Still, the lack of water damage was no proof that his story was a lie. She'd seen for herself that the "water" of the magic pool had had no power to dampen the warlock's hair or clothes, even when he'd nearly drowned in it.

"Strange though the episode was," Verek went on, "it was not the first time such a thing had happened."

He's unusually talkative this morning, Carin thought. *Is it the liquor talking?*

"Some years before the book washed up in the pool," the warlock said, "another item—albeit less fascinating—appeared in like manner."

Verek set his half-empty glass down and went again to the liquor cabinet. From it he removed two clean goblets, which he set on a nearby shelf that Carin's labors had cleared of books. Then he reached deep into the cabinet and gave a sharp tug. He brought out a narrow slat that looked like it came from the cabinet's wooden back. Again he reached in, deeper still, accessing what Carin took to be a cavity within the wall-space behind the cabinet. From it, he withdrew a wand of what looked like honey-colored wood.

The wand was the length of Verek's arm from wrist to elbow and about as big around as his thumb. It was highly polished, either by hand or as if it had been driftwood on the sea, smoothed by the action of winds and waves. In the sunlight that slanted through the library's windows, the honey tones shone as if waxed.

Verek handed Carin the wand, then resumed his seat.

"I was not at home when this artifact emerged from the pool," he said. "While out riding, I sensed in the very air the workings of unusually strong magic. I could not reach the cavern in time to discover the wizardry's nature or source. But I believe the disturbance of the waters then was as violent as it would be later, when I 'scried the vortex that carried you between worlds.

"When I reached the cavern after that first disturbance," Verek added, "I saw no sign of anything amiss except the wand you now hold. I picked it up from the pool's rim, marveling at the odd manner of its arrival. I admired its luster but could see nothing of significance in it. Having no clear idea of its importance, I put it away and all but forgot it ... until my first meeting with the woodsprite, in the forest near here, a year and a half later."

"The woodsprite!" Carin exclaimed, intrigued that the sprite would crop up in the history Verek was relating. She rolled the wand between her hands, feeling its satin smoothness, and wondered: Had the sprite also arrived in this world twirling madly in a whirlpool? Could this wand be a relic of the creature's home, as the puzzle-book was purported to be a vestige of hers?

"Sir, have you talked to the sprite about this?" Carin asked. "Have you shown it this stick? I'm sure the creature would want to see it. Maybe the sprite can tell whether the wand comes from its home world. If it recognizes the wood, then I'll have more reason to believe what you say about *me* being from somewhere else."

Verek snatched up his goblet so abruptly that some of the liquor sloshed out and splattered.

"You declare the sprite trustworthy and in the same breath accuse me of deceit—is that the way of it?" he snapped, his eyes flashing. "You doubt the proof of your own eyes, calling it a sorcerer's trick. What all your senses tell you, you deny, for you allege that I conjure it all to lead you astray. But you accept the woodsprite's claim that it is from elsewhere, and you say you're ready to believe the same of yourself—if only the sprite shall tell you that it must be so."

The warlock glowered at her, and Carin paled once more as she realized what she risked to question Lord Verek so brazenly. Doubting a nobleman's word or calling him a liar outright—it was an offense punishable by drawing and quartering, should the offended noble choose to apply the law's severest sanctions.

That Verek was thinking along the same lines was obvious when he spoke again.

"As I've sworn not to murder you today, I won't hold you to account for taking the word of a nameless fay over the testimony of a sovereign Ruainian lord," he said icily. "I know you look upon the creature as a friend, even while you think of me as your enemy. Whether the sprite will prove to be a true friend to you, I cannot say, for the slippery creature has eluded all my attempts to know its nature.

"But you trust the creature," Verek said. "Then let me use that trust to support my claim. On the night when it helped you escape the dogs, didn't the fay speak to you of the spells it sees, the things of power curtaining off a forbidden portion of my land? Didn't the sprite marvel that you passed through the barrier at will, never sensing the magic's existence?

"And how did the creature explain this uncanny ability of yours?" the warlock asked. "Did it weave fantasies of lost parents who taught a half-grown child an unknown tongue—a tongue that bears no resemblance to any ancient language of Ladrehdin? Could the sprite say why those same devoted parents would abandon their child dangerously near water in the dead of winter? Did it waste words on such whimsy, or did it tell you plainly that you, like it, are from elsewhere?

"Answer me!" Verek demanded, as though Carin could have slipped in a word before then. "What do you say to the woodsprite's assertion—which echoes my own—that you are not of this world?"

Carin put the wand down and reached for her goblet. She drained it of the last ruby drops, then twirled its stem in her fingers. Verek had her. The combined weight of his arguments and the woodsprite's overwhelmed her resistance. She could not hold on to the pretense.

"I know I'm not of this world," Carin said, rather testily. "I've known it since I saw the little girl's bedroom in the mists of the magic pool. After the image died away and you asked me about it, I told you I didn't see anything familiar. But actually, there was one thing in the room that I think I recognized. The egg-man toy that was sitting on the top shelf of the bookcase had a little sign hanging from his foot.

"Did you notice it?" she asked. "It had two words on it that were in the same language as the looking-glass book. They said 'Karen's Zoo.' I haven't been able to get that sign out of my mind. I think I remember writing those words. I didn't recognize anything else about the room or the other objects in it. But I remember a hand—I think it must have been mine—being *so* careful to make that sign neat, to print the letters clearly and to fit the short word perfectly under the longer word. The word on top, the longer word … it's my name. In the language of the puzzle-book, 'Carin' is 'Karen.'" She pronounced the second name with a harder initial sound and without the slight trilling of the middle letter that characterized Ladrehdinian speech.

Verek stared at her. Slowly, he shook his head.

"I glanced at the sign but took no particular notice of it," he admitted. "Had I been more in the habit of calling you by name, perhaps I would have seen a hint of a similarity."

The warlock drained his goblet and set it on the table. Then he leaned back and studied Carin, the expression on his face a mixture of faint annoyance and something unreadable.

"You've known from that moment the truth of your origins," he said. "You've known that the truth must be thus, and not otherwise. Why, then, have you seen fit to waste half the morning in pointless argument?"

Because I cross barriers you don't want crossed, Carin thought, meeting Verek's gaze. *I open doors you don't want opened. And with the words of an alien tongue, I conjure a killer dragon. You must feel threatened by me. You do, don't you? No matter what you say.*

But putting it so bluntly to Verek would only help to build the case against her. If Carin meant to run through the list of reasons Verek might have for wanting to be rid of her, she'd need to take care with her phrasing.

She began with understatement. "I know you don't like how I can walk through the spells that screen your woodland. I know it gets under your skin, me not even seeing them, or barely feeling them."

Gets under his skin? That is putting it mildly, Carin thought, remembering his fury and how exquisitely close he had come to handing her her head.

Verek said nothing to this, but seemed to be waiting for her to go on.

So Carin waded in deeper.

"You tell me I shouldn't be here," she muttered, still eyeing the warlock. "You talk about threats to Ladrehdin and about using the puzzle-book dragon to … remove them. When I put one thing with another, I don't like what I get." She picked up the book and riffled its pages. "I'm not natural to this world. Does that make me dangerous to it? Could I do something, without meaning to do it, that would hurt people? The same way I called up the dragon without even knowing—the first time—that that's what I was doing?"

The sky Carin could see through the library's windows was cloudless, a bright blue. She studied it for a moment, then turned back to Verek. He was watching her, his head slightly atilt, silent, letting her talk.

Carin's voice was getting softer as she went. "And about that dragon I've conjured from the wizards' well … You must be wondering why a monster would come when I call it. Why in Drisha's name *would* it come—unless I've got some kind of evil power over it?

"—But I don't." Carin leaned toward Verek for emphasis. "Whatever spellcraft this is, I know nothing of it. I just read what's written on the page. I don't even *understand* the poem that conjures the Jabberwock."

She watched Verek, searching for a sign that he believed her. But the warlock only regarded her with a kind of detached interest, as though Carin were an insect of the summer forest that had scurried out of a snow-draped woodpile in the heart of winter.

His coldness cut into her.

What did I expect? Sympathy? From him? Carin bit the inside of her mouth. *Not likely.* What was it to Verek if Carin's sense of self had been shattered piecemeal down in that cave? Her understanding of who she was had always had its blank spots, true.

But she'd chosen to think of herself as a traveler — never suspecting that, in fact, she was an alien castaway in a world where she didn't belong.

And never dreaming that she could conjure dragons.

Sighing, Carin leaned back and continued, speaking frankly now.

"I'm sorry I ever came anywhere near you, Lord Verek. If I'd kept away, I never would have found out how really lost I am. Or how *strange* I am. I wouldn't have known about that other world, where I guess I used to live. I wouldn't be wondering who I was — or who I used to be. And I wouldn't be feeling like such an outsider, here in this world."

Carin looked at her hand, the one that Verek's spells had failed to burn off when she touched the hidden latch to his cave of magic. Right now, her own flesh seemed alien to her.

"I'm sorry your sorcery didn't stop me coming here," she muttered. "If I'd gone on my way instead of hiking up into your trees, those filthy dogs might have torn out my throat before I got far. But I would have died still knowing myself, and still thinking I had a right to live in this world."

"You would have died uselessly," the warlock retorted, rousing, "and with your questions all unanswered."

Verek looked impatiently at her. "Come!" he snapped. "Throw off this melancholy and spare me any more of your self-pity. This mood doesn't become you. Vilify me if you will — scream at me, if you must — but don't whine. It makes for poor company on one of the last bright mornings that we'll see this autumn."

He stood, rounded the table between them, and reached across Carin's lap to snatch the polished wand from the seat beside her. His move was so sudden that she barely had time to gasp. The artifact, as it left her, made a blur through the air.

Then Verek was at the cabinet. He replaced the relic in its hiding spot, and with the slat he'd earlier removed, sealed the opening at the back of the cabinet. He returned the two clean goblets to their places within the nook and snapped the doors shut.

Restlessly the warlock strode back to his bench, but he stepped behind it, to grasp the high seat-back with both hands and lean his stomach against it.

Carin stayed where she was, watching him. His rebuke had stung. She sat up straighter and wordlessly vowed to never again let her captor see her so deeply unsure of herself.

Verek leveled his gaze at her.

"That you do not summon the dragon to the well through any wizardry of your own making, I believe," he said. "The power lies within the words of the rhyme. Rare is the incantation that carries its magic utterly within the syllables themselves, and therefore needs no magician, only a native speaker to give it voice. But such magic does exist in the wizardry of this world. Hence, I am disposed to accept that the rhyme from the looking-glass book is magic of that sort. As you say, you merely read the words that lie upon the page. Such recitation doesn't make you a worker of magic."

"Of course it doesn't." Carin tried to sound dismissive of the whole idea. Nevertheless, she felt some of the burden of responsibility lift from her shoulders, to know that being a conduit for otherworldly witchcraft did not implicate her in the working of it. She closed her eyes and swallowed, only now fully realizing how heavily that dragon weighed on her.

Verek spoke again. Carin opened her eyes.

"As for your impudent inattention to *my* spellwork: I believe the matter will not trouble either of us for much longer. Do you recall what I told you yesterday? That with each day you spend under my roof, you feel more acutely the magic within these walls? Plainly, you are susceptible to the wizardry. You hear a summons when I conjure visions in the chamber of *wysards*. Twice, you have succumbed to the spell of stone."

At this, Verek lifted two fingers of his right hand from the back of the bench he was leaning against.

Carin grabbed the *Looking-Glass* book and held it to her like the breastplate of a suit of armor. She wasn't sure why she did it. The book wouldn't stop Verek from turning her to stone if he chose. But she had an idea that Verek might not want to risk any spell of his striking the book that held a potent specimen of alien magic. He had no way of knowing what might result.

He seemed to appreciate that fact. Something flitted across Verek's face that might have been a half-smile. Then, with a dip of his head — a nod to Carin's small victory — he let his fingers drop to the seat-back.

"Also, there's the magic that healed your cheekbone," the warlock went on, as if nothing had passed between them. "Were you invulnerable to my wizardry, the fracture would not have knit under its influence.

"All of this leads me to suppose that you're not as outlandish as you think you are," he said. "To quiet you on the subject — for I wish to hear no more bemoaning of your lot — I will tell you my speculations. But take them only as such, for I do not claim to have a perfect understanding of the matter."

Verek quit leaning on his bench and came around it to take his seat. He laced the fingers of both hands behind his head and went on unhurriedly.

"Perhaps you've known of a man who, bee-stung, suffered no ill effects beyond the momentary pain. Twice stung, he was little harmed. Thrice stung, however, the wretch swelled up and died. Repeated exposure to the venom of the bee's sting had built in him such a sensitivity as to finally provoke a marked response.

"I think it's likely that oft-repeated experience with the wizardry within these walls has built in you a like susceptibility — though not with like results. Do not mistake me on that point. I use the example of the bee-sting for no other reason than it is an instance from nature that serves broadly to explain the quickening of your senses.

"A week ago," Verek went on, "you could not perceive the powerful wizardry that curtains my woods. Yet now, you surrender to the simplest of spells — the spell of stone. You hear the whisperings of magic in the chamber of enchantment, yet the spells that guard its portals do not touch you. Maybe you are like the patient whose injured eyes have been well wrapped to block the light and promote healing. As the wrappings are removed, layer by layer, you sense — at first — only the simplest patterns of light and shadow. But as the bindings come slowly away, you see more distinctly. You begin to discern shapes and colors. The time shall come when the last wrappings will be removed, and all wizardry, from the simple to the consummate, will be present to your senses with perfect clarity. And then perhaps you will know who you are, and where you belong."

Verek dropped his hands from his head and reached for the flagon on the table. It held just enough liquor to refill his goblet a final time.

"I've talked until I'm hoarse," he said between sips, "and in consequence I have drunk too much. You must take the blame for an idle morning given over to drink, for you've forced me to spend it dispelling doubts that you never harbored. As for your fears ... perhaps there is less pretense in those, but no more substance. You've conjured them from a mind over-full of suspicions. It belongs, however, to your age and your nature to entertain such fancies.

"Enough!" Verek put down his goblet and flung himself full-length on his bench. "Read! Take up the tale of Alice through the looking-glass, from the moment the incantation ends. I trust you'll say nothing to call the monster back — if it's not your intention to summon the dragon."

Slowly, Carin thumbed open the puzzle-book, mentally chewing on everything Verek had just said. His words had not eased her mind. Quite the contrary.

She fumbled her way through the pages, found Alice's thoughts on the *"Jabberwocky"* poem, and read them aloud:

"'It seems very pretty,' Alice said when she had finished it, 'but it's *rather* hard to understand! … Somehow it seems to fill my head with ideas — only I don't exactly know what they are!'"

Feeling as if the passage had filled her own head with nameless notions, Carin lowered the book and looked at Verek.

"Excuse me, sir," she said. "But do you know the name of the master wizard who sent the whirlpool that snatched me away — and took the woodsprite, too — from the worlds where we used to live?"

Verek raised onto his elbow and glared at her. A fierce frown darkened his face. "In time, your questions will be answered. Do not plague me with them. I bid you *read*."

He dropped back and lay looking up at the ceiling. "Or shall we see," he growled, and raised his hand threateningly, "whether you are now subject to subtler spells that not every novice magician knows? Most especially I call to my mind the spells of sores and scabs."

Hastily, Carin read, picking up where she'd left off in Alice's musings. "'However, *somebody* killed *something:* that's clear, at any rate — '"

Verek rolled again to his elbow and looked at her. Carin kept her eyes glued to the book and read on without pause.

The warlock, apparently satisfied that the talk of killing didn't spring from Carin's own thoughts, lay back and lowered his hand. With a sigh that sounded almost contented, he settled himself more comfortably on his cushions.

When Myra bustled into the library to call them to the midday meal, Carin was reading the Red Queen's directions to Alice as the girl became a pawn in the living game of chess. The sorcerer Verek was sound asleep, snoring gently.

Chapter 17

The Magic of Life

Carin woke from a long nap. She threw open her bedroom curtains and found the sun hanging well past its zenith. She'd passed out after lunch, drugged by the single glass of liquor she had drunk with Verek in the library.

The warlock, after four brimful goblets of the stuff, might still be sleeping. Carin and Myra had tiptoed away from the library, leaving Verek snoring on his bench. There was no sense waking him to feed him, the housekeeper had said. Her "good master" would call for his meal when he wanted it.

Carin splashed her face with cold water, pulled on her boots, and went downstairs. Turning first to the kitchen and finding it unoccupied, she secured a sturdy broom and a knife that had a broad blade. She returned with these to the stair foyer, left them on the bottom step, then walked down the hall to the library.

Cautiously she cracked the door and stuck her head in. Good. Verek no longer slept in front of the cold hearth. The room was empty. Carin crossed to the desk and retrieved the book on archery that she'd been reading when Verek brought in his bag of "unfortunates" fated for the Jabberwock's jaws.

With the book and the tools she'd gathered, she climbed again to the landing that fronted her bedroom. From there Carin took the upper passageway that led to the double doors separating this part of the house from the master wing beyond. As she reached the head of the wide, dark staircase that descended to the cave of magic, she did not look down.

Quietly she lifted the doors' latch and passed through. She strode down the dusty corridor beyond, then squeezed herself and the tools through the narrow opening at the corridor's end.

A few paces took her across the balcony to the head of the steps that descended into the long-abandoned great hall.

Sweeping trash from each step before setting foot on it, Carin worked her way down the stairs to the equally dirty floor of the hall. There, she used the broom to clear dirt, dead leaves, and bird droppings from an aisle between two of the tables that ran the length of the room. Brooming the filth aside vigorously, she made no effort to clean the whole floor. All she needed was enough space to try her hand with a new weapon.

Taking the knife and the archery book with her, Carin went outside, through the servants' entrance and past the rowan tree that partly blocked the doorway.

"Sprite!" she called. "Are you there?"

A spark leaped from tree to tree, racing toward her from the direction of the outer wall where the huge oak breached it.

"I — am — here — my — friend!" came the thin, disconnected voice of the traveling woodsprite.

Carin walked to meet it. Her feet sank into a carpet of autumn leaves that was damp and springy after yesterday's drenching. Almost together, she and the spark reached the same nondescript oak where they had talked two days before.

"I hoped you'd come this afternoon," piped the reedy voice from a mouth working in the tree trunk. "So fierce was yesterday's storm that I did not venture from the coppice of sweet myrtle that gave me refuge, for fear that I'd roast in a lightning strike. I sorely doubted you'd be abroad on such a day."

Carin settled on the exposed root that had been her seat before. She cradled the book in her lap to keep it out of the moist leaf litter. A rich, rain-washed scent enveloped her, the earthy perfume of the wooded wilderness that had grown up on this side of the house.

"Sprite, I need your help," she said, impelled in the fast-waning day to speak and act quickly. "I've lost my sling, and it was the only weapon I knew how to use. Verek took it from me.

251

He's not likely to give it back. What I need now is to make myself another weapon — something better than my sling."

She opened the archery book to a page showing different types of bows. "See here?" Carin pointed to a picture of bowmen, some of them shooting from the ground, some from horseback. "I don't think I could handle a longbow, but I'm sure I could learn to use a short bow. Like this one." She pointed out a horsed archer who was drawing and shooting while spurring his mount to a gallop. "That's the kind of bow Verek uses. He didn't miss with it when he was wiping out the pack of dogs."

"That he didn't," the sprite agreed, attentive. "And I've seen him use it equally well at other times. The mage and that boy of his were in the habit, until not a very long while ago, of riding and shooting ofttimes of an afternoon. Many days I've watched them practice, but always from a safe distance. I confess myself unwilling to feel an arrow pierce any tree in which I dwell. But I digress. What were you saying?"

"I was about to ask you to jump through the trees, the way you do, and find me a branch of yew or elm that's the right length for a bow staff. In this book, it says that an unstrung bow for someone my height should reach from my neck to my knee." Carin stood and demonstrated the length needed. "Can you look in the trees back here and find me a branch that long? The book says the wood should be limber, but strong."

"At once, my — friend!" the sprite cried, leaping enthusiastically to the task. "In — no — time — you — shall — have — your — limb!"

While she waited, Carin studied the book. She pored over the method for thinning a bowstave from belly to back, leaving more width at the center than at the notched and tapered ends. She was weighing her grip options — leather-wrapped? a carved handle? — when the woodsprite came sparking back.

"A young yew-tree grows nearer than an arrow's flight from this spot," the creature reported, sounding a shade breathless.

"I've found among its lower limbs a branch that will serve you admirably, unless I'm much mistaken. Come! Let me lead the way."

Carin wedged the book into a crotch of the oak. Knife in hand, she followed the flashes of the sprite's leaps.

The creature led her to an entire grove of young yews. The particular tree the sprite had chosen grew well above her head. But at a height easily reached from the ground, the tree had produced a straight, slender limb that seemed made for her purposes.

"It's perfect, sprite!" she exclaimed. "Thank you. Now, please go to some other tree while I cut this limb off." She frowned. "After what happened when those dogs chased me and you broke the branches to help me get up high, I'm a little worried that I'll hurt this tree. But I guess you'll be all right if you'll move."

When the creature had leaped to safety, Carin put her knife to the branch and sawed. Many strokes and a sore hand later, she sliced through the last fibers that held the limb.

"Sprite, I've got to go now," she said, eyeing the lengthening shadows. "The day's getting on, and I'll be missed."

She hurried to get the archery book. With it, the knife, and the yew limb filling her hands, she turned to reenter the great hall through the weather-fretted door that hung on one hinge. But the feel of the slender branch in her hand reminded Carin of another stick she'd handled that day: the wand that Verek kept behind the liquor cabinet in the library.

"Sprite!" she called. "Wait a minute. I just remembered—I've got some news for you."

Carin wasn't ready to tell the creature everything she had learned since their last meeting, least of all what Verek had said about the "master *wysard*" who had whirled her to Ladrehdin. Though Verek had not given her an answer when she'd asked— only a look that could raise blisters—Carin felt certain that he knew the name of that master of magic. The all-but-confirmed existence of such a blackheart might be enough to set the wood-sprite off hunting for the agent to send it home. Carin wanted the sprite with her, not carried away on a quest for a shadowy figure who might or might not help the creature. That Verek stood in awe of the master wizard's powers also argued for keeping quiet. The sprite was safe in the warlock's woodland. But if the creature actually found and entered the domain of one whom Verek called a *master*, the sprite might confront a sorcerer it could not escape as easily as it eluded the lord of Ruain.

No, now wasn't the time to talk of the blackheart who wielded the power of passage between worlds. In good conscience, Carin could keep the excitable woodsprite in the dark for a while. But the sprite deserved to hear about the wand that might have the same origins it did.

As she stood at the rowan door, Carin described for the sprite the wand's smooth luster and honey color. She related Verek's story about the manner of its arrival years ago, and how the war-lock hadn't known what to make of a gleaming stick that was tossed up like driftwood on the rim of his magic pool. She re-peated what Verek had said about first meeting the sprite in his ensorcelled woods a year and a half after the wand washed up.

"I remember you telling me, sprite, that for a while after you came to this world you wandered around," Carin added. "And then you found Verek's woods and settled here because they made you feel protected, the woodcutters not being able to bother you here.

"It seems to me," she said, "that you and the wand probably came to this world at the same time, but not in the same place. It's interesting, isn't it, how you started out wandering but you wound up here, where the wand has been all this time. Maybe it's not just a coincidence that both of us ended up in Verek's cursed woodland. And we both found him keeping things that might have belonged to us where we used to live: my book and — maybe — your wand."

Carin's news threw the sprite into such a frenzy of sparking that she feared for the creature's safety. The sprite leaped from root to bole to branch of the rowan, then back again — all the while piping in its shrillest and most broken voice. Soothing it as best she could, gently stroking the rowan's trunk, Carin managed to make the creature stay still enough that she could understand what it was saying.

"My friend!" the sprite gasped. "I beg you to help me. You must bring me the wand so that I may see and feel it. You must help me to discover whether it truly is a piece of my homeworld. I wish to leap within its heart. I want to press myself into every pore of it. Please, dear girl — you *must* bring it to me!"

"I'm not sure I can do that," Carin replied, alarmed by both the creature's frenzy and its request. "Verek has it locked away with his liquor — which tells you how much he values it. He's already got me down for a thief. If I broke into the cabinet and stole the wand … I don't even like to imagine what he'd do to me. You know how bruised he left me, the last time he caught me stealing from him."

Out of the rowan came a whine like a lost litter of puppies crying for comfort.

"Do help me!" the sprite pleaded. "If you cannot bring the wand to me, then carry me to it. I'll leap into a sprig so small that you may put it in your pocket and take me to the treasure. Please, Carin! I beg you to not deny me this."

The sprite's second plan was better than its first one, Carin thought. But even so, the venture would have its dangers.

"All right," she said, and patted the rowan's trunk. "Maybe I can take you to the wand, if I can sneak you into the library in a twig that's too small for anyone to notice. But remember what Verek said. He threatened to 'use you for tinder and laugh as you burn' if he ever catches you. So if we're going to do this, we've got to be sure that warlock is out of the house and not coming back for a while. I won't risk your life, sprite."

She gave the rowan a final pat. "I have to go. And you have to be patient. The next time you see Verek riding off into the woods, wait for me here. If I'm sure that we'll have enough time while he's away, then I'll take you to see the wand."

Carin slipped past the tree and shut the tottering scrap of a door. In the great hall, she retrieved the broom. Carrying the book, knife, and yew limb also, she ran up the steps to the balcony. Along its back wall, in a dark alcove, she hid the knife and the cut branch. Then she made her way back through the dusty corridor and the double doors, to return to the wing where life kept a foothold in this crumbling mausoleum of wizardry.

At the door to her bedroom, Carin slowed and checked her clothes for tell-tale signs of her afternoon's errand in the garden grown wild. The breeches Myra had made for her and the shirt borrowed from Verek were still respectably clean. But the damp leaves and catkins that clung to them, and the resin staining her hands, would inform even a casual glance that she had been outdoors. Better to rid herself of the evidence and stop any questions before they were asked.

In her quarters, Carin whisked off the plant debris, cleaned her hands, and brushed her hair. When she had made herself presentable enough for kitchen duty, she retrieved the borrowed broom and went downstairs.

Myra was tending a pot of poultry and veal, slicing bread with which to thicken the broth. "Here you are, dearie!" she exclaimed as Carin entered. "Done with your nap and standing before me fresh-faced and rosy-cheeked, with hardly a hurt to show for that folly in the stable. The master's medicines work their good for foolish heads the same as for wise. Put aside that broom, dearie—have you been tidying your room?—and take this knife, and trim the crust from all this yesterday's bread. I'm glad to have you here at just this moment, for with your two hands and mine, we'll soon have the broth properly drawn and put to boil."

Carin put up the broom, glad for the housekeeper's ceaseless patter that made no reply necessary to the woman's question about the broom's use. While Carin trimmed the bread, Myra skillfully drew off the broth from the meat, tipping the heavy kettle on its iron pot-hanger so the hot liquid poured without splashing into a second kettle. Carin put the bread to soak in the broth, then helped the cook crush a large bunch of parsley in a mortar. When the bread had soaked up most of the liquid, Myra pounded the parsley and a handful of other spices into it, then put the mixture through a strainer. Adding wine, she returned the seasoned and thickened broth to the pot and put it back on the fire to simmer.

And all the while, Myra talked: of yesterday's storm, and of Carin's red, rain-soaked kirtle—"Dearie, the master dyer of Fintan shall have my thanks for a fine bit of cloth; 'twas soaked through but the color held as rich and true as when it left the vat." Most especially, Myra talked of Carin's foolishness in going out in such weather, while wearing her best.

Carin submitted tight-lipped to the scolding, and grabbed her chance when the housekeeper paused to stir up the fire.

"I noticed that Jerold hasn't come after his oilskin," she said, and pointed. "It's still hanging by the door. If you don't need me anymore just now, Myra, I'll take it out to him. We could get another storm any day, and he might get soaked without it."

"It would do the old goat good," Myra said, "to be caught in the rain with no hood. Might soften him up, as a pot of fair broth will soften a loaf that's gone hard and dry. But you've a good heart, child, and I'll not stop you doing what you think you ought. So go on now, and run your errand. A boiled salad is all that's needed to finish this meal, and I've my own two hands for chopping spinach. And with them also," Myra added, more to herself than to Carin, "I'll put in a good handful of currants for savor."

Carin's throat tightened at the housekeeper's mention of currants. After her morning with Verek, drinking currant-flavored liquor with him—and wondering with each sip why the Jabberwock's proven abilities as a killer would delight the warlock—she never wanted to taste those tart fruits again.

She draped Jerold's oilskin over her arm and left the kitchen through the side way. The yard felt almost firm underfoot. The day's bright sun had dried the quagmire more thoroughly than Carin would have thought possible in such a short time. Only scattered pockets of mud remained to catch a careless step.

As she paused on a dry mound halfway out to the stable, Carin scanned the grounds for some sign of Jerold—or of Lanse. Though Verek had warned the stableboy of dire consequences if he hurt her again, Carin wasn't sure the threatened punishments would stop Lanse. He might choose to remove his "rival" first, then seek his master's forgiveness afterward. Lanse had served the warlock much longer—and much more willingly—than Carin had. If loyalty counted for anything with Verek, he might show his stableboy more leniency than his heated words from yesterday suggested.

Carin remembered how Lanse had stood up to Verek, straight-backed and self-assured. If the boy had felt fear, some hint of it would have shown in his hazel eyes. She'd seen nothing there but anger and defiance.

Forget Lanse, Carin told herself. *He won't help you. You need Jerold.*

The old gardener apparently had no reason to be afraid of Verek. Though he worked and lived in the warlock's household, Jerold was clearly not a servant. When the grumpy elf stopped Verek from lending Carin his own rain-cloak, Jerold's manner had had nothing of the "craving m'lord's pardon" or "by m'lord's leave" about it. What was it he'd said? "No point you taking a soaking, Theil." *Theil* — a name spoken familiarly, as an equal might speak it.

With eyes as restless as her thoughts, Carin searched the stableyard but saw nothing of either Jerold or Lanse. Hiking the oilskin up to her shoulder, she went around the back of the stable and silently approached the cut in the hedge that opened to the hidden orchard beyond.

Jerold was there. High on a rickety ladder, the old man was harvesting by the setting sun's last light what few apples remained on the trees after yesterday's storm. On the ground were several baskets full of dirty fruit — the bulk of the crop, salvaged from the mud into which torrential rains and winds had dumped it.

Carin approached cautiously and stopped at a discreet distance from Jerold's ladder. The wisp of a gardener, working on in silence, ignored her. Soon he filled the basket that teetered on the ladder's top rung. He started to climb down with it.

"Be careful, Mister Jerold!" Carin exclaimed, alarmed into speaking first. Basket, ladder, and white-haired elf all seemed in imminent danger of tumbling to the ground. She rushed to the ladder. "Let me help you."

"Much obliged," Jerold growled. He sounded more peeved than grateful. But he didn't take another step down the rungs until Carin had draped his cloak over a handy tree limb, then stationed herself to brace him.

Jerold descended far enough that he could lower his apple basket to Carin's hands. No word passed between them as she set it on the ground, found an empty basket, and handed it up to him. Then she steadied the ladder again while he climbed into the tree's upper branches to pick the last of the fruit.

This time when Jerold descended partway, he handed Carin a half-full basket. When she had put it with the others and resumed her post, the old man clambered the rest of the way down.

Carin let go of the ladder then, and stood looking at him through its rungs. They framed his thin, wrinkled face in an odd portrait.

"I'm obliged," Jerold muttered, though he looked and sounded disapproving.

Take heart, Carin told herself with forced cheerfulness. *If the old elf petrifies you the way he did Emrys, who'll help him put up all these apples?*

She smiled at him. "I'm glad I found you, Mister Jerold. I wanted to return your raincoat." She retrieved the oilskin from the tree limb and held it out to him. "Thank you for letting me use it."

Jerold lifted his chin and jerked his head toward the stable. "I'll be wanting that put back where it was, missy."

He turned from her and stacked one apple basket atop another. Awkwardly lifting the double load, he shuffled to the cut in the hedge and disappeared through it, not speaking another word.

Carin sighed. She draped the cloak around her neck to free her hands, picked up a basket, and followed. Though Jerold hardly seemed to want her help, offering it gave her a reason to be around him. She still nursed hopes of making the gardener her ally. Lanse, she knew for an implacable enemy. Verek, she suspected of plotting something diabolical for her and "her" dragon. If there was a friend to be found among the men of this odd household, it would have to be the old elf.

She got to the back of the stable just as Jerold emerged, now empty-handed, from the low store-shed that was set against the wall. With a curt nod, he reached for the basket she carried.

"Mister Jerold." Carin delayed him with the first thought that came to mind. "Emrys loves apples. I see a couple in this basket that are so bruised from the storm yesterday that they'll go bad fast. May I have them, please, for the mare?"

Jerold grunted, a sound that might as easily have meant "no" as "yes." But Carin took it for consent. She picked out the two apples and handed the rest to the gardener, not daring to hold him with another question.

As Jerold reemerged from the shed, however, Carin matched her steps to his and walked with him back toward the orchard. When he didn't shoo her away, she ventured further onto his turf.

"Your garden is beautiful, Mister Jerold. Myra says there's not another one like it in all of Ruain. She says you keep a garden where things grow even in the winter, and flowers bloom in the snow. She said there's magic in the garden. Would you tell me, please, what kind of magic can keep things from getting killed?"

Jerold stopped in his tracks, turned, and scowled at her.

"That old woman talks too much. I can't abide a talker." Grumbling, he walked on, leaving Carin to wonder if that was the only reply he would make.

But a few steps later, Jerold stopped again. Turning to her, he gave Carin an answer that only deepened the garden's mystery.

"'Tis the magic of life, missy," he snapped. "And when I die, it dies with me. Ask me no more," he growled as he disappeared through the cut in the hedge.

Carin obeyed. Leaving Jerold to bring in his crop alone, she walked back to the stable. She carried an apple in each hand and the old elf's cloak round her neck.

At the stable's entrance she paused, listening for any hint of Lanse's presence. Hearing none, she stepped inside. A railing near the doorway served to hold Emrys' two apples while Carin hung the cloak on the peg where Jerold kept it. Then she took the treats to the mare, and noticed as she passed their empty stalls the absence of both Brogar and Lanse's gelding.

Were the stableboy and his master out riding? Or were both horses with Lanse, as they had been on market-day when he had taken both of them to the village, tied to the wagon's tailboard?

Maybe it was Lanse's job to see that Verek's big hunter had exercise when the warlock didn't ride regularly.

"Whoa, horse," Carin murmured as Emrys stretched a sleek black neck between the rails of her stall to claim the apples. "You should eat these slowly and make them last. I can't promise that I'll ever bring you any more. The boy who takes care of you is my sworn enemy. Your master, that warlock Verek, has murder on his mind. One or the other of them could make sure that I'm not around to bring you apples. You ought to enjoy these while you can."

Her advice went unheeded. The mare finished off both apples almost before Carin had finished speaking. And as the sound of her voice died softly away, a noise came from the direction of the stable's wide doorway.

Carin whirled.

Two figures stood in the opening, silhouetted against a luminously twilit sky. Though matched in height, in build one was a willow to the other's oak. Both were armed. Beside each dusk-shrouded, featureless face rose the outline of a shouldered bow.

In the whole province of Ruain, there were only two who might want Carin dead. Both of them now stood before her.

Chapter 18

Visions

With a show of self-confidence that was entirely feigned, Carin trod toward the doorway where the two figures stood in the soft light of evening. Neither of them spoke, but both turned in her direction. Though she could not see their faces, the change in their outlined shapes told her they now stood looking into the shadows of the stable from which she would momentarily emerge.

"Good evening, Lord Verek," Carin said in her politest way as she approached the pair. She gave the stableboy no notice—not a word or a look.

Verek returned her courtesy but, mercifully, paid her no further attention. Turning back to Lanse, he said, "We'll resume the lesson on the morrow. Tonight, give thought to what I told you. To starve yourself profits no one."

Carin made to slip past the pair, keen to avoid them both. But as she crossed the threshold and stepped into the yard, and into an evening rapidly growing chilly, Verek fell into step beside her.

Two horses—Lanse's gelding and the warlock's hunter—stood in the yard, sleepily awaiting the stableboy's attentions. As Carin and Verek walked by, Brogar nickered and stretched to nuzzle the warlock's shoulder. He paused to scratch the horse's forehead, then rejoined Carin and walked with her toward the kitchen door.

"I had almost forgotten how much simpler the world looks," Verek said, "when one is sighting down the shaft of an arrow from the back of a good horse. Things come into focus.

"I will need you again this evening," he added as they reached the door and he pushed it open for her. "You must join me in the library, to read again from the looking-glass book. I was too gone with *dhera* this morning to keep up with the story. Tedious though you may find it, I will require you to reread the events that follow the footsteps thumping through the 'garden of live flowers.' I remember nothing of the tale beyond the meeting of the girl Alice with the bantam queen who had grown half a head taller than Alice herself."

Carin mumbled assent, but her words were lost in Myra's cheery greeting.

"Here you are, my lord!" the housekeeper exclaimed. "And my fair helper too, whose hands are quick with every task I set them. Make ready now, I pray you both, and in a twinkling the meal will be before you."

Verek unshouldered his bow and leaned it against the wall. He shed his coat, rolled up his shirtsleeves, and crossed to the kitchen's hand-pump to scrub at the basin. Carin followed his example rather than climb the stairs to her bathing room. Meat, broth, and salad were on the table, as Myra had promised, by the time both had washed the horse off their hands.

In her weariless way, the housekeeper supplied most of the dinner-table conversation. From Verek's few comments, however, Carin gathered that the warlock—after rousing from his somewhat intoxicated stupor—had spent the afternoon testing Lanse's bow arm. While the boy's technique was sound, in stamina he was lacking; hence Verek's parting admonition about Lanse's unwise effort to starve himself.

"Oh my! The foolish boy!" Myra exclaimed at this news. "So he'll go hungry, will he, before he'll come again to this table for his meals? We'll see about that, we will!" Falling atypically silent, the woman heaped chunks of chicken and veal into a bowl and drowned them with broth. On a serving dish she piled a generous helping of salad. So forgetting herself that she failed to ask her master's leave, Myra marched to the side door, a dish in each hand, and disappeared into the dusk.

"Good," Verek muttered, more to himself than to Carin. "The cub's not been born who can defy that mother bear."

After Myra's departure, the two ate in silence. Verek devoted his attention to his plate like a man who had slept through his midday meal. Carin, finishing first, sat quietly and watched him.

Myra hadn't yet returned when the warlock, with a satisfied sigh, pushed away from the table. He stood, and motioned for Carin to join him. Down the dark passageway and hall she followed him to the firelit library. Sometime that afternoon, while Verek was coaching Lanse and Carin was scheming with the woodsprite, the capable Myra had kindled a fire in the room.

Few words passed between Carin and her captor for the rest of the evening, except those of the looking-glass book as she resumed her reading, by the sorcerer's conjured witchlight. Two chapters later, and two verses into the long rhyme called *"The Walrus and the Carpenter,"* Verek stopped her, declaring her evening's effort satisfactory and himself better able to appreciate poetry after a night's sleep. Leaving her to her own devices, he disappeared into the library's perpetual shadows.

Carin wandered back to the kitchen to find the dishes cleared and Myra sitting by the hearth. A needle flashed as the housekeeper mended a tear in a faded pair of pants — Lanse's, to judge by the slimness of the long legs.

Let's not talk about him, Carin thought. *Let's talk about something interesting*—like Jerold and his enchanted garden.

"Myra," she began, "when I saw Jerold today I asked him what keeps his garden green all fall and winter. He told me it's the 'magic of life.' And he said it would die with him."

Carin leaned forward. "That reminded me of something you mentioned when you were first telling me about the garden. You said there's magic in it 'still.' So I've been wondering about the seeds of enchantment, how and when they were planted in Jerold's garden. What does he mean by the 'magic of life'? And about the garden dying when he does? — Which won't be any-time soon, I hope. But Myra, does Jerold really give the garden its life? Does he have that kind of power, to stop it from dying in the winter? I'm beginning to think Jerold may work magic that's as strong as Lord Verek's."

The housekeeper let her mending rest idly in her lap. She stared into the flickering fire with eyes that looked backward in time, as though she saw an almost forgotten past. For a time she was silent. But then Myra turned to Carin and spoke, with an air of gravity that seemed misplaced in one who was generally light-hearted.

"Nay, dearie," she murmured. "Jerold's skill in the *art magik* is to my good master's as a fine mist to a driving rain. He has a gift but slight. Though both learned at the knee of the same teacher, they were years and leagues apart. Jerold as a young man had got all he could of the craft, before my good master had begun *his* studies while yet a boy.

"You know, don't you, dearie," Myra added, "that Jerold is of an age to be my master's father? Aye. He was born in the same year as my master's sire. Jerold came to this household as a lad apprenticed in wizardry to old Lord Legary."

Leg-a-ree. Carin rolled the unfamiliar name around in her thoughts. "Excuse me if I sound foolish," she said. "But coming from southward, I don't know about the noble families who own the land in the north. Who is Lord Legary?"

"To be sure, dearie," Myra replied, "you wouldn't know of him. The old lord was my master's grandsire. He taught young Jerold all the magic an artless lad could learn. And after Jerold, he schooled my clever master in the craft for a score of years, from infancy to manhood — and glad the old lord was, I tell you, child, to have a pupil as quick as my master proved to be."

Myra picked up her needle and resumed her work, as though unwilling to add the crime of idleness to her weakness for talk.

"Now there was a wizard beyond compare!" she murmured. "Lord Legary could make the snow to fall and the fog to creep over the land so deep 'twould bury mountains. He conjured visions and told the meanings of dreams, and cured ills grievous and mortal. On the battlefield he could raise a mist, and in it make one man seem like a hundred. He could enchant the trees and stones so that they became a host and routed his enemies."

A master wizard – absolutely! Carin thought. Could this be the master magician who awed Verek?

"Where's Lord Legary now?" she asked. "Is he still in Ruain?"

"Nay, dearie." Myra shook her head sadly. "The old lord has been dead these twenty years. He died on an autumn night as chill as this, not six months after my master's lady and their dear little son drowned in the lake. Though he was past eighty, still he was a vigorous and powerful man. Wizards live long. Eighty is the prime of life, the very pinnacle of strength for those who are filled with the *art magik*. We never had a thought that his time had come." Myra sighed heavily. "But 'tis not in the natural way of things for a man to outlive his children. Already he had lost a son. Then to see the bodies of his grandson's young wife and his great-grandbaby laid on the funeral bier … 'twas more than his brave heart could stand."

For a time both were silent, the housekeeper intent on her needlework and Carin giving careful consideration to her next question. This household's history was tragic enough to make even Myra dole out the details charily. The picture that was emerging, however, discouraged Carin from pinning much hope on Jerold. The old elf's "life magic" – his seeming ability to ward off death – did not appear to extend beyond garden plants.

She thought it through. Lord Legary could not be the "master wizard" who made the whirls that had brought Carin and the woodsprite to Ladrehdin. He had died years ago, soon after the drownings, apparently overcome with grief. The drownings had driven a maddened Verek to lay a curse on the woodland, so

Myra had told her earlier. The "life magic" must have been in Jerold's garden then, to save it from the desolation that blighted the woods.

But magic that could keep plants alive was evidently not enough to save a family of wizards, since all of them—except the one—were dead now.

"Myra," Carin said gently, "I'm glad you told me about Lord Verek's grandfather. It helps me understand Verek better, I think, knowing about his family … especially what you said about how deeply he loved his little boy. But I'm wondering how Lord Verek lost his father too. What happened? Can you tell me that?"

Myra nodded, and again she let her hands fall idle as she stared into the fire.

"I'll tell you all I know, child, for it's a tale that can be told in a twinkling. The lad's name was Hugh. He married at eighteen, fathered my good master at nineteen, and was dead within the year. It fell to Lord Legary to be both grandfather and father to my master. A babe not yet seven months old could hardly be remembering a sire who was nothing to him but a name—a name writ in black on a leaf of the holy *Drishanna* where they write the births and deaths and marriages of all the family. Aye, dearie. The old lord, though he be grandfather, was all the father my good master ever knew."

But what about Verek's mother? Carin wondered. *Did he have one?* Try as she might, she couldn't picture the lean-faced warlock as an infant in his crib or suckling at the breast of a young mother. But Myra had mentioned a marriage, so there must have been a bride.

"That's sad about Hugh dying so young," Carin said. "He must have left a young widow. It was hard on her, I'm sure, to lose her husband and have to raise their baby alone. Well, not completely alone, if she had the grandfather, Legary, to help her. But still, she couldn't have had it easy."

Myra put aside her mending and rose from her seat at the fire.

"I can't say, dearie," she muttered, and busied herself with setting the table for tomorrow's breakfast. "I hadn't come to service in this household then, when my good master was but a babe. 'Twas not to be until the boy's tenth year that I took the post of housekeeper to Lord Legary. And by that time, my master's father was dust in the tomb, and the widow no longer lived under this roof. What became of her was a mystery then, and 'tis a mystery still. I never asked. 'Twas enough for me to do the old lord's bidding and watch the young master grow into the fine man that he's become—a wise man and a healer, so like his noble grandsire."

Carin saw, with an uneasy feeling, that Myra's eyes refused to meet hers. The housekeeper paused, empty serving-platter in hand, to stare past Carin into the fire. Then she plunked the platter down and turned for the door to her bedroom.

"'Tis late, child," she said, still avoiding Carin's gaze. "It's time I took these old bones to bed. You be up with the sun, or you'll hear me tapping at your door. There's work enough to be done in this house that we needn't go back two-score years to find aught to occupy ourselves."

The door to Myra's room shut solidly, leaving Carin in no doubt that their conversation was equally closed.

She sighed. Again she had gained two new questions for every one answered. Now she understood more clearly Jerold's place in Verek's household. Both were sorcerers. The powerful younger wizard showed his weaker elder a polite respect—as much in deference to Jerold's age and long affiliation with the family, Carin guessed, as out of regard for his presumably slight mastery of magic.

But now, Carin found herself acutely concerned with Lord Verek's parentage—a subject that had in no way interested her before tonight's talk with Myra. Who was Verek's mother? Where was the lady now? Was she still living, or was she in the tomb with every other member of the warlock's star-crossed family? Not one of them had made it to a ripe old age—not by wizardly standards, anyway. According to Myra, Verek's grandfather had died in his prime. His father had perished before reaching his majority. Verek's wife and son had also died young. Carin shuddered at the memory of their macabre images, sculpted from the waters of the magic pool, floating like dead fish over the warlock's head.

Why was Myra so reluctant to talk about her master's missing dam? That the housekeeper knew more than she was telling, Carin didn't doubt. On such an open countenance as Myra's, the struggle to hide a secret was plainly written. What was there about Verek's mother that Myra thought Carin shouldn't know?

Shaking her head in frustration, she climbed the stairs to her bedroom. When she had shut the door behind her, Carin eyed the room's furnishings, looking for some way to block the door against the murder-minded Verek. She wrestled the small table into place, wedging it under the latch, and loaded it with unlit lamps from Myra's multitude. Any attempt to force the door would send the lamps crashing, and wake Carin from the soundest sleep.

Lying in bed with her eyes shut, she tried not to think of the many deaths—past and future—that were linked to this household. But they haunted her.

As she drifted off, Carin's dreams brought an image of a windowless stone tomb. She seemed to stand in its arched doorway. On the keystone above her head was chiseled the name "Verek."

Looking first to the left, Carin saw a crypt inscribed "Legary." On the wall-crypt to her right was the name "Hugh."

Directly in front of her was a double chamber. It was adorned with the deeply carved images of a crescent moon and a radiant sun. One of the paired vaults bore the name "Alesia." Overlapping that vault and the other was a tablet of white bronze. Upon the tablet was inscribed the name "Aidan" and the joined sun-moon symbol that Carin had seen at her captor's throat on the day he found her in his woodland. Into the stone of the vault touching Alesia's was cut the name "Theil."

Even asleep—if, in fact, she was asleep—Carin could recognize the family tomb of the House of Verek. Did she see it as it was now, with the current lord's grandfather, father, wife and child buried within, and only the warlock's own vault empty ... awaiting the corpse for which it had been prepared? Or did she see it as it would be in the future, when all the crypts had received their eternal occupants?

A roar sounded behind her. Carin turned with the slowness of a flower unfurling its petals. In her dream state, time crawled. When at last her back was to the tomb and she faced the direction from which the roar had come, she saw the dragon of the puzzle-book ripping apart a woman's body.

Blood dripped from the monster's talons and fangs. The woman's mutilated limbs disappeared down the dragon's maw ... first an arm twisted violently from the shoulder socket, then a leg sliced off as easily as if it had been the succulent root of a *paelgra* bush.

Carin's scream put the vision to flight. But even as she sat bolt upright in bed, pushing away the sweat-soaked linens and panting for breath, she knew hope for her own survival. The woman in her nightmare, the woman the dragon tore apart, had not been auburn-haired like Carin. The victim's hair was long, straight, and crow-black—in both texture and color, quite like Theil Verek's.

* * *

Morning came, and the warlock's promise held. He did not ask her again to summon the dragon to the wizards' well. In fact, Carin hardly saw Lord Verek for the rest of that week and most

271

of the next one, except in the evenings when he had her read to him from the puzzle-book.

Carin's days took on a pattern that began to feel almost comfortable in its familiarity. Each morning she assaulted the chaos in the sorcerer's library, slowly bringing order to the jumbled books. At midday, Myra called her to an always excellent meal. Mostly they ate alone, though occasionally the master of the house joined them at the table. Never did Jerold or Lanse make an appearance. Whatever Myra or Verek had said to the stable-boy, it hadn't persuaded him to drop his self-defeating hunger protest against his rival.

Afternoons began with exercising the mare, always within the confines of the manor's encircling stone wall. While prowling the grounds, Carin realized that the urge which had kept her walking over miles of grassland and high into Verek's woods had entirely left her. Verek's statement that "You've come as far north as you can" had wormed its way in, supplanting Megella's long-ago injunction to "Go north, girl." Had Carin won her freedom now, she would not know which direction to turn.

Even so, she searched for ways over or through the wall. But she found none.

When her daily session with Emrys was done, she stole away to the abandoned great hall to work on her new weapon. Guided by the archery book and using a hand adze "borrowed" from Jerold's woods-tools, Carin shaped a serviceable bowstave from the yew limb that the woodsprite had helped her get. She strung it with catgut stolen from Myra's mending chest. She made a half-dozen crude arrows from straight, sharpened stems of hazel, and fletched them with the pinion feathers of a goose that had given its all to one of Myra's finest meals. From a scrap of leather, she fashioned a guard to protect her wrist against the slap of the bowstring.

A torn pillowcase thieved from the housekeeper's mending basket and stuffed with hay made an excellent target. Carin hung it on a wall of the long-deserted banquet hall, near the servants' entrance where she could talk to the woodsprite and the creature could watch her practice from the safety of its rowan tree.

Excited though the sprite had been at the prospect of making a new friend in Myra, the creature had never worked up the courage to approach the housekeeper. Myra was seldom outdoors alone, and the sprite had enough discretion not to speak to the woman when Jerold or Verek was present. Their hostility toward the sprite would have poisoned the woman against the creature. The one time, however, when the woodsprite found Myra out of her kitchen and alone in the outdoors, the gray-haired matron had been pulling up weeds with such a passionate zeal for their destruction that the creature's nerve failed it.

"The woman was *ripping* the soft little mites up by their roots!" the woodsprite told Carin, its distress obvious. "She threw the poor things onto a bonfire to burn while still green. The last juices of sap-filled life had not left their veins. It was foolish of me, I suppose, to be so horrified at the savaging of mere *weeds*; a weed isn't a tree, after all. But a weed isn't so *very* different from a sapling that I couldn't be moved to pity for the woman's victims."

Half sickened by the stench of burning foliage, the sprite had forfeited its opportunity to make the housekeeper's acquaintance. And so Carin remained the creature's only friend in Ladrehdin, and the sprite joined her each afternoon to encourage her attempts to master the bow.

The two of them went sometimes to the enormous oak that breached the wall beyond the main wing of the house. Carin tried lofting her arrows into the tree's steeple-high canopy. If she could put a shot over a limb, the arrow might be equipped to trail a string behind it; a dangling string might be used to hoist a rope over the limb; with a rope to climb into the oak's crown, she might get over the wall and down the other side.

But all her arrows fell back as though they struck a springy but impenetrable, invisible barrier. They didn't carom from a hard surface but returned along graceful, not at all natural, arcs.

The woodsprite noticed their odd trajectories. "Give me a moment," the creature said to stop Carin's shooting. It sparked up the tree's trunk and disappeared among the branches high above her head.

Presently the sprite was back on Carin's level, and making a puzzled report.

"I see nothing among the limbs that might send your arrows along such curious paths. But when I try to leap from limb to limb, I cannot advance any better than the arrows do. There seems to be a skin of sorts. It's stretched between the branches like the wing-skin of a huge bat in unseen flight. It is not of the tree's flesh, I'm certain, or I could enter it the same as I press myself within a leaf. Nothing more can I make of it, except that it's very strong. There is something in the crown of this giant oak that I have not encountered in any other tree."

Carin was not terribly surprised. The oak that chinked the wall had been her best hope for making her escape. Of course Verek would know about the imperfection in his defenses, and he would secure it. Or maybe the magic was older than that—as old as the oak itself. The tree had breached the wall centuries ago. Maybe it was Verek's ancestors who had webbed a spell like bat-wings through the oak's branches. Whether it was new magic or old, it was effective.

Wondering what the woodsprite would make of her own new "talent" as a conjurer, Carin eventually told the sprite how she'd summoned the Jabberwock to the wizards' well. She spoke of her flight through a driving rain to reach the supposed safety of the stable, only to be greeted there by Lanse's fist.

The sprite was appalled, not by the bloodthirsty dragon Carin had conjured, but by Lanse.

"I can't bear it!" the creature shrilled. "The thought of that youth raising a hand to you has me quivering with rage."

It was true. Carin felt a tremble in the tree trunk under her fingers.

"I promise you the boy's crime will not go unpunished," the sprite fumed. "I'll put myself in a tree above his usual path through the woods, and as soon as my chance comes I'll make a great bough fall and crack open his worthless head!"

With effort, Carin persuaded the sprite to restrain itself—at least for now. She was encouraged, though, to think that the creature could be capable of killing. Though its range as a weapon was limited—the intended victim had to pass under the sprite's tree—having it and her bow in reserve made Carin feel less powerless against Verek and the forces that swirled around him.

After practicing with her bow, then helping Myra with the evening meal, Carin spent the close of each day in the library, reading the puzzle-book to Verek. To her surprise, the warlock didn't seem at all disappointed when she reached the book's twelfth and final chapter, which revealed the whole affair to have been only a child's dream. Instead, Verek had her read again those snippets that he seemed especially to like, including the poem *"The Walrus and the Carpenter"* from the fourth chapter.

Carin wondered, as she reread the rhyme, why it appealed to Verek. Remembering the badge at his throat, she thought he must appreciate the verse about the sun shining in the night while the moon sulked:

> *"Because she thought the sun*
> *Had got no business to be there*
> *After the day was done—"*

For herself, Carin liked the imagery of the sandy seashore where the poem was set. But why that should draw her, she couldn't say. There were no sandy beaches in Verek's woods, or on the southern plains that Carin had crossed to reach Ruain.

One happy fact about *"The Walrus and the Carpenter"* was that she could translate it word for word. Every term in the other-worldly rhyme had a match in the language of Ladrehdin. In reading the poem to Verek, Carin never had to substitute a Lad-rehdinian word that conveyed a meaning close to, but not exactly the same as, the sense of the puzzle-book term.

She wasn't so lucky with another of Verek's favorites from the book: Alice's provoking of Humpty Dumpty the egg-man, in the sixth chapter. When Carin reread those pages to the warlock, she couldn't remember how she'd first translated the alien word *"cravat."* This time, when she gave it the meaning "scarf," Verek stopped her and complained that she'd said "neck ribbon" before.

This led Carin to make a mumbled confession: that, lacking a perfect mastery of either the puzzle-book's language or the tongue of Ladrehdin, she had given him only a rough translation of some passages from the book.

Verek threw up his hands, stalked to the liquor cabinet, and poured himself a stiff drink of the ruby-red *dhera*. After throwing it down—and evidently swallowing some of his displeasure with it—he tersely bade Carin to begin again, from the beginning, and reread the entire book to him. This time through, she was to tell him whenever she came to a word that might have more than one meaning—or no meaning at all—in the Ladrehdinian tongue. They would discuss the sense variations, and together decide the true and proper translation.

And while they were at it, Verek declared, they'd work out the moves of the "chess" problem that underlay the book's action. He hadn't recognized the game, at first, as having its par-allel in an ancient pastime from the west called *Tanod*. When "pawn" Alice reached "the Eighth Square," however, and found herself crowned, the warlock saw the similarities between Alice's living game of chess and the nearly forgotten Ladrehdin variant.

"It's a very old game," he told Carin, "not played here for centuries. Somewhere I have a game-board and a few pieces. They're little more than broken fragments, but perhaps they will add to your second reading of the 'chess' problem."

Thus speaking, he strode into the library's shadows and rummaged in a wooden chest, lit by one of his witchlight orbs. Verek's conjuring of the useful lights no longer startled Carin. She'd come to expect an orb's appearance whenever she or the warlock needed the illumination.

When he returned to their seats at the hearth, Verek carried a small, flat box. Its top was decorated with alternating squares of white and red. He tipped out the box's contents on the table between the benches, then set up the game-board. Consulting the puzzle-book, which had a drawing of a chessboard with eight pieces on it, he picked out tokens from the box's meager contents that resembled, in color and shape, those of the drawing. These he placed on the red and white squares to match the illustration.

Satisfied with his effort, Verek leaned back and gestured sharply at the book, indicating that Carin should take it up.

"Read," he ordered. "From the beginning. Omit nothing— except the incantation that calls the dragon. Invent nothing. Stop at any word that eludes your complete understanding."

Obeying this order kept Carin—and Verek—occupied for several evenings. They debated the Ladrehdinian translations of puzzle-book words from *"telegraph"* to *"Macassar-Oil."*

And although they talked much together, they did not grow more comfortable with each other. Verek often showed his temper, and he allowed no questions about any of the mysteries that bedeviled Carin: his plans for the puzzle-book dragon that only she could conjure ... the identity of the "master *wysard*" who could send uncanny whirlpools spinning between worlds ... why that blackheart had brought Carin here where she didn't belong ... what power kept winter's grip away from Jerold's garden and repelled the curse that deadened the woodland beyond

… and the newest puzzle of all, the name of Lord Verek's mother and what had become of that lady.

Myra was no further help. The housekeeper hardly paused for breath whenever she had Carin's company, but the woman never again touched on any of the subjects that Carin wanted her to talk about. In fact, Myra's endless prattle seemed designed to keep her helper from slipping a question in edgewise.

Jerold was even less cooperative. The old elf avoided Carin, although she tried to draw him out with a book of brightly painted flowers from Verek's library — the pictures "done up in glorious colors," as Myra had advised. One chilly but sunny afternoon, Carin took the book to the grassy lawn that edged Jerold's garden and sat looking at it for an hour. But the onetime sorcerer's apprentice didn't rise to the bait. And no amount of Carin's poking about the grounds could uncover the elf's hiding place. Jerold seemed determined to deny her any opening to ask him more about the "magic of life" that held sway in his enchanted garden.

On her twenty-first morning under Verek's roof, as Carin mounted a ladder to pull dusty books from one of the library's topmost shelves, she felt keenly vexed by her many unanswered questions.

"Why won't anyone in this house talk to me?" she muttered under her breath as she yanked an ironbound volume to the shelf's edge, then slid it onto her head. "Really talk, I mean. It's like everyone here is afraid of my questions. There's something they don't want me to find out."

Balancing the heavy volume with one hand while tensing neck muscles that were barely up to the task of supporting it, Carin descended with the book. When she had gained the floor and stood above the bench she called her own, she canted her head and let the volume fall.

"Agh!" What hit the bench's cushions wasn't a book, but a coiled, writhing mass of snakes. Two of the serpents sank their fangs into Carin's hand.

Even as she jerked away and ran for the hall door, a corner of her mind added this new mystery to all the others that troubled her. *How could a book transform itself into a nest of vipers?*

Chapter 19

The *Book of Archamon*

Her shrieks echoed down the passageway. Both Myra and Verek were on their feet when Carin burst into the kitchen.

"Look!" she gasped, thrusting her palm at Verek. "I'm snake-bitten! They were in a book. They *were* a book. I don't know where they came from. But they bit me. Sweet mercy, it *hurts!* Can you do something? Drisha almighty, my hand's on fire."

Verek stared. He took Carin's proffered hand and studied it. He turned it over to examine the back as well as the palm. Then he held it out to Myra's view.

"Tell her," he instructed his housekeeper. "Maybe she'll listen to you. The girl doubts every word I say."

Myra bustled over, wide-eyed, briefly struck dumb by the commotion. She took Carin's hand between her warm, pudgy palms, examined it as closely as Verek had, then raised wondering eyes to her master's.

"I think the lass has been struck out of her wits. Does she dream a waking dream? Or is it a vision she sees?"

Carin jerked her hand from Myra's grasp and cradled it against her body. The hot, throbbing pain was rapidly spreading up her arm. If Verek didn't soon produce a remedy—whether natural or magical—she might lose a limb to the venom.

"I can feel the poison in my blood!" she cried. "If either of you can make an antidote, then please hurry and do it. I need help!"

Verek looked at Myra, one eyebrow raised. Then he grasped Carin's shoulder on her uninjured side and steered her toward the passageway.

"Come," he said. "Show me these vipers that you've disturbed. I must know the species of venom if I am to prescribe a remedy."

280

Carin broke away from him and raced to the library. The war-lock followed on her heels. She half expected the snakes to have slithered off the bench and scattered about the room, hiding themselves in dark corners. But the serpents writhed on the cushions exactly where she'd dumped them.

Staying back near the desk, she pointed. "There! Right there."

Verek made straight for the bench. Before Carin could shout a warning, he had plunged his hands into the nest of snakes. He lifted the twisting coil.

And as he did so, the serpents reformed themselves into an ironbound book.

"The *Book of Archamon!*" Verek cried, alive with excitement. "You've found it! How? Where? Tell me!"

The warlock lugged the heavy volume to the desk and set it down. Carin drew back, confused. She cradled an arm that throbbed hotly.

"But—there were snakes! They bit me, and it hurts *really bad.*"

Verek reached for her so quickly that Carin could not elude him. He caught her wounded hand and pulled her to the desk. Firmly he pried open the fingers that she clenched in pain. His hand felt cool as it pressed hers flat to the book, his palm cover-ing her nails, his long fingers reaching to the back of her wrist.

Her pain subsided. The fire no longer swept up her arm. When Verek lifted his hand from atop hers and Carin jerked her palm off the book, she found no trace of an injury. The angry redness had faded away.

"Magic," she muttered as understanding dawned.

The warlock nodded. "A spell … laid on the book to ward off the touch of the unbidden."

Verek opened the top cover to reveal a brightly inked frontis-piece of no definite design. At least, Carin could see no pattern in its random lines and colors. But as Verek paged through the volume, she began to suspect that more sorcery hid the book's contents from her view. Frequently the warlock paused in his skimming and studied a few lines, one blunt-nailed forefinger ranging over the page as if to pin down what the text told him. Carin, however, could see only jumbled letters and meaningless marks.

If she concentrated on any section, looking for characters to make sense, the indecipherable text seemed actually to *move*. Like a troupe of tiny stick-insects and long-legged water striders, the marks whirled and gyrated across the page until, dizzied by their acrobatics, Carin had to avert her gaze. When she looked back, the characters were still. Their motion—like the writhing of the spectral "snakes"—was a magical illusion.

"Where did you find this book?" Verek asked again, looking up from it. "It's not been seen in this house in twenty years."

"There, sir." Carin pointed out the high shelf from which she had pulled it. And as she looked up at the empty ledge, she recoiled. Earlier, distracted by her thoughts of the morning, she hadn't noticed how near to the shadows she worked. Her ladder was leaning against a bookcase not an arm's length from the gloom that lay like black smoke over the library's recesses.

While she stared, the edge of the darkness crept nearer the windows. Then it paused, and gradually drifted in the opposite direction, toward the hidden door to the cave of magic. As she watched the black pall undulate with funereal sluggishness over the shelves, Carin realized that the space from which she'd taken the enchanted volume could have been cloaked in shadows only a day—or an hour—earlier.

Verek seemed to think the same thought.

"A fortunate happenstance," he said, "that you should choose to clear *that* shelf, when so many others await your labors. Tell me: was the book plain to view? Or did it have the aspect of something deliberately hidden?"

"It was hidden," Carin replied, nodding. "If the morning hadn't been sunny, and if the light hadn't hit the shelves just right, I probably wouldn't have seen it. The book was lying flat, and it was pushed way back. It looked lost."

"It *was* lost," Verek said. "Or mislaid, when my grandfather died. It's a book more ancient than this house, and filled with the wisdom of generations of *wysards*. My grandfather taught me from this book. I lamented its disappearance. I now delight in its recovery."

Verek lifted the opened book with both hands, hefting it, and set it down quickly. "It weighs no less than I remember. How did you manage to get it down without breaking your neck or some part of the furnishings below?"

Carin let a little pride show as she described her method, worked out over a fortnight of book-sorting, of sliding the heaviest volumes onto her head, then balancing the load with one hand while the other steadied her descent down the ladder.

The warlock shook his head and placed both hands on his hips in an attitude of disapproval.

"Such folly is hard to excuse," he snapped. "Didn't I tell you, a week ago or more, to call me to any task in this library that is beyond a young woman's strength? I am better employed — I assure you — in shifting these books than in mending your bones."

Carin couldn't think of a reply that wouldn't add to Verek's irritation, so she only nodded. Then she turned away and resumed the endless job of sorting and stacking.

But while she worked, she cast frequent sidelong glances at Verek as he sat at the desk, bent over his book. Twenty minutes of observing the warlock's absorption in the volume made Carin wish for the chance to study it herself. Full of the wisdom of wizards, Verek had said it was. Maybe that book named the master blackheart and explained the magic that had spirited Carin and the woodsprite from their natural homes to this …

She didn't finish the thought. The groan that escaped Verek's lips arrested her utterly. It seemed to come less from his body than from a fissure in his soul. The sound of it stopped her breath, it conveyed such a depth of sorrow.

Carin dropped the books she was sorting and took a step toward the warlock. Verek's forehead rested on the desk on one arm. His other arm fell across the back of his skull as if to ward off a blow from behind. His shoulders shook with the force of his emotion.

Confronted by such an extremity of distress, Carin hesitated. What could she say to Verek? How could she presume to comfort him, when she had no idea what had brought on his sudden anguish?

And why are you feeling sympathetic toward your captor anyway? wondered the voice of cool reason as it checked her first impulse of concern for the man across from her.

Verek jerked his head up and shoved back from the desk. He lunged to his feet and made for the room's shadowed recesses. As he stumbled past her, Carin glimpsed his face. She didn't think it could have expressed a deeper pain if he'd been lying disemboweled on some mad priest's sacrificial altar.

He disappeared into the shadows. The hidden door creaked sharply on its hinges and thudded shut.

Stunned by the intensity of Verek's grief and the speed of its onslaught, for a moment Carin could only stand and stare after him. Then she walked to the desk and looked down at the over-sized, iron-wrapped *Book of Archamon*. What had Verek read in its bespelled pages to cause him such torment?

With a start, Carin realized that the right-hand page — of the two facing leaves to which the book lay open — held words she could read. The left-hand leaf was a riot of marks without meaning. But whatever enchantment shielded it from her view did not lie upon the right-hand page.

Carin fingered a corner of that page, tensing to jerk her hand away if the book reformed itself into a nest of vipers. A book, however, it remained.

She thumbed through its few remaining leaves. All were blank. The legible page was the last entry.

From a drawer of the desk, Carin took two sheets of Verek's fine linen writing-paper. With these she covered the unreadable left-hand page. Deciphering the spidery handwriting that slanted across the facing leaf would be hard enough without the added distraction in the corner of her eye of the weirdly uneasy letters that seemed to shiver across the opposite page.

Carin settled into the chair that was still warm from Verek having occupied it. She studied the thin, infirm handwriting. The date on the page was twenty years past. The signature alongside the date read "Legary."

What had Myra said? "The old lord has been dead these twenty years." Judging by the state of the handwriting, Legary had been on his deathbed when he made this final entry in the *Book of Archamon*. It seemed to be a lay—a narrative poem something like the verses in the puzzle-book, although lacking their rhythmic, rhyming qualities.

Barely had Carin made out the date and the authorship when the name "Alesia" jumped out at her from the text, as boldly as if written in blood. *Alesia*. It was a name from her nightmare—a name on a vault in the family tomb of House Verek.

"First I dream about it, and *then* I find it in a book of magic?" Carin whispered, the hairs rising on her arms. "How's that possible? What's happening to me in this wizards' lair?"

Suppressing a shudder, Carin made herself ignore the implications and bent to the task of deciphering the unsteady hand. On a third sheet of paper from the desk, she carefully copied each line as she puzzled out the archaic language:

> *"The evil toucheth not this child!"*
> *I rejoiced in the knowledge of it.*
> *I cried it from the turrets,*
> *I declared it from the treetops.*

The blood of my son's blood is clean!
The evil that slew the first
And tainted the second
Hath no power over the third.

The raven heard my shouts of joy;
The black raven carried my news abroad.
Of my happiness, the enchantress did learn;
All my joy, the sorceress did blight.

From weak seed, and flawed,
Sprang innocent youth.
From the womb of guiltless Alesia
Came the child of shining spirit.

To the lake of the lilies walked mother and child;
From waters ensorcelled came never they home.
Dead was the first by guileful craft;
Dead was the third by blackest art.

The second—the troubled, the tainted seed—
Vented wild rage upon the living wood.
Dead and barren, as his heart within,
Left he the woodland with fury spent.

"Stop him!" shrieked the man of the green.
"Wilt thou suffer the spread of his venom
O'er all the Land of Ruain, and the blighting
Of all bright flowers within thy vast domain?"

"Stop him!" I cried to the four winds.
"Halt this furious plague.
Stem the life-force's ebbing;
Let not the curse prevail!"

The winds took heed:
An edge was made.
Within these walls and past the wood
The poison floweth not.

But I have paid the dearest price
To invoke the forces primal;
They draw me now into the tomb,
Where lie the first son and the third.

My crimes are great, my penance vast;
What punishment can harm me now?
The lad is slain, the infant drowned;
The tainted seed is future's hope.

By the oath of my House, I command thee:
Touch him not, Morann!

Carin's hand faltered over the final line. She guessed that Lord Legary's pen must have shook badly as he reached the end of his narrative; the script of the last ink-blotched stanzas was as jagged as saw teeth. He had trembled from exhaustion, but also from heartsickness, she thought. Given what she knew of this family's past, Carin could imagine the sorrow that had attended the dying wizard's penning of the poem.

Rereading the copy she'd made in her own clear hand, Carin felt a firm—if dismaying—conviction that she understood most of its lines. What "evil" Legary alluded to in the opening stanzas, she didn't know. But clearly the gist of the narrative dealt with the deaths in the family that Myra had told her about.

"'The evil that slew the first ...'" Carin muttered.

If "the first" meant Hugh—the first son of this house to be laid in the tomb—then the line made the ominous suggestion that Legary's nineteen-year-old heir had died by violence. And if "the

first" was Hugh, then the "tainted second" was the present Lord
Verek. "The third" must be Verek's young son: "The blood of my
son's blood," as great-grandfather Legary had called the child.
This was the little boy who drowned … and the child was untouched by "the evil that tainted the second."

The tainted second. The phrase hinted darkly that Carin's mis-
givings about the warlock were fully justified.

"You can defend him till you're blue in the face, Myra," Carin
whispered to the absent housekeeper, "but now I know what
Verek's own grandfather said about him."

Studying the poem further, Carin decided that nothing in
what Myra had told her of the family's history would serve to
explain the "enchantress" or "sorceress" of the third stanza. Nor
could she guess the meaning of "weak seed, and flawed" in the
fourth. But the references to Alesia, her "child of shining spirit,"
and the lake of the lilies spoke clearly of Theil Verek's wife and
son and the waters in which they had died.

"'From waters *ensorcelled* came never they home.'" Carin read
the line in a whisper. Had the lake been hexed? Had the pair
drowned not by accident, but through sorcery?

"'Dead was the first'" — Hugh, if she were right — "'by guileful
craft.'" Could this mean the cunning craft of a sorcerer? *But not
Verek's spellcraft*, Carin thought, *because he was just a baby when his
father died.*

"'Dead was the third'" — Verek's young son, if she correctly
read the clues — "'by blackest art.'" This certainly was a reference
to black magic. Again, however, Carin discounted the possibility
that the warlock Verek was the blackheart responsible. Half mad
he might be — mad enough to enjoy the spectacle of an alien
dragon snacking on the local poultry — but surely he wasn't evil
enough to cause the drowning deaths of his wife and only child.

Indeed, the next four stanzas of Legary's narrative seemed to
confirm Myra's account of a bereft and grieving Verek, so un-
hinged by his family's death that he had cursed the woodland —

leaving it the desolate place Carin had stumbled across three weeks ago.

The "man of the green," who had begged Legary to use his magic to keep Verek's curse from devastating all of Ruain, had to be Jerold, Carin thought. And the "edge" that was made to halt the spread of Verek's venom must be the boundary where enchantments twined through the trees … the boundary she could not see … the borderland built of spells that were potent enough to consume her, the woodsprite had said, and yet powerless to touch her. Carin shivered despite the warmth of the late-morning sun through the windows.

Here also, she realized, continuing down the page, was the answer to the riddle of Jerold's enchanted garden. *Within these walls and past the wood / The poison floweth not.* The "edge" that confined Verek's curse to the woodland must also bar it from the garden inside the manor's walls.

"So Jerold didn't make the 'magic of life,'" Carin muttered. "It's the work of his master, Lord Legary. I wonder if Jerold realized, when he begged his master to make the magic, that it would end up killing Legary?"

For that was the clear implication of the tenth stanza. In calling on "forces primal" to stem the ebbing of life from his domain, Legary had sacrificed his own life. Had it been a trade of sorts? The great wizard's potent life-force in exchange for the vitality of the land itself? And was Jerold's life also a part of whatever unearthly bargain had been struck? "When I die, the magic dies with me," the old elf had said.

Carin gazed long at the poem's final lines: *The lad is slain, the infant drowned; / The tainted seed is future's hope.* With his son and his great-grandson both dead, the only heir left to Lord Legary — his only hope for the future of House Verek — was "the tainted seed": his grandson Theil.

That's a sorry basket to have all of your eggs in, Carin thought, convinced now that she wasn't the only one to have a low opinion of the current Lord of Ruain. Why else would Legary have hidden the *Book of Archamon* so that his heir and pupil hadn't come across it in twenty years? Verek's failure to locate the volume was not for want of trying, Carin suspected.

But what should she make of Legary's parting behest on his grandson's behalf? *Touch him not, Morann!* Who was Morann? Did this person still live, or was the name an echo of the past, as dead as Hugh and Alesia and Legary himself? At the time of the narrative's writing, maybe this Morann had posed a threat to the present Lord of Ruain—and, by extension, to the future of his noble house. But did the threat of Morann still hang over Verek's head?

With a frazzled sigh—*More questions,* she thought; *always more questions*—Carin folded the fair copy she'd made of Legary's narrative and slipped it deep into a pocket of her breeches. Preparing to close the *Book of Archamon,* she removed the two sheets of paper she'd used to cover the enchanted page that faced the unmasked final entry. And as the concealing sheets came away, Carin clearly saw, for the briefest instant, a date and a name at the bottom of that page.

The work, again, was signed "Legary." But the author had written his name boldly. His signature was hardly recognizable as belonging to the same hand as on the facing page.

The date gave the reason for the firmness of the leftmost signature. It had been penned fourteen years earlier than on the right-hand page. Legary would have been in his sixties—the springtime of life for a wizard, apparently. And young Master Verek, Carin determined with a quick mental calculation, would have been ten years old.

Ten. Myra had said that Verek was in his tenth year when she took the post of housekeeper to Lord Legary. What else had the woman said? Verek's father "was dust in the tomb, and the widow no longer lived under this roof."

What had Legary written on the page that preceded his narrative of evil? Had he named the evil that put his son in the tomb and "tainted" his grandson? Had he mentioned his grandson's absent mother? Whatever Legary's subject had been, he'd taken care to conceal it. Carin had barely glimpsed the signature and the date when all the characters on the page jumbled themselves and resumed their uneasy gyrations.

Hoping to read more of the bespelled writing, she re-covered it. Then she looked up into the sunlight over the desk and counted to five. As quickly as she could drop her gaze back to the book, she snatched away the two sheets of paper.

The trick worked, but very briefly. In the split second before the page again became indecipherable, Carin tingled with excitement as the phrase "wife of Hugh" rose to her eyes. Legary had indeed written of his grandson's mother—recording, perhaps, her name and possibly her fate. Was it written, on that page, why she had left the household? Had Legary penned his daughter-in-law's obituary? Or had something other than her death taken the widowed lady from her ten-year-old boy?

Carin had re-covered the ensorcelled page and was about to repeat the trick when the library door opened, and in came Myra.

"Here you are, dearie!" the woman exclaimed, a slight frown creasing her brow. "And how is it with you, child? Have you your wits about you again? Are you seeing serpents still, or did my good master banish those frightful visions?"

"I'm all right, Myra," Carin said. "Lord Verek broke the spell I was under."

"And where is my master?" Myra asked, looking around the room. "Is he not here with you? The meal's on the table, and I would call you both to eat it before it grows cold."

Carin took a moment to think before she answered. How much of the morning's events should she tell the housekeeper?

Verek's warning from days ago jumped to her mind: "That simple woman is not so privy to my affairs as you may suppose … If you care for her, hold your tongue."

Deciding to err, if error it was, on the side of caution, Carin replied casually: "Lord Verek left me after he looked at this old book I found." She closed the *Book of Archamon* and walked to Myra. "I'm not sure where he went. Just off to be by himself, I suppose."

Myra stared past Carin at the bespelled volume.

"Is that the book," she softly asked, "that had you struck out of your wits, thinking you were seeing serpents?" When Carin nodded, a tremor seemed to shake the housekeeper. "Then I'll be wanting nothing to do with that musty old book. And if you'll take my advice, dearie, you'll not touch it again. Such things are not for you and me to meddle with."

Hurrying from the library, Myra led the way to the kitchen. During lunch, the housekeeper was uncommonly subdued. Before she sat down to her plate, she tried to take a tray to Verek in his rooms. But there was no reply, she told Carin with a worried air, when she rapped at her "good master's" door.

Myra's unusual silence, under other circumstances, might have prompted Carin to ask more questions about the nameless widow who'd disappeared from this house. But Carin resolved to seek her answers now in Legary's ensorcelled account. Maybe if she worked patiently with her two sheets of paper and a quick eye and hand, she could eventually make out the concealed text.

Her trick of hiding, then revealing, the enchanted page had its limitations, however, as Carin soon discovered. The text refused to be deciphered in an orderly way, beginning — as she thought reasonable — with the first word Legary had put to paper and continuing line by line. Instead, Carin found her eyes drawn randomly to words and phrases that were scattered over the page. Whatever popped out at her, she noted down on a sheet of Verek's writing paper, in approximately the place it had seemed to appear on the ensorcelled page. But she could not be certain of any word's location within the text, so quickly did the spell of concealment reassert itself and throw the characters into disarray, twitching them across the page like agitated ants.

After two tedious hours, Carin had on paper a tantalizing collection of words and phrases that, for all their disjointedness, piqued her curiosity almost beyond bearing. Among the terms that had bobbed up like corks from murky water were *a worthy heir, the adept*, and *ungifted*. Also rising to view was the enigmatic name "Morann," but nothing to say how it might be related to any of the uncovered terms.

Maybe her eyes grew tired, or her method of extracting legible words began to fail. In any case, as the afternoon wore on, Carin found it increasingly difficult to make headway against Legary's spell. After another half-hour of struggle, she softly swore "Drisha take it!" and gave it up for the day. But before she abandoned the library and slipped away for a session with her bow, Carin shut the *Book of Archamon* against the sunlight that spilled through the windows. Sun could fade the inks in which ordinary books were written. She didn't like to think what Verek's reaction would be, if such damage befell this ancient treasury of wizards' lore.

Adjourning to the great hall at the far end of the house, Carin took weapon in hand and shot holes in the hay-stuffed pillowcase. The woodsprite, as was its habit, lodged in the rowan at the doorway and called encouragement while she practiced. Between rounds—they were short: she only had six arrows for her bow—Carin told the sprite how she'd found the book, and she described Verek's anguish upon reading its last pages.

She pulled out her copy of Legary's final entry, read it to the sprite, and gave the creature her thoughts on the text's meaning. Now, too, seemed the right time to tell the sprite what Verek had said about the "master *wysard*" who had brought them both to Ladrehdin.

The sprite hung on her every word. Though eager to find in Legary's narrative some clue to the identity of the blackheart who awed Verek, the sprite had to agree with Carin, after lengthy discussion, that nothing in the poem pointed definitely to their elusive quarry.

"But you'll keep looking, won't you, my friend?" the wood-sprite pleaded. "With each bit of news you bring me, my hope grows that you may yet discover the power that will send me homeward. You won't let me down, my friend. I know you won't."

"I … right," Carin murmured, trying to be kind but noncommittal. Even if she did learn the name of the power, would it be possible — or wise — to seek an audience with a wizard who out-magicked Verek?

At the table that evening, it was again only Carin and Myra. The housekeeper, now thoroughly worried about her absent master, tried to pry details from Carin about the written passages that had sent Verek into seclusion. She feigned ignorance, uncertain how much she could or should tell.

"I'll ask this of you, then," Myra said when Carin gave her no satisfaction. "Will you sleep lightly tonight? Your bedchamber being so close to my master's private rooms, you can hear better than I can when I'm tucked away in my cozy chamber aft the kitchen. Will you come for me at once if you hear the lightest footstep on the stair, or the faintest creaking of a door, or any sound of my master abroad in the night? For I'm sorely troubled, dearie, that my good master doesn't take up the dishes that I leave at his door, or answer me when I tap and call his name. I fear some ill has befallen him."

Quaffing her ale to quiet a fit of nerves, Carin composed herself. Then she asked the one question that she'd never wanted answered in all her weeks under the warlock's roof.

"Uh, Myra, where *are* Lord Verek's private rooms? You said my bedroom is close to his, but I've never seen his door."

Myra lifted her bulk from the kitchen table with more agility than Carin would have credited her with.

"Oh my, dearie!" the woman exclaimed as she lit a candle. "I quite forgot. To be sure, you wouldn't know. 'Tis no wonder that you've never seen the doors to the master's rooms. Those who do not know where to look can hardly make shift to see. Come, child, and I'll show you the secret." She beckoned for Carin to follow her. "And then I'll be wanting you to give a little tap and call out the master's name. Maybe he'll answer to the one who makes his evenings pass so pleasantly with her reading from the puzzle-book."

On legs unwilling, Carin followed the woman into the dark ground-floor hallway. Halfway along it, Myra stopped and pointed to the interior wall. In the smooth stonework, Carin could see nothing that resembled a door. But the housekeeper, with one plump finger, silently traced out a width of wall. Then she stretched her arm over her head, and by candlelight swept out a half circle as though indicating the arch of a doorway.

As reluctantly as if the wall were made of human skulls, Carin stepped closer and felt the stones where Myra had outlined the shape of a door. Her hands detected what her eyes could not. There was indeed a break in the stonework. And filling that break were what felt like the planks of a timber door.

Even the walls of this wizards' lair are bewitched, Carin thought, running her fingers over the planks.

"There, dearie!" Myra exclaimed. "You've found it. 'Tis the lower door to my master's chambers. Give it a good knock, won't you? And speak his name. Drisha willing, he'll answer you."

Carin rapped at the invisible door as firmly as she dared, and called out for Verek. She got no answer, only an echoing silence which the thudding of her heart seemed to fill.

Myra, fussing like a mother goose with a lost gosling, led the way back to the foyer, then upstairs to the landing that fronted Carin's bedroom. As Carin had feared she would, the woman turned down the corridor that led to the double doors between the minor and master wings of the house. But only a few steps down the passageway from Carin's bedroom, Myra halted and pointed at a section of wall opposite one of the hallway's high windows.

Here, in fact, there was no need for the housekeeper to point out an invisible portal. Though Carin could no more see it than she could see the lower door to Verek's apartments, an untouched tray of food on the floor announced the door's location.

Myra clucked over her master's refusal to eat. She picked up the tray, then urged Carin to rap at this door as well. Carin did so and called out the warlock's name. He didn't answer.

Returning with Myra to the kitchen, Carin spent the rest of the evening trying to convince the woman that her "good master" was unlikely to come to harm in his own house. Myra went to her bed still worried.

And secretly, Carin didn't blame her. How dangerous this house could be, with its serpent-fanged books and its dragon-spawning pool of magic, she had seen and experienced for herself.

She crept silent as a moonbeam up the stairs to her room, and there lay awake for some time. For reasons unrelated to Myra's request, Carin listened intently for any sound from the direction of Verek's rooms. She couldn't stop thinking about the dozens of times that she had slunk past Verek's invisible doors, all unawares. Every walk down the lower hallway to the library, to steal an hour reading when she should be working, and every skulking along the upper corridor to reach the great hall for her private archery practice, had been done practically under the warlock's nose. How she'd avoided getting caught, only Drisha knew.

Slipping into Carin's thoughts, just before sleep came, was the realization that Verek's rooms must have at least one more secret door. How many times had she known him to exit through the library's creaky portal to the cave of magic, when what he sought was the privacy of his apartments? He wouldn't descend all the way to the cave, cross its considerable expanse, then climb three long flights to reach the upper corridor and his upstairs door. It was more likely, Carin supposed, that the library's shadowed portal opened not only upon the spiraling stairwell to the cave, but also to a bespelled doorway by which Verek could gain his private rooms.

This house, she thought sleepily, *suits its master perfectly. The one has as many twists, and dark and secret places, as the other.*

* * *

Sunrise did not bring the warlock down to breakfast. An anxious Myra took trays to both of his hidden hall-doors, trusting to the aromas of fried bacon, poached eggs, and fresh-baked bread to draw her master from his retreat. The sight of food piled at each unseen entrance to Verek's den made Carin think of baited traps at mouse holes.

In the library she neglected to sort books, but instead pricked holes in the spell that cloaked Legary's account of "the adept" and the "ungifted." It was a risk. If Verek chose to end his seclusion at just that moment and caught her trying to read the *Book of Archamon,* Carin might feel his wrath as never before.

But the warlock did not appear. His absence, and what might account for it, was the sole topic of Myra's monologue—Carin could not call it conversation—when the women ate together at midday.

After lunch, she volunteered to take a fresh offering to Verek's upstairs door to save the housekeeper the climb. Carin found the invisible entryway by feel, and rapped briskly. She waited awhile for an answer. Getting none, she continued along to the unused wing. She retrieved her bow and handful of arrows from their hiding place in an alcove of the balcony and descended to the floor of the great hall.

There, Carin shot her six arrows as quickly as she could put them to the string and let fly. Sighting down each shaft kept her from seeing, in her mind's eye, the pain that had contorted Verek's face as he'd fled the library and the *Book*. Concentrating on the target, Carin couldn't think about the manic excitement that had gleamed in Verek's eyes when the Jabberwock proved itself to be a killer. Roughly she yanked her arrows out of the hay-packed pillowcase, then stalked back to the shooting line and squared her stance.

As she raised the bow and took more careful aim for the next round, a clipped voice called down from the balcony at her back:

"Hold firm! Don't let the arrow creep."

Carin convulsively released the arrow and jerked her head toward the voice at one and the same moment. The shot went wild. The missile sped to the rowan that grew in the servants' entrance. The sound of it thudding into the bark was lost in the woodsprite's scream.

Chapter 20

The Truth

She dropped her bow and sprinted for the doorway. The rowan stood like a sentry with her arrow protruding from its silvery-gray livery. Carin put her fingers to the wound and called frantically for the woodsprite. Had she killed the creature?

She had not. The sprite answered her, not from the rowan but from the nearby oak that was their frequent meeting place.

"Carin!" the creature exclaimed in a voice shriller than usual. "What a fright you gave me! I was shaken to the roots when the arrow hit my dwelling-tree. But the rowan had hardly roused to the first inklings of its pain before I sought the comfort of this familiar bole."

"You're all right?" Carin demanded as she joined the creature at their tree. "You're sure you're not hurt?"

"Be easy, my friend. I've suffered no damage," the sprite assured her. "And look who comes in your wake. The mage himself trails you out the door."

In her worry for the sprite, Carin had temporarily forgotten the sharp voice of instruction that had startled her into shooting wild. Turning now, she discovered Verek standing in the servants' entrance. He was inspecting the arrow she'd embedded in the thin-barked rowan. In one hand, he held her homemade bow. From his trousers' pocket protruded the five shafts that Carin had left on a table in the great hall.

Verek pulled her arrow from the tree. He nocked it and made a few experimental draws, with the missile pointed groundward, testing the stiffness of her greenwood bow. Then he raised the weapon and sent the arrow flying into the wooded wilderness behind the hall.

Carin, feeling as if a beloved caged lark had been lost to the open skies, dug her fingernails into her palms. She would never find the precious thing in the undergrowth.

The warlock took another of her arrows from his pocket and fitted it to the bowstring, but kept it pointing at the ground as he walked to the oak where she stood. Carin steadied herself with a hand on the sprite's tree.

Unlike his wild-man's reappearance after he nearly drowned in the wizards' well, this time when Verek rejoined his world he was neatly groomed and dressed. His long hair was combed; his beard and mustache trimmed. He wore a fresh white shirt under a russet-red woolen vest that Carin coveted for its warmth. The chill of the late-autumn afternoon was quickly banking the fire that restlessness and brief exercise had built in her muscles.

Traces of yesterday's anguish showed in Verek's face. Under puffy, red-rimmed eyes, his mouth was tight. The pain of his reading from the *Book of Archamon* might be duller today, but the words had made a wound that still gaped.

"Good day to you, mage!" the sprite called heartily at Verek's approach, startling Carin. The creature might have been welcoming a dear friend. "How does this crisp, bright, fall day find you? In good health and spirits, I trust?"

"I'm well enough," Verek snapped. "How is it, sprite, that you dare to trespass so brazenly on my private grounds? By whose leave do you come here?"

"By your own," the sprite said. Its reedy voice sounded unconcerned. "Have you forgotten? On the morning when I led you to the ancient oak that gave sanctuary to my friend Carin, I exacted a promise from you. In return for my help, you gave me your word that you wouldn't hinder my speaking to her, once you'd returned her safely to your house. And so it is that I come here to visit my friend and offer her what comfort I can. For it seems that this traveler from a far country regards you with a sentiment akin to horror."

"And well she should," Verek growled. "For I threaten her daily with bread and meat and featherbeds, and order her to take such care in her duties as to do herself no injury." He flexed the bow again, still pointing its nocked arrow downwards. "Against these mortal threats, she arms herself, I see. From whence came this rough-made bow and these sticks that serve it for arrows?"

Carin's face burned, and she was glad when the sprite replied as though the question were meant for it alone. She didn't mind the woodsprite talking about her as if she weren't standing there, if it saved her answering the warlock's gibes.

"Isn't her bow a pretty thing?" the sprite exclaimed, with more enthusiasm than Carin's inexpert effort merited. "Our traveler made it herself ... with my help. *I* found the yew-tree that gave up a limb to the purpose. Carin has practiced diligently with it," the creature added. "Rare now are her misses—if no voice comes from above to surprise her off the target."

Verek shot Carin an annoyed look.

"If you still possess the power of speech," he snapped, eyeing her with a directness that silenced the sprite, "oblige me, pray, with the name of the one from whom you learned to shape a bowstave. A wheelwright's bondmaid could have had no need of such training."

Carin shook her head. "No one taught me," she snapped back at him. "I learned it from a book." She named the dog-eared volume that had been her sole source of archery lore, and was surprised to see a look resembling pleasure cross the warlock's face.

"An excellent text," he muttered. "In my youth I consulted it daily as I learned the song of the bow."

Verek questioned her no further, but raised the weapon and sent the second of her arrows to lose itself in the wilderness. With a frown, he shortened the string—Carin's light bow obviously lacked the power he required in his own—and then he shot her remaining armory into the overgrowth. To complete her disarmament, he took her bow with him as he returned to the rowan-guarded doorway and disappeared through it. Not another word did the warlock say to either Carin or the sprite.

Leaning against the oak, Carin swore vehemently. "I hate him! I wish he had strangled in the wizards' well, or starved himself to death."

"Do not speak so!" the woodsprite shrilled in her ear. "Without the mage's help, my friend, how do we find the master wizard? Without the one to lead us to the other, how shall we make our passage home?"

Carin pushed away from the tree and took her leave of the single-minded creature. "I'll be back tomorrow," she said. "And if you'll find me a limb that's as good and strong as the first one was, I'll make another bow. Verek won't stop me, not as long as there's a tree left standing around here."

When the sprite had promised to help, Carin told it good-bye and stepped inside the servants' entrance. She waited in the great hall until the creature had sparked away, leaving her alone with her thoughts. She wished to nurse her disappointments privately.

And she wanted no more meetings with Verek this afternoon. Since he'd returned to the occupied wing through the upper corridor, she might hope to avoid him by way of the remnant path through the wilds, which would take her to Jerold's garden. From there, both the stable and the door to the kitchen would be within reach.

First, however, Carin meant to search for her armory. Finding six arrows in the verdant snarl would be like combing a haystack for toothpicks. Making replacements would be much easier than locating the originals. But Verek had thrown away her work with such contempt, he'd forced her to at least *try* to find her arrows.

Heedless of damage done to her breeches and Verek's borrowed shirt, Carin pushed her way through the tangle behind the house, in the direction of the warlock's last four shots. The arrows, if they hit no trees, would have traveled far. Verek's expert shooting had coaxed more distance from her bow than Carin had thought it could give.

With only guesswork to guide her, she pressed on into the wooded wilderness until she'd gone a distance roughly equal, if luck were with her, to the arrows' flight. Then she began a careful search, ignoring the voice of reason that declared it hopeless.

What Carin soon glimpsed through a screen of knotty vines was no arrow, but moss-covered stonework. She had found— what? A back part of the kitchen facilities that had once served the great hall?

Among her earliest discoveries at Verek's house, during her free afternoons of roaming the grounds, Carin had stumbled across the ruins of the main kitchens—crumbling, roofless, overgrown, their gaping windows staring past the foliage like blind eyes. Those kitchens—way larger than Myra's domain at the opposite end of the house—adjoined the great hall, however. The stonework Carin could just make out now, through the vines, seemed much too distant from the house to have served any purpose in the family's long-ago festivities. Perhaps she was seeing the back wall of the fortifications that enclosed the manor grounds.

But no—

As Carin drew nearer, she found no high wall stretching away in both directions. The mossy stones that peeked from the greenery formed one corner of a low building. The face of the building that she could see through the undergrowth had no windows. Its one wide door was secured with a massive padlock. Wrought of black iron, the door curved along its top edge to fit the arch of the portal that it sealed. And upon the keystone of the arch was cut the name *Verek*.

Carin gasped. She backed away with immoderate haste, tripped on an exposed root, and sat down hard, nearly landing in a thornbush. Horror reached for her like a bony hand. But she fought off its grip and forced herself to calmness as she extricated her clothing from the brambles and got to her feet.

The structure before her was without doubt the Verek family tomb, just as Carin had dreamed it—except these stones were hoary with age. The tomb of her nightmare had seemed newly built. Carin didn't need to see past the iron-shackled door to know that the mortal remains of Lord Legary rested in the left-hand vault, and those of young Hugh to the right. Directly opposite the door was a double chamber, in one vault of which lay the Lady Alesia and her child—dead "by blackest art," if Carin correctly interpreted the narrative from the *Book of Archamon*. The vault at the dead woman's right hand was empty ... gathering dust against the day when it would receive the corpse of the current Lord of Ruain.

With a shudder that traveled her from head to toe, Carin turned and rushed back the way she'd come, abandoning her search for the lost arrows. As quickly as she could, she made her way past the great hall and found the enormous oak that over-powered the outer wall of the grounds. There she picked up the remnant path from Jerold's garden by which she'd first discovered the tree. The path took her to the edge of the elf's domain. She put out her hand to part a way through a curtain of hanging vines, and then she froze.

Footsteps approached down the garden's graveled walk. A familiar voice reached Carin. Verek was talking to a companion she couldn't see through the greenery and didn't dare try to glimpse. Any movement or sound from her, and the warlock would know that an eavesdropper lurked in the bushes not a stone's throw from him.

"As Drisha is my witness," Verek was saying, "I did not grasp the truth until I read my grandsire's dying declaration in the book that curious *fileen* discovered hidden on a dark shelf. Or have I deluded myself, Master Jerold?"

So — he's gone to talk to the old one, Carin thought, glad that Verek hadn't kept her guessing. Already growing uncomfortable in the cold and damp of her green-shadowed hiding place, she nonetheless thrilled at the prospect of gaining answers from both the warlock and his gardener without their realizing it.

"Have I known the truth these past twenty years," Verek said, "while refusing in my heart of hearts to confess it? Many times I have asked the waters of the *wysards* for an account of that terrible day, but all that I am given to see is the image of their deaths. How can I impress upon you the horror of it? To view again and again that hideous scene … relentless … inescapable …"

As the warlock's voice trailed off, Carin remembered his frenzy in the cave of magic on the night of his near-death in the wizards' well. *"You have shown only this brutal image in answer to my every plea!"* Verek had cried to the spirit-being of the well. Though he begged for a glimpse of his wife and child as they had been in life, the mirror pool would show him nothing but their drowned, bloated bodies.

"Can it be, Master Jerold," Verek went on quietly, "that the waters obey — not my commands, which I scream with what seems desperate earnestness — but rather, my most secret, silent wishes? Can it be that the all-knowing power descries my desire for self-delusion, deeply hidden though it is even to myself, and thus denies me the thing that I seem to demand of it? Perhaps I *have* known, deep in my soul, what evil drew my lady and the child to their deaths … but I could not admit such knowledge, for fear of the delirium of mind that would follow upon a recognition of such truth."

What evil? Carin wondered, thinking of the neat copy of Legary's poem that nestled in her pocket. *What truth?*

Any reply Jerold might have made was lost in a sudden, cold gust of wind that rustled through the leaves. Under cover of the breeze's passage, Carin settled deeper into the vines and creepers—preparing for a wait of hours, if that's what it would take to hear everything Verek had to say.

The warlock's voice reached her again as the breeze died away. "But I swear to you, Jerold," he was saying, "never did I suspect that my lord held himself to blame for *summoning* the evil that took my wife and son. It is painful to think on … that my grandfather's declarations of joy at a child's innocence would fly on wicked wings to the demon's nest, and bring down on our heads the *daēva*'s envy."

Joy flying on wicked wings. The imagery rose vivid in Carin's mind. She could almost see the "black raven" of Legary's narrative winging its way to some demon's lair, carrying the old lord's happy news of a child untouched by whatever scourge lay upon other members of this household.

"And by the oath of my House," Verek went on, so quietly that Carin could hardly hear him, "I swear I did not know what price was paid to stop the curse born of my madness. Barely had I laid Alesia in the tomb, with our boy in her arms, when my sorrows were multiplied by the swift decline of my grandsire. *I never knew, Jerold.* For twenty years, I had thought my lord succumbed to the same unbearable grief that drove the reason from my brain. Never did I understand, until I read the final words from his hand, that my grandfather died halting the curse I had invoked upon his lands."

Verek fell silent, and for a long moment no one said anything. Then Carin heard the dry rasp of the elf's voice.

"Do not blame yourself, son," Jerold said. "The death of my lord Legary can be laid to no single cause. 'Tis true, he felt deeply the loss of her ladyship and the child … the untouched heir. 'Tis true, the magic he wove against the blighting of Ruain took all his strength—and what little I could offer of my own slight powers. But know you this also, Theil: On his shoulders alone rests the blame for the harm that has been done to this household."

Verek must have started to protest. The gardener's voice harshened, as though the old man meant to tolerate no interruption.

"Aye—'tis true, son," Jerold growled, then went on in a milder tone. "Though you loved him greatly and would forgive him any conduct, there's no denying the wickedness of the deed he did—the deed that haunts this household still. He knew the sin he'd committed, and 'twas the guilt of it that put him in his grave, as much as did any other of these matters we discuss. I mean no disrespect to Legary's memory, for I loved him as I would a father. I must say these things, Theil, so that you shan't take upon yourself—as you are wont to do—the blame for the misdeeds of others."

Carin marveled, not only at Jerold's words but at the quantity of them. She hadn't been sure the old elf could speak more than two sentences together. His words called sharply to her mind a line from Legary's narrative that bore out this "gardener's" accusation: *My crimes are great, my penance vast*, Legary had confessed.

"What's done is done," Jerold continued. "As you now know the true source of this garden's magical life, I'll press you to its service. My days are fewer in number than yours, Theil. I'll not live to see a new age. Either an apprentice is found to learn the magic and take this duty from me, or this garden dies when I die. That knuckleheaded Lanse has neither the gift nor the temperament. What of the girl? She comes often to this garden, and she has a fondness for flowers. On a cold day of this week just past, I saw her sitting on the greensward studying a book of blossoms as though she meant to conjure living petals from the page."

Verek laughed. The sound of it was so unfamiliar, Carin couldn't put it to the picture she had built in her mind of the two wizards speaking together on the graveled walk. Verek laughing, or Verek as the doting father of a young son: either state seemed too normal, too ordinary for the moody warlock.

"You are deceived, Master Jerold," he said, amusement brightening his voice. "I, too, saw our peculiar guest sitting on the grass with a book. In my puzzlement, I asked Myra why a *fileen* who is possessed of some wit would take her reading outdoors on a chill autumn day and sit there shivering, when she might stay by the fireside in my library. And this was Myra's reply: 'Why, she means to charm Jerold! The girl regrets provoking the old goat, and she knows—for I've told her so—that she may put things right with him, if she doth but speak to him of flowers!'"

"'Old goat,' my eye," Jerold growled. "But why should the girl wish to 'charm' me? What does she wish of me?"

"I believe, Master Jerold," Verek replied, "that she means to make you an ally against ... What is it that she calls me? A fiend, she's named me with conviction, and also a madman and a murderer.

"And do you know, Jerold," Verek added, his voice losing any hint of mirth, "that I cannot in good conscience deny the truth of any charge that she has laid at my feet?"

Gravel crunched, and their voices faded as the two wizards walked on down the path, leaving Carin to mull over what she had heard. Evidently, the final entry in the *Book of Archamon* contained much information that was new to Verek. Carin felt oddly privileged to have read Legary's narrative after only three weeks in this house, when Verek had waited twenty years to learn what his grandfather's words could tell him.

She rose stealthily to her feet, backtracked along the remnant path, and returned to the great hall. Obviously she couldn't follow her original plan to regain the house through the kitchen door. To step boldly from hiding into Jerold's garden could land her in the hands of both wizards, who might still linger on the graveled ways, discussing an "apprentice" for the old elf.

Would they press her into such service? Carin doubted it. Verek seemed bent on another course for his "peculiar guest."

From the great hall, Carin hurried along the wide "V" of the upstairs corridors to her room. She hid her copy of Legary's poem, and the notes from her tedious deciphering of his preceding work, in a drawer of the dressing table. Then she brushed twigs from her hair, and changed into the kirtle and shift that Myra had restored to wearability after their drenching in the thunderstorm.

The return of the woman's "good master" had Myra in high spirits, Carin discovered as she arrived in the kitchen to help with the evening meal. Apparently Verek had mentioned that it was Carin's knock on his door which had roused him from his "meditations." The housekeeper expressed her gratitude with such expansiveness that Carin had no need — or opportunity — to say a word.

When supper was on the table, however, and she took the seat across from an obviously hungry Verek to dine on a pigeon and bacon stew, her silence finally attracted Myra's notice.

"What ails you, child?" the woman asked. "You haven't said three words all evening. You'd not be catching a fever, would you?"

Carin shook her head. "I'm all right, Myra." She aimed her next remark at the warlock opposite, but she didn't look at him. "I'm just unhappy that I lost something this afternoon, out in the wild part of the garden behind the house. I'd made it myself, and I'm not pleased that it's gone."

"Oh my, dearie!" the housekeeper exclaimed, oblivious that Carin meant to get at Verek over a confiscated weapon. "Whatever were you doing out there? That tangle of brambles is fit for nothing. It's Jerold's fine garden that you're wanting, child, when you've a mind to be out-of-doors. Forsake the unkempt green and take the sun in Jerold's flowerbeds — that's what I'm advising you."

And be watched by every eye in this house? Carin thought, but said nothing.

Verek didn't acknowledge her grievance against him. He went on deliberately spooning up the stew. Myra, finding her master too fixed on his plate to join the conversation, and her helper too glum, happily filled the rest of the hour with her own wide ramblings.

The warlock, when he'd eaten his fill, summoned Carin to the library to resume her second reading of the puzzle-book. She finished the eighth chapter, about the clumsy White Knight and his curious inventions. It was when she started to revisit Alice's coronation and madcap dinner-party, in the ninth chapter, that Carin's smoldering resentment at Verek flared into her thoughts and would not be suppressed.

He steals my bow, she fumed, *and he doesn't tell me why he did it or — Drisha forbid — apologize for taking what's mine.*

Knowing it was madness, but unable to stop herself, Carin lit into him with the most incendiary question she could think of. The subject of the stolen bow would have been far safer ground than the off-limits arena she chose to fight him in. She lowered the puzzle-book and abruptly demanded:

"Who — or what — is the spirit-being that I heard you talking to in the wizards' well? The one you called 'Amangêda'."

Verek sprang to his feet. His eyes were wild. His hands stretched toward her, palms out, as if desperate to silence her before another syllable could pass her lips.

Carin had no time to enjoy her question's striking effect on the warlock. The hidden door to the cave of magic burst open, and from the shadows that cloaked the library's depths came a strong wind. It blew open the covers of her stacked books and riffled their pages noisily, like hosts of frogs jumping one after another — *plop, plop, plop* — into their ponds. It blew at Verek's back, sweeping his hair into his face. The wind gusted with such stinging force directly at Carin that it brought tears to her eyes. Her hair streamed out behind her, over the back of the bench she occupied. And accompanying the wind was a bright, tinkling, musical sound, such as seashells make when they dangle on strings under house-eaves, chiming in the breeze.

Then the wind died; the music died. The tempest that welled up from the cave of magic ended as abruptly as it had erupted.

Verek put back his hair with both hands and stood gaping at Carin, his eyes agog, as if expecting her to either disappear or grow horns. But when nothing untoward befell her, he staggered to the liquor cabinet and poured himself a tall drink of the red *dhera*. He gulped it down, then held his empty glass up to Carin in a mock toast.

"I salute you," he said, husky-voiced. "The last mortal to speak that name burst into flame upon the spot, and was nothing but ashes a heartbeat after committing the offense."

Carin suddenly found breathing difficult, as though the warlock's words had knocked the wind from her lungs. She watched him lower his glass, his hand trembling, and in that instant she understood three facts.

First: Verek was honestly shaken. Carin's continued life and health not only astonished him, but filled him with a sort of horrified awe.

Second: she had uttered a forbidden name, a name sacrosanct.

And third: for her transgression, Carin should, by rights, be dead now.

When the meaning of what she'd done—and the potential consequences—fully sank in, Carin tasted horror like bile rising in her throat. How close she had come to an awful death was apparent from Verek's reaction. But why hadn't she provoked a similar—or deadlier—response before, when she'd spoken the forbidden name?

"I, um, hesitate to admit this," she whispered, "but that's not the first time I ever said the name aloud." Carin thought back to the afternoon when the house was empty, Myra away, Verek missing … last seen dragging himself half-drowned from the wizards' well.

The warlock threw himself onto the bench across from Carin's, ran the fingers of both hands through his windblown hair, and softly demanded an explanation.

Carin told him how she'd murmured the name in Emrys' ear as she walked the mare around the grounds, as if hoping the horse might know what manner of spirit-being haunted the mirror pool. Verek pressed her for details by which to know the hour of her deed, until he established that he had still lingered in the cave — battered, but still seeking answers in the wizards' well — when Carin said the name to Emrys.

He shook his head. "So intent was I upon the well — and it upon me — that your first utterance went unheeded." Sitting forward, he fixed Carin with a gaze that had the force of physical restraint. "*Never* speak the name again. Twice you have been spared. Do not tempt providence by a third repetition of such folly."

Verek leaned back and rubbed his face vigorously with both hands, as though to rid himself of something unreal. Then he laced his fingers together and slipped them behind his head, visibly relaxing after Carin's brush with the supernatural.

"I find myself indebted to you," he said crisply. "You have subjected yourself to a test that I would not — dared not — deal you … though I longed to know what would result, were you to speak aloud the name of power. I was confident that the outcome of such a test would tell me much."

"And what *has* it told you?"

"That the well of the *wysards* regards you as other than mortal."

Carin's heart sank. Were they back to that?

"No!" she protested. "I thought that question had already been answered to your satisfaction. Other than not always falling under your spells the way you'd expect me to, I'm just as mortal as any other … scullery maid." Carin had a moment's hesitation before describing herself thusly, as other possible labels flashed through her mind: "alien misfit" and "accidental conjurer" among them.

The warlock shook his head. "Entirely mortal you might be, on that world which is your natural home. Here, in Ruain, you are otherwise. That you still live, having uttered aloud the name of power, is proof enough. But remember also that you have entered the cave of magic through a door bespelled to prevent such intrusion. The deed would not have been possible for a mortal of this world."

It was Carin's turn to shake her head. "You wouldn't read too much into that if you'd seen how petrified I was, right after I opened that door. Scared? More than I can tell you. But you know what I'm saying: I did not escape the spell that made me a statue on the doorstep."

Verek slipped his hands from behind his head and laced them around one knee. He eyed Carin speculatively. Did her argument echo thoughts that he'd mulled over in his own mind?

"If I recall aright the story you told of your spying," he said, growing guarded in his look, "the spell of stone held you from the instant that I was swept into the well. The moment I was free, you were released."

Carin only nodded agreement, suspecting that any words of hers might hit him wrong. Her night of spying was, she thought, a sore subject with him.

"I believe it likely," Verek went on, "that the well of *wysards* is not altogether certain what to make of you, or how much trust to place in you. Though I cannot speak for the voice of power, I suspect that the well thought it prudent to turn you to stone, to assure your right behavior in its presence, at a time when I was not in the cavern to govern your conduct."

He talks about the mirror pool like it's alive, Carin thought with a little shiver. *He hasn't mentioned a spirit or a ghost, or a goddess or a demon, that comes up from the well. Is the water itself alive? Is it aware? Does it think?*

Verek stood, signaling his intention to end their conversation. But as his gaze sought the *Book of Archamon* on the desk where he'd left it yesterday, he paused, and frowned.

Carin didn't need to look behind her to know the reason for Verek's scowl. When he fled the room yesterday in a state bordering on shock, the book lay open to the two facing entries that Lord Legary had penned. Now, its cover was closed. Verek could suspect no hands but Carin's had dared to touch the book.

Before she could explain about protecting the volume's bright inks from sunlight's ravages, Verek had shot her a look that held her tongue. He resumed his seat opposite.

"It is past time you understood that names have power," he said with quiet intensity. "From the looking-glass book, you have conjured a dragon by speaking its name. In the tumult of the well this evening, you have seen the folly of voicing a forbidden name. The lesson you must learn is this: *Never utter aloud* a name you do not know. Names call those who wear them. If you cannot be certain what being—or manner of being—will answer to your call, do not speak its name."

Carin took his meaning even before Verek glanced again at the *Book of Archamon*. Only one page of that volume had yielded to her scrutiny: the final entry, Legary's poem, which no spell of concealment kept her from reading. And in that narrative were two names: Alesia, and the mysterious Morann.

The warlock couldn't know that Carin had discovered, by uncanny dream and odd luck, the identity of the woman called Alesia. He must think the name was as obscure to her as that of the unknown Morann. Clearly, he was worried that Carin might say aloud one or both of those names. Because she had overheard him speak of his dead Alesia in the garden, Carin was all but certain that it must be the other name—*Morann*—which the warlock dreaded to hear.

Speak it aloud, she would not. The name might call an entity that would show her less forbearance than did the spirit—or whatever dwelled there—of the wizards' well.

Verek got to his feet. He dismissed her. Carin's rereading of the puzzle-book's ninth chapter would await another evening. This instructive day was done.

* * *

Carin slept badly and woke with a headache. A thousand dismal fancies had filled her dreams through the night: the heavy, suffocating darkness of a dungeon ... a forest of shadows and deathly silence ... bones rattling behind the iron door of the Verek family tomb ... a pit of icy black mire that turned into the maw of a sea serpent that was half puzzle-book Jabberwock. The monster had called her name and spoke other words she couldn't make out. The sky outside her bedroom window had barely begun to lighten when Carin threw off the covers and headed for a warm bath, glad to escape the province of nightmare.

She felt better after a hearty breakfast from the hands of a still-buoyant Myra. The morning passed uneventfully as Carin bent to her task in the library. She made good progress in arranging Verek's books, and also stole half an hour to decipher, by her laborious cover-and-reveal method, a few words of the ensorcelled page from the *Book of Archamon*. Evidently Verek trusted the spell of concealment to keep it hidden from her eyes. He didn't take the book to his private rooms, as Carin had expected he would.

After lunch, she headed upstairs. She needed a nap, but she wouldn't waste time catching up on sleep. Making a new bow was more important. She planned to get the archery book from her room, and seek out the woodsprite to find her another limb of yew.

As Carin topped the stairs, however, the sight that met her eyes banished all thought of handcrafting another weapon. Leaning against the door of her bedroom was a bow, beautifully lacquered in indigo blue. The elegant curves at the ends of its limbs declared this weapon's superiority over the simple straight-limbed bow that Carin had fashioned from unseasoned wood. She knew, from studying the archery book, how the curves at the bow's tips would open with the draw, then spring back when the string was released, casting an arrow with great speed and power.

I find myself indebted to you. Verek's remark from last evening jumped to Carin's mind. Was this the warlock's way of repaying a debt? If so, she was pleased to accept it.

Elation turned to displeasure, however, as Carin checked the landing outside her bedroom door and confirmed her first impression: her new bow had no arrows. For all its smooth, sinuous beauty, the weapon was useless without missiles.

But arrows she could make, in less time than it would have taken to craft a bow. With almost the speed of the thought, Carin was down the corridor, through the double doors, and into the dusty master wing, all her sleepiness forgotten. She slowed only when she stood on the balcony above the great hall.

Standing below looking up at her, his bow in one hand and a quiver of arrows in the other, was Verek.

Carin's excitement died.

"Good. You're here," he said gruffly. "Come outside."

"Beggar it all," Carin swore under her breath. She gritted her teeth and scuffed her way down the steps. Until now, the great hall had been hers in privacy. Verek might own it, but he was not welcome in it.

Two paces outside the rowan door, Carin stopped and stared. In the wooded wilds behind the hall and its kitchens, half hidden in the trees, waited the outline of a deer. Though realistic, it was easily recognizable as a wooden practice target. What the warlock had lured her to, Carin realized in astonishment, was archery practice.

Verek handed her the first of many arrows from his quiver, and proved himself to be a demanding and impatient teacher. Carin's numerous errors of technique, her every break in form, and all her misses earned biting criticism. But at the end of three exhausting hours, she had a greater mastery of the weapon than many days of self-study had given her.

When the warlock called a halt, he collected her bow and all of his razor-sharp, jasper-tipped arrows. Carin gave them up reluctantly, expressing her wish to keep the weapons and train on her own.

Verek wouldn't hear of it.

"Those who school alone," he said, "school their mistakes. Errors become so deeply ingrained that no amount of correction can remedy them.

"Besides," he added, scowling at her, "I do not wish to feel my own arrow in my back, or see the boy Lanse fall victim to you. Knowing how you detest us both, I would show myself to be a greater fool than I am, to permit your going armed about these premises."

Carin didn't argue further. She couldn't fault the warlock's reasoning. It had never been her intention, were she to master the weapon, to limit her shooting strictly to deer.

In the late afternoon, finding that neither Verek nor Myra required her for an hour, Carin had her much-needed nap and awoke refreshed. After supper, she reread the last four chapters of the *Looking-Glass* book to Verek, and with him worked out the closing moves of the chess game that took Alice from pawn to queen. "Peaceful" was a word Carin could seldom apply to time spent with the warlock, but this evening was as tranquil as any she had known under Verek's roof. Dismissed from her reading, she went straight to bed and fell soundly asleep.

Hours later, far into the night, something jolted her awake. Carin sat up in bed, her heart pounding. What had roused her? Another nightmare? Or the force that she felt reaching for her from the landing outside her door.

Carin's feet hit the floor. From Myra's multitude she grabbed a heavy candlestick in each hand. She was rushing to try to position herself beside the entrance, hoping to surprise the intruder, when the door burst open and a gust of wind hit her in the face. The blast brought tears to her eyes.

"*Come,*" chimed a silvery, seashell voice. "*The wysard needs you.*"

Chapter 21

The Trap

If the iridescent colors of mother-of-pearl could make a sound, it would be the shimmery sound of that voice. In it, Carin heard the play of the colors of polished shells, of sunlight flashing on ocean waves, and silvered, jewel-like fish. She heard the glittering liquid glass of the mirror pool in the cave of magic.

It was the voice of the wizards' well that she heard, the voice of power, and she knew it at once.

Barely had the echo of its chimes died away when Carin felt a great disturbance that rolled in through her open bedroom door like an invisible flood of seawater. This flood threatened not to sweep her away, but to pull her with it back to its source. It had the same compelling, inexorable quality of the summons that had drawn her to the cavern of the enchanted pool to witness Verek's travails.

Do not heed the summons, the warlock had warned her after that episode. *Resist those unfathomable feelings that call you to the chamber of magic.*

But Carin could not resist the voice of the wizards' well. She would have had an easier time stopping her own heartbeat. There was no holding back.

She put down the candlesticks and got dressed, hardly knowing that she did so. Her hand closed on the bail of a candle lantern. Lighting it from one of Myra's multitude that always burned in her room at night, Carin steadied her courage. She stepped out into the corridor and walked down it toward the three long flights of stairs, toward the hidden door in the dark paneling that opened to the cave.

What I do or see in that chamber does not concern you, Verek had cautioned her. *If ever I require your presence in that vault, I will summon you by means unmistakable.*

Whether this was his summons or the mystic well's alone, it was unmistakably meant for her. This time Carin had not caught an echo of a distant conjuring, as when Verek invoked his intimate visions from the wizards' waters and she had felt the force of his appeal. This time the voice of power had itself bespoke her, and she must answer, though it lead straight to ruin.

At the foot of the wide, dark stairway, Carin did not need to risk a hand to the guard-spells of the door's concealed latch. The portal opened silently at her approach, and swung closed behind her as she stepped into the redly glowing vault of magic.

Verek was there, standing near the backless bench that was carved with a crescent moon. He stared steadily at the mirror pool. He seemed not to notice Carin's arrival. But then, without taking his gaze from the pool, he reached his hand toward her. The gesture was more an invitation than a command.

Warily, slowly, Carin set her lantern down and crossed the smooth expanse of floor to stand at the warlock's side. Still he didn't look at her, but kept his eyes on the pool.

Carin, following his gaze, inhaled sharply. An image seemed to hang, or float, just under the pool's surface—an image of a swiftly spinning whirlpool. And as she watched, it grew vastly larger and nearer.

Abruptly the vortex broke through, shattering the pool's glassy surface. It whirled in midair above the wizards' well. With its ascent came thunderous noise.

Carin clapped her hands over her ears and backed away, but she kept her eyes glued to the vision. Near the whirlpool's center were two black forms, so large that she could make out details despite the speed of their swirling around the vortex's eye. These were not mere specks, as the child in blue and green had been only a spot of color in the first whirlpool that Carin had witnessed in this cave. The black figures rode the frothing waters like warships on a tempest-tossed sea.

But ships, they only resembled. Wonderingly, Carin picked out stumpy, muscle-bound legs, splayed to the sides and sharply bent at the middle joint. All the legs—four on a side—were clawed, but the forelegs ended in swollen, heavy claws like lobsters' pincers. The creatures' bodies were long and low; their snouts, long and pointed. The powerful tail that curved like a misplaced ship's prow over each scaly back was tipped by a stinger. Though she could scarcely credit the thought, Carin could only conclude, as she stood staring at black forms against gray water, that the vermin in the vortex were part crocodile, part scorpion, and as long as two-masted schooners.

The whirlpool spun ever faster and larger, hissing and churning with such violence that Verek joined Carin in backing away, until they both ran up against a cave wall that halted their retreat. The image then broke up in a wave of white-capped water that swept over it from the wizards' well below. As it drowned the image, the magic pool seemed to acquire the vortex's fury. The usually glassy waters roiled and tumbled, like seawater in a hurricane.

Now Carin understood what Verek had meant when he'd talked about a "storm of magic" whipping the well's waters to foam. He had witnessed such a storm once before—five years ago. Then, the enchanted pool had been so fiercely agitated that it could form no clear likeness of the vortex which had swept Carin between worlds. Yet, the power in the cave—the power named Amangêda?—had been able to impress upon Verek's mind, or so he'd said, images of the whirlpool that bore the green-and-blue speck.

Did he still see, in mental image, the vortex that carried the vermin? Carin looked up at him and couldn't help flinching as she glimpsed the warlock's eyes. They burned with an inner and unworldly luminosity. Though they stared toward the pool, it wasn't the seething waters they saw. Verek's eyes were fixed on something only they could perceive. He held himself perfectly still, a mooring post that was lashed by a hurricane but would not yield. All of his senses, magian and mortal, seemed trained on an image that was as lost to Carin as a paper kite in a gale-force wind.

After what felt like hours but might have been minutes, the storm subsided. The stock-still warlock at her side roused from his vision. He turned to her.

"I asked that you be brought here," he said, looking at Carin gravely, with his eyes now subdued, "so that you might witness the vortex before it drew so near to this world that the waters of the *wysards* could no longer contain the image of it. Tell me: what did you make of the shapes that were darkly paired in the midst of the whirl?"

Carin shook her head. "I didn't know what to make of them," she whispered. "They seemed to be half reptile and half scorpion. But they were huge." She tilted her head to one side, reminded of something. "I heard a story once—a man was telling it to my master, the wheelwright. He talked about monsters he called *mantikhora*. They're fairy-tale creatures that have the feet and tails of scorpions. Maybe those things in the whirlpool were the real *mantikhora*."

Verek's eyes bored into Carin's. Though they no longer burned with magian fire, their steady gaze made her uneasy. When the warlock looked at her with such intensity, some part of Carin's inner resolve failed, leaving her submissive to his will. Her breath came short. If he were to fix her with such a gaze as this, then order her to conjure the dragon of the puzzle-book, would she find the strength to refuse? Or would she obey him, as she had heeded the summons that he'd conveyed to her tonight though the voice of the wizards' well?

"Think carefully," Verek said. "Seek to remember. Strive to picture that world which is your natural home. My charge to you is more urgent than you now realize. Though you trust me in no other matter, trust me in this and give me the truest answer that it is in your power to give. *Do such monstrous creatures as you have seen here tonight live on that world from which you sprang?"*

Carin could only shrug. "I don't know. I really can't say. When I try to remember 'my world,' I get nothing. It's a blank. That place you call my 'natural home' is a mystery to me.

"The woodsprite," she added, "is desperate to get back to its 'homeworld.' That's almost all the sprite talks about. But since I don't remember ever living anywhere except Ladrehdin, I really wouldn't want to leave here. This is my home." Carin was surprised to hear herself say that. She hurried to add, in case Verek thought she'd meant *his* house: "Ladrehdin is, I mean. It's the only place I can call 'home' … even if other people don't think I belong here."

Why she told the warlock about her and the woodsprite's conflicting goals, Carin couldn't say. Something in the perfect stillness of the wizards' well after its raging of moments ago, and something in Verek's own manner made her speak more openly than might be wise.

"But getting back to your question," she said, realizing how far she'd strayed from the subject, "I can't tell you anything about those *mantikhora* monsters in the whirlpool. Maybe they do come from the same world I do. Or maybe they exist only in fairy tales — or magical visions. They might be demons from hell, for all I know. I just can't say."

Verek nodded, looking more resigned than displeased.

"It is as I thought. What memories you may possess are buried so deeply that even the power of this place cannot recover them." He gestured toward the concealed doorway by which Carin had entered the cave. "The day will soon break. Seek your bed while night still reigns."

Glad out of measure, this time, to do as she was told, Carin wheeled and headed for the door. It was only as she walked away from the warlock that she realized how tautly strung she was. Her hands shook and her legs quivered. As she skirted the well of magic, she minded each unsteady footstep, taking pains to avoid tottering into the liquid glass.

Only by paying such close attention to what lay under her feet did Carin notice the artifact. It rested on the pool's rim, so perfectly flush with the smooth stone floor as to be nearly invisible, like a sheet of paper-thin, translucent glass.

Carin acted before she thought: she picked it up. The sheet was no heavier than a like-sized windowpane of thinly split, polished horn would have been. It had horn's toughness and pliability. But as she studied the long, teardrop shape and picked out a tracery of veins radiating through the sheet, Carin suddenly knew the thing in her hands for what it was: the flexible, transparent wing of a creature like a dragonfly. And it was as long as she was tall.

* * *

When she woke again, the sun had climbed to midmorning. Carin hadn't got back to bed until nearly dawn. Mercifully, no tap on her door had roused her at the usual early hour. Myra must have learned before cockcrow of the night's events, and pitied her enough to let her sleep.

That woman may know more about your affairs than you think she does, Carin silently addressed the secretive Verek. Then: *Since I'm late already, why hurry?* She decided to take time for a bath even though it would further delay her getting to work in the library.

No one reprimanded Carin, however, when she finally descended for a late breakfast. Verek was nowhere to be seen, and Myra bubbled with too much news to bother chiding her slug-abed helper.

"Oh my, dearie!" the woman exclaimed as Carin entered the warm, richly scented kitchen. "What a fuss there's been this morning. My good master took a notion, all on a sudden, to sally forth with his bow on his shoulder and bread and meat enough in his saddlebags to keep a company of men on the road. ''Tis high time, woman,' he said to me, 'that I bestirred myself from this house and got out among the freeholders and my tenants. It's to the far ends of Ruain that I'm riding. You needn't look for my return before the month is out.'"

Carin's hand paused in the act of spooning porridge to her mouth.

"Lord Verek will be gone that long?" she asked as casually as she could.

"Aye, dearie. I'd hardly kindled a fire this morning before my master came stumping down the hall in his heaviest boots, dressed for the ride and carrying his warmest cloak. A man fit and eager for travel, he was. We'll not be seeing him for a good two weeks—unless I've grown too old and blind to know a man who's making for the road, when he's come to the table for the last home-cooked meal that he'll likely see in a fortnight."

Two possibilities sprang at once to Carin's mind. The first was that Verek rode out, immediately after last night's storm of magic, to discover whether the vermin they had seen in the image now infested his own lands.

Why should he think the creatures were here? Carin buttered a piece of bread while she thought it through. Last night, the wizards' well had burst its bounds when the whirlpool *drew so near* to Ladrehdin, Verek said, that the mirror pool could no longer hold the image of the vortex. From that idea, it was a short leap to suppose that the vortex had actually, physically reached Ladrehdin, the same way the whirlpool of Carin's own passage had reached the millpond on the southern plains. And just as that other vortex had discharged its cargo—her—maybe the whirlpool they saw last night had delivered two huge, venomous monsters to terrorize Ruain.

Was that what had drawn Verek straight from the cave of magic into the saddle and through the manor's gates? By Myra's account, the warlock had barely had time to don his riding leathers and call for his horse. He couldn't have gotten even a half-hour's sleep. The sun had been poised just below the horizon when Carin left him puzzling over the translucent wing that had washed up in the magic pool.

Another artifact which, years before, had come like flotsam to the pool's rim was the honey-colored wand that interested the woodsprite. Verek's absence raised the second part of Carin's deliberations over breakfast: whether to take the woodsprite into the library to see the relic. What better time for such a risky venture, with the warlock away?

It would be best to avoid drawing notice to her plans, she decided. Carin kept to her usual routine. She spent what was left of the morning at work in the library, enjoying the warmth of a fire on the hearth and the glow of her own anticipation. She stole time from her duties to investigate the liquor cabinet behind which Verek kept the wand. But as it had for nearly two weeks, the cabinet defied Carin's attempts to open its slat-wood back. The sprite would have to be content with whatever the creature could learn of the wand through the thin wooden wall that concealed it.

After lunch, she walked Emrys around the grounds. The mare was impatient for exercise. Carin had neglected the horse for the past three days, in the disruption that finding the *Book of Archamon* and losing her homemade bow had inflicted on her routine.

When she stabled the mare and returned to the house, Carin peeked in at Myra, confirming that the woman napped in her room off the kitchen. The way was clear to smuggle the woodsprite into the library. Quickly she passed through empty corridors to the great hall at the far end of the building.

"Carin!" the sprite greeted her excitedly. "How I hoped you would come! The mage must be leagues away by now. I saw him ride out at first light—and well-equipped he was for a journey of many days. I followed for a time, to be certain that he would keep to his course and not circle back to surprise us in our intrigues. For this is the day—isn't it, my friend?—that you'll take me up in a seedling and bear me within the mage's house to see the wood that might be—could be—*must* be a part of my home-world!"

"Take it easy, sprite," Carin said, laughing while she tried to calm the creature that sparked in the rowan at the servants' entrance. "Yes, my strange friend, I will take you as close to the wand as I can. But you may be disappointed. We can't be sure the stick has anything to do with the world you come from. Everything about it might feel wrong to you.

"I also need to warn you," she added, "that I've tried several times but I can't find a way into the wand's hiding-hole. Verek made it look easy to open, but I haven't discovered the secret. So, I can take you only as far as the liquor cabinet. If that's not close enough, tell me now. I'm still worried about taking you indoors. It's dangerous, and we shouldn't do it if there's no point in it."

"The cabinet will be near enough, Carin," the sprite said. "Though the trees in which I dwell must be of living wood, I may press myself for stretches of time into lumber that's dry and seasoned. Take me as close as you've said, and leave all else to me. Follow me now to the twig that will be my vessel for this voyage."

The sprite led her to a hazel seedling. Carin pulled it up by the roots, taking care not to shake off the damp dirt that clung to them. The roots must be kept moist, the sprite warned. Else, the seedling would wither and become perilously unsuitable as a dwelling-tree for a woodsprite.

When the creature had leaped within, Carin rushed it into the great hall and along the connecting passageways to her quarters.

At the washbasin in her bathing room, she rinsed and filled an empty cider-mug and plunged the seedling's roots in it. The woodsprite nearly wriggled with delight at the sensation of warm water and saturated soil enveloping what it called its feet.

Carin took the potted sprite downstairs. No sound came from the kitchen. Myra would probably enjoy a long nap after the morning's madhouse of getting her master fed and provisioned for his journey.

In the library, on a roomy shelf next to the liquor cabinet, Carin set the sprite's cider-mug. She wanted both hands free to snap open the cabinet's doors and empty it of glass flagon and goblets. One fumble while juggling mug and glassware could send the whole lot crashing to the stone tiles, with disastrous consequences for the sprite and for Verek's expensive crystal.

But as she placed the goblets with the sprite's mug, a single small object on the otherwise empty shelf caught Carin's eye. It was a round, polished piece of red quartz.

That it hadn't been there yesterday, she was certain. She had used that very shelf to hold books she was sorting for the "B" section of Verek's collection.

But whether the rock had been there this morning, Carin couldn't say. So intent had she been on probing the wand's hiding place for some secret fastener or fingerhold, a coiled snake on the shelf might well have escaped her notice. A rock as small as this almost certainly would have gone unseen.

Suspicions prickled like hackles on her neck. Carin picked up the quartz. It exuded an unpleasant sort of moist heat. As soon as her fingers closed upon it, the stone began to glow with an eerie inner light—much as the warlock's dark eyes glowed when they saw things no mortal could glimpse.

Carin had a sudden and powerful urge to fling the thing as far as she could throw it.

A seer's stone! She doubted it could be anything else. She had read in one of Verek's books that sorcerers used such devices to watch from afar. And she knew, from the moment her hand touched the thing, that she had borne her trusting woodland friend into a trap.

"Drisha's mercy!" Carin swore through clenched teeth. She grabbed the sprite's cider-mug. Wasting no breath on explanations, she made to flee.

But she'd hardly cleared the room's paired benches when the library's door opened. Over the threshold stepped Verek, wearing his riding leathers but unarmed except for the dagger at his belt.

"You—!" At the sight of him, Carin almost lost her footing. She swerved toward the desk and skidded to a stop behind it. She stood there glaring at the fiend, gulping increasingly shallow breaths as the muscles in her throat knotted up.

"I thank you for not disappointing me," Verek said acidly as the door closed behind him. He did not move farther into the room. "As the hours passed and I saw by the 'scrying crystal that you had not fetched the sprite here, I began to believe that my plan had failed. Without a doubt, I had thought, you would have told the creature of the wand, and no less certainly it would beg a look.

"'Will the girl not bring her weirdling friend,' I asked myself, 'to storm the wall that hides their prize, the moment they believe themselves safe in their venture?' It pleases me to know that I did not take the mismeasure of the one or the other of you. And now, I'll claim *my* prize: the irksome creature that has so long eluded me."

Verek advanced toward the desk. From the mug in Carin's hand, the sprite gave a shriek of terror.

Carin thrust the seedling behind her back. She drew herself up to her full height—which brought her brow even with the warlock's chin—and shook her head.

"No," she snarled, eyeing Verek with what she hoped was determination. "You're not going to get the sprite this way. I'd die before I'd let you hurt my friend."

Whirling, Carin raised the mug as high as her shoulder and started to heave it through the window over the desk. The mug would shatter, as would the windowpane. But if she could hurl the sprite in its seedling through the glass, the creature could leap to the safety of a tree in Jerold's garden.

Barely had her arm begun its upward thrust, however, when Carin's body hardened to a rigid, compact mass. She could not move.

The spell of stone! screamed panic inside her head.

She banished terror before it could rout the last of her wits. Carin filled her mind instead with imagining that her body was rising from a pool of watery mud. In her mind's eye, the mud on her skin looked like a thin honey and brown-sugar glaze. She conjured a hot desert wind to blow the glaze dry, and called down a shower of pebbles to crumble it to powder.

The imagery was swift and powerful. Shattered utterly, the spell released her. Carin's arm heaved the sprite's cider-mug toward the window. Her fingers opened to cast it through the glass —

— And Verek's hand closed around it, snatching the mug in flight. Though the spell of stone had held her for not more than two seconds, it had given Verek the time he needed to reach the desk and stretch an arm between Carin and the window.

"No!" she screamed, and grabbed for the mug.

But already it was beyond her reach. Verek's long strides had carried him to the fireplace. He gripped the seedling and let the mug slip away and crash to the floor. The mug broke with a wet, fleshy sound, like a pumpkin rupturing, and covered the hearth in mud and pottery shards.

The sprite shrieked, then whimpered like a frightened child.

"Hold!" Verek ordered as Carin took a step toward him. "Would you provoke me further and see the creature die? Begone—or I'll toss your cowardly friend in the fire." As he uttered the threat, the warlock passed the seedling's bare roots through the flames. The sprite screamed—whether in pain or terror, Carin could not tell.

She threw up her hand, silently imploring the blackheart to stop torturing his captive. She edged to the hall door. With her hand on the latch, Carin tried, through hot tears, to look daggers at the warlock, but she knew the look she gave him was more wretched than menacing.

In a voice choked with passionate hatred, she flung at Verek the words he had screamed to protest the cruelty of the wizards' well: "You are a *monster!*" Then Carin pulled open the door and passed through to the hallway, abandoning her one true friend to its fate.

Chapter 22

One Dolphin

When the door had thudded shut behind her, Carin slid down it, to collapse in a defeated heap on the floor. For a long time she stared down the hallway, seeing nothing, feeling nothing except the tears that trickled over her cheeks. The trickle grew to a torrent: Carin cried as she had not cried since the first year of her life in the wheelwright's household, when she'd lain awake nights, sobbing in terror and confusion, filled with a deep, aching loneliness.

Gradually the deluge slowed, then stopped. Carin wiped her eyes with the tail of her shirt, which had caught enough of her tears to be hardly less wet than her face. She was wearing the oldest garment in her sparse wardrobe, the once ivory-colored shirt in which she had walked from the wheelwright's service into Verek's.

If I'd never come to this cursed land, Carin raged inwardly, *the sprite never would have fallen into the hands of the blackheart who rules it. I've brought the creature to its death.* She winced, remembering her brave words: "I'd die before I'd let you hurt my friend," she had told Verek. Yet here she cowered at the door — too frightened, too much in awe of him to do anything to save the creature.

What *could* she do? How could she challenge a wizard whose power would overwhelm her the way a lightning bolt outshone a candle? What weapon did she have that could prevail against Verek?

The Jabberwock. She had the Jabberwock.

Objections crowded into Carin's mind as quickly as the thought took shape. Her own chances of dying in the dragon's jaws far exceeded Verek's. He wanted the monster turned loose against an enemy of Ladrehdin. He wouldn't be the dragon's victim in his opponent's stead.

But supposing, for the sake of argument, that Carin dared to summon the monster against him: then the problem became *how*. The puzzle-book dragon seemed inextricably tied to the enchanted waters that gave it form. Verek would be vulnerable to the monster's talons only when he stood in the cavern of the wizards' well. And to conjure the beast, Carin must recite the whole of the incantation, including the lines that called the dragon's heralds: the "toves," "borogoves," and "raths" of the opening stanza. At the sight of those creatures rising from the mists of the magic pool, Verek would know at once that Carin sought to call the dragon against him. Speak the incantation as fast as she could, and still the sorcerer would have time to dive for the safety of the stairwell, where Carin had seen that the dragon's claws could not reach him.

And what about the sprite? If the fay was still alive, and Verek held it prisoner in the cave, then Carin's summoning the Jabberwock might prove deadlier to the woodsprite than to the warlock.

No, she could not use the dragon against Verek—not until she was sure he couldn't escape it, and the woodsprite could. To know those things beyond a doubt, Carin would have to be in the cave—to conjure the dragon at the precise moment that would see the warlock fatally trapped and the sprite safe.

She stood and shoved open the door against which she'd huddled—for how long? To judge by the waning sun through the library's windows, she had sat for at least two hours, by turns vacant, numb, and sick with despair.

The fear crawling up Carin's spine was a strength-sapping parasite that she must pluck out lest it cripple her. If she had found Verek in the room when she flung open the door, she might have lost the battle before it was joined. The library, however, was empty. And in the time it took to search the hearth for the burnt remains of the woodsprite's seedling, Carin wrested her courage from terror's grasp. The ashes in the fireplace revealed nothing recognizable as a charred hazel twig — providing no proof that the sprite was alive, but offering a glimmer of hope that it hadn't died in the flames within seconds of her abandoning it.

Carin strode into the perpetual shadows opposite the windows and made for the hidden portal to the cave of magic. She spat on the door's creaky hinges, then eased it open.

All was silence. If Verek waited in the cavern below, he would not *hear* Carin approach, at least. By how many other senses, magian and mortal, he might detect her presence, she couldn't guess.

She wound her way down the steps. From the foot of them, she peered into the vault. It was empty.

Carin ground her teeth in frustration. Having made up her mind to conjure the Jabberwock against Verek, she counted the time all too long until her chance to act might come.

She started to put a foot on the cave's floor, to make her way across it to the concealed doorway beyond the pool. But Carin's foot dangled in midair as caution whispered a warning: *Will you risk offending the power of this place, and by your recklessness lose all hope of saving the woodsprite?*

Verek's words came to her: "The well of *wysards* thinks it prudent to turn you to stone when I am not in the chamber to govern you." Maybe Carin wouldn't break free of the well's enchantment as easily as she had Verek's spellcraft.

She turned and raced back up the steps. The pool of magic, if it was aware of her now as it had been before, might already have informed its servant that Carin sought him.

Through the library she ran, and down the hallway to the stair foyer. On sudden impulse Carin continued along the passageway to the kitchen, thinking of a particularly sharp, narrow-bladed knife that she had used for boning meat.

"Oh my, dearie!" Myra greeted her arrival in the kitchen. "'Tis an odd turn this day has taken. My good master rides away at sunrise, as ready for the road as any man I ever did see and promising a fortnight's absence as surely as a day's. But what do my eyes behold as I'm throwing out the washing-water from noontime's dishes? None but my own master, hurrying back like a man with urgent business who daren't delay a moment. 'Ask me no questions, woman!' he bids me as he passes, and I hold my tongue, though fair I am to bursting with them.

"But dearie!" the housekeeper exclaimed, now catching sight of her helper's face. "Whatever is the matter? You've been cry-ing—in a fair way to cry your eyes out, by the look of it. What ails you, lass?"

Carin shook her head, loath to waste time on the woman's chatter. "Something has been taken from me," she snapped as her hand closed on the hilt of the boning knife. "It's something important, and I mean to get it back. Don't try to stop me, Myra."

Then she was back down the passageway and at the foot of the bedroom stairs. Two at a time Carin took them until she reached the landing that fronted her door. Without slowing, she turned along the corridor that hid the upper entrance to Verek's rooms.

And as she took a step down that hallway, a section of its stone wall melted. The stonework reshaped itself into a door of braced timbers. The door opened inward, and out stepped the warlock. He no longer wore his riding gear, but had changed into his usual garb of dark trousers, a white shirt, and a vest. This one was gentian blue.

Carin raised her knife and rushed him.

Verek stood relaxed in his doorway. He watched her come at him with neither surprise nor anger on his face. He didn't bespell the knife and send it flying from Carin's grasp. Nor did he make a statue of her. He only waited until she had closed the distance between them. Then his left hand flew up, caught her wrist, and wrung it, hard.

The knife fell from fingers made nerveless. He kicked the weapon aside.

Carin jerked her wrist from his grasp and backed away, nursing bruises to her knife-hand and to her pride. Her attack, foolhardy, had been less to the warlock than a fleabite. But why hadn't he wielded magic against her and saved himself the trouble of physically disarming her?

As he so often did, Verek seemed to know what Carin was thinking.

"Small use casting the spell of stone upon you," he said. "I have seen you break it with the speed and skill of a practiced magician. But would you expect to prevail against me with a kitchen knife? There aren't many alive in this world who would be so bold as to challenge me with any weapon so slight."

Go down to the cave, you fiend, Carin thought, seething, *and you'll see a more terrifying weapon.*

Aloud, she answered him in a voice dripping malice. "There aren't many people in this world that I would like to kill with my own hands. In fact, you're it—you evil warlock. I hate you so much that I would willingly put a knife in your heart. To feel your blood on my hands—oh! I would enjoy that."

The sorcerer's face darkened. "Your words are empty. You know nothing of such matters. Until you have killed, you have no right to speak of taking pleasure in spilling another's blood."

"And did you have a pleasant time murdering the woodsprite?" Carin retorted. "Or was the juice in its veins too thin, too much like water, to satisfy your taste for blood?"

Verek sighed. "Such would be the weight of all the bloodguilt that you lay to my account, that did I truly bear it, by no effort could I lift my head higher than the grasshopper's knee." He pushed open the still-visible door at his right hand, then jerked his head to indicate the room beyond. "Your friend is here, un-harmed and disposed to talk. Go to it, and satisfy yourself that whatever sap the creature uses for blood has not left its veins."

The woodsprite was alive? Or was Verek setting another trap?

Carin approached the open door as if it were the web of a spider that had invited her into its parlor. The warlock stood motionless, holding the door and watching her as she brushed past him.

Verek allowed her to pass untouched. Wordlessly, he closed the door behind him as he ushered her into the antechamber of his secret apartments.

The room, gallery-like, was longer than it was wide. The hall door through which Carin had entered claimed a good part of one short wall. Opposite it was a tall window, deeply recessed into the thick exterior wall of Verek's house. The window reached to the floor, giving the narrow space ample light and an airy feel. Draping either side of it were curtains of a rich crimson silk, thrown open to the late-day sun. The window, Carin knew without crossing to it, looked out over Jerold's enchanted garden.

Both long walls of the room were covered in a silky, silver-tinted fabric that created expanses of paleness. Brightening them were thin, sweeping brushstrokes laid on randomly in the same crimson hue as the curtains.

In the wall to Carin's right was a closed door—leading, she supposed, to other rooms of Verek's private suite. Beside that door was a low sofa covered in crimson silk. Next to the sofa stood a round table that was formed entirely of gold-threaded marble. The same marble made up the mantelpiece of a grace-fully proportioned fireplace in the long wall opposite the sofa wall.

That expanse was otherwise blank except for four paintings in richly carved frames. They hung, two by two, on either side of the mantelpiece. The first pair were landscapes: one with snow-capped mountain pinnacles; the other with a calm blue lake ringed by flowers in a sheltered oak woodland. The second pair, to the right of the fireplace, were portraits.

Carin stared. One was the face of a beautiful young woman whom she recognized at once, from the macabre image that had floated above the mirror pool, as the dead Alesia. The other portrait was of a bright-eyed, dark-haired little boy of about five — the drowned "child of shining spirit," he had to be.

Verek, following Carin into the room, dropped onto the sofa. He heaved a weary sigh.

Carin tore her gaze from the portraits and walked to the window, watching a leafy tree that grew in a stone tub in front of it. The sunlight that touched the tree through the open-curtained window picked up the faintest motion of its leaves, like the trembling of an aspen's.

"My friend!" cried the woodsprite at Carin's approach. Its reedy voice sounded nervously subdued. "Words fail me. I am more pleased to see you than I can say."

She reached her hand through the tree's middle branches and gripped the trunk. For a long moment, Carin couldn't speak. She was choking on the tears that spilled down her face and dripped onto the leaves. She stood clinging to the tree trunk, offering up silent gratitude to whatever gods watched over defenseless woodsprites.

"Don't cry!" the creature begged, its distress evident in its thin voice. "I am quite undamaged. And though your tears touch me deeply, I must beg you not to drop them on the soil under this shrub. Salt water, you know — it's bad for the roots. If I'm to dwell in this potted plant, then I'd best keep my host healthy!"

"Sorry," Carin mumbled. She released the trunk, backed away half a step, and wiped at her face. "I'm just so happy to find you alive and talking. When that motherless sneak put your 'feet' in the fire, I was sure he'd kill you." Verek, sitting on the couch not half the length of the room behind her, could hardly help hearing what she called him. Carin didn't care.

"As was I, friend!" the sprite exclaimed. "As was I! But the seedling's roots were wet enough, or had enough soil still clinging, to protect them from the flames. I was terrified but little harmed. Yelping as I did was cowardly. You were so brave in my defense, it makes me all the more ashamed of myself."

Carin shook her head. "I ran and left you in the fiend's hands. I'm the coward, not you."

"Do not reproach yourself. If you had disobeyed him, the mage might well have thrown me on the fire. I confess I thought you sometimes stretched a point in our talks together, Carin, when you told me how the magician made you fear for your life. I was free to have my doubts as long as I leapt unhindered through the trees. But now that I'm in his power, I see what you mean. This wizard can set one's leaves to fluttering."

"Yes, he can," Carin muttered under her breath, reluctant to let the warlock at her back hear them so freely confess the terror that he inspired in both his captives. "But tell me, sprite," she added, louder. "What happened after I left you alone with the fiend? What did he do to you?"

"Nothing so very terrible," the sprite replied, beginning to sound more like its usual, affable self. "Once I had mustered wits enough to know that I was not roasting, I told the mage I fared poorly in withered wood. I asked for dirt and water to shore up my seedling. He filled a crystal goblet with the wet soil from my broken mug and set my roots down in it. I thanked him then— as I do now, sir," the always-courteous creature called over Carin's shoulder to the warlock behind her.

"And then," the sprite added, "the mage drew from its hiding place the wand that I have longed to see."

The bait that Verek knew would draw two fools into his trap, Carin thought, biting the inside of her mouth to keep from interrupting the sprite.

339

"Eagerly I gazed at the wand," the creature went on. "When I asked him to, the mage pressed the staff to my seedling so that I could force myself into the wand's pores and fibers. But just as you had warned me, Carin, I could feel nothing of my home-world in the beautiful thing. Inside the wand were only empti-ness and silence. I have felt more kinship with the sun-dried lumber of this world than I sensed in that featureless stick."

For a moment the sprite was quiet. Carin fingered a leaf of its prison-tree, knowing she had no words that could soften the creature's disappointment.

"But hope was not all lost," the sprite went on, with a forced cheerfulness in its voice. "The mage then took me deep into the ground — deeper, it must be, than any tree ever thrust a root — to the pool like a perfect mirror of which you have told me, Carin. My excitement was high when the mage proposed delving into my buried memories, the way he has looked into yours.

"'By all means!' I cried, eager to see in the pool's magic mists a world I cannot remember but long to know. Again, however, I was frustrated. Though I filled my thoughts with everything I could recall of my first days on this world called Ladrehdin, no image rose from the pool. Its surface never rippled.

"'Your mind is too alien,' the mage told me. 'The waters of the *wysards* can make nothing of your memories. The way your mind works — the way it weaves its thoughts — is so strange, the waters cannot join with it. For all her otherworldliness, the girl reasons and comprehends with a mind that is much like any the well-spring would find in Ladrehdin. With her thoughts, interplay is possible. But your mind is too outlandish — too peculiar for even the power of this place to penetrate.'

"Am I giving a fair account of your words, Lord Mage?" the sprite called over Carin's shoulder.

The woodsprite's efforts to include Verek in their conversa-tion thwarted Carin's attempts to treat the warlock like house-dust. She suppressed a sigh at the creature's misplaced courtesy, and turned to see how Verek would respond.

He only nodded and gave a brief, listless wave of his hand, as if indifferently sanctioning the sprite to continue.

Carin intervened, however, before the creature could say more.

"That's it, then," she snapped at Verek. "This whole thing is a mistake, and you've admitted it. You don't need to keep the sprite locked up. You can't learn anything from the creature. Your sorcery doesn't work on it." She sniffed contemptuously. "You didn't even need to lay a trap to catch the sprite. All you had to do was show it the wand, and invite it to go with you down to the wizard's well. The creature would have told you everything it knows and done anything you'd asked. It *wants* you to help it find its way home."

She sneered at Verek. "All that trouble to get your hands on the woodsprite, all that effort to trick and threaten both of us — it would have been easier to just *ask*.

"So what are you going to do now?" Carin demanded, slinging her words at Verek, giving him no chance to answer. "I'll tell you what you *should* do. It's what a 'noble lord' who deserves the title would do. Turn the sprite loose. The creature isn't useful to you." Carin pointed at the window and the fading daylight outside. "Right now, before the sun goes down, act like you've got a streak of decency in you, and set the creature free. The sprite will excuse the wrongs you've done it. It knows you can't help your black heart. It doesn't even seem to hate you. Whether Drisha — or whatever dark god you pray to — will pardon you, though, I can't guess."

"But *you* assuredly will *not* forgive me!" Verek exclaimed, breaking his silence. He sat forward on the sofa. "Isn't that the meaning you wish me to find in your witless words? Perhaps you will pardon me, however — you presumptuous wench! — if I confess myself untroubled by your censure. It's not your good opinion that I require."

Shaking his head—whether at her insolence or his tolerating it, Carin couldn't say—Verek sat back and resettled himself. Then he fixed her with a look so black that even the sprite in its prison-tree beside her felt the force of the warlock's gaze. Carin heard a thin, whistling gasp from her fellow captive.

She steeled herself, knowing from three weeks' acquaintance with the sorcerer that such a look boded ill.

"What I require of you," Verek said in a voice like flint, "is that you complete a certain task which I am sure you will wish to refuse. Though I might threaten, imprison, starve or shackle you, still you would resist. Weeks would be lost—months, perhaps—as you defied me.

"Weeks and months cannot be spared. The time to act is now. The task of which I speak cannot await your pleasure. It cannot await my winning your trust—a thing I begin to think impossible, given your vast and fantastic suspicions of me. The task cannot await my subduing—by force, persuasion, or enchantment—the obstinacy within you that retreats to guardedness when what is needed is a sworn covenant between us.

"Therefore, I mean to use the sprite to compel your obedience. Do as I command, difficult though you may find the task, and the creature goes free. Refuse me, and the sprite dies. My terms are simply those."

He wants me to walk into the jaws of the Jabberwock. The conviction rose firm in Carin's heart, and made a cold sweat pop on her forehead. *That is the price of my friend's life. Verek wants me to admit that I don't belong in this world, I should not be here—I've no right to be here. To remove the threat I pose to Ladrehdin, I am to throw myself—like a sin offering to Drisha—into the dragon's mouth. With me dead, the Jabberwock can never again be summoned to this world. All here will be safe from any harm I might do. And the woodsprite will live. But refuse my own destruction, and the sprite will die.*

342

Maybe … *maybe*, came a whisper from a corner of Carin's mind where fear did not rule, *there's another possible outcome.* Verek would be with her in the cave of magic when she conjured the dragon. He would want to see Carin sacrifice herself with his own dark, accursed eyes. Could she trick him? Could she be the one sheltering in the stairwell, safely out of reach, while the dragon ripped the warlock apart?

Find a way, whispered a cold little voice. *The Jabberwock is your only weapon against this sorcerer. Use it.*

Struggling to keep her thoughts off her face, Carin bent her gaze past Verek's shoulder—there was no looking into those glinting eyes—and nodded assent.

"I will do what you tell me to. Just don't hurt the woodsprite. And as soon as I've done what you want, you've got to set the creature free like you promised. Do we have a bargain?"

"We have," Verek said shortly. He rose from his couch and walked to the door, to pull it open and stand waiting for her.

"Carin!" cried the woodsprite from its prison at her side. "I do not like this bargain that's been struck. Promise me that you won't put yourself in danger for my sake. My gratitude would be boundless if you could do some arduous but innocent chore and thereby gain my release. I'd forever be your devoted servant. But in your eyes and in the mage's dark looks I see hints of things that are not only arduous, but perilous. Promise me, Carin! Swear that you will not endanger yourself in my behalf. Were harm to befall you in this, I could never forgive myself. Throw myself onto the plains, I would. There to perish with no twig for shelter."

"Hush, sprite." Carin reproved the creature gently, stroking a leaf. "Don't talk like that. I'll be fine, and so will you. Whatever the warlock needs me to do, I'll do, to get you out of here." She tried to smile. "When this is over and you're free, I'll meet you in the back garden. All right?"

Not for the first time, Carin wished she were a more accomplished liar. She sounded unconvincing, even to herself. In a last attempt to reassure the sprite, she gave the tree a squeeze.

Then she joined Verek in the doorway, leaving the creature spluttering: "But I—you— *My friend!*"

Just before the warlock shut the door behind them, Carin called into the room, cutting across the creature's stammer: "Stand up to him, sprite! Tell the son-of-a-hag if you need more sun or water."

The object of her aspersion reached past her to pull the door closed in Carin's face. And as Verek's hand left the latch, the cross-braced timbers dissolved. Stonework indistinguishable from the rest of the corridor took the door's place. The upper portal to the warlock's private haunts had disappeared.

Carin stood in the hallway quivering like a taut bowstring. Her fists were clenched. At least, the left one was; her right fist wouldn't close all the way. At a movement from Verek, she jerked her hand behind her back.

"Is your wrist sprained?" Verek growled. "If it pains you, I will bind it."

Carin shook her head. She'd rather hurt than have him touch her again.

The warlock studied her for a moment. Then he bent to retrieve the knife he'd made her drop. He used it like a pointer to indicate the invisible doorway.

"Do not tarry here, grieving for your odd friend and plotting its deliverance. You will find my chamber doors proof against your scheming."

He stalked to the landing above the foyer stairs and gestured down them. "Myra will soon have the kettle on the fire. She'll be wanting her helper." Verek stood for another moment scowling at Carin, then descended, saying nothing more about the "difficult task" he planned for her.

She trailed him, straggling along, the weight of her apprehension dragging Carin down the stairs. Did the warlock not mean to usher her immediately underground to meet what awaited her in the cave of magic?

He should, she thought, *and get this over with — this "bargain" I've struck with the devil.*

At the foot of the steps, Verek turned down the hallway toward the library. Carin fled along the passageway in the opposite direction to the kitchen.

"Oh my, dearie! Here you are!" Myra greeted her. Anxiety was written on the woman's face as she rushed to take Carin's hands in hers. Perhaps the housekeeper had read enough in Carin's tears and her master's gruffness to know that trouble was brewing. Maybe she felt the tension in the air. In any case, the woman did not speak of Verek's aborted journey to "the ends of Ruain" or of Carin's sudden need for a knife. Instead, Myra seemed bent on lifting her helper's spirits with a wordy speech on the merits of using parboiled kidney in any recipe that called for calf innards.

Carin suffered in silence and helped the woman get the evening meal on the table as quickly as possible. Then, excusing herself on the pretext of a vicious headache, she slipped upstairs to her bedroom before Verek called for his meal.

Despite the warlock's warning, she detoured down the corridor with the intention of trying the invisible door to his sitting room. But the blackheart's spells held firmly against her. Although Carin knew, from the location of the hallway window opposite, where the door must be, she could feel neither its timbers nor its latch, only the stonework of the wall. Verek's sorcery now concealed the portal from her touch as wholly as from her sight.

In her room, Carin paced and thought. She threw herself on her bed and agonized. She splashed water on her face and tried to scheme. But she could devise no definite plan for making the warlock, not herself, the dragon's most probable victim. Inaudibly Carin rehearsed the *"Jabberwocky"* incantation, over and over, until she could deliver the opening stanza in the space of four heartbeats. Verek would not need more time than that, however, to remove himself from danger. At the first sight of the dragon's heralds, he would make for the safety of the stairwell. Conjuring the monster quickly enough to catch him unawares did not seem possible.

The answer, Carin decided, would be to keep Verek out of the stairwell, just long enough for one razor-sharp dragon's talon to lay him open from collarbone to groin. How?

Carin raked through Myra's multitude, seeking a candlestick that might serve her as a spear. If she could sneak it into the cave of magic … if she could plant herself within the stairwell to wield it even briefly against Verek … if she could keep him at bay until the dragon roared up in answer to her summons …

There was no end of "ifs," but an end came to Carin's reprieve. A knock, firm and insistent, sounded at her bedroom door.

When she didn't answer, there was a moment's pause. Then the latch was lifted and the door opened wide. Verek stood on the threshold, looking as refreshed as Carin felt expended. The sleep-short warlock, she surmised, had been taking a nap while she'd been walking the floors.

On Verek's shoulder rested a glowing witchlight orb. In his left hand, he held the puzzle-book.

Why have the book with him? They were done with the second reading of the volume. Over the past week and a half, they had discussed shades of meaning for every word that Carin could not translate with absolute certainty into the Ladrehdinian tongue. She could tell him nothing more about the book. What reason might there be for the warlock to have the volume with him tonight? Carin could think of only one:

He assumes that I don't remember the incantation that calls the Jabberwock. He believes I will have to read from the book those words that will mean my extinction.

"Come," Verek murmured. "It is time to begin."

Carin wiped her sleeve across her forehead. Then she followed him out the door without a backward glance at Myra's multitude, which had yielded nothing she might use against the warlock in the moments before the dragon materialized.

Along the corridor under high, dusk-darkened windows they walked without speaking. Down three long flights of stairs they descended, passing at some unknown point from the surface world to the underground realm of the wizards' well.

This time, the concealed door to the cave did not swing open. Was the power of that place not expecting them?

Verek reached into the secret opening in the dark paneling, lifted the latch, and pushed the door in upon its unseen hinges. As the cave's ruddy light spilled into the stairwell, the witchlight orb vanished from the warlock's shoulder.

Carin trailed her captor into the magical space, feeling as much alarm at her own passivity as at the prospect of facing the dragon. Had she grown resigned to her fate? Or was this what it felt like to be numb with terror?

The door closed behind her. Carin looked over her shoulder at the place where it had been. Nothing met her eyes but a surface of stone.

Across the vault was the opening that gave upon the spiraling steps up to the library. It would be in that stairwell that either Carin or the warlock would find sanctuary from the dragon's claws.

Verek did not take himself to that refuge. He sat on the nearest bench—that of the carved key—and gestured for Carin to join him.

What's he waiting for? She studied him through narrowed eyes. *Does he enjoy stringing this out?*

"Sit," Verek instructed when Carin ignored his silent gesture. "There are matters we must speak of before the work begins."

Carin unwillingly obeyed, perching on the bench as far from the warlock as possible. Did he intend to bring up "noble acts" and "reluctant killings"?

The thought of my death must hurt his conscience, if he needs to tell himself again that I have to die for the good of this world.

But when Verek continued, it was not on the subject of the puzzle-book dragon as "an instrument for good."

"You told me last night—or was it in the small hours of this morning? Night and day lose their meaning when one goes sleepless. You told me that you did not wish to return to that world which is your natural home, a world you do not remember. Tell me now, and speak the plainest truth that lives within you: Is it your definite wish to remain where you are? Or, if you were given the chance to go back to that other world, would you take it?"

Carin stared at the warlock. What did this have to do with her conjuring a killer?

Slowly, she shook her head. "No. I wouldn't go there even if I could. That other place means nothing to me." Carin looked up at the cave's rough, high ceiling, imagining other worlds far beyond. "I would try to help the woodsprite find its 'home-world,' if I knew how to do that." She glanced back at Verek. "But for me? No. For me, Ladrehdin is 'home.'"

The warlock nodded. "Good. That will render the task ahead of you less distressing. If you longed for that other world, great would be the temptation to lose yourself in the image of it. *But that, you must not do.* Though it will seem as if you tread firmly upon the surface of that world, only an intangible part of you will walk there. Your essence, your being—your life's breath I'll call it, for want of better words—will remain here with me, in this cavern, on this world.

"*Remember that,*" Verek ordered, leaning toward Carin. "Your safety will depend on it. *You must not attempt to linger* in that other place. You will cross to it; you will lay the looking-glass book upon the desk in the child's bedchamber; you will take the crystal from the head of the bed and place its chain round your neck. And then you will return here. You will do *only* these things that I have said—no more and no less."

Verek put the puzzle-book on the bench between them, then rested his weight on that hand and leaned across the volume, bringing his face to within inches of Carin's. "Before I relinquish this strange book and send it back with you, back to the world from which it came, there is one thing that I must know. Have you committed to memory the words that call the monster?"

Now we're getting there! He's sure taking the long way around to the dragon.

Though she had thought herself prepared for it, Carin felt her mouth go dry at Verek's question. In reply, she could give only a half nod.

"Good. I expected as much," the warlock said as he studied Carin's face at uncomfortably close range. "One who arms herself with bow and knife would not have overlooked the dragon's promise as a weapon. I don't doubt that you learned the rhyme by heart on the day you first contemplated conjuring the beast against me. How many hours have you devoted, I wonder, to seeking a means of calling the creature without first summoning its heralds? It is an inconvenient sort of incantation, is it not, that gives itself away and grants the would-be victim time enough to flee? I am moved to commend you for the restraint you have shown, in attempting to this hour no loosing of the beast against me. Hasty and rash as is your nature, I have looked every day for the dragon's appearance."

Carin struggled against the wave of hopelessness that threatened to undo her. So—the warlock was already on his guard.

What chance did she have now of denying him the safety of the stairs?

Verek pulled back to his end of the bench. He slid the *Looking-Glass* book along the seat until it touched Carin's hand. Hardly aware that she did so, she picked it up.

"There shall come a time, unless I am much mistaken," the sorcerer said, "when you will have good and urgent cause to conjure your otherworldly dragon against a *wysard*. That time is not now. The task before us tonight will, however, take us into the realm from which the dragon springs. I strongly counsel you to say nothing that would summon the beast. That it would find you a more tempting morsel than myself, I don't doubt. Young flesh is the most desired by any eater of meat."

Verek stood and reached his hand to help Carin to her feet. He escorted her around the mirror pool, in the direction of the bench that bore Carin's preferred image, that of a fish.

She was unresisting. Outwardly she must appear to him almost dazed. But her thoughts were spinning:

How was this possible? Could she be so wrong, so far off the mark? In a complete reversal of Carin's expectations, the warlock had ordered her *not* to summon the dragon of her death. Her mind seemed hardly able to accept this turn of events. Did she understand Verek correctly? She was to enter the dragon's realm for no reason except to return the puzzle-book and steal a crystal trinket? What was this unpredictable sorcerer *thinking*?

He guided Carin to a spot midway between the pool and the bench of the fish. Standing behind her, Verek drew Carin's hair back off her shoulders and put his hands firmly on them. His forefingers pressed against the sides of her neck. Into her right ear, he whispered his commands.

"Gaze into the pool. Breathe deeply and slowly. Clear your mind of all thoughts but for the child's bedchamber with its many bright-hued fish, its books and playthings on the shelves. Picture it: the desk and the chest of drawers … the bedpost from which a crystal hangs by a golden chain. Think of the room as it appeared when you summoned its image once before from the waters of the *wysards.*"

Carin stared at the pool's glassy surface. As she recalled the bedroom in all the detail of its first emergence from the well of magic, the pool lost its mirror sheen and grew transparent. She saw the steps that led down from its rim, down into crystalline water, ever downward into an abyss that seemed eternal.

Then the water fogged. The pool's surface grew misty. Out of the mist rose the small room with its four-posted bed and the tall shelves above a child-sized desk. The great egg with piglike eyes looked down from the topmost shelf, the sign for *"Karen's Zoo"* dangling from its booted foot. The scores of colorful fish that hung from the ceiling swayed gently, as if a breeze wafted through the room from an open window. The crystal suspended from one cornerpost of the bed caught and reflected light, perhaps from that same unseen window.

In only one respect did the room differ from Carin's first glimpse of it, when a fiercely spinning vortex had retreated through time and space from the millpond of southern Ladrehdin to this bedroom on an unknown world. In that first image, a child wearing blue and green had slept under the bed's fish-patterned coverlet. Now, the bed was empty. Its linens were in disarray, as if the sleeper had cast them off in a panic.

"Good," Verek breathed into Carin's ear. "Now ... walk into the room. Place the book upon the desk. Take the trinket from the bedpost and put its chain around your neck. When you have done these acts, return immediately to me. *Do not linger,* though countless be the things that intrigue your eyes and ears."

Carin, stirring from the state of numb confusion that had gripped her, started to turn toward the sorcerer at her back, with a protest on her lips. How could she "walk into" the child's bedroom? It was an illusion formed of the mists that swirled above the wizards' well. The room had no substance. Carin's slight movement as she started to turn to Verek sent one edge of the image shredding off like a wind-tattered cloud. She could have fanned away the vapors with a wave of her hand.

"Stop!" the warlock exclaimed. His hands rose from Carin's shoulders to pinion her head and keep her gaze directed forward. "Do not look at me. Look only into the child's room. When you have done as I have said, to replace the book and retrieve the crystal, *then* you will turn your face to me and rejoin me on this spot."

At a loss, Carin peered into the mists and through them, and saw the wizards' well rippling below the image. The ripples, steadily rising higher, gave the pool an upheaved and billowy look, like the surging of a stormy sea. Did Verek expect her to walk on those waters? To step into the floating mists of illusion would be to plummet beneath the waves that were now white-capping the pool—there to drown in depths of liquid glass.

"I have not misled you," the warlock hissed in Carin's ear. "I have said that you would wish to refuse me in this. I have spoken of the difficulty of the task. But what I ask is not impossible. Do as I say. Walk into the child's room ..."

... *Or the woodsprite dies*, Carin finished the thought, feeling her heart flutter in her chest like a trapped sparrow.

Clenching the puzzle-book in both hands, she fixed her gaze on the mist-shrouded surface that was to receive it. Then she gulped a breath ... and stepped into the magic. Toward the child's bedchamber Carin walked as though it were only another room in Verek's labyrinthine manor house.

"Good!" she heard the warlock call to her. His voice sounded far distant.

Carin did not glance at the waters below, for fear of blinking her destination out of existence. But she heard the whitecaps breaking, with a sound like windowpanes cracking. And with every step, she tensed, steeling herself for the plunge into the pool. Would it be as cold as it looked? Would the sorcerer pluck

Carin from the billows? Or would he watch her drown, pleased to finally be rid of his "peculiar guest"?

But step after step, there was no plunge into quicksilver swells. There was no loss of solid floor under her feet. When Carin stopped walking, she was standing at the desk in the bedroom.

In wonder, she risked a look down at the book in her hands. Gazing past it, Carin saw her feet—in her worn, shabby, square-toed boots—resting on the floor of the child's bedroom. This floor was as highly polished as the stone of Verek's great cavern of magic, but it was made of alternating squares of blue and white tiles.

Carin felt estranged from her mind, as if she weren't quite all there. Prodding herself back into motion, she dropped the *Looking-Glass* book on the desk. Then she crossed to the bed and lifted the winking crystal from the cornerpost.

The crystal was the pendant of a heavy necklace. Carin slipped the trinket's chain over her head, then raised the ornament to her eyes for a closer look and saw the sleek, rounded form of a stylized dolphin. The undersea theme of this fish-bedecked room was complete to the smallest detail.

As she started to face away from the bed to return to Verek, she spotted the corner of a book peeking out from under the pillow. The room's occupant—Carin as a young girl, so she understood but couldn't really accept—had evidently been in the habit of reading at bedtime.

She drew the book into the light. The title made her gasp. It was *Alice's Adventures in Wonderland*. Another puzzle-book? A mate to the volume she'd just returned to this room?

Carin flipped through the book, scanning chapter titles. "'*The Pool of Tears,*'" she muttered, drawn to a chapter that seemed appropriately named for her present situation. She read Alice's thoughts on a saltwater pool into which the girl had fallen, and was brought up short: "I wish I hadn't cried so much! ... I shall be punished for it now, I suppose, by being drowned in my own tears!"

Drowned ...

Carin jumped, suddenly remembering where she was and what she was engaged in. *"Do not linger,"* Verek had warned her.

She tossed the book onto the bed and spun on her heel to seek the warlock who had been standing at her back. Nothing was there now but a wall. In it was a large window, open to the salt-scented breeze that teased the dangling fish and admitting the watery sunlight that flickered in Carin's crystal necklace.

Sunlight? In Ruain at this hour, long after the evening meal, it was nighttime.

Carin rushed to the window. Immediately below it, ocean waves lapped at the wall. There was not so much as a footpath between the sea and the child's bedroom.

She gazed far out across the waves and glimpsed the vault of magic. Standing within it, hardly bigger than a seagull in the distance, was Verek. He seemed to gesture to her but Carin couldn't be sure what he signaled, he was so far away.

From that distance, his voice couldn't possibly reach her. But it did somehow. *"Hurry!"* came the faint cry. "Return to me this instant, you young fool!"

If she hadn't already crossed water once, Carin would have counted it quite unthinkable to heed the warlock's summons. But with the woodsprite's life depending on her, and all of Verek's warnings ringing in her ears — *"You must not lose yourself in that other world"* ... *"Your life's breath remains with me"* — what choice did she have? She must trust to an untrustworthy sorcerer and his enchanted pool, and whatever magic had taken her on this journey.

Carin climbed through the open window and crouched on the sill. As she flexed her right wrist, she noticed that it didn't hurt from when Verek had twisted it. Maybe the warlock wasn't tricking her. He had said that only an intangible part of her would walk on this world. Maybe her true being—the part that could be bruised and feel pain—was, in fact, waiting with him in Verek's cave of magic. The idea was just comforting enough that Carin could bring herself to make the blind leap into the ocean below—

—Where her boots found solid footing in the water, though waves brushed her calves like tall grass rippling in a meadow on a breezy day.

You are in a meadow, Carin told herself, and fixed her mind on that illusion as the salvation of her senses. To admit otherwise, to admit that she walked on the sea, to acknowledge that she crossed … what? The unnatural waters of the wizards' well, grown from a pool to an ocean? Or the vast, unbounded void between the worlds themselves? To admit such possibilities would be to lose her grip on reality. This realm … this ocean … this infinite void was a thing far beyond her grasp. Only in her imaginary meadow could Carin subdue the substance of her terror, and leave just its shadows to occupy the shuddering corners of her mind.

Nearer she drew to Verek. But her progress was slow. Though she "walked" through the ocean waves as easily as through a tall-grass prairie, the distance between Carin and the warlock seemed immense. She would be a year reaching him, at this rate.

But in an instant—she missed both the means and the moment of it—Verek was there in front of her, not a stone's throw away. His long, lank hair was plastered to his skull. Sweat ran down his face and neck. His stripped-off woolen vest lay crumpled at his feet, and his shirt clung to him, soaked through. His face was ashen. The strain of his more-than-mortal effort showed in its taut, distorted lines.

And Carin knew: her easy striding through ocean waves was entirely the warlock's doing. She did not buoy herself up. She did not close the distance between them on her own two feet. It was Verek who conducted her along this return journey, drawing her back to the cave from ... wherever she had been. And the struggle to reclaim her was crushing him.

"Throw me the crystal!" he cried. Pain hoarsened his voice. "Quickly! I cannot withstand its pull upon you!"

Its pull?

Carin yanked the necklace over her head. With a few quick turns, she wrapped the chain tight around the dolphin pendant, making a ball that she lobbed to the warlock's waiting hands.

His fingers closing over the crystal were the last things Carin saw. Under her feet, there was suddenly — nothing. She plunged into a frigid liquid, down into a blackness without form.

The shock of it drove every thought from her mind, except for one glimmer: *He only wanted the crystal. And now that I've brought it to him, he's done with me.*

Carin drifted through a thick, achingly cold, ebony ocean. She was going to drown. When her lungs filled with this liquid that was more glass than water, she would die in the glacial nothingness of this supernatural void, where all was silence ... and stillness ... and ...

Betrayal, was the last clear idea in her mind before existence ended.

END of BOOK ONE of WATERSPELL

About the Author

Castles in the cornfield provided the setting for Deborah J. Lightfoot's earliest flights of fancy. On her father's farm in Texas, she grew up reading tales of adventure and reenacting them behind ramparts of sun-drenched grain. She left the farm to earn a degree in journalism and write award-winning books of history and biography, including *The LH7 Ranch* (University of North Texas Press) and *Trail Fever* (William Morrow, New York). High on her bucket list was the desire to try her hand at the genre she most admired. The result is *Waterspell,* a complex, intricately detailed fantasy about a girl and the wizard who suspects her of being so dangerous to his world, he believes he'll have to kill her ... which poses a problem for him, since he's fallen in love with her. The story begins with *Book 1: The Warlock* and *Book 2: The Wysard,* continues in *Book 3: The Wisewoman,* and concludes (the author claims) with *Book 4: The Witch.*

Deborah J. Lightfoot is a professional member of The Authors Guild. She lives in the country south of Fort Worth, Texas. Find her online at www.waterspell.net.

CPSIA information can be obtained
at www.ICGtesting.com
Printed in the USA
BVHW050029051122
650904BV00001B/20